A TWISTE

BOOK TWO

Bound

R. PHILLIPS

Bound

Bound

Bound, A Twisted Tale #2

Edited by: Ellie McLove, My Brother's Editor
Proofread by: Rosa Sharon, My Brother's Editor
Cover design by: Clarissa Kezen - ckbookcoverdesigns.com

ISBN-13: 979-8-9860684-3-5 (Paperback)
ISBN-13: 979-8-9860684-2-8 (Ebook)

www.rphillipswrites.com

Playlist

Falling Apart by Michael Schulte

I Found - Acoustic by Amber Run

Add It Up by Violent Femmes

cinderella's dead by EMELINE

…Ready For It? by Taylor Swift

Stay with Me by Vitamin String Quartet

Jamie All Over by Mayday Parade

Powerful by Major Lazer, Ellie Goulding, Tarrus Riley

Trouble by Valerie Broussard

Young And Beautiful by Lana Del Rey

Issues by Julia Michaels

Poison & Wine by The Civil Wars

To Build A Home by The Cinematic Orchestra, Patrick Watson

Bound

VI

For anyone who has ever felt a little lost.

Remember that life is all about the journey.

And often, it's when we don't know which way is

up or down that we discover who we're truly meant to be.

It's the climb that teaches us everything.

“These violent delights have violent ends

And in their triumph die, like fire and powder.

Which as they kiss, consume.”

-Shakespeare

Prologue

Coop

Present Day

Everything in life has a price.

Death is the price demanded for the gift of life. Madness the price that stalks at the edges of genius. Heartbreak is the inevitable price for even the purest, most innocent of loves. Crumbling reality under your feet the price for letting yourself become lost in the fantasy.

Nothing is ever freely gifted. The universe always comes, whether in the brightest, cheek-aching second of the day or the darkest, most plaintive hour of the night, to collect its payment. To rattle and shake your world.

To slither into the illusion of Eden painted by strokes of lies and deceit.

And I had left the door open for it, welcoming the thief into my house to steal what was dearest to me. That one decision that I couldn't amend, paving the path for the inevitable loss of the thing, the person, who meant the most to me.

Even if I had done every unthinkable, irrational, detestable thing to prevent it.

To fight the inevitable loss of the base mistake I had made.

The princess that was never supposed to be mine.

The deception that had slowly bled darkness into my soul.

Eating away at the back of my mind in a cackling mockery.

Throttling my throat with the words I had chosen not to speak.

Because the love I had found, the one I had never expected, never foreseen, was a tale I had woven full of lies to keep.

And the greater the love, even as twisted as mine may be, the greater the price. The greater the deception grew, the longer it had gone on, the further redemption had fled from my reach.

She had been right. She had always been right. Love had killed her parents. She just didn't have all the facts. I *hadn't* told her all the facts. Looking back, it was hard to discern between the truth of reality and the deception of fantasy that was that very first moment. Of whether I had ever really meant to tell her or whether that was just as much of a lie I had fed myself as the one I had thrust us into.

Maybe I had. Maybe I hadn't.

Maybe I'd never be sure of anything now.

Except that, when I had finally met her… when I had seen that little teasing spark in her eyes, that defiant jut of her chin and challenging cock of her brow, those smirking lips that just begged me to join in on her game.

I had been terrified that she would turn away.

And in those deceptively coincidental moments of that first night… instances filled with that first lock of eyes, catch of breath, the intangible pull of something cellular between us… my life had finally started to make sense.

With her, order had fallen among the chaos filling my brain, leaving nothing but a calm that had ordered the world into beautiful poetry.

I had finally understood.

What it meant to breathe for someone, to need them like the gravity grounding me. Understood how a person could forsake all others and fall to their knees, sacrificing everything for one being. How the importance of one person could outweigh that of the rest of the world.

Because she, out of all the people in the entirety of the world, had been the one to finally make me understand. And she was the one person I should have allowed to remain out of my reach.

So I had hidden the truth, buried it under darkness and love. Tying her to me in the most intimate of ways. Abject terror of her loss driving me to do the unthinkable. Impulsively, stupidly thinking I could hide the secret away for eternity.

And then reality collided with fantasy and shattered everything.

An insane bark of a laugh leaves my mouth as I flip my phone closed, quickly turning into a quiet gasp as pain stabs through my chest.

I stare at the pages and volumes strewn across the floor, sitting on our bed that still reeks of tequila, hearing the words of the voice mails I just listened to run on a loop through my mind.

"Oh, big brother. I have news for you. Our cousin has finally gone and fallen in love. You know, the cousin who used to have a different girl for every day of the week. Yep, that one. You wouldn't believe it, he's absolutely smitten, and she's…"

"Hey man, I don't know where you are or when you'll check your phone. And I don't know, maybe Jace is right and I'm crazy, but… there's this girl in town. Eleanor Delacroix? Anyway, I just found out she was in Cahuita last summer and she has this tattoo, and fuck, man… I don't know, hopefully I'm wrong, and you're still with your girl… you never fucking call us anymore, so I wouldn't know. But Coop, those words, I've seen your broody-ass poetry and they—they just feel like yours. Just call me, okay? Tell me I'm crazy and that you're still fucking away on the beach with the love of your life."

I could still feel the slight rise of the freshly tattooed script under my lips as I ran them over the skin under her breast. Could still hear in my head the way her breath caught as I did it again. And again. Worshiping her and the words that were ours. My greatest deception and my entire world held in the delicate body of one girl.

I flip my phone in my hand and stand, jaw clenching at the absence of a voice mail from the cousin I loved like a brother. The one I had killed for. The one who had loved her first, even if he was too young to understand it at the time and thought of her as only an annoyance.

And now… apparently, he did understand it now.

"When the fuck are you going to clean this place up, man?" Alec's sardonic voice calls from the kitchen.

"When she's here to do it with me."

"Right," he scoffs. "Well, here's your cut from the job. Let me know when you need cash to keep you going again, and I'll try to find another."

I pocket my phone and turn, walking to the kitchen to collect the bundle of cash off the kitchen table. "That won't be necessary."

"And why is that?" Alec asks, narrowing his eyes at me.

I meet his curious stare, body strung tight as a bow with the urgency to move, to finally have her in my sight again. "Because she found me."

She had gone home, to the one place I never thought to look, never thought she would venture to in all my obsessive imaginings.

There was always a price. For everyone, in everything. Innocent and guilty alike.

And now I'd learned mine.

But what would theirs be?

Chapter 1

"Hey, Princess."

A deep, stuttering breath leaves me at the sound of the old familiar name, the realization that this isn't another dream he's haunting. That all of his harsh beauty is real, tangible, standing right before me. Back from the dead and close enough to touch. The sight of him cracks my heart in two all over again, sending me right back to that moment of lying on a book-covered floor as pain and loss shredded who I had become with him.

I stare into his night-forest eyes as every memory from last summer, every shared dream barrels down on me like a tidal wave. Leaving me as speechless as the first time I saw him, except this time, by way of an absurd new reality. And I can see them there in his eyes too. In the pain and the love there… and I fucking hate it. I hate that I can see, that I can feel the infinity of all that we once were and lost reflecting right back at me.

I watch his eyes drop back down in answer to my shocked silence, snagging on my bare legs again and turning dark before they slide to Jace.

His voice comes out deceptively soft. Every word laced with quiet fury. "And tell me, cousin, how long have you been fucking my wife?"

My heart just about stops, and I reach out, placing a hand on the door to steady myself as a roaring starts in my head. "Cousin?" I breathe the question of a word hardly loud enough to be heard, jerking my gaze to Jace for some sort of answer. Needing him to stop this, to tell me this is some kind of twisted joke, but his eyes are locked on Coop as a shocked expression spreads across his face.

"She's—she's your wife?" His voice wavers with disbelief.

A humorless kind of scoff leaves Coop, and he turns purposefully back toward Jace as if he's about to hit him. "Don't tell me you didn't figure out who I was to her, who she was to me, in all the time you've been with her."

Jace finally meets my gaze, and I can see the horrible truth in his eyes, in the way they're already begging for forgiveness before he speaks. "Not until a couple weeks ago." He swallows visibly and turns back to meet Coop's gaze. "I didn't know for sure until a couple weeks ago."

"Really?" Coop mocks viciously. "There wasn't a single moment? A single phrase on her body that made you think of me?"

I see the spark of anger flare in Jace's eyes as they narrow. "You're reaching, cousin," he answers quietly before heaving a breath and pulling his bottom lip through his teeth. "Even if there was a second, I thought there was no way she was the girl from last summer and you wouldn't have told me." His eyes flick back to mine, the hurt and accusation in them front and center, aimed straight at me. "And I sure as fuck didn't know y'all were married."

Because I hadn't told him.

The betrayal doesn't need to be spoken. It's reflecting back at everyone on this boat as we're all trapped in a house of distorted mirrors, leaving me dizzy in the world of deceit I've awoken to.

"Yet I'm guessing you still had no issue sticking your dick inside of her even after you figured out who she was to me," Coop bites out. "And tell me, did you tell her? Once you knew, Jace, did you tell her?"

"Don't put all this on me." Jace shakes his head, eyes filling with anger as he looks back to Coop. "Why the fuck wouldn't you have told me it was her?!" he shouts in frustration, waving a hand in my direction. "You were here. We were in the same fucking hospital room. You knew I knew who she was!"

"My mother and I... have a complicated relationship, you could say."

The words ring through my head as I'm still lying on that bed with him in Cahuita and I see the way Coop's body locks up with tension when Jace continues.

"You said her name was Della. Why the fuck would you lie to me? Why the fuck wouldn't you just bring her with you?"

"My dad was a writer, among other things, and he... he kept a lot of secrets. And I guess, in a way, when he died, they became my secrets to bear."

No... it can't be...

Please. Please, god no. Please. I can't... it can't be.

Coop turns his head, eyes raking my face and finding the look of horrible, dawning realization there. "Shut the fuck up, Jace," he snaps.

"How did—how did she not know?" The blood drains from Jace's face as his eyes dart back and forth between us, sensing there's something more to this story that he's missing. "What the fuck did you do, Coop?" he finishes quietly, fearfully.

"He had an affair."

My heart races as the puzzle I've been trying to figure out all summer slides sickeningly into place. Each pump of blood sends the piercing pain deeper and deeper as the horrific pictures of my parents' bodies flash through my mind in time with each of his remembered confessions from last summer. I look into Coop's eyes and see the fear there as the ghost of his voice rings through my head once more.

"He destroyed a lot of lives."

That almost nothing blank space in the splatter of my mother's blood. Her head turned toward the doorway. Seeking the attention she had loved so much even in her last seconds of life.

The silence that follows in the boat is deafening, thick with the weight of secrets discovered but still not voiced.

I bite down on my lip hard, using the pain to ground me and push through the sick feeling in my stomach. Trying to steel myself against what's to come as I take a step into the cabin and clench my sweating hands. Grasping desperately for any kind of armor to deflect the damage I can feel these answers will bring me.

Barely keeping it together as it is.

"Your father?" I guess softly, voice coming out raspy from the horrible tightness in my throat.

Coop's eyes drill into mine for a moment, the silence stretching taut between us before his plush lips tighten and he nods the confirmation. As if he can't bear to speak the words.

I heave a breath and look up at the ceiling, eyes pricking and fists shaking at my sides. Trying to work through this horrible truth in my head. To figure out where exactly our story had become so tainted.

"Why wouldn't you tell me?" I finally ask, dropping my eyes back down to him as the first embers of anger flare to life inside of me. "Why the fuck wouldn't you tell me once you knew who I was?"

His jaw clenches before he shakes his head. "Because I couldn't lose you."

"You couldn't lose…" I scoff in disbelief, rapidly blinking to keep everything from becoming blurry. "You didn't know that would… we might've…" I shake my head, trying to order my thoughts amid the fog of anger and confusion. Try to bring my world back into some kind of focus. "You fucking told me that was a pretty name!" An insane kind of laugh bursts from my lips at the memory. "When I told you my name, you said it was pretty. A fucking pretty name, really, Coop?" I mock scornfully. "That was your only reaction? Like—like…"

His night-forest eyes I've secretly longed for so many nights fill with dread and my stomach gives a sharp twist in response. Intuition whispering up my spine with a knowledge that has me gulping for air as hysteria starts to creep in, slowly closing me in its grasp.

"Did you know?" I whisper in horror, almost unable to force the next question out. Almost not wanting to know the answer. "When you met me… did—" My voice cracks and I feel the first tears fall, gulping desperately for more air to get the words out. "Did you know who I was already?"

His expression crumbles, utter desolation blanketing his face. "Eleanor…" He seems to choke on my name as his chest heaves, and his hands clench at his sides, mirroring mine.

Silent in response to my question as he drops his head.

But I don't need him to say it. I have my answer.

Even after a year apart… I can see the truth in him, feel it in the torture radiating out of his body and into mine. In the shadows and dread that I saw in his dark eyes.

The horrible truth I somehow missed all along.

All those carefully worded phrases that were lost among that first falling of love.

He loved me even if *I wouldn't* tell him my name.

Not that he didn't already *know it.*

That singularly beautiful, infinitely precious moment of our becoming in the Costa Rican rain is shattered in an instant. And I feel myself shatter right along with it. Something inside of me snapping at the realization that I know nothing of the truth of our story.

"You fucking knew." I spit the words out in disgust, taking another step toward him as sickening rage pumps through me.

"Ellie…" Jace ventures cautiously, taking a step closer to us, sensing the impending explosion. "Ellie, tell me what the fuck is going on here."

Coop lifts his head. "Eleanor… let me explain—"

"You sick fuck!" I shout furiously, closing the distance between us and bringing my hand down across his face with a hard slap that whips his head to the side. "You fucking knew. How could you do that? You—you knew—" A cry rips from the deepest part of me, cutting off my words and I feel like I can't draw enough breath into my lungs. As if I'm suffocating. Suffocating on the choked sobs and lies and betrayal. He turns his head back to me, meeting my gaze with eyes that hold nothing but pained understanding.

"Y-y-you knew all along," I manage to stutter out, the desire to flay him open driving me forward. "How could you?" I gasp. Fuck his understanding. He can't possibly understand what he's done to me. Yet again. "You stay the fuck away from me." I sob raggedly, tasting the salt from my tears.

"Eleanor… I—" His gravelly voice breaks and he clears his throat. "You have to let me explain."

I stare at him for a moment, at this beautiful deception of a man who once owned every part of me. At the torment laid bare in that dark Adonis face I never thought I'd see again. And it dawns on me that he's chiseled entirely out of lies.

"No, actually, I don't," I gasp, swallowing down my sobs as I turn and walk back to Jace's bedroom. I dig the keys from the back pocket of my shorts before pulling them on and walking back out to the cabin. To get the fuck out of here, away from this insanity. Away from him. Away from both of them.

Right fucking now.

I steadfastly avoid both of their gazes as I walk out, not stopping until I come up beside Coop and his hand shoots out to lock around my arm. Bringing me to a stop beside him, close enough that I catch the faintest hint of his almost forgotten sandalwood scent, but I refuse to meet his gaze.

"Let go of my fucking arm," I snap furiously.

"Princess." He drops his head closer to mine, voice low and quiet as his gaze burns into the side of my face. "Where are you going?"

An insane noise bursts from me as I try to yank my arm from his grip. "Isn't that irony for you?" I turn my head and look up, giving him a vicious, tear-filled smirk. "Guess what? I get to be the one who leaves this time."

I see his eyes spark with dark possession as his grip tightens on my arm. "I've chased you across this fucking earth for almost a year, Eleanor," he growls at me. "You're not going anywhere."

Jace moves up next to us in the tight space, reaching out and putting a hand on Coop's shoulder. "Let her go, Coop. She's not going to leave town."

Coop keeps his eyes locked with mine. "How do you know that?"

"Because I'm guessing from what I've seen, she needs either you or your mom to get her answers. And she wants those answers more than she might hate either of us right now." He sighs wearily, turning his gaze on me. "Isn't that right, Blondie?"

My stomach churns with rage at the truth of his words, sending my breathing straight into a panicked pace, because he's right.

Goddammit, but he's right.

"Both of you can fuck off," I snarl, yanking on my arm again in his steely grip.

"Coop." Jace edges between us, cutting off my view as he brings himself eye to eye with his cousin. "I wouldn't let her go either if I thought she would be gone for good." He reaches down and grasps Coop's wrist, emphasizing every word as he continues. "Now let her go."

Another beat passes before Coop slowly, one finger at a time, lets go of my arm, and I waste no time squeezing myself behind Jace and racing from the boat. Gulping down the fresh air and squinting my eyes against the harsh sunlight as I leave the cabin behind. I throw myself over the side of the boat, hitting the dock hard and falling to my knees before shakily standing on my bare feet. Trying desperately to force the sobs back down my throat as I walk down the dock. To contain the broken shards of me until I get somewhere safe to let them fall where they may.

It's only a few moments later when I hear someone land on the dock, footsteps coming up quick behind me.

"Ellie. Please stop," Jace begs softly.

I can't. If I stop, if I look at him… I will drag him right into this pit of darkness and despair alongside me.

He comes up beside me, keeping pace as I power down the dock. "Just stop for a second."

I see him reach out for me out of the corner of my eye and whip around, chest heaving as I step away from his outstretched hand. "You don't get to touch me either!"

His brows drop down, eyes crinkling at the corners in pain. "Ellie… please, just talk to me."

So be it.

"Why?" I scoff, voice dripping poison. "So you can keep more promises, Jace?"

"Ellie…" He breathes roughly, taking a step toward me again. "I didn't—"

"You," I cut him off, voice cracking. Looking up into his pleading firework eyes and hardening myself against them. "The worst part about you is that you already loved me when you betrayed me." I shake my head, feeling fresh tears fall on my cheeks. "At least with him, it was all a fucking lie from the start. But you… even after everything we had built, you still chose to betray me. The person you claimed to love."

"I do," he argues imploringly. "I do love you, Ellie." His voice cracks on my name and he shakes his head, a few strands of his messy blond hair lifting in the ocean breeze. "I'm so sorry. I should have told you the minute—"

"But you didn't," I interject, voice coming out choked from how unbearably tight my throat is. "Even after you knew how bad I had been hurt before." Another sob tries to work its way free, and I swallow down both the cry and pain in my throat. "Which makes you just as bad as him as far as I'm concerned." I turn away from him, throwing out over my shoulder as I walk away, "So you can stay the fuck away from me too, Jace." It turned out even the brilliant light of the sun was as deceptive as the promise of stars in the dark. "I want no part of that kind of love."

I can feel the agony in him at my back, and it pushes me into a run. Racing down the dock in a futile attempt to escape these horrible revelations. I make it to Franny and throw myself into the car, screeching out of the parking lot in a mirror of my arrival this morning. The safe haven I had run to only hours ago now a poisoned place.

Clenching my teeth to fight the cries trying to escape, I make the drive back to Gram's on autopilot. The echoes of everything that just happened playing over and over in my head with every turn and stop. As if their confessions are the most horrible song I don't want to hear stuck on repeat. By the time I pull into Gram's driveway, my head is pounding, jaw aching, and I hardly know how I got here. The drive nothing more than background noise to my mourning.

I force myself from the car, wanting nothing more than to crawl underneath the covers of the bed and, quite possibly, never come out to face this new reality. My hand fumbles on the doorknob only once before I manage to push it open, walking into the house and coming to a halt at the sight of the horrific photographs on the living room floor waiting to greet me. I walk slowly into the room, staring at the disheveled pictures as the sense of déjà vu overwhelms me. Leaving me as dazed as the last time Cooper Monroe had shattered me and left me staring at a kaleidoscope floor.

It feels as if my head is about to split in two as I look at the photographs, seeing everything about them in a whole new light. A horrible pressure in me building as I wonder what actually happened that night. What role Coop's father played in the night that had robbed me of my fictitiously happy family. I drop to my knees, body giving out as a hundred rushing voices whisper answers that only lead to more questions in my head all at once. My gaze snags on one of the displaced photographs that shows the hallway that leads to my childhood room and a barely remembered dream from this morning hits me full force.

A little boy's scared voice and a small pair of night-forest eyes seen through the grogginess of sleep.

"It's okay. Everything's going to be alright. You're just dreaming. Like Sleeping Beauty. I'll read you a fairy tale so you can go back to sleep."

The pressure becomes unbearable and I crack, a scream ripping its way from my throat as I swipe furiously at the pictures in front of me. A scream of frustration and rage and pain and betrayal. A scream of being set adrift from the sureness of reality. Lost in this horrible new black hole of a world where everyone's masks have finally been ripped away.

I run out of breath to fuel my cry of agony and gasp for air as tears slide down my cheeks, throat aching and sore. Staring blankly at the floor and realizing that this is worse than when he disappeared last summer, because this time, I don't even have anything of our story to hold on to. No secret hope that it had all been real.

Our whole story was nothing more than a carefully crafted illusion.

Every memory, every word, all of our love written and spoken, was now a question of truth or lie. Tainted. Twisted. Broken. Quite possibly, never real at all.

I'm not sure how long I've been sitting there when a banging starts up on the front door, and I know I should probably get up. To at least lock the door if not answer it, but I just can't. I can't make my body move. Every part of me hurts and the only parts that don't hurt feel utterly removed. Blissfully, utterly, removed. And those are the parts I'm trying to cling to.

"El!" I hear Tiff's voice call. "El! Open the door!"

She's his sister, the removed part of me muses. Sheriff Reynolds, his mom. Reynolds, Monroe, that part doesn't make sense still. Maybe he lied about that too though… along with everything else.

"El! I swear to god you better open this door," Tiff shouts. "I answered mine. Now it's your turn!"

Doesn't she know I can't move? If I move, if I face any more of this, I'm going to fracture again.

I know it.

"Fine! Have it your way!"

I hear the door open and turn my head to see the look of agitation on her face fall at the sight of me.

Her eyes slowly take in the mess of photographs on the floor and widen.

"El…" she whispers, bringing her now worried eyes back to mine. "El, what's going on? Are you okay?"

Sure. Fine. Right fucking peachy.

Totally removed and trying to stay that way.

I jerk my head once into a nod, hurriedly trying to swallow down the emotion attempting to break free again at the sight of her.

Tiff takes a slow step into the room, as if I'm an injured animal she's trying not to scare. "What's going on, El?" she asks softly. "I just went by the boat and Coop and Jace wouldn't stop yelling and—" She sucks in a breath, brows shooting down as she stares at me. "Do you… do you know my brother?"

Do I know her brother?

I'm not sure anymore.

"Coop, El," she presses. "Do you know Coop?"

"I have a little sister. Had to watch more princess movies growing up than I care to admit."

Coop's voice echoes through my head as great, heaving sobs rip their way from my soul. The last of his haunting words striking their final blow as I crumble to the floor and feel the pieces of me land at her feet.

Chapter 2

I can't seem to stop the sobs all day, curled up in Tiff's arms as she murmurs nonsensical, soothing words in an attempt to comfort me. Slowly purging the poison of both men's betrayals from my being. Until I feel at least somewhat better, more in control, if not completely put back together again. More bruised than broken though, and I'll take what I can at this point. At some point during my breakdown, Tiff had managed to coax me to the bed, which is where we are now. Both of us silently staring outside at the darkening sky.

And I'm pretty sure she's worried that if she speaks, she's going to break me or something.

And you find that shocking, El? Really?

I shoot her a curious glance through my swollen eyes and see the tension lining her face where she lies next to me, absentmindedly running her fingers through my hair. She's such a bright, innocent contrast to Coop, but now that I know they're related, I see the similarities I didn't pick up on before. The plush lips, the arching line of cheekbones she shares with not only Coop but Jace too.

The features she must have gotten from her father and not her mother.

It takes me a minute to work up the courage to ask the question nagging at me. "What's…" I rasp, causing her gaze to jerk to me in surprise. "What's your last name?"

Confusion clouds her face. "Monroe, why?"

"Your mom's name is Reynolds…" I clear my aching throat, blinking against the pricking in my eyes. "I just assumed yours was the same."

"Oh. Yeah." Tiff's lips pinch up for a moment, pursing in a way that only brings her brother to mind and does nothing to help the aching in my heart. "She went back to her maiden name after my dad passed away."

"Oh." I nod.

Guess he wasn't lying about that.

And you just blindly assumed everything was as it seemed again. Thought you claimed to be smarter now, El?

"Thank you," I tell her softly, reaching down to grab her hand. "For today."

"Of course." She sighs, squeezing my hand with a concerned look. "Is it okay… do you think you could clue me in on what's going on now though?"

"I…" I swallow, trying to figure out what to even tell her. If I should tell her anything. "I'm not really sure where to start. Or if… there are just some things you can't unknow, Tiff."

"Please, El," she pleads. "I'm feeling so lost right now. Like everyone is keeping secrets from me, and I hate it." She squeezes my hand again. "Please."

"They're bad secrets, Tiff," I warn her.

"And I'm not a child," she argues softly. "So how about I just start with the questions I have and we go from there?"

I pause for a moment, looking into her serious blue eyes and seeing the resolve there, knowing I owe her at least some answers after today.

"Fine."

A small smile flashes across her face for a second before it falls, and she starts hesitantly. "I'm… I'm guessing you know my brother?"

That damn sharp pain shoots through the center of my chest as I answer her. "Yeah." I sigh. "Yeah, I know Coop."

"And um…" Her face pinches up with an awkward look. "I'm guessing you, uh, know him *really well* by all the yelling and crying that happened today?"

I give a humorless snort. "That would be correct."

"Then uh—what happened with y'all?"

"The only thing that can ever cause this much pain." I dart my eyes away from her, my voice cracking on the word. "Love."

She pauses for a moment, voice coming out quiet when she speaks. "Why did it end?"

"Why did it begin?" I whisper to myself before looking back at her. "It's complicated." I shrug. "Even I don't have all the answers."

She opens her mouth to reply when a loud pounding starts on the front door and we both jerk in surprise, our gazes flying to the bedroom doorway.

The pounding pauses for a moment before starting up again, harder than before.

"Do you think—"

"If it is, you can tell him I said Satan isn't welcome here."

Tiff shoots me a shocked look and I grimace, trying to remember that Coop is her big brother, even if that means she's related to Satan.

"Sorry," I mumble.

"Princess!" his demanding voice shouts from outside, loud as fucking possible. "You have about two minutes before I start checking to see if any windows are open!"

Fucking great. Doreen was probably out on her porch eating this shit up and on the phone with half the town already.

Tiff shoots me a nervous look. "Do you want me to get rid of him?"

"Yes, please," I answer softly. "If only to save the last shred of my sanity."

"Right. Okay," Tiff mutters nervously, getting up from the bed and walking out of the room.

I hear the pounding cut off a moment later and slide out of the bed, trying to be as quiet as possible as I go to listen in by the bedroom door.

"Tiff?" Coop's surprised voice filters back to me. "What are you doing here?"

"The better question, brother," Tiff whispers angrily. "Is what the hell happened between you and my friend back there?"

A beat passes before I hear Coop speak again. "Is she okay?"

"No! She most definitely is not okay, Coop! She's been sobbing almost all day."

"Let me in, Tiff," he demands quietly.

"No." Tiff pauses. "I don't think I will."

"Why the hell not?"

"Well, for one, the crying that happens at the mere mention of your name. And two… she told me to tell you Satan isn't welcome here."

A dark scoff sounds. "I'm sure she did. Regardless, let me in, Tiff."

"No. And then there are all the pictures…" Tiff rambles. "I wouldn't have been surprised if those had made her break down, but I think it was you that—"

"What pictures?" Coop cuts her off sharply.

"Uh… of—of her parents."

A long moment passes, and I can practically feel Coop's agitation skyrocket.

"Let me in the fucking door, Tiffany," he orders her, voice tense.

She's going to break. I know it then. This is her big brother, after all, and ultimately, she probably thinks he's still a good person. Totally unaware that he really is fucking Satan.

"Coop…" She drags out his name indecisively. "I really think she needs a few days to—"

I hear his heavy footfalls sound against the wood floor of the house before coming to a stop, and I can guess he just pushed past her before the sight of the living room brought him to a halt.

A minute passes before his voice sounds again, coming out empty. "You can leave now."

"Uh—"

I hear some shuffling before Coop speaks again. "Goodbye, Tiffany."

The sound of the front door shutting hits me like a lightning bolt and I slam the bedroom door shut in response, quickly flipping the lock. My heart thundering in my chest as I stare at it, breathing hard, the silence on the other side telling. He knows. He knows I just locked him out. And part of me hates it, wants to be strong, go out there and rip him apart… but I just can't.

I can't face him. Not yet.

Not when I've only just begun to pull myself together again.

I hear his heavy footfalls walk toward the bedroom slowly. Each step louder than the last until they stop right outside the door and I watch the doorknob in fearful anticipation but it never turns. Instead, after a few minutes, I hear him lean against the outside of the door and slide down before the wood floor creaks loudly. Clueing me in to the fact that he just sat down on the other side of it.

Well, fuck. What the hell am I supposed to do now?

Open the door and let Satan in?

No, thanks. Think I'll pass.

Another minute passes before he speaks, voice low and rough. "I'm not going to beg, Princess." He pauses for a moment again before continuing. "What I did is unforgivable. But… I do need to explain. For you to understand."

Understand? Fucking understand? Really?

I bite my lip to keep from either yelling or crying, unsure of what will come out of my mouth if I allow it to open.

"Can you please open the door?"

I don't even consider it. I just continue to stare at the white wood silently. Waiting to see what he says next as my stomach flips with trepidation and a sick desire to know more.

"Come on, Princess, I said please, I just—" His voice breaks, and it's a few seconds before he speaks again, voice rough with feeling. "You have no idea how badly I just need to see you. What this year—" He cuts himself off.

I stare at the door for a moment, hating that the brokenness I can hear in his voice still pulls at some part of me. Even now. Even after I know everything that he's done to me. Even after he's broken me time and again. I hate that I just can't be numb when it comes to him.

Numbness would be so much better than this twisted heartbreak.

"I can't even look at you, Coop," I finally rasp quietly. "I don't want to look at you."

It hurts too much.

A heavy pause passes before he answers. "Okay." I hear his head softly thud against the door and can picture him dropping it back, clenching his jaw in frustration. "But I need you to listen." Another pause. "I know you, Eleanor, and some part of you wants to know why, so let me tell you. Allow me that."

My heart thuds against the bones in my chest, terrified that if I give him this one inch, it will open the door, somehow allowing him to shatter the remaining shards of me I'm desperately trying to protect. But he's right. I want to know why. I want to know why he deceived me, forced me to love him only to abandon and break me.

To know the truth of our story.

"Okay," I whisper, so quiet that I'm not sure he can even hear me as I take a tentative step toward the door and mirror how I imagine him as I sit down on my side of it. My body too aching and tired after the emotional beating I've taken today to remain standing. I draw my knees up to my chest and loop my arms around them, trying to physically hold myself together as I wait for him to speak. My head spinning with questions that I hate him all the more for holding the answers to.

But when the silence continues to stretch on, I can't help but snap at him in agitation. "Are you going to talk?"

"I'm just…" He clears his throat. "Trying to figure out where to start."

"Here's an idea," I mock. "How about at the beginning?"

"Of us?" he asks, voice rarely hesitant. "Or them?"

Us or them. Them…

My stomach twists sharply at the thought.

"Them," I tell him quietly, hating the answer. Hating that there ever was a them.

It's a minute or so before he starts softly. "It started at the park."

A soft cry escapes my lips at his words, at the memory of my mother's last journal entry ending with her making a new friend at the park. I press my lips tightly together as my eyes prick, filling yet again with unshed tears.

"Eleanor," Coop breathes, voice pained.

"Keep going," I croak.

"Just let me in, Princess."

"Keep going!" I snap, voice cracking as I swipe angrily at the few tears escaping onto my face.

I hear the thud of his head against the door again and a tense silence follows before he starts. "From what I've figured out through the years… it started about a year before they all died. Your mom used to take you to the park so she could write in her journal while you played. My dad… I told you he was a writer, along with owning the bar, and one day… he took my sister to the park and saw her writing."

Adam's place.

Adam Monroe, the writer, the bar owner. Handsome, if his children are anything to go by. And Nadia Delacroix, the woman who had always selfishly craved more, more of everything, sitting on a park bench writing about her boringly happy, ordinary life.

The deck was stacked perfectly.

"It spiraled from there like you would imagine," he finishes flatly.

"Did," I start after a moment, having to clear my aching throat to get the words out. "Did he love her, at least?" Not sure why it even matters to me. It's not like it changes anything.

A long pause sounds from the other side of the door and I can imagine how tightly Coop's brow is drawn with tension. "Yes, Eleanor," he answers softly, voice catching. "From what I remember of everything, I think—I think he loved her very much. And…" He pauses and I hear him suck in a harsh breath. "I know that she loved him too."

"How?" I turn my head to the side, laying it against the door.

"Because I was an angry kid who wanted answers." I hear his head rub against the wood of the door and know he's shaking it. "So one night when I got drunk in high school, I broke into your parents' house and found your mother's journal."

"The last one," I whisper in shock.

"What?"

"She had others," I mumble hurriedly. "Where was it?"

"Inside a copy of *Madame Bovary* on the bookshelf in the living room." He sighs. "I only even picked it up because—"

"Because you love the tragedies," I interrupt with a short, bitter laugh.

"Because," he responds after a moment, voice tense. "I remembered it being one of my father's favorite books." Another beat. "I still have it, the journal. If you want it."

My stomach clenches violently at the idea. "No, thanks," I snap. "I'd rather not read about our parents fucking. Don't think I need to add that to the damage you've done."

A long silence sounds on the other side of the door before I hear him lay his head against it. Somehow knowing it'd be laid against mine if not for the wood between us. "They did love each other, Eleanor," he echoes softly.

"Right," I scoff. "Because love excuses people's deceptions and betrayals, right? Excuses the damage done in its name?"

"That's not what I'm saying," he argues back. "I just—"

"It's fine. I asked," I cut him off, not wanting to go down the road of what, exactly, is forgivable in the name of love. Because the truth is I don't know anymore. I'm not sure I ever really did in the first place. "At least they loved each other, and my whole fucking world didn't end for only lust. What happened that night?"

"I can only tell you what I remember."

"You mean that you were there?" I taunt softly. "That you told me it was all a dream?"

A long pause follows filled with so much tension I can practically feel the door vibrate between us.

"You remember."

"Barely."

Another soft thud of his head against the door. "I don't know much, Eleanor."

"You know more than me," I shoot back sharply.

"My dad was driving me home from baseball practice," he starts slowly. "His phone rang. I could hear a woman shouting on the other end of it. I remember him saying it would be okay, that he would be there soon. He looked at me and told me we had to go help someone."

I hear him suck in a sharp breath, but when he speaks again, his voice is empty, lost in tragic memory.

"The next thing I knew, we were pulling up at your house. The only reason I knew it was yours was because Jace was always bitching about having to play with you and had told me what it looked like. My dad told me to stay in the car, that he would be right back, but a few minutes after he went in, my patience was gone. I was only eight and figured if this was somewhere Jace played, I should be able to go inside too. So I went inside." He pauses. "And I could hear the shouts as soon as I made it to the staircase."

"What happened?" I gasp, uncaring now of the tears falling onto my cheeks. Heart breaking impossibly more for the little boy who lived through that terrible night with me. Even if the man doesn't deserve it.

"I honestly don't know," he answers brokenly. "It wasn't long after I made it to the top of the stairs that I heard the first gunshot. I couldn't move for a minute. I remember being frozen. So fucking scared I almost pissed my pants, but then…"

I hear his voice choke and swear I can feel him sink into the door. Like the wood is pressing harder against my skin as he tries to work his way through the barrier to me. To get impossibly closer.

"I heard you calling for your mom… and I couldn't leave you."

I swallow down the tightness in my throat, trying to make room for the words I want to speak. "And you told me I was dreaming," I finish, voicing the part of that night I remember now. "That you would read me a fairy tale so I could go back to sleep." The one part of our story that might be entirely real. Unblemished by any deceit.

"I thought you would be scared," he continues in a soft voice. "But you weren't. I didn't even get a book. Just made something up, tried to talk loud enough to cover up the—the crying… and you went right back to sleep."

"Then the second gunshot happened?" I guess.

"Then the second gunshot happened," he confirms. "My dad came out not long after that, found me in your room, and dragged me out of there. I told him that I wasn't going to just leave you. I didn't know exactly what had happened, but I knew it wasn't good. He told me we would call the police and that you would be fine. And he did," he finishes tensely. "He called my mom after that."

"Did she know?" I ask curiously. "What had been going on?"

"I don't know," he answers shortly. "He put me in the car but stayed outside to call my mom, and I was too freaked out to pay much attention. Too—too distracted and worried about you. I knew you mattered to Jace, and I had seen you, in some way—it doesn't matter." He sighs. "Then the next thing I knew, we were driving home, and the car was sliding off the road."

Shock fills me. "He died that night?"

"Yeah," Coop answers roughly. "He was pretty beside himself. Definitely shouldn't have been driving, was crying, actually, and well, it was raining." He clears his throat. "I woke up the next morning in the hospital, and my mom told me that my dad had died and that we were never to speak of that night again."

I can feel the wood of the door sticking to my face in the silence that follows. Silence filled with the horrible truth of our start, and the fear filling me up to ask him to tell the rest of our story. I can feel the shared pain between us because of that night and everything that followed winding its way through the door. The wooden material holding no dominion over such a thing. I can feel him, our pull, his presence, the shattered entity of us trying to find some kind of purchase for repair.

Because he's right there. Closer than he's been in a year. And I can practically feel his heart beating in tune with mine. It's excruciating. A breaking kind of thing to my soul in a way only he has ever managed to be.

"Why?" I finally rasp softly, forcing it from my aching throat. "Why did you do it, Coop?"

He knows what I'm asking. I don't need to explain.

There's only one truth left now, as far as I know.

"I…" A long moment passes before he sighs wearily and starts again. "I checked on you throughout the years. After I was old enough to wonder about you, the girl who had survived that night with me. The only other person who might've—" He stops suddenly, and a tense beat passes through the door. "From what I could tell online, you seemed totally fine. Honor student, your photographs on display at your high school and college. A promising future. Life of the party on social media. Completely fine, thriving even."

I feel that wood press into my skin even more.

"And I-I couldn't help but wonder how you could go on with your life so unaffected by what had happened when I was so fucking haunted by it." His voice chokes. "I never—I think I would have left you alone, Eleanor. But then… fuck." He sucks in a harsh breath. "But then I checked one day, and you were right there." His dark, humorless laugh vibrates the door under my cheek. "Practically on my front porch in Costa Rica, and the temptation was finally too strong to resist." He pauses for a beat. "I thought if I met you, maybe I could make sense of it somehow. Maybe I could figure out what your secret was. And then…" He trails off and I know he's remembering that first night of us like I am.

The shared memory a living thing flowing between us.

"Then you met me," I whisper, hating that some sliver of me understands.

If he's telling the truth, that is.

"Then I met you," Coop echoes softly. "And I knew how wrong it was. Knew I should have turned around and walked away the second I laid eyes on you. But fuck, like I told you before, Princess… I was captivated by you. You had me that very first night, at that first cock of your brow and smirk of your lips."

He pauses as if waiting for me to say something, but I can't.

Those words, that memory, I can't even allow myself to think of it. Of us like that.

He clears his throat. "I told myself it was just for one night. Lied to myself. Rationalized that even though I could never have you, I'd allow myself one night. You seemed okay. Maybe a little more reckless than most girls your age, but still okay. Then I woke up, and you were gone and I realized something." He pauses, voice unapologetic when he speaks again. "That you were just as damaged as me, because nobody could have had a night like we did and just walked away unless they were." I hear him heave a breath, almost a laugh. "And that, that I couldn't let go."

The tears are falling freely down my cheeks as he finishes, dripping down to puddle on the floor as I suck in a stuttering breath and wait, breaking bit by bit, a little more with each of his words that had built me before.

"And day after day," he continues, voice quietly reverent. "You brought me to my knees. And as each of our broken pieces fit perfectly together, my life finally made sense. I finally understood how someone could ruin so many others' lives for one person, because you—" He chokes. "You... damn, but there was no fighting that. No reasoning with it. So I met you and that was it. I was done for." A dark scoff sounds against the door. "There was no going back after that."

"What did you think?" I wonder out loud. "That I would never find out?"

"I honestly don't know. You were—" He exhales harshly. "You were the most impulsive thing I had ever done. The one thing that had spiraled out of my control faster than I could keep up. And I was so fucking terrified of losing you, of you finding out, so I-I did everything in my power to keep you."

A pause of shared memory, of promises broken and dreams shattered.

"It was…"

"A mistake," I surmise softly.

"No," he shoots back without pause. "No, Eleanor, you could never be a mistake. And even if you were, you'd be the best damn mistake I ever made."

Fuck him. Pouring out all this love on me after doing everything he did to break me. I can't stand it. The claims of love to justify deceit. Abandonment.

"Then why did you leave?" I ask harshly, giving in to my anger. "If you loved me so much, Coop, what the fuck happened?"

It takes him a minute to answer, voice dark and conflicted when he does. "Jace happened."

His words spur me to remember Jace's comment about being in the hospital together this morning and trepidation floods me. "His accident?" I guess fearfully.

"He needed part of a liver," he answers flatly. "No one here was a match."

My heart cracks open at his words. Worse than this morning. Worse than when I was staring at those pictures of my parents last night. Even worse than it did in Costa Rica.

"Fuck!" I shout, dropping my head back against the door and screwing my eyes shut against the pain slicing me in two. The horrible truth found in this reality.

"Princess?" Coop calls tensely.

"Fuck," I gasp raggedly, tears continuing to pour no matter what I do.

Because the girl in love with the stars in Costa Rica, brokenly wishes he had never left, that we had stayed on that beach forever. But the one that had fallen in love with the brilliance of the sun… she was eternally grateful that he had.

"I never abandoned you," Coop rushes out quickly as if feeling his time ticking down. "I had to decide, Jace wasn't going to last, and I did come back as quick as I could. But things happened along the way that you don't understand, and when I got there, you were already—"

"It doesn't matter," I interject, nothing left to me but heartache. "It doesn't matter. The truth is…" I open my eyes, staring blankly at the ceiling through blurry eyes as everything in me pulsates with agony. Eyes, body, heart, soul, and everything in between. Even the lost dreams ache. "The truth is you treated me like I was a mark, Cooper. You pulled me in and made me fall in love with you like I was a damn job."

A tense beat passes before he responds tauntingly. "You made yourself unforgettable, Eleanor. Or did you forget that part?"

The door between us turns into a universe the instant he utters the words.

That ember of anger sparks within me, fanned by his tone, in the last vestiges of feeling my being has to give for the day. But I know him. I know how we used to operate. Feed off and on one another. And I know he's fucking pushing me. Trying to force a reaction. Flaunting that demanding dominance in my face in hopes of getting me to crack for him like I used to.

Not anymore.

"Even if you are telling me the truth." I keep my voice purposefully emotionless, cold. "Even if it wasn't just some kind of sick mindfuck. You had already abandoned me the instant we met in that bar. Your deception ensured that."

I push myself shakily from the floor, digging down deeper than ever before and gathering the last of my strength as I flick the lock, opening the door.

He barely catches himself in time to keep from falling before his head whips around, night-forest eyes locking with mine as he slowly stands. Body tense and gaze full of uncertainty.

"So unless you find your mother, we have nothing more to say to each other, Cooper." I don't even bother trying to hide the last few tears that fall, voice full of contempt. "And I have no desire to see you in case that wasn't clear earlier." I jerk my chin toward the front door. "So you can leave now."

His eyes narrow on me dangerously, and I see his jaw clench, nostrils flaring.

"Get the fuck out of my house." I lift my chin at him defiantly, not backing down. "Like I said, Satan isn't welcome here."

Chapter Three

I sip my shit instant coffee the next morning with aching eyes, leaning up against the kitchen counter, wondering what the fuck happened to my life. Coop had surprisingly left last night after I told him to get the fuck out, but I knew it wouldn't be long before he and Jace were at my front door again. Demanding to be let in. Determined to earn forgiveness. Or at least Jace would be determined to earn forgiveness, Coop… fuck, I didn't even know what to think when it came to Coop anymore.

Besides that, I hated him.

That much I knew. Could feel it in the tight fury in my chest and the sureness of my mind as soon as I opened my eyes this morning. The kind of hate that ran right down to my very bones. I didn't care how sad his story might be. He had fucking deceived me from the start and I hated him for it. For ruining us before there ever even was such a thing. For loving me and destroying me. For leading us down this dark, twisted path that anyone could have seen would lead to only brokenness.

Even if some small part of me understood… I still hated him for it.

Jace, well, Jace was more complicated. He was harder to hate. He shouldn't be, it wasn't fair, but it was the reality of them and me. I still didn't know what the fuck to do with him though, still furious with him for hiding the truth from me.

Cousins.

I shake my head at the thought and take another sip of coffee, grimacing at the taste. Fucking cousins. Cousins that had been tied to me almost from the very start in such contrasting ways. Cousins that had ultimately betrayed me in their attempt to keep me.

What the fuck was I going to do?

I look down at my phone on the counter beside me, fighting the urge to call the guys like I had been all morning. All I wanted was to hear their voices right now. To spill the whole horrible truth to them and reach out for the familiar comfort of family. But that would only lead to more drama and quite possibly, violence. They would lose their shit if they knew Coop was here, much less what had happened with Jace too. And I didn't have it in me at the moment to calm them down while keeping my shit together too. So I resisted the urge. Even though it left me feeling unbearably alone.

Alone and furious… and embarrassed. Embarrassed that I had allowed myself to be so blinded by the pretty lies of two boys.

It was a volatile combination. One that had my chest feeling too tight. As if all the pain had settled there overnight and turned into nothing but an unbearable, poisonous pressure. Setting me on a tightrope, one push away from falling off and diving headlong into a magnificent plunge of self-destruction.

The sound of a car door closing distracts me from my turbulent thoughts and my hand tightens around my mug in response, tensing as I prepare for the next wave of assault.

But which one will it be?

I feel my shoulders tense up as I wait for the knock that takes longer to sound than it should, answering my question before I even hear his voice. And when the soft knock finally sounds, it sends a pulsing kind of ache through my furious heart.

"Ellie," Jace's melodic voice calls softly.

I hold myself stiffly in check, not moving an inch, hardly allowing myself to breathe because all part of me wants to do is go throw myself into his arms and soak up all the comfort his sea-spring scent has to offer. To not feel so alone for just a moment.

"I'm not picking your lock, Blondie," he calls after a moment. "That's got to count for something, right?"

I hate it. That I can't be weak with him right now. That I can't allow myself to be vulnerable with this boy who became my rising sun. That he ripped that away from me as surely as Coop lied to me that very first night when he pretended to not know who I was. It makes me so fucking angry with him it physically hurts.

"I love you, Ellie. I'm sorry and—" His melodic voice catches and I know he's in pain too but I have nothing to offer anyone but me at the moment. It's taking everything in me to just stay standing. "I know you can hear me," he continues, voice just a touch rougher than before. "But I also know you need space, and fuck, if anyone's earned the right to a little space right now, it's you."

I blink my eyes rapidly as they begin to prick at his words. I made a promise to myself this morning that there would be no more crying today. These boys didn't deserve any more of my tears and I didn't particularly like the habit I was getting into of becoming a sobbing mess when it came to them either. No matter whether it was justifiable or not.

"I'm leaving coffee and breakfast for you and—and Coop." He pauses for a moment, and I know he's pulling his bottom lip through his teeth nervously, unable to tug on the lip of his boot since he's standing. "I'm going to head over to Coop's because he thinks he found his mom. So when you're ready to talk about that… just reach out, okay?"

Of course he did.

I scoff and roll my eyes before taking another sip of my coffee. Satan probably took my words last night as a challenge instead of the fuck off back to hell they actually were. Twisted bastard that he was.

"And Ellie…" Jace's pleading voice sounds again. "Just please be careful, okay? Kyle and Kurt are still out there somewhere, so just… I don't know. Stay here, please, okay?" He knocks on the door again. "That was just in case you weren't already awake… I love you, pretty girl."

It takes a minute, as if he lingered, hoping I would come to the door, but eventually I hear the sound of him getting back into his jeep and pulling away. I let my body slowly relax back against the counter, wondering how much Coop told him yesterday. If he told him the truth of what happened between us. From what Tiff mentioned about them yelling at each other… I'm guessing so.

And I'm guessing Jace was firmly on team El when it came to that one.

Fucking Coop. He had found his mom to force the issue between us, and I knew what price he would demand for the information. Time with me, in some form or fashion, would be the expected payment. It was all a play to drag me back into his hemisphere and all it did was solidify my view that he really was fucking Satan. Possibly Satan with a heart, but still Satan, determined to wreck me, soul and all.

And it was going to work because I needed to know what happened in that room that night. Needed it to hopefully quell some of the fury in me. Although what I was hoping to hear, I still wasn't exactly sure.

Fuck it.

If I was going to have to venture into hell to get what I wanted, the least I could do was load up on some ammunition beforehand. Pushing off the counter, I sip my coffee while walking back to Gram's bedroom and open the closet door. Running my eyes along the clothes hanging there out of habit before grabbing a T-shirt and some sweatpants at random. Not really giving a shit what I look like. It's not like I'm exactly trying to impress anyone today.

Foregoing a shower because, again, something about it just seems so pointless right now. I quickly change and throw my hair up into a messy bun before grabbing my keys and heading out the door. Grudgingly making sure that it's locked behind me this time and steadfastly ignoring the coffee and breakfast Jace left for me. I will not be wooed by coffee this time and it's not like I have any kind of appetite anyway. Hopping into Franny, I pull out of the driveway and turn the music up to blaring as I head toward the marina.

At least Jace had done me the courtesy of letting me know he wasn't going to be there so I could stock up on my ammunition in peace. For a while at least.

I pull into the marina and park in my usual spot, figuring there's no need to hide my presence since I'm going to let them know exactly where I am here shortly. Meandering down the dock to Jace's boat, I pull myself up onto the deck and let myself into the cabin with an eye roll that he doesn't feel the need to lock *his* door before heading directly for the bedroom. I steel myself against the smell of his sea-spring scent before crawling onto the bed and reaching for one of the compartments lining the walls that I know he keeps his stash in. Grabbing the wood box out of the compartment, I sit on the bed and open it up, quickly pushing aside the weed pens in favor of the rolling paper and green.

Surprisingly, Jace usually didn't have the patience for it when we smoked, but I appreciated the art of a perfectly rolled blunt. And after the hell I had endured the past couple days I had sure as fuck earned one. I set the contraband on top of the box and carefully roll up the blunt, taking the time to make it into the perfect little baseball bat shape that I love so much before grabbing a lighter and heading up the deck. Pausing to snag his speaker and a mug to ash in along my way.

I climb the stairs and sit down on the lower deck, leaning back against the bars and setting my collection of goodies down next to me. Pulling my phone from the pocket of my sweatpants, I sync my phone up to the speaker before starting up one of my angrier playlists and turning the volume up to an ear-splitting level. My teeth almost rattling as I grab the blunt from the deck and light it, taking a deep inhale of the sweet smoke and holding it in for a minute before exhaling.

I can feel the tension ease from my body as the familiar buzz fills my head. Feel that horrible poisonous pressure in my chest ease just a bit. I take another hit and grab my phone, pulling up the messages and clicking on Jace's name before typing out a message and pressing send.

El: I'm at the boat.

That should give me just enough time to finish the blunt if they're at fucking Leah Reynold's house. God knows they're probably running for their cars already. I close my eyes and take another deep hit, leaning my head back against the railing of the deck to soak up the sun in hopes that it'll improve my mood somehow. Little do they know I plan to get so gloriously high that even their betrayal doesn't bother me… well, that'd be impossible, but at least it won't bother me as much. Allows me to be in their presence and look at them without breaking.

Are we diving off that tightrope then, El?

Not quite. But close… so incredibly close.

It's right when I'm getting to the good part of "Add It Up" by Violent Femmes that I feel a light kick to the bottom of my Converse-clad foot. I crack my eyes, looking up into a pair of amused firework-green ones staring back at me. Jace nods to the speaker at my side, and I reluctantly reach over, turning the volume down to a more bearable level and seeing Coop staring back at me from where he stands at the bottom of the stairs. The disapproval in his dark gaze is evident.

Apparently, Satan didn't approve of my coping mechanism.

Go figure.

I skate my eyes over him as if he doesn't even exist before turning back to look up at Jace, seeing the grin he's trying to hide pulling at the edges of his lips.

"You trying to get me in trouble, Blondie?" he drawls playfully.

"Needed something to take the edge off," I respond tonelessly, taking another hit of the blunt before continuing, knowing I'm being an epic bitch but unable to stop the poison in my heart from lashing out. Even if the weed has dulled it some. "Plus, I figured we've fucked up here, and if your neighbors didn't mind that then this wouldn't be an issue either."

You could cut the tension with a knife in the silence that follows my words and I see the reproach fill Jace's gaze. His body tenses, eyes flicking to Coop before coming back to me. "Ellie…" He drags out warningly.

Well, fuck him too then. I flick the ash off the blunt into the mug at my side and take the last hit as Coop speaks.

"It's okay, Jace," he says, low voice filled with insolence. "If Eleanor wants to act like a brat and lash out with her feelings, let her." He pauses purposefully. "She knows I can take it."

I jerk my head to meet his challenging night-forest gaze, anger striking at the memory of his words. "Satan," I snap, looking away to stub the blunt out in the mug. "Satan… doesn't get to speak." Taking a deep breath, I look back up to Jace. "So he found his mom?"

Jace's eyes search mine for a moment, as if taking stock of my mental state before he nods. "Yeah, Blondie, he did."

"Where is she?"

"He thinks she's at a cabin about two hours from here that his dad used to go to write at."

Something of a humorless laugh leaves me. "How appropriate." I grab my phone and push up off the deck to stand, finally meeting Coop's gaze again as I look between the two of them. My stunning liars. "So what are we waiting for?"

"We were waiting for you," Coop answers, narrowed eyes locking with mine. "One question first though."

I roll my eyes, voice dripping sarcasm when I speak. "Of course there is."

He nods to Jace at my side. "How come he gets to speak?"

I give him a half shrug as I come down the stairs. "Because the sound of his voice makes me feel just a tad less violent than yours."

Chapter Four

The silence in Jace's jeep is damn near unbearable. We've been driving for just over an hour now and so far, no one has spoken a word. I had thought about putting on music when we got in but had quickly discarded the idea, opting to let them suffer with my silence instead. It was uncomfortable as hell and would probably kill me more if it wasn't for the fact I was still just a little too high to care. That was the only thing keeping the tension from invading my body at the thought of what answers we were about to face next.

That and the game I had come up with to pass the time of betting on which one of them would break the silence first. It was such a toss-up. Jace was the one who would beg for my forgiveness but he also understood the need for space, whereas Coop was undoubtedly the most stubborn out of everyone in the car but he also couldn't help but always push me. I feel Jace's eyes dart to me again as they have been every few minutes from where he sits in the driver's seat while Coop's gaze practically drills a hole in my back.

Hmm. Jace, definitely Jace.

I see him open his mouth next to me out of the corner of my eye and then close it before giving a weary sigh.

So close.

My lips twitch with the first thread of amusement I've felt since opening that godforsaken file two days ago. Not exactly the time for the apology tour, Dawson.

Reaching out for the bottle of water in the cup holder, I quickly uncap it and chug half, trying to get rid of the cottony dryness in my mouth as Coop's mocking voice sounds from the back seat.

"Coming down from your high, Princess?"

Goddammit. He couldn't even let me win my own bet.

I slowly twist the cap back on, trying to focus on the movement and not the thought of him at my back before setting the bottle back in the cup holder.

"I'm actually surprised you're not blasting Taylor Swift," he continues tauntingly. "You know, for old times' sake."

Jace's curious gaze darts to mine but I shake my head just the barest hint, letting him know to leave it alone. I'm not fucking going down memory lane any more than necessary today. And I'm also not speaking to Satan if I can help it. Grabbing my phone from the center console, I plug it into the aux cord and launch *Spotify*. Quickly scrolling through my library in search of the song I want before finding it and pressing play. The first notes of "cinderella's dead" play through the speakers, quickly followed by the lyrics and I can feel the pissed-off energy pouring off Coop at my back in response to them.

I feel him grab on to the back of my seat before hauling himself forward and grinding out into my ear. "You weren't fucking nineteen… Princess." He emphasizes his name for me, voice low and dark as my whole body tenses at the feel of his breath at my ear. The sudden intrusion of his sandalwood scent.

I reach for the water bottle again to put some distance between us while mumbling. "Close enough."

Jace's low burst of laughter next to me draws my attention and I narrow my eyes on him. "I don't know what the hell you're laughing at, Dawson," I snap irritably. "Your apology breakfast is currently rotting on the front porch, so you have about as much reason to laugh as him."

His surprised eyes meet mine and I see a flash of hurt in them as he visibly swallows, tightening his grip on the steering wheel.

But what the fuck did he expect? That a little breakfast and caffeine would erase his deceit?

Try harder, Jace. This goes beyond your usual charms.

I reach out and turn the volume up to a deafening level before leaning back in my seat again. Done with dealing with their shit for the moment. Especially now that my high has most definitely faded due to the forced interactions.

The rest of the drive passes in tense silence, my song choices growing angrier as that poisonous pressure fills my chest again until it's back in full force. Sitting right there behind my breastbone and just waiting to crack it open.

Un-fucking-bearable.

Coop taps Jace's shoulder before pointing to a dirt road coming up on the right and I reluctantly reach out to turn down the music. Figuring we probably shouldn't blare our arrival since she's trying to hide out. Jace takes the turn, and we drive down the bumpy road for a mile or so before coming up on a wood cabin that has my stomach clenching up on sight.

It reminds me of the shack in Cahuita for some reason. Maybe the size or shape, the similar color of the wood or some intangible essence of it. But regardless of why, the structure brings on a whole flood of memories that I'm trying to avoid like the plague.

I hate it on sight. The whole fucking peaceful setup in the woods and all.

And I wonder if they ever came here.

Jace parks his jeep a little ways from the cabin and we all get out, closing our doors softly. The boys pause at the front as I do and look at me, Jace for direction and Coop probably just to piss me off impossibly more.

Well, maybe not, but that's what I'm going with anyway.

"How do you want to play this, Blondie?" Jace asks softly, taking a step closer to me.

Bold move, Dawson.

I give him a shrug and nod toward the cabin. "Nothing left to do but see if the witch is home."

Coop scoffs a laugh and I turn my head to meet his darkly amused gaze in time to catch his lips ghosting up. "You'll find no argument from me on that, Princess."

I jerk my eyes away from his and start to walk to the front door, trying to leave all those memories behind me.

But Jace quickly catches up to me and reaches out, grabbing my arm and bringing me to a halt. "Maybe let Coop go first? She'll probably be more likely to open the door for him."

I suck in a deep breath, purposefully flicking my gaze down to where he's holding my arm and his eyes flash with that pain again as he lets go. "Fine."

Coop's eyes slide between us with a dangerous kind of curiosity as he walks past us and I make sure to give him my best go-to-hell look before he looks away. I watch him walk up and knock on the door, my body practically vibrating with tension as we wait to see if she'll answer. But it only takes a moment for it to open and I start forward again as soon as I see that coppery hair flash over his shoulder.

"...I still don't know what you're doing—"

I'm almost running by the time I make it to the front door and she notices me, surprise flashing over her face and stopping her midsentence.

It doesn't take long for her gaze to turn icy though as she flicks it to Coop. "What are you doing with the Delacroix girl?"

"Oh," I interject snarkily before Coop can get a word out. "Didn't you know, mommy dearest?" She waits a beat before bringing her eyes back to mine when Coop doesn't respond. "Surprise! I'm your motherfucking daughter-in-law."

I see her nostrils flare as Jace comes up to stand at my side and she continues to stare at me for a moment, as if her brain can't seem to grasp the concept before she flicks her eyes back to Coop.

"What is she talking about?" Her voice lashes out angrily.

Coop clears his throat next to me. "It's complicated."

"Complicated?" She laughs viciously. "Complicated? God, Cooper, you really are just like your father." She shakes her head, still smiling humorlessly. "Despite everything I did to try and change that—"

I sense Coop tensing up more with each of her words at my side and quickly snap my fingers in front of his mother's face, stopping her tirade.

"Right here, Leah." Despite everything between us, I can't stand to see her break him apart. Only I get to do that now. "I think it's time we take this family reunion inside. What do you say?"

She hesitates, sweeping her eyes across the three of us, and I watch as her brow tightens with tension. Hitting me hard as it reminds me of the same way her son's does.

"You don't really have much of a choice here." Jace drawls the quiet threat on my other side, leaning in the barest hint and letting her know we're not about to be turned away.

Leah meets Jace's gaze and I see her chest expand with a deep breath before she snaps. "Fine." Turning away from the door, she leaves it open and walks into the small cabin, leaving us to trail in behind her.

I step into the cabin first, breathing in the neglected smell in the air and seeing the sparse furniture dotting the space. There's nothing but a kitchen table with a few chairs and a bed. A small kitchen jutting off to one side, bare of anything on the counters and it's clear the place hasn't been visited in years by the thick layer of dust and cobwebs covering everything. The boys follow behind me as I watch Leah walk to the table, taking a seat before her eyes move between her son and me curiously.

"How did you two even meet?"

I bite the inside of my cheek in the silence that follows her question, keeping my expression flat and not backing down from her gaze despite my refusal to answer.

A cold smile spreads across her face and I can see the wheels in her mind turning as her eyes land on her son, filling with a cruel kind of interest. "Damn, Cooper. You must have really been more damaged by that night than I ever realized."

Her words spark that fucking unreasonable desire to shield him again and I take a step forward, mustering up a bratty smirk. "But that's not what we're here to talk about, Leah."

She watches me carefully as I pull out the chair across from her and take a seat. "So enlighten me, Eleanor, what is?"

I pause, staring into her eyes and seeing the swirling hate there that she's still trying to hide. "The truth."

Her lips purse at my words. "You didn't get enough of that from your parents' file?"

"Oh I got plenty of it," I scoff snarkily. "Just not the truth I'm here for today. Not the truth you're hiding."

Her eyes flick to Coop and narrow before coming back to land on me. “And I’m guessing my son had no problem enlightening you?”

“Your son…” I take a deep breath, trying to ease some of that pressure in my chest and choose my words carefully. She doesn’t know how much I’ve figured out and I don’t want to give her any ammunition to hold out on me. “Your son only gave me the last piece of the puzzle. You gave yourself away in those photos though. Standing by the door and trying to cover it up.”

Her eyes slowly roll over my face, picking it apart and making me feel like an insect under a microscope. “Maybe you are smarter than Nadia after all.” That cold smile pulls at her lips and she looks to Coop purposefully. “Then again, maybe not.”

Fucking bitch.

“Careful, Mother.” Coop’s low, deadly voice threatens at my back. “Spew your poison at me all you want but leave Eleanor out of it.”

“God.” She leans back in her chair, crossing her arms with a bitter laugh. “What is it about Delacroix women and Monroe men? I never understood what had put Adam so completely under Nadia’s spell.”

“Maybe that they actually have a heart,” Jace drawls out sarcastically, walking around the table to stand at the head of the other chair and brace his hands on top of it.

Leah raises her brows at him, eyes considering. “And apparently Dawson men too.”

"So you knew?" I question curiously, trying to get this conversation back on track so we don't spend the next hour dissecting my fucked-up love life or lack thereof.

Her eyes come back to me, tone annoyed when she speaks. "Of course I knew." She shakes her head. "A blind man would have been able to see the change in Adam. He was absolutely smitten with Nadia. Head over heels." She scoffs before breaking my gaze and looking out the window. "The funny thing is we had run into them, Nadia and Cane, throughout the years. At the grocery store, at the Dawson's for a birthday party a couple times. We weren't friends, but it wasn't like we didn't know of each other either. I just…" She sighs, eyes narrowing in thought. "I don't know where it changed. How it started."

Well I sure as fuck wasn't about to clue her in.

I clear my throat, drawing her gaze back to me. "Did my father know?"

"No." She purses her lips with a disgusted expression. "No, like my husband, Cane was too obliviously in love with Nadia to see what was happening right under his nose." She pauses. "That is until I told him."

My heart stops completely in my chest for a moment at her words. At what they could possibly mean. "You-you told him?" I stutter out in shock.

She gives me a look like it's the most obvious thing in the world. "Of course I told him. After Adam wouldn't stop the affair no matter how much I warned him to… I went to Cane, hoping he could make Nadia see sense."

"When—" I pause, staring into her blank eyes and knowing what her answer will be already. "When exactly did you tell him?"

"The day they all died."

The air whooshes from my lungs and I reach for the seat of the chair I'm sitting on, gripping it tightly to keep from flying across the table at her.

"Jesus Christ," Jace mutters, staring at her with a horrified expression for a moment before his eyes move to me with concern.

"What happened in that room?" Each of my words is spoken purposefully, slowly, and quietly in sharp contrast to the rage pumping through my veins.

"Exactly what I told you before."

"I don't believe you."

"What do you want me to tell you?" She tilts her head at me quizzically. "That Adam did it?" A small smile plays across her face as she shakes her head. "No, Eleanor, Adam was many things but he never had that in him." She slides her eyes to Coop before bringing them back to me. "My son gets his more lethal tendencies from me."

"Don't try to distract me with him," I snap angrily. "What the fuck happened in that room?"

"Why do you care so much? Why not just move on with your life?" She narrows her eyes at me. "Is it the little girl in you? Longing for some fairy tale of a family that you never really had? Longing for some fantasy that your parents didn't really choose to abandon you—"

"Mother." Coop's voice lashes out at her from behind me, bringing her tirade to a halt as he walks to the table and looks down at her with eyes that are filled with dark fury. "I won't warn you again."

She sighs, shaking her head at him as if he's nothing more than an errant child before bringing her gaze back to me. "The truth, Eleanor, is that when Adam showed up, Cane pulled a gun from the nightstand, told him to leave and threatened him with it, and then Nadia stepped in front of Adam at precisely the wrong moment. The moment Cane's finger must have slipped on the trigger, I'm not really sure of the order of events to be honest." She shrugs carelessly. "Maybe he really was going to shoot Adam."

That pressure in my chest continues to build with each of her words, fingers tightening on the chair until I'm sure my nails are probably bleeding.

"And then, when he realized what he had done… Cane couldn't live with himself." She gives another careless shrug as if this entire discussion is just a waste of time. "Or so Adam told me before he went and died too."

She's a fucking monster, I realize, staring into her uncaring gaze. It doesn't matter how justified her actions might have been, what they led to, the malicious intent she set out with… she's a monster, plain and simple.

And in a way, so were my parents. My mother with her selfishness and my father with his careless or purposeful actions. Either way, he still chose to leave me too. To leave me alone in the world with no answers. To leave me with this fucking mess of me to clean up.

I was always right, regardless if it had been a lie or not. Coop's and my darkness had called to each other because we were born of similar monsters.

"Ellie?" Jace's soft, melodic voice pulls at me and I look at him, realizing that I must have been blankly staring for a while because everyone is looking at me. "You ready to get out of here, Blondie? I think we got what we came for."

I stare into his firework eyes for a moment, eyes that are filled with pain for me before jerking a nod. Unable to find my voice despite the fact that my brain feels utterly empty for the first time since I set out on this journey.

She really was telling some form of the truth all along. If I choose to believe her, which I do, her whole speech was entirely too carelessly cruel to be fake.

Coop walks to my side and leans down, bringing his fingertips to press against mine, gently encouraging me to let go of the chair. I somehow manage to make my aching fingers loosen their grip, looking at him as I do but his night-forest gaze isn't waiting to greet me like usual. Instead his head is bowed, eyes glued to the floor and body tight with tension. I take a deep breath and stand while Jace moves to my side as we begin to walk out of the cabin. Leah's chair scrapes as she does the same, trailing behind us to the door.

We've made it a few steps away from the threshold when I hear her voice call out behind me. "A word of motherly advice, son… get away from the Delacroix girl as fast as you can."

Just keep walking, El. Don't let her see how her words get to you. They shouldn't get to you.

"If you don't… well." She laughs that horrible sound. "Mark my words, she'll spell nothing but death and destruction for you just like her whore of a mother did for your father."

That pressure in my chest finally explodes and I whip around, charging back toward her before either of the boys can stop me. I see the shocked expression spread across her face at my abrupt change in demeanor about a second before I bring my hand down across it with the hardest slap I can muster.

"You shut your fucking mouth," I spit the words in her face, body shaking. "You bitter bitch. You shut your fucking mouth."

She brings a hand to her cheek that's quickly turning an angry red and then lifts it away, looking at it in disbelief for a moment before turning her hate-filled eyes to me.

"You know," I scoff at her. "I would actually feel sorry for you if it wasn't for the fact that you're such a massive cunt."

She goes to take a step toward me right as I catch a whiff of a sea-spring scent at my back and her eyes move over my shoulder, the sight of Jace bringing her to a halt.

He wraps an arm around my middle, dropping his head down next to mine, voice coming out soft and soothing. "Leave her to her misery, Ellie. It's worse than anything you could do to her."

I allow him to pull me away from her and guide me to the car because deep down, I know he's right. He keeps his arm around me all the way to the jeep this time, and I allow that too, because I'm too caught up in the rage to protest his touch at the moment. It's just as he's tucking me into the passenger side of the jeep that I see Coop still standing in front of the jeep, staring at his mother.

"I did warn you," he tosses out at her before turning and walking away. His shuttered gaze catches mine for a second as he passes by before quickly darting away.

As we pull away from the cabin, I can't pull my eyes away from Leah Reynolds who is still standing in the open doorway. A hand pressed to her cheek again with an expression of disgust on her hate-filled face.

I don't think it's an image I'll ever forget for some reason.

No one tries to speak on the way home. No music is played. All of us are too lost in our own thoughts for me to even try to play any games.

Chapter Five

When I push open the door of Adam's place that night, I know I've stepped off the tightrope, executing a perfect swan dive headlong into the glorious pit of self-destruction. But I just couldn't sit in Gram's house for a second longer with nothing but the sound of Leah Reynolds's voice echoing through my head to keep me company. And the sad truth is I didn't really have anywhere else to go. I had gotten out of Jace's jeep after we had got back today and driven away in Franny without speaking a word to either of them. The mess of both relationships at the back of my mind for once.

And surprisingly, they had left me alone since.

I take in the bar, seeing that it's not as busy as usual considering it's a Sunday and that suits me just fine. I'm here to drink, not socialize. To fill that now empty space in my chest with enough alcohol to ensure a dreamless oblivion when I fall asleep tonight. I walk to the bar and see Tiff do a double take when she spots me, her eyes widening as they take in my disheveled appearance. Can't say I blame her though. I'm rocking the same careless combination that I had put on that morning and don't really give a fuck what anyone thinks of me at this point.

She gives me a small smile as I slide onto the barstool in front of her. "El."

"Tiff." I manage to twitch my lips a bit at her in return.

"How—uh," she starts nervously. "How are you?"

I wonder what they've told her. Truth or lie?

"I'm…" I sigh, eyes moving across the bottles behind her. "I'm surviving, Tiff."

She scrunches her nose up. "That's good, I guess?"

I look at her confused expression, the picture of blissful ignorance, and for a moment, I wonder if it's really better off to be that way. If I really was a masochist for seeking these answers to begin with and digging up graves, demanding their ghosts speak to me. And if I ever would have felt the urge if it wasn't for a darkly arrogant guy stumbling into me at a bar in Costa Rica. Dropping that rock in the pond that sent me on a desperate search for closure.

"I'll take that bottle of tequila and a glass, please." I point to the one I want behind the bar. "You can put it on Jace's tab. He owes me."

Tiff's eyes widen and she hesitates for a second before mumbling. "Ah, okay."

I cast my gaze around the bar as she turns to grab the bottle. "Where are they by the way?"

I don't need to specify which they I'm talking about.

"Um…" She brings the bottle back and places it on the counter in front of me before reaching for a glass. "Jace left a little bit ago, said he would be back soon. And Coop, uh…" She sets the glass down. "Coop hasn't left his room since he got back today."

I pull the cork from the top of the bottle and nod before pouring a generous amount into my glass.

That's good. Should give me the time I need to get shit-faced before they know I'm here. Because they will come once they know. Unfortunately, they both know me too well and will be able to spot my self-destructive spiral a mile away.

I take a gulp of the tequila I usually so enjoy sipping and see Tiff press her lips together in front of me.

"What?" I rasp, feeling the liquor burn down my throat.

"It's just…" She hesitates and I wave my hand in a motion for her to continue. "We never finished our conversation from yesterday."

"Fuck." I roll my eyes, taking another gulp of the tequila. "They really don't tell you anything."

"But you could—"

"No, Tiff," I snap, softening my voice at the hurt expression on her face as I continue. "Listen, it's just, he's your brother. Your family." I shake my head. "I'm sorry but it's too complicated and I'm not going to be the one to wreck your world. You need to talk to Coop."

A crestfallen expression fills her face but she nods in acceptance before turning and walking to the other end of the bar.

I sip down the rest of the tequila in my glass in record time before pouring myself another. Trying to not think about the fact that I'm drinking in a bar owned by the man who had played such a huge part in wrecking my world. Not paying attention to anything around me except the steady buzz of sound that's drowning out the wreckage in my head. I almost miss it now that it's gone, that furious pressure in my chest. The empty ache it's left only adds to the terrible loneliness that's plagued me since the boat.

I'm halfway through my second glass of tequila when someone sits down on the barstool next to mine, drawing my attention. I lift my gaze to Andrea's worried one and squint a little as everything becomes wobbly for a second.

She gives me a small smile. "Well, this certainly looks like a cry for help if ever I've seen one."

A burst of laughter leaves my lips at her words. "Not exactly." I dip my glass at her in cheers. "More of a well-earned bender."

She tilts her head at me in question. "Want some company?"

I turn my head and skate my eyes along the bar, picking out Zane and Tommy where they're sitting at a table with fucking Sam of all people. All of them staring at me with open interest. And if Zane and Tommy are here.... It won't be long before my stunning liars arrive.

"I guess I wouldn't mind yours." I give her a careless shrug. "As long as you don't make me talk about my feelings."

"Done." She nods before reaching over the bar and helping herself to a glass.

I pour some tequila into her glass, having to focus hard on the task to avoid spilling. The difficulty of the act letting me know that I am well on my way to the gloriously drunk state I set out to achieve. Putting the bottle back on the counter, I see Tiff staring at us from the other end of the bar and I narrow my eyes at her, quickly sending her gaze darting away.

"Did Tiff text you?"

"Yep," Andrea answers easily, giving me another smile when I look back at her. "She thought you could use a friend who wasn't her."

"Hmm," I respond noncommittally and maybe a little drunkenly.

Andrea pauses for a beat before going right for the gold. "So you and Coop, huh?"

I dart my eyes away, taking another sip of tequila to buy myself time before answering. Trying to force away the aching in my heart that's becoming harder to contain in my inebriated state.

Maybe this wasn't the smartest idea.

But it was too late now though and I wasn't a quitter.

"I thought we weren't talking about feelings."

"We're not," she replies quickly. "These are facts."

A soft scoff leaves me and I meet her curious eyes. "Who told you?"

"As soon as we knew Coop was back in town… and then Jace dropped off the radar, well, we knew something was up, so…" She shrugs. "We cornered Tommy, and he fessed up. Although none of us know exactly what the story is."

"Perfect." I tip my head back and finish off the remaining tequila in my glass with a large gulp that has me pulling a face as I set it back down. "More fodder for the Delacroix rumor mill. Should keep the town going for at least another decade."

"If not two." She laughs softly. "So are you going to put me out of my misery over here?"

I pour more tequila into my glass before taking another large gulp. "Trust me, Andrea." I shake my head. "You don't want this damage. I—" My voice catches and I have to clear my throat to keep going. "I can barely handle it myself."

A worried expression fills her face and she opens her mouth to respond right when a melodic voice sounds at my back.

"Then give it to me."

I turn in my seat slowly, locking eyes with Jace and seeing the devastating heartbreak in them laid bare for all the world to see.

He turns to Andrea and nods over to where Zane is sitting. "Give us a minute, would you?"

"Of course," she answers softly, standing and patting his shoulder as she walks by.

Jace keeps his eyes on me as she leaves and then slowly steps around the barstool, reaching over with one arm to cage me in before dipping his head down close to mine.

"Give it to me, Ellie," he repeats, the pain in his voice matching the expression on his face. "I know I fucked up in the worst kind of way. I know I betrayed your trust and I will spend the rest of my life regretting not just coming clean with you in that moment. I just," He pauses, blowing out a stuttering breath. "I heard his name fall from your lips and it fucking terrified me. I didn't know what had happened with y'all. I didn't know what would happen if…" He trails off as if he can't even handle the thought.

"If you told me," I finish quietly, squinting as I try to keep him in focus.

"If I told you." He nods. "All I knew was that I had just found you, we had just found each other again, and that those lips that his name had just fallen from were mine now and it—it was wrong." His gaze flicks away for a moment before he lifts it back to mine and moves even closer. Heart in his eyes and voice low and intimate when he speaks. "Fuck, it probably still is wrong, I know that, but I can't. I can't just let you go, Blondie." He brings his hand up, lightly playing with the strands of hair escaping at the base of my neck as he pulls his bottom lip through his teeth nervously.

"You know, I used to stand up on that stage." He nods his head in the direction of the small stage in the bar. "Or just play some songs at the beach and part of me loved it. The attention. The act of performing. But then I fell in love with you, and you became everything to me." His firework eyes search my face as if committing it to memory before continuing. "You're the intriguing intro that draws me in. You're the verse that just barely gives an inch before your chorus fucking memorizes me. You're hidden between every heartbreaking cord that I pick at the bridge and your laughter plays in tune with every note of the song in my mind." He brings his hand around, brushing a few strands of hair behind my ear with a soft caress. "You're the whole damn melody to me, Ellie."

My lower lip is trembling by the time he finishes and it takes me a minute to reply, having to fight to get my words out. Fight against the overwhelming urge to just give in and crumble into his arms right then and there.

"I'm so mad at you, Dawson," I finally tell him, voice breaking and cracking all over the place.

"I know, pretty girl." He nods, eyes crinkling at the corners as if in pain. "But do you think you can forgive me?"

"I don't know," I tell him honestly, shaking my head. "I want—I just don't know. I'm so mixed up right now, Jace, so—" So full of betrayal that I don't know where Coop's ends and Jace's begins. And I'm definitely not going to figure anything out in my current state. "I need time to figure that out. Figure it all out. Okay?"

I can see the questions filling his eyes, but after a moment's hesitation, he nods slowly. "That's fair." He lifts his hand, tugging lightly on one of the strands of hair escaping from my messy bun and some of that old playfulness winds its way back into his eyes. "Now, how drunk are you?"

"About a sip of tequila short of blackout territory."

A hesitant grin plays across his face with a quick flash of dimples. "Then how about we go get you some food, yeah?"

I open my mouth to respond but hesitate, wanting to go with him but not wanting to face any more of our broken reality today.

His face falls at my silence. "Give it to me," he repeats, trailing his fingers down my side to lightly rest on my hip. "We don't have to talk anymore. I'm not asking you to forgive me tonight. Just let me be there for you, please. Give me the pain tonight and just think about the rest, okay?"

I see the naked honesty in his expression and know I'm in no position to turn down his offer, nor do I want to, I want his comfort tonight. Maybe, subconsciously, that's why I came here in the first place instead of going anywhere else I could have to escape him.

"Okay." I nod, trying to slide off the barstool and almost eating it as my foot catches on one of the legs.

Jace's hands shoot out, gripping my hips and steadying me as he sets me on my feet. "You are trashed." He looks down at me worriedly.

"Can you blame me?"

"No," he answers in a soft voice. "But I wish you would have just come to me instead."

"You have to earn it," I mumble, reaching out to grip his arm as the whole bar starts to sway now that I'm standing. "Forgiveness."

"I will," he promises seriously, looping his hand around my middle to help balance me as he turns us toward the front door. "Come on, let's get you home."

Jace is pretty much half holding me up as we start to make our way out of the bar, keeping me steady on my increasingly failing feet. And we've made it about halfway when I notice Sam walking toward us with a definite sway in her hips, an overly confident expression on her bitchy face. She comes to a stop in front of us and cocks her hip, barely sparing me a glance as she tilts her head at Jace flirtatiously.

"Not now, Sam," Jace snaps at her when she opens her mouth.

"Ahh. Come on, Jace." She juts her bottom lip out at him. "We used to have so much fun together."

Andrea walks quickly up to Sam's side and grabs her elbow. "Excuse her." She darts her eyes to us nervously. "El's not the only one who's had one too many tonight."

"Hey," I mumble in protest, pretty much sounding exactly as drunk as she called me out on being.

Sam rips her elbow from Andrea's grip, shooting her a dirty look. "And I told you." She drags out, looking back to Jace. "Wouldn't he rather have me than Coop's sloppy seconds?"

"Jesus fucking Christ, Samantha," Jace says, shaking his head and pulling me along as he goes to step around her.

She steps halfway back into his path, placing a hand on his shoulder and stepping into the side of his body opposite from me. "She's a fucking train wreck, Jace. Always has been. And now she's Coop's used goods to boot. Let her go," she whispers huskily, earning a look of disgust from Jace.

Sam turns her gaze on me. "Tell him, El." She smiles nastily. "Tell him how good Coop probably beat that pussy up. I mean." She laughs. "I wouldn't know, but I can imagine it probably leaves you with some interesting comparisons at the end of the day, right?"

"Oh my god!" Andrea shouts in a mortified voice. "Shut the fuck up, Sam."

"God, Sam." I sigh wearily, resisting Jace's pull when he tries to tug me away. Already knowing there's no turning back by the rage her words have brought back to life in me. "You really are just an epic bitch, aren't you?"

Pushing through the tequila-induced haze as much as possible, I squint to bring her into focus and clench my fist. Then using Jace's hold on me for leverage, I quickly pull back my arm before clocking her right in the face as hard as I can.

Sam's high-pitched scream echoes through the bar immediately, drawing everyone's gaze as she brings her hand to her nose and leans over as Andrea's mouth pops open. Her eyes flicking between her friend and me as if she can't believe what just happened while Jace just stares at me with a stunned expression.

"What?" I give him a careless shrug. "She was asking for it."

Sam lifts her livid eyes to mine. "You fucking whore!" she spits out at me, still holding her nose that I can now see is dripping blood.

"Call me a whore again!" I clench my fist again, taking a step toward her. "I fuckin—" My words are cut off when Jace quickly dips down and throws me over his shoulder, walking past Sam and making me have to lift my head to keep her in my sights. "Dare you, Sam!" I laugh tauntingly as Jace's long strides eat up the distance to the door. "You're just jealous that neither of them wants your trampy ass! They wouldn't touch you with a ten-foot—"

Jace pushes through the door to the bar, letting it swing shut behind us and effectively ending my threats. I let my head drop, hanging loosely over his shoulder as the whole world starts to tilt and sway again. The sound of a motorcycle pulling into the lot draws my attention and I turn my head, watching it pull up alongside us before the driver cuts the engine.

Two guesses who the driver is, El. And I really hope you don't need both even in your drunken state.

Jace turns toward the motorcycle and I lean my head to the side, peeking out from behind his waist to watch Coop sit up and pull the helmet off his head.

He takes us in with shuttered eyes, the only clue that what he's seeing bothers him is the way his expression is so carefully blank. "What's going on?"

Jace pauses for a beat and it's killing the inherently curious side of me that I can't see his face. "What are you doing here, Coop?"

Coop's jaw clenches, but he just continues to stare at him silently, waiting him out for an answer.

Well fuck. I can't just hang here upside down all night while they see who gets to piss on me. Plus, all the tequila sloshing around in my stomach is definitely starting to protest Jace's shoulder digging into it.

"Satan's probably here to collect my soul as punishment for my recent slew of violence."

There.

Coop's brows drop down in confusion as he stares at me, and I give him a bitchy smirk.

"She's trashed, don't." Jace sighs wearily. "She just decked Sam on our way out of the bar."

"She called me Coop's sloppy seconds!"

Why does no one see the appropriateness of my response here?

I see the surprise flash across Coop's face before his lips ghost up. "She hit her?"

"Decked her right in the nose," Jace answers as if he still can't believe it.

Why are they so surprised after I already slapped his mother today? And Coop too, for that matter.

I had never been a violent person, actually abhorred it for most of my life because of my parents. But now I was three for three in as many days and punching Sam might be the most satisfying thing I'd done all day. Even more so than slapping Coop's mom.

These boys were turning me savage.

"Shit," Coop breathes and I watch him duck his head as those lips ghost up again. "Well—"

I hear the bar door open and turn my head toward it, seeing Tiff coming out with a panicked expression on her face. "Jace—" She comes to a halt at the sight of Coop, eyes darting between us all. "Um…" She trails off uncomfortably.

"What, Tiff?" Coop prods her gently.

"Uh…" Her eyes land on Jace. "Sam is in there pitching a fit. She says she's going to call the police and press charges and I thought maybe you could—"

"Jesus fucking Christ," Jace groans again. "This day just gets better and better."

"She wants to press charges?!" I shout, my stomach giving a hard roll of protest. "You can tell her I did her a favor! Now she can get that nose job—"

"I got it, Tiff," Jace cuts me off. "Go back in and make sure she doesn't call them."

Tiff shoots me a wide-eyed look before turning and going back into the bar, leaving a tense silence in her departure.

"It's fine," I tell Jace as my stomach starts rolling with increasing urgency. "Just put me in the car and come get me when you're done."

"I could take her," Coop offers, avoiding my gaze as he steps off his motorcycle.

Oh hell no.

"Or you could go handle Sam," Jace shoots back. "It is your dad's bar after all."

"Wrote this place off a long time ago." Coop smirks savagely. "Plus, she's your ex, not mine."

"She's not my ex—"

"You fucked her, not me. I knew better than to mess with that crazy."

And I seriously can't help myself despite the fact my body is warning me to keep my mouth shut. "Because you recognized one of your own species?"

"Goddammit." Jace sighs, shaking his head. "Just watch her for a minute while I deal with Sam, and then I'll take her."

"You know, little cousin." Coop takes a step toward Jace right as my stomach gives a violent lurch and the whole world spins. "I knew how to take care of her long before you did."

Fuck, I should've kept my mouth shut. "Jace, put me down." I breathe shallowly.

Jace laughs lightly. "You said it right there, old man." He pauses, eyes locked with Coop's as he gives him a wicked grin. "That was before me."

"Jace!" I hit his back. "Put me the fuck down!"

"What, Blondie?"

"Now!"

Jace pulls me back over his shoulder, setting me down, and I drop like a weight to the ground beside him. Landing hard on my hands as I gloriously expel all the tequila I had so eagerly consumed, vomiting right there between them.

"Fuck." I hear Coop mutter as Jace crouches down beside me and starts to rub circles on my back.

My eyes water as I continue to heave up nothing but bile for a few minutes and they both remain silent until it passes.

"Jace." Coop's voice comes out low and concerned. "Let me take her home."

"Goddammit," Jace breathes.

"Please. Let me—" Coop clears his throat. "Let me *do* something. I'm…" He trails off.

Don't you fucking dare, Dawson.

The heaving in my stomach subsides, and I take shallow breaths, trying to regain my bearings and stop the world from spinning.

After a moment, I feel Jace move a little beside me. "Here, take my keys. She can't ride on that death machine right now." He pauses and I tilt my head, squinting and watching him pass Coop his keys through watery eyes. "And I swear to fucking god, Cooper," Jace warns in a low voice. "She better not be in a worse state tomorrow because of your bullshit."

Coop gives him a short nod, pocketing the keys and remaining silent as his eyes slide to me.

"Hey Blondie." Jace dips his mouth to my ear. "I'm going to text you as soon as I have this shit cleared up, okay? Make sure you haven't killed him."

I give him a nod, worried that if I open my mouth, I'll start to puke again.

He drops a kiss to the top of my head. "And then I'll bring you breakfast in the morning, yeah? It'll help with the hangover."

I try to nod again but the motion is too much and I start to heave again, stomach cramping painfully as nothing comes up. Jace stays by my side, waiting until it subsides to drop another kiss on the top of my head before he stands.

“Take care of her,” he orders Coop in a hard voice.

“Like I said, little cousin.” Coop walks up, dropping down to slide his arm under mine before standing and swooping my legs up in his other as he picks me up. “I learned the art of Eleanor long before you did.”

He starts to walk toward Jace’s jeep and my head lolls on his chest, my eyes finding his night-forest gaze that’s spilling over with a whole world of feeling now that Jace can’t see us.

“Satan…” I try to mumble in protest.

“I know, Princess. I know.” His chest heaves under my head with a sigh. “Satan doesn’t get to touch you either.”

Chapter Six

Jace

Present Day

I watch Coop put her into my jeep as if she were made of glass instead of flesh and bone. My gut churning with unease at the sight, at the way he's keeping his head turned away from me to hide his face. As if I don't already know how fucking in love he still is with her. It's in every move he makes in her presence, as if he's the shadow following each of her moves. And the thing is, I don't even think he realizes it. The way his body automatically trails her, even in the smallest of gestures. And I'm positive Ellie doesn't notice it.

But I… I noticed it, even that first time I saw them together on the boat. It was obvious in the way they moved together without being aware of it.

How strangely they echoed one another.

I'd never seen anything like it before.

And it scared me. Not because I was threatened by it… well, okay, maybe a little. But it scared me because I was worried what would be left when we all eventually made it to the other side of this, one way or another.

Ellie and me, we contrasted each other, the light and the dark as she would say, we balanced each other out. But Coop and her were nothing but a song of darkness, their chords the layers of shadows and suffering.

It could so very easily spell nothing but destruction for us all.

I had remembered something today, when Leah was spouting her bullshit and mentioned my birthday parties. About my seventh birthday party at the beach. It had been my last birthday Ellie had been at, and Coop had been there too. I had been so annoyed that my mom insisted on her being there. Too stupid to see what my mom probably already knew my future held. And we had all been playing in the water together, my friends, Ellie, Coop. I had wanted to wade out farther, but Ellie couldn't come because she was too little still and Coop…

Coop had looked between her and me, and I had known as soon as his eyes met mine that he wasn't going to leave her.

So he had stayed, and I had waded out deeper.

That memory… it fucking terrified me worse than that night on the beach when I'd first heard his name from her lips. Terrified me more than my worries over what would be left of us all at the end of this. And I couldn't figure out why.

She loves you, I remind myself, trying to ease the churning in my gut as I watch them pull away. Some part of her might still love him even after everything he'd done. But she loves me too, I'm sure of that. I think she might even love me more in some ways too. Only time would tell. But if my cousin thought I was just going to let her go, step back and let him take her from me, he had a rude fucking awakening coming his way.

Because she might have been his princess once upon a time, but she was my Ellie now. And he only had himself to blame for that. I watch the jeep until it turns out of sight before turning to walk back into the bar, hoping like hell they don't push each other into a symphony of pain and despair before the light of morning washes away the darkness of the night.

Chapter Seven

By the time we make it back to Gram's house, my head has stopped spinning and my stomach feels considerably calmer than when we left the bar. I spent the drive forcing myself to recite the ABCs backward and I'm definitely still drunk, but not anywhere near the level of trashed I was at the bar. Coop pulls into the driveway and cuts the engine, turning his darkly amused eyes on me.

Those ridiculously full lips twitch. "The ABCs?"

Guess I was reciting out loud.

I give him a half shrug. "Kai taught me the trick in high school for when I had to get past Yvie after drinking too much."

In the silence that follows, I'm hit with the weird realization that there are so many things Coop and I never knew or had the chance to know about one another. Our entire relationship had existed in a bubble, completely removed from reality, tucked away on a dark little slice of paradise in Cahuita. Almost as if the us we had become had never really existed at all, even if it had been without the lies and deception.

Coop opens his door, getting out of the car and closing it behind him before walking around to open mine. "Come on." He reaches out for my hand. "Let's get you inside."

I let him help me from the car because my hands are already scraped up from my fall in the parking lot and I'm not looking to repeat that decidedly embarrassing move again. But as soon as my feet hit the driveway, I give a hard tug, pulling my hand free from his grip and walking past him.

"I can take it from here." I throw out over my shoulder, totally dismissing him.

"Not a chance, Princess," he responds, catching my elbow when I trip on the first porch step. "I'm not leaving until you're safely tucked in for the night."

"Fuck you, Coop," I snap.

"I would say please," he muses as I take the key from my pocket and unlock the door. "But I think you might puke on me still."

"I hate you."

"I know."

I walk into the house with Coop on my heels and head straight for the bathroom, knowing that I most likely have vomit on me somewhere after my epic regurgitation of tequila in the parking lot. Opening the bathroom door, I step inside and turn around, narrowing my eyes at him in warning.

"I'm going to shower now so you can go find some other way to amuse yourself." I give him a bitter smile. "Jack off, find some other girl to fool, I don't really care. Just go away." And with that, I slam the door in his smirking face.

I turn on the shower, letting the water warm up while I strip off my clothes and drop them into the corner before stepping under the hot spray.

Tilting my head back, I let the water wash away all the grime coating my body from the hellish day. Imagining all the negative feelings washing down the drain as well. I grab my shampoo and quickly wash my hair, ignoring the stinging in my hands from the various cuts before moving on to give my body the same treatment. Allowing myself to stand under the water for a solid ten minutes after I'm done and let it loosen all the tension my muscles have accumulated over the past few days.

Turning off the shower, I push back the curtain and grab my towel hanging on the rack beside it, using it to scrub my hair dry before wrapping myself up in it. Sighing happily at the scent of my amber soap hanging in the air, clean and more relaxed than I have been in days. Not to mention more sober. It's amazing what a good shower can do for you after some serious emotional trauma. Should've just started with that in the first place. Saved myself the vomit and sore palms, but then I would've never gotten to deck Sam and what a shame that would've been. I open the door and step out into the hall, turning toward Gram's bedroom to find some clothes.

"Hey Princess, I found some—"

I peek over my shoulder and see Coop round the corner of the kitchen before coming to a screeching halt at the sight of me. His eyes widen in surprise, entire body going tense and jaw clenching to a degree that just looks painful.

Cocking a brow at him defiantly, I look away and step into Gram's room before kicking the door shut behind me. Effectively ending his little perusal of my towel-clad body. Nothing but silence sounds through the house as I dig through my clothes and pull on a baggy T-shirt and some sleep shorts. I sit on the bed when I'm done, trying to decide whether to just ignore him or not, weighing the chances that he'll just leave if I do.

There's no chance. Despite his abandonment of me in Cahuita, I don't believe that he'll actually leave me alone now that the secret is out unless I force him to.

I grab my phone from the nightstand to put off the inevitable, hoping there will be some dire emergency to deal with but unfortunately for me, the screen is blank of any notifications. Useless, utterly useless. I briefly consider texting Jace before discarding the idea, deciding instead that I'll text him after I get rid of Coop. Standing from the bed with a resigned sigh, I head for the door, opening it and walking down the hallway in search of the devil himself. Cursing myself as ten kinds of stupid along the way for letting myself end up in this situation. I quickly find him in the kitchen, back to me as he sets out some things on the counter I can't quite make out. Leaning against the entry to the kitchen, I take advantage of the opportunity to watch him unnoticed. Seeing the way his body moves with that familiar grace I'd almost forgotten, our words wrapping their way up his left arm.

He is leaner than before though, my first instinct was right about that. The soft black shirt he's wearing that I used to steal from him all the time before sliding into bed hangs more loosely on his body than it used to. I can still see the cuts of his muscles underneath it but they're sharper than they were before. His body all harsh angles now with nothing forgiving to be found in it.

“Come here,” he demands without turning around, making me startle in surprise.

“Why?” I push, that bit of tequila left in my system leaving me unable to resist the urge even as I lift off the wall and walk toward him.

He shoots me an unamused look as I come up beside him and see the first aid supplies he’s laid out on the counter. “Because…” He turns to me, dark eyes dropping to my hands before returning to mine as he arches a brow. “I’d rather you not die of some infection you picked up in a bar parking lot.” He reaches out and grabs my waist, lifting me up onto the counter in front of him before I can get a word of protest out. “Especially when I’ve just found you again.”

My heart is thundering in my chest as he smoothly grabs the bottle of disinfectant on the counter and pours some onto a paper towel before reaching for one of my hands. I can’t even open my mouth to tell him to fuck off because my stomach is flipping too wildly, and it’s taking everything in me just to keep my breathing even. He starts to carefully wipe down the cuts on it and the slight sting barely fazes me. My sole focus is on keeping my hand from trembling, my body in sharp check. The last thing I need is for him to think he has the upper hand here, to realize how affected I still am by his presence.

He would use it against me without hesitation.

He moves to wipe down my other hand and I stare at his bowed head to give myself something to focus on. But all that does is make me notice how his new buzzed hair only serves to accentuate the angles of his face even more than the short length I used to tug on. And the whole thing, the different hair, the familiar way he pushed in and demanded to care for me… everything about the moment sends an ache through my heart with the remembrance of how acutely I missed him for so long.

It makes me hurt and hate him all over again.

He tosses the paper towel onto the counter and grabs the ointment, darting his eyes to my face and slowing as he sees the expression there. I know what he sees. The pain and anger. I'm too tired right now to try and hide it from him. Plus, it's better to let him see that than the desire attempting to flare to life inside me.

"Trust me, Princess." He drops his head back down, voice pitched soft and low as he starts to gently rub the ointment on my hand. "As much as you may hate me, I hate myself more."

"I actually believe that." I watch him, thinking about the way he's been so hesitant to meet my gaze at certain times… like today with his mom. "You undersold what a bitch your mom is in Cahuita."

His lips ghost up as he screws the cap back onto the antibacterial ointment and sets it on the counter. "Yeah, well." He shrugs, lifting his head and locking eyes with me. "Describing her can be difficult."

"And you were under a limited ability to tell the truth." I cock a brow and he gives me another careless shrug. "Why does she dislike you so much?"

"I think," he sighs, placing his hands on either side of me. "It's just what she said. I always reminded her too much of my father and she couldn't deal with that."

Some perverse part of me can't help but ask. "Do you look like him?"

Coop stares at me intensely for a moment. "Yeah." He nods hesitantly. "Pretty much the spitting image."

"You do." I dart my eyes away from his too-intense gaze. Taking a deep breath to steady myself before looking back at him and starting again. "You do realize that even if it weren't for the lies… how wrong the concept of you and me is, right?"

"Then why…" He steps in closer, boldly moving into the space between my legs and causing me to damn near stop breathing. "Did it feel so right?"

I keep my eyes on his, not backing down and fighting like hell to keep the attraction from my gaze. "Destruction can feel good, Coop." I scoff lightly. "That doesn't mean you partake."

His eyes narrow and rake my face. "You've changed."

"Maybe. I don't know." I give him a half shrug. "If today is anything to go by I'd probably say no but…" I suck in a shallow breath. "A year is a long time."

He shakes his head. "Today was an extraordinary circumstance." The dark in his eyes sparks before he looks down and lifts a hand, bringing it to the inside of my wrist to ever so lightly trail his fingers up my arm. Leaving fucking goose bumps I hate in his wake. "Tell me something, Eleanor…"

He lifts his hand when he reaches the bottom of my sleeve and brings his eyes back to mine as he reaches up. "Does this feel like destruction to you?"

And there it is... that thumb on my cheek. Lighter than before though, as if it's an echo of what it used to be. Just like us. But the stark need I see in his night-forest eyes, in the way they dilate as he looks at me, is very much real and present. It pulls me in, drowning me in memories of what he used to feel like inside of me. Of what it felt like when that indefinable pull of ours burned hot and bright for those precious moments. Coop keeps his eyes locked with mine as he moves in even closer and drops his head, bringing his lips a breath away from mine.

And I remember the last time he kissed me. The last time we were so close that I could feel the heat radiating from his body like I do now. The shattered vision of our future he had painted in my mind with his beautiful words that day.

"Don't you see it?"

I look down quickly, ending the moment and clearing my throat. "You need to leave." He moves back slightly and I lift my eyes back to his, seeing the frustration there. "You need to leave," I repeat, voice soft but firm. "None of that should have just happened."

He clenches his jaw, heaving a breath as he drops his head and I watch as his entire body goes still. "I've been meaning to ask." He reaches out, ignoring my request and pressing a thumb against the sun on the inside of my right wrist. "What's the story behind this?"

I shake my head, knowing he's probably already guessed and is just trying to pick a fight. "Don't ask questions you don't want to know the answers to, Coop."

A quiet laugh leaves him and he keeps his eyes on the tattoo as he speaks. "Jace has always liked to fix things, people. Take care of them." He lifts his eyes to mine. "I should've figured he'd take one look at you and fall hard."

"Don't go there," I warn him, narrowing my eyes. "Don't lash out at me with your jealousy."

"Why not?" He arches a brow. "Isn't that what you do?" He drops his head down close again, voice threaded with anger when he speaks. "Tell me, Eleanor. How long did you wait? A day, two? Before you gave in to your damage and left?"

It feels like acid has been poured into my veins at his words. Each of them digging into the wound that was ripped open at his reappearance and setting fucking fire to my heart. Eating away at me from the inside out.

Fine. He wants to fight, we'll fight. This isn't one he'll win.

"I waited almost a week for you, Cooper," I grind out viciously. "Five days. Five days where I paced the floors, called hospitals, and called you so many fucking times I lost count." I push off the counter, forcing him to take a step back as I land on my feet. "So don't stand there and ask me how long I waited when you were *gone*."

His brows drop down, whole body tight with tension. "You should have known I was doing everything I could to come back to you. You should have had more faith."

A mocking laugh bursts from me. "Coming back to do what?" I cock my head to the side. "Lie to me some more? What exactly should I have had faith in Cooper? Tell me, please. I'd really like to hear it."

"You should have believed in us!" he argues, nostrils flaring with anger. "You should have waited longer!"

"There never was a fucking us!" I shout, sweeping my hand between us. "It was just all fucking lies and—and…" My chest heaves and I shake my head. "There never was an us as much as you might have deluded yourself into believing there was."

"That's bullshit and you know it," he growls, stepping in close. "I may have lied. But every fucking thing between us was real, Princess, and deep down… deep down, you know it."

"Right," I scoff, tilting my head back to look him in the eyes. "Except for the truth. Except for the basis of our entire relationship! Except for the most important thing." I lift my hand to the side of my head before flicking it out. "But let's live in your deluded reality for a moment," I mock with quiet anger. "You saw that place, right? Saw what you did to me? Even before I knew the truth about you."

His expression shutters as he looks at me and it's a moment before he gives me a nod of confirmation. "I saw."

"You fucking broke me, Cooper," I whisper, voice nothing but pain as I let him see all the agony in my eyes at the memory.

"Eleanor," he breathes, lifting a hand to reach for me. "You don't understand—"

"No." I shake my head, batting his arm away. "No, Coop. You don't get to lie to me, break me, and then show up here and expect to have some kind of place in my life still. It doesn't work that way."

"Right," he mutters darkly. "Because my cousin took that spot, right?" He steps back, fists clenching at his sides and lips twitching up into a mocking smirk. "Yeah, you sure did wait, Eleanor. I bet Jace had fun picking up the pieces."

"I waited a fucking year!" I scream, wiping the smirk from his face. "I could barely look at anyone for a year! I was a fucking ghost!" My words catch in my throat and I force a sob back down it. "You have no idea—no idea what I was like. How haunted I was by you, by the damage you did… even a year later." I shake my head, angrily swiping at the lone tear running down my cheek. "So you don't get to judge me. Judge us. You don't get to act jealous and lash out at me for this!" I swallow down the urge to yell and rage at him more, needing this to be done. "I needed someone to bring me back to life after you. So you don't get to stand there in righteous anger at me for loving the person who pulled me back into the light."

Coop freezes, body utterly still as shock plays out across his face. "You love him?"

I watch as a deep kind of hurt fills his face, starting at the center of his night-forest eyes and spiraling out as my silence continues. "Coop," I whisper, unable to stop how my hand reaches for him automatically.

"No." He takes a step back. "No. It's fine. I left, and he picked up the pieces and… of course you love him."

"Coop."

"It's fine." He lifts his head. "He's a great guy. All uh—" He shakes his head, brow drawing tight as his eyes land on my tattoo again. "All sunshiny and shit, right? Why wouldn't you love him?"

"Coop," I hedge, taking a small step toward him. Hating seeing him this way despite everything between us.

"Not at all like you and me," he whispers, eyes lost. "I'm going to head out."

"Coop," I say his name again but he's already turning.

He pauses by the entrance to the kitchen, calling out softly over his shoulder without looking at me. "I'll come by tomorrow to… I don't know." I see his shoulders tighten up impossibly more. "I'll just be by."

With that, he disappears around the corner and it's only seconds before I hear the front door slam hard behind him. As if he put all of his pain into that one act.

"Fuck!" I scream, turning and slamming a hand down on the counter, sharp pain shooting out from each of the cuts and reminding me that I'm injured.

I cradle my hand and walk to Gram's bedroom, throwing myself onto the bed before curling up into a protective ball against the feeling left in Coop's wake. It's fucking horrible. As if all the heartache and hate are tearing me apart from the inside out. And guilt… there's guilt there too, because that part of my heart that didn't understand hate, well that part wanted to give in to him.

I can't stand it…

And then it occurs to me that I don't have to.

At least not for a little bit.

I know I'll have to deal with Coop eventually. Figure out if what I have with Jace is salvageable.

But I have my answers now…. So really, what the fuck am I even still doing here?

I reach for my phone and quickly unlock it, pulling up my recent calls before tapping on his name without hesitation. Calling one of the three guys I know would storm hell itself to get me out of here at a moment's notice, especially once they find out what's going on. The phone rings three times before he answers, the sound of his deep voice shouting loud over some deafening metal music that was definitely chosen by Kai.

"*Cara*?"

"I'm ready to come home."

Because the truth is, nobody won that fight. Not really.

Chapter Eight

Coop

One Year Ago

I open my eyes to the sterile white of the hospital room, squinting at the harshness of the fluorescent lights filling the space. It takes me a few blinks to remember where I am and why. Why I'm not waking up wrapped around the woman that I love like usual. The ache in my side from the surgery sends a sharp pain slicing through me in the next instant and has me drawing in a harsh breath, smelling nothing but the antiseptic hospital air.

God, I fucking miss her smell already. The way it hits me first thing in the morning before I even open my eyes. Causes me to roll over and bury myself in her every damn time. Wanting nothing more than to fucking live inside of her body. The sweet taunts that fall from her bratty lips when I do that only make me need to drive myself into her deeper. So that she can never be rid of me.

Damn. No way was I spending the whole week here like the doctors demanded. I needed to get home. Although how the fuck I was going to explain this away… I wasn't sure yet.

"So the conquering hero awakens."

I jerk my gaze to the side and see Alec sitting in the chair beside my hospital bed, a wide smile flashing across his face.

"Welcome back, brother."

"What the fuck are you doing here, man?" I croak, my throat sore and dry from surgery.

"Bainbridge gets notified anytime one of our people is hospitalized, Coop. You know that." He nods at me. "I'm your emergency contact at work, so I thought I'd come up here and see what the fuck was going on."

"My cousin—"

"I know." He holds up a hand to stop me. "The doctors already filled me in. I'm sorry, Cooper."

Dread fills me at his words. "Has he woken up yet?"

"No." He shakes his head. "No, he made it through surgery though, and that's something."

I nod in response, unable to give voice to the fear filling me up at the thought of losing him. Jace had been my partner in crime from the time we were in diapers together, but being older than him, he had also always been my responsibility in a way and it fucking killed me that I couldn't fix this.

Alec's eyes sweep the room. "So why isn't your girl at your bedside?"

"She, uh—" I suck in a sharp breath as shooting pain throbs through my side again. "She doesn't know I'm here. She can't."

He cocks his head at me, narrowing his eyes and reminding me eerily of Eleanor with the look. "Why not?"

"She—" She would never forgive me. Not if she figured out the truth. "She just can't. I'll tell her what happened when I get home."

"Well you might have a problem then because she called you about an hour ago," Alec drawls sardonically.

"Fuck." I cough, throat aching and my stomach seizing up with fucking agony.

"Let me get you some ice, man, and call her back for you." Alec stands, grabbing the plastic pitcher and my phone from the hospital table. "You sound like you're about to die and she'll definitely know something's wrong if she hears you right now."

"What are you going to tell her?"

I hate it. Hate that I can't call her and hear her voice but he's right. She would know something was wrong the minute she heard me right now.

He shrugs. "I'll just tell her you got roped into a quick job to save my ass and are already undercover. That you'll call her as soon as you can and be back in a week, right?"

"You called on the way back from my family emergency," I correct him. "That it turned out everything was fine."

"Sure. Whatever." He nods, walking toward the door.

"Be nice," I call out before coughing again, my whole body seizing up in pain as the door closes behind him.

Chapter Nine

A loud, incessant banging jolts me awake the next morning and I shoot up in bed, the hangover hitting me hard as my stomach rolls and head pounds. I sweep my blurry eyes across the room, trying to push through the haze clouding my head and remembering Jace's promise from last night to bring me breakfast. Fucking hell. Jace really should know better than to wake me up so early, breakfast or not. Although, Jace typically didn't bang on my door quite so loudly so it could be Coop waking me up at this ungodly hour in retribution for last night.

I push the covers off just as the banging cuts off, ignoring the flip my stomach gives as I stand along with the twinge in my heart at the thought of last night. These boys were going to tear my heart to shreds if I didn't get out of here soon. Between Jace with his heart-wrenching pleas for forgiveness and Coop with his pushing remembrances. Good thing I solved that problem last night though. I only had about six more hours left in Landing Point if the bright morning sunlight shining through the house was any indication.

I turn the knob and open the front door, brow dropping in confusion as I stare at the empty air. Not a person in sight. Sweeping my eyes up and down the street, I come up empty in my search for Jace's jeep or Coop's motorcycle. Well, that's fucking weird. Maybe it was Doreen getting back at me for undoubtedly being a bad neighbor with my constant string of people shouting and banging on my front door. Just as I go to shut the door though, my gaze dips down and I freeze at the sight of what's sitting on the front porch mat.

Two birds, one very vulnerable stone.

My blood runs cold, heart skipping in my chest with fear as I slam the door shut and throw the lock in the next instant. I sprint back to Gram's room, throwing myself across the bed and reaching for my phone, fumbling as I try to unlock it the first time and fail. Adrenaline flooding my body and causing my breath to stutter out in uneven pants. I finally managed to unlock my phone and pull up my recent calls, tapping Jace's name hard before bringing the phone to my ear.

"Pick up. Pick up. Pick up," I order as it rings, breaking into a cool sweat.

"Hey Blondie," Jace answers delightedly. "Didn't expect for you—"

"Kyle and Kurt are here." I choke out the words, pushing through the feeling of panic trying to suffocate them.

Dead silence sounds over the phone for a second. "I'm on my way," he tells me, voice tense and strained. "Where are you?"

"I uh—" I stutter a breath. "In my gram's room. I locked the front."

"Good," he pants through the phone, heavy footfalls sounding and telling me that he's running. "What happened?"

It takes me a second to respond, to actually voice it. "They left something on the front porch," I whimper, hating how weak I sound but unable to help it. "I thought it was you."

"It will be, Ellie," he answers firmly and I hear the door shut to his car before he starts it up. "Five minutes, that's all," he soothes. "Now I want you to do something for me. Okay?"

"O-okay," I stutter.

"Go into the bathroom."

"Why?"

"Come on now, Blondie." He laughs lightly, trying to calm me even though I can tell it's forced. "Now really isn't the time to argue with me, yeah?"

I stare at the doorway, trying to muster up the courage to move.

"You got this, Delacroix," Jace urges. "Prove to me you're as much of a badass as I already know you are."

"Fuck," I mutter, forcing my body to move off the bed, peeking out the doorway to make sure it's empty before darting into the bathroom. "Okay, I'm here." Closing the bathroom door, I turn the lock on it with a shaking hand. Not like that's really going to stop them if they're determined to come for me though.

"Alright," his voice answers hesitantly. "Now open the cabinet below the sink and reach up."

"What?"

"Just do it," he orders with uncharacteristic sharpness.

Despite my confusion, I kneel down and open up the cabinet, crooking my neck to hold the phone against my shoulder as I reach up. Feeling around for a second before cold metal meets my fingertips and I immediately jerk away.

"What is that?" I breathe, dread filling me because I already know what his answer is going to be.

Jace pauses for a beat, voice coming out soft when he speaks. "A gun."

"You put a gun in my house?" I snap, anger at yet another deception momentarily edging out the panic in my veins.

"Two minutes," he tells me, ignoring my question. "Stay by it. If you hear anything before I get there, you grab that fucking gun, Ellie."

I don't bother responding, but I don't hang up the phone either. Torn between the lifeline he is and the newfound anger sparked at my discovery. He knows damn well I would never be okay with having a gun in the house and he hid it here anyway. Totally disregarding my feelings on the matter and hiding yet another thing from me. It didn't matter whether it was serving me now in my current situation, with everything else that had gone down lately, I was one lie away from cutting him off completely. Then he and Coop could go live in fucking Cahuita together with only themselves to blame.

The minutes pass slowly, crawling along with the silence sounding through the phone until I eventually hear him cut the engine to his jeep and close the door.

"I'm here," he tells me and I hear him walking up to the porch. It takes him a minute to speak again and I'm assuming he's taking in the grotesque present left for me there by the way his voice comes out with quiet anger when he speaks again. "At the door."

"Okay." I breathe in relief, standing and opening the bathroom door.

I poke my head out, making sure I don't see any intruders before darting to the front door. Flipping the lock, I throw the door open, not allowing myself to look down at what Jace's gaze is set on. He stares at it for another second, wet hair hanging around his head before lifting his eyes to mine and stepping over the front porch mat. I take a step back to let him in the house, seeing the way his movements are tight with tension underneath the gray T-shirt and low-slung black sweatpants. He lets himself in before closing the door behind us, wasting no time in stepping right up to me and reaching his hands up to cup my face.

"I'm sorry," he whispers with a pained expression as his fingers thread through my hair.

I feel my heart give another little twinge as I look up at him, at the honesty and care for me laid bare on his face. It quells some of the anger inside of me regardless of whether I want it to or not.

"For what?" I question, not ready to forgive him yet. "The gun or the Morrisons?"

"Both." He gives me a small shrug. "I just wanted to keep you safe."

I shake my head with a small, humorless scoff. "I'm so tired of the men in my life using fear to justify their lies to me."

His eyes crinkle at the corners and I see the regret fill his gaze. "You're right." He nods, tucking me into his chest. "You're right, and I'm sorry for hiding it from you. It won't happen again." I feel him press a soft kiss to the top of my head before continuing quietly. "But Ellie… don't make me apologize for trying to keep you safe. I'd give my beating heart if that's what it took, even if it meant you never speaking to me again."

Fucking hell. He was just so hard to stay mad at.

Pulling back, I look up into his eyes and feel my own heart clench up painfully in my chest at the absolute love I see there. "No more lies, Jace," I tell him seriously. "If you even want a chance at mending this between us… there can be no more secrets. And I can't tell you that there even is a chance, I don't know—"

"I know." He nods, dropping his hands to wrap around my back and pull me into his body again. "I know, Ellie." His soft, melodic laugh sounds under my head. "You kinda have a lot going on right now."

A small puff of laughter leaves me and I give in to the urge I've been fighting since that day on the boat to lean into him and the comfort he so willingly gives. Sinking into his body and breathing in his sea-spring scent as I crack the door to my heart just a bit. Letting his light invade me and ease the burden of darkness weighing me down.

He reaches up after a long moment and tugs on the back of my hair. "Sorry I forgot breakfast."

My lips twitch at his playful words and I open my mouth to respond but the sound of a motorcycle rumbling up to the house stops me. I tip my head up to look at Jace, watching as his face goes tense and all that lightness I had just allowed myself to bask in leaves me in one fell swoop. Leaving nothing but trepidation in its wake.

I feel his body lock up in my arms as the rumbling of the motorcycle cuts off. "You didn't…"

"Sorry, Blondie." He takes a step back, arms dropping from around me as he grabs the handle of the front door with a small shrug. "I didn't know what I was walking into and it seemed like the smart move."

Jace opens the door, and I watch as Coop climbs the steps to the front porch, frantic eyes running down the length of me as if checking for injuries. But when his gaze lands on what was left for me on the front porch mat, he grinds to a halt. Body stilling so completely that I can hardly tell if he's breathing as he stares at what the Morrisons left me. And I can't help but drop my eyes to look at it once more, like a car accident you see on the side of the road. You can't not look.

My stomach rolls at the sight of the two doves, necks cracked and stomach split to reveal all of their bloody insides. But it's the picture they're framing that really sends that jolt of fear through my system again. It's a picture of me last night, sound asleep and dangerously unaware someone was watching me. My phone clutched in my cut-up hand and held against my chest as if I had just ended my call with Stef before falling asleep. I can tell it's taken through the window of Gram's room that I never close the curtains to and written across the top of the picture in bright-red marker are the words that had my blood running cold to begin with.

Coop takes the remaining few steps to the picture in the next breath and reaches down to snatch it up, revealing another photograph beneath it that was impossible to see before. I see what it is in the seconds before he grabs that picture too. It's a picture of him leaving Gram's last night with a look of utter desolation on his face. And as he snatches his photograph up, yet another is revealed. A picture of Jace, walking out of the bar last night, running a hand down the back of his head with a weary expression on his face. The last picture is of the three of us, me puking and the boys looking at me with worry clear on their faces in the bar parking lot the night before. By the time Coop picks up the last photograph, my hands are shaking at the thought of just how close I was to a very unfortunate end last night.

But why the hell didn't they just do it then?

Don't look a gift horse in the mouth, El. You do like being alive, right?

"What the fuck is this?" Coop snaps, looking to Jace for an answer.

Jace pauses for a beat and I can feel the tension pouring off him, can guess how much he hates that this all leads back to him.

"The Morrisons," he answers in a clipped voice.

Coop's eyes widen a fraction before they slide to me, and I can see the way his shoulders tense up under the white T-shirt he's wearing.

"The Morrisons?" he echoes quietly, not breaking my gaze. "How?"

"I guess they got out of jail." Jace reaches for the photographs in Coop's hand and starts to look through them himself as he answers. "Came back to town about the same time Ellie got here and…" He pauses as he comes to the photograph of me sleeping, pulling his bottom lip through his teeth as he stares at it. "Started making threats, causing trouble."

Coop's jaw clenches and he finally breaks my gaze, looking back to Jace. "What kind of threats?" he grates out.

"Threats against Ellie."

I dart my eyes between the two of them in the silence that follows, seeing the heavy look of challenge fill both their eyes when the other doesn't back down.

Coop narrows his eyes at Jace, voice quietly furious when he speaks. "And you let her stay here?"

"Let," I scoff, drawing his intense gaze. "Nobody lets me do anything, Cooper. I made an informed decision."

"Then you made the wrong one." He dismisses me shortly and turns back to Jace. "And you should have known better."

"Fuck you, Coop," Jace snaps. "Don't act like you're the all-knowing savior. You wouldn't even be here if it wasn't for her."

"And now that I am, what, Jace?" Coop shoots back. "You expect me to clean up the problem? Kill for you again?"

"Kill?" I mutter, looking between them both in confusion and seeing the anger fill Jace's face as neither of them bothers to answer me. "That was who you killed?" I demand, looking to Coop as yet more puzzle pieces slide together in my head. "The smuggler guy?"

He breaks Jace's gaze after a moment and looks at me with a shuttered expression before jerking his chin down with a single nod.

"Holy shit," I whisper as the weird reality of my life shifts beneath my feet again.

"I'm not asking you to kill anyone," Jace snaps out. "There's a BOLO out for them already."

Coop's brows drop down in confusion. "For what?"

Jace pauses again before admitting. "They made a play for Ellie at the bar already, beat me up pretty good before she got my gun and stopped them."

Coop's body stills to that scary degree again as his eyes find mine and this time I can tell he's not even breathing for a few seconds while I watch the wheels turn in his mind. "Right." He breathes quietly as if he's speaking more to himself than us.

And with that, he steps over the doormat, pushing right through us as he walks into the house and heads straight to the end of the hall.

I stare at him in shock for about two seconds before charging after him. "What the fuck are you doing?"

He doesn't bother answering, just continues into Gram's room, and I watch his head turn as I come up behind him.

"I repeat, Coop—"

"Packing," he answers distractedly, cutting me off and walking to the closet door.

My mouth drops open as I watch him open the closet and duck down, pulling my suitcase out from where it sits below the hanging clothes. He reaches up and grabs the first piece of clothing his hand touches from the rack and throws it inside the suitcase before repeating the process.

I hear Jace come up behind me before stopping to take in the sight. "Fuck," he mutters in a worried voice.

Clearly, Satan has lost his freaking mind.

I march forward and slap the lid to the suitcase down, halting his moves as he goes to throw another piece of clothing in.

"You need to chill out," I order, standing and crossing my arms. "We'll call the police and they'll—"

"They'll what, Eleanor?" He turns to me with a humorless laugh, clenching my shirt in his hand. "Tell me what my mother will do for you now?"

I push through the trickle of fear his words spark, shaking my head. "There are other police officers there, they wouldn't just—"

"I won't lose you again!" he roars.

My head jerks back at the sudden outburst, eyes widening as I see the way his chest heaves and the screwed-up expression on his face. And for the first time since he came back into my life, I really look at him. Am forced to by the absolute terror I see in his night-forest eyes. Terror at the thought of something happening to me. I see the buzzed hair and weight loss for what they probably are, uncaring acts that he would have never let happen if not for existing in the same pit of misery I did for a year. I see the pain on his face at not having a place in my life to really have a say. And when he drops his head, eyes darting away from mine, I see the self-hatred

I know he feels over his actions, over losing me. I see him for what he is, what he doesn't want me to see, the creature he became without me. A man toeing the line, one push away from plummeting right over into the never-ending abyss of what he thinks is insanity. His world without me.

I see it in a way that forces me to acknowledge it.

To acknowledge the fact that some part of him probably did and does love me.

And I don't know what the fuck to do with it.

I turn to look at Jace behind me, seeing the unsureness in his eyes as he watches us. The insecurity he's probably feeling over his place in my life right now to some degree. How it has his body locked up with indecision over whether or not to intervene. That little bit of loss in his face because of the fact that he wants me too and that means hurting his cousin, which goes against the grain for him. But that maybe for the first time in his life he's too selfish to let me go, because he does love me.

They both do in their own way.

And I know I can't leave them. To leave them right now… as much as they might deserve it and I might like to because it's the easy choice. It'd be fucking vicious of me. Cruel in a way that I think I'm just incapable of when it comes to both of them. At least so far. Because the truth is, I wasn't the only one hanging on by a thread here. All of us were and until I figured out what the fuck to do. I couldn't abandon them and expect that thread not to snap.

I had grown, and my world had grown with it. And that world now encompassed two people's feelings who weren't my own. That world left me a little less selfish because of the two men I had let into it. At least on my good days.

"Fine," I quip, impulsiveness in full force as I come to the decision. "Keep packing then. You're only doing me a favor anyway."

Coop's eyes narrow on me. "What do you mean?"

"My train out of town is leaving today." I give him a careless shrug. "So no need to freak out. I'll be out of the Morrison's reach."

"What are you talking about, Blondie?" Jace asks, taking a step toward us and drawing my gaze. "We weren't supposed to leave until tomorrow before…" He trails off.

Before everything went to shit. Yeah, I know, Dawson.

"Change of plan." I look down and play with the edge of my baggy concert tee, not wanting him to see the guilt in my eyes. "The plane leaves at three."

I feel both of their gazes on me in silence that follows like a probing weight. Working out what the fuck I actually mean.

"You were running," Coop guesses, voice low and accusing.

I look to Jace first, knowing it'll hit him harder and hating the flash of pain I see in his eyes because of me.

"I just—" I breathe a weary sigh and feel my shoulders droop as the fight leaves me. "I just needed some space. I wasn't—" I shake my head. "It doesn't matter anymore." Looking between the two of them, I manage to muster up a small smirk. "So, who feels like running with me?"

Chapter Ten

The bickering was going to drive me to grab a parachute and jump from the plane any second now. And it wasn't manly, hot, argued debates. No, it was nothing more than childish bickering. As if they had both reverted back into their six-year-old selves the minute we stepped onto the plane and decided to fight over their favorite toy, except their favorite toy was me and instead of actually arguing over me… they chose to bicker over every other possible thing.

Whether to keep the AC on or off.

Jace's music was too loud from his headphones.

Coop shouldn't get so distracted by music while reading. Obviously, if he did, his reading material wasn't that great.

Jace wouldn't know good reading material if it hit him in the face.

I sat across from them on the private plane Stef had sent for me, watching as they slowly devolved from grown men in their midtwenties to surely children during the course of the six-hour flight. And the private plane… that alone had taken up the first thirty minutes of our flight as they both shot me hard stares brimming with silent curiosity after I had driven us to the small airstrip.

But at least then they hadn't been devolving yet.

The first hour or so of it hadn't even bothered me that much honestly. It had been interesting even, in a weird way, to watch their familiar dynamics with each other. How these two men who had played such huge roles in my life at different points in time naturally interacted with each other. The thread of affection I could see between them and in how even when they were arguing, neither of their verbal blows really struck that deep. It was the same way I sparred with the guys from time to time. You could say things to each other you might not say to anyone else because of a surety of the love there.

But after hour two, when the pettiness had really kicked in, I had started to become annoyed by it. And now that we were coming up on the tail end of hour six… my head was officially pounding and I was done.

Next time I'd have to tell Stef to send a bigger plane if it would keep this at bay.

"I'm not saying that," Jace argues back to Coop's latest retort. "All I'm saying is that doesn't it feel a little too calculated for Kyle and Kurt?"

"Then who else would it be, Jace?" Coop laughs mockingly.

"Oh, I don't know," Jace muses, tilting his head to the side in dramatic consideration. "Which one of us has a list of enemies a mile long from their mercenary days?" He looks side to side as if searching for the person before widening his eyes when they land on Coop. "Oh, that would be you."

Coop stares at Jace for a moment and I see his nostrils flare with anger. "I never used my real name with Bainbridge jobs."

"Right," Jace scoffs. "Because those types of people don't have resources or anything."

"There would be no reason for them to come after both of us."

Jace rolls his eyes. "There would be—"

"Oh my god, stop!" I exclaim, causing them to both jerk their gazes to me in surprise. "I swear I will turn this plane around and have it drop you both back in Alabama if either of you utters another word."

They both stare at me with looks of confusion following my threat, as if they can't possibly grasp what caused me to lose it on them and I roll my eyes.

"You both do realize that I haven't spoken a word since around the time we crossed over the Mississippi River, right?"

Jace at least has the decency to cringe. "Sorry, Ellie," he mutters, drawing Coop's narrowed-eyed gaze.

"Suck-up."

I shoot him a warning look at the verbal jab and he just arches a brow at me, face all kinds of insolent.

Jace gives his cousin a long-suffering look before opening his mouth to speak.

"Uh-uh-uh." I hold up a finger, cutting him off. "Blessed silence, Jace. Unless you want me to start drinking."

"But this is helpful," he argues.

I heave a weary sigh and narrow my eyes at him in consideration for a moment. "It better be, Dawson."

“Promise, Delacroix.” He winks, shooting me a playful grin and causing me to roll my eyes again as I fight against the twitch of my lips.

But on the way down my gaze catches Coop’s narrowed one darting between the two of us and I see the reluctant curiosity there. The way his brow tenses up as his eyes land on his cousin still grinning at me and hold there, the barest hint of a frown taking form on his full lips. And I know he’s trying to figure out our dynamics, comparing them to the ones he and I once shared.

I clear my throat, not liking having Jace’s and my relationship under his microscope. “So what is it?”

Jace turns his gaze back to Coop. “Uh,” he starts, the grin slowly falling from his face as he takes in Coop’s expression. “I was just thinking maybe you could call your people at Bainbridge. Have them at least look into finding Kyle and Kurt, if not double-check that it’s no one from your dealings with them.”

Coop stares at Jace for another beat before shifting uncomfortably in his seat. “I can’t.”

“Why not?” Jace asks, brow pulling down in confusion.

“Because,” Coop starts tightly. “I quit Bainbridge.”

“What?” The question slips from my lips in shock and his gaze meets mine for a second before darting away.

“Why?”

Coop looks back to his cousin. “Because I couldn’t have both.”

I beat Jace to the punch this time, curiosity getting the better of me. "What the fuck does that mean?"

Coop's eyes meet mine reluctantly, and I see him take a deep breath. "Looking for you." He slides his eyes back to Jace. "I couldn't work for Bainbridge and look for Eleanor, so I made a choice."

I watch Jace's face go slack as he stares at his cousin, silence settling over the plane as a conversation flows between them that I'm not privy to.

Well, this just became a bit awkward. I should have just let them keep bickering.

It's also an uncomfortable reminder that he may not be completely full of shit. That his pain might have compared to mine, even if it was self-inflicted. Another reminder that leaves me drifting in a world of unknown feelings for one of the two men sitting across from me. But the next moment I feel the plane start to descend, saving me from having to delve too deep into my newfound realizations.

"Thank god," I mutter, drawing both of their gazes and giving me the nudge I need to go over a few, ah, logistics with them. "So a couple of things before we land."

I bite down on my bottom lip to buy myself a second and watch as both of their gazes zero in on the act, making me quickly let it go. Clearing my throat in the silence that follows, I cross my legs at the desire I see in both their gazes. Totally not mentally equipped at the moment to deal with it or the answering pulse of need I feel shooting straight to my core. Clearly, my libido did not understand the terms of betrayal.

"So…" I start slowly and see Jace's eyes fill with amusement, lips pulling up just a bit as if he can guess what's causing my current brain fog. "Uh, Stef will be picking us up at the airport and he may not be too pleased to see that I brought you two along."

Coop's expression shutters at my words. "You told him?" He guesses in a low voice.

"Yeah." I nod. "Last night when I called him. All of them."

"Well," Jace sighs dramatically and leans back in his seat. "There goes any chance we had of winning the family over, Coop."

I scoff quietly. "I think that chance went out the window for Coop about a year ago." Coop jerks his gaze back to me, and I see the spark of irritation in it before I shake my head, not wanting to get into it with him here. "I'm just giving you both a heads-up that you may not receive the warmest of welcomes. But be nice regardless because we're staying at his place."

Jace's mouth pops open before they both speak at the same time.

"What?"

"The fucking Italian?"

I shoot them both a warning look. "Well, I can't very well drag you both into Yvie's without offering up an explanation now, can I?" Pulling a sarcastic face, I muse mockingly. "Oh, hey Yvie, here's that guy I told you about earlier this summer, the one I was dating. Yep, this is him. And this is his cousin, the guy I didn't tell you about from last summer, who, who," I sputter for a second before deciding it's best to just cut that explanation short. "And that's without all the tragic history that I still have to find a way to explain." I roll my eyes at them. "Yeah, that would go over great."

A beat passes before Jace squints his eyes at me and tilts his head in question. "Was?"

"Seriously?" I stare at him in exasperation. "That was what you got out of that?"

He leans back in his seat, shooting me a playful grin. "You can't blame a guy for trying."

"Incorrigible." I laugh softly before catching the possession in Coop's eyes as he stares at us and quickly continue. "Besides, I was planning on staying there anyway. I have a room there that Nona set up for me in high school when everyone finally realized nothing was ever going to happen between the guys and me. Then after she passed when we were in college." I shrug. "Well, I pretty much moved in, can't remember the last time I slept in my childhood room at Yvie's honestly."

The curiosity in both their gazes is up front and center as the plane touches down, jolting me in my seat as it skips across the tarmac. And I'm yet again hit by the realization that while I may know pretty much everything about both of their lives now, there's still a whole side to me that neither of them has gotten to experience. Jace, well, I have a feeling that he'll slide into my world as if he was always a part of it if he can ever get the guys to forgive him. But Coop…

And, why oh why, do you care if Coop fits into your world, El? Isn't he Satan?

Old habits, I reason, before giving myself a firm reminder that he is Satan. It doesn't matter whether he fits or not. I don't owe him anything besides the opportunity for closure and even that is gracious on my part. As the plane comes to a stop, I give myself a nod of understanding that has both guys giving me a confused look which I choose to ignore and instead peek out the window.

And the sight of a white McLaren Spider with its red leather interior sitting against the California evening sky has a wide grin splitting my face instantly. I hurriedly reach down to unlock my seat belt, completely ignoring Coop and Jace across from me as a pure kind of happiness fills my heart. The happiness of family.

Grabbing my phone from the table beside my seat, I stand and dart to the jet's door, bouncing on the balls of my feet as I impatiently wait for it to open. When the door cracks and lets in the first breath of LA air, exhilaration fills my veins at the smell of the dry air laced with desperation. Jace and Coop come up behind me just as the door touches down and I bite the inside of my cheek to check my grin, keeping my expression carefully blank as I walk down the stairs.

He's about halfway between his McLaren and the plane. Phone in hand and swiping away as if he couldn't give a shit that I've just landed when we both know better. His golden hair is cut shorter than when I left and an artful mess on his head, most likely from whatever model of the week was running her hands through it at some point today. The fine fabric of his white V-neck and tailored black chinos finished off with a pair of leather driving loafers practically screams understated wealth. As one would expect of any Astor. But the tattoo of wings made of flame peeking out of the top of his shirt and wrapping up around his shoulders that becomes visible as I draw closer reminds me that he and I are the same.

I stop a good five steps away, crossing my arms and jutting out a hip before tapping my foot impatiently. He makes me wait a few more moments before lifting his eyes to mine and I see the way his cheeks suck in with the smile he's trying to fight. His gaze quickly finds Coop and Jace at my back and he heaves a sigh while dropping his eyes back to the phone.

"So." He slides up to close out whatever app he was using before sliding the phone into his back pocket and finally lifting his head, revealing that all-American beauty the girls have always gone crazy over. "The bitch brought home strays."

I wait a beat, feeling the sudden tension pour off Coop and Jace at my back because of his words before stilling my foot. "And surprise, surprise." I take a step forward and cock a brow. "The bastard is overcompensating for a lack of something by bringing the McLaren."

We stare at each other for a few more beats before breaking into wide, mirror grins. He quickly closes the distance between us in the next instant and grabs me up, swinging us around in a circle that has my feet leaving the ground and an open laugh escaping my lips. When he finally sets me down, I feel a million times lighter, more myself, and so incredibly happy to be home. Truthfully, it's even better than when I came back from Europe because I guess, finally, I have some closure on all fronts. I tip my head back to look up at him, unable to keep the grin from my face even if I cared to try.

Mac brings a hand up to cup the side of my face, his sinful sapphire eyes practically glowing with happiness as they look into mine. “I fucking missed you, Els.”

Chapter Eleven

The rare show of vulnerability from him has my heart turning all kinds of soft and I reach up, wrapping my arms around his shoulders and pulling him into another tight hug. "I missed you too, Macallan," I tell him softly. "Sorry I left again."

"You're forgiven. Just no more trips without *me* at least, okay?" He gives me a squeeze and a low chuckle before whispering. "The strays are looking a bit feral."

Stepping back, I turn to see Jace and Coop both tense and looking at us with eyes that are filled with all kinds of possession. I roll my eyes at them and wave a hand between my two worlds, making the introductions. "Mac, the strays have names, and they are Coop and Jace."

Mac gives them a smile that's more disdainful than welcoming. "I figured."

"Be nice." I smack his arm.

"Why?"

"Because I said so and I'm home, so that should be reason enough for today." I look to Coop and Jace before jerking my head toward Mac. "Obviously, this is Macallan."

Mac slings an arm around my shoulders before speaking and I see the way Jace's whole body locks up and Coop's jaw clenches. "And you can refer to me by full name until I tell you otherwise, which given your track records, will probably be never."

"Shut the fuck up," I snap, rolling my eyes again and bumping his arm off my shoulders. "And stop antagonizing them."

He just laughs in response.

I narrow my eyes at him. "And there go my warm and fuzzies at seeing you again."

"You'll be all warm and fuzzy once you see what Kai rolled you at the house."

I shake my head but can't help the twitch of my lips. "And how are we all supposed to fit in that car of yours?"

"Exactly my thoughts." Coop muses in a low voice as he takes a step toward us.

"Oh, don't worry." Mac smirks and pulls his phone from his back pocket. "I called you an Uber." He looks down at the phone and unlocks it. "Estimated arrival time is… now." He looks up and to the right, eyes on the long road that leads up to the tarmac and I turn my head to see the black escalade making its way to us.

"An Uber?" I ask, trying really damn hard to fight the twitch of my lips.

"What?" He shrugs. "I called them an Uber black."

And there goes that fight.

I shoot a guilty look at Coop and Jace, finding nothing but agitation pouring from Coop's narrowed-eyed gaze as I expected, but Jace's eyes flick between Mac and me for a moment before they spark with wickedness.

"It's okay, Ellie." He flashes those dimples, drawing Coop's disbelieving face. "Go. We'll be right behind you."

"There you go." Mac nods as if it's a done deal before giving me a nudge and jogging to the driver's side of his McLaren.

"Are you sure?" I ask nervously, still feeling a little guilty even though I really shouldn't, given all that they've put me through.

Coop looks down and shakes his head as if he can't believe what his cousin just agreed to before lifting his eyes to mine and arching a brow. "You heard him, Princess. I guess we'll be right behind you."

"Okay," I mutter, darting my eyes between both of theirs and making sure of what I see there before turning toward Mac's car.

My hand is on the door handle when the sound of Jace's voice stops me. "Oh, Ellie?"

"Yeah?" I turn my head, watching as he walks up and closes the distance between us.

He steps right up against me, grabbing my hips and pulling me against him, making sure there isn't one part of our bodies that's not touching before sliding a hand around to rest right above my ass. Reaching up with one hand, he pushes the hair behind my ear and dips his head down, putting his lips right up against the shell of my ear and causing my heart to damn near stall in my chest. And even then, he waits, prolonging it and letting me feel his breath fan out against the sensitive skin as I breathe in his sea-spring scent.

"Nothing," he finally whispers, voice all playful sensuality as he trails his fingers down my neck. "Just felt the need to lick you a little."

His words have my stomach flipping and he lets his hand drop back down my hip before giving it a light squeeze. And just to top it all off, he slowly and ever so lightly trails his lips across my cheek before he brushes it with the barest hint of a kiss and steps back. I stare into his firework eyes for a moment at a total loss, completely under his thrall with the sudden lust pooling in my veins before Mac clears his throat pointedly and jolts me awake. Shooting a slightly embarrassed look to him, I see the reluctant amusement in his eyes from where he sits watching the show in the driver's seat. But when I jerk my eyes to Coop, I find nothing but dark fury in his gaze that's resting on Jace.

Fuck, not good.

"Sometime today, Els," Mac drones impatiently.

I dart my eyes to Mac before looking back to Jace and seeing the challenging grin he's shooting Coop's way.

Well, it seemed they were going to have an interesting car ride. One that I wanted no part of, thank you very much. Plus, it wasn't like my presence would exactly make things less tense between them after that little display.

"Right," I drag out awkwardly, darting my eyes between them again but neither one of them is paying attention to me now. Their gazes are locked on each other and neither of them is backing down. "Well, uh, see you guys there."

I open the door and slide into Mac's car, sinking into the buttery leather as he starts it up and revs the engine over the sound of Drake blaring from the speakers. The loud purr finally makes Jace and Coop quit their stare off and look at the car, both of their gazes finding mine before I look away. Mac guns the engine then, peeling out and sending us rocketing down the tarmac with the smell of rubber filling the air. And it's not till we're already a quarter of a mile down the road that I realize he's chuckling.

"What?"

"Nothing." He shoots me a smile. "You're just so screwed."

I groan, sinking farther down into the seat which only makes him laugh harder as the ridiculously fast car continues to eat up the road, sending all kinds of exhilaration through my veins along with a dawning realization.

Apparently, Jace Dawson had come to LA ready to play the game.

To play it smart. To play to win.

***

Mac pulls up to the ornate iron gate of Stef's house in the Hollywood Hills and throws the car into park as we wait for the Uber to catch up. He had hauled ass here, whipping us around the winding roads of the hills, much to my delight, so I was guessing it would probably be a few minutes before it got here. I look through the gate to the Italian-esque villa and can't help but smile. The three-story stucco home had sat vacant for a year before Stef's nona had bought it as most buyers in the area were searching for the more modern look the houses around here were designed in. Even the little snippet I can see of Yvie's home next door doesn't fill me with the anxiety it probably should with all I had to explain to her.

I was just so fucking happy to be home. Especially after everything that had happened the last several days. Rolling my head to the side, I find Mac's worried eyes on me and give him a small grin. Letting him know I'm doing okay despite my call for help last night.

"So how in the world did you convince the other two to let you pick me up alone?" I narrow my eyes on him teasingly. "I thought Stef was picking me up."

He flashes me that troublemaker smile before reaching down and opening up the center console, revealing three sets of keys there. I quickly look them over and identify them as Stef's keys to his Pagani, Kai's to his G-wagon, and the extra Audi RS Q8 they kept on hand.

"You stole their keys?" I laugh.

"Fuckers were taking too long." He shrugs. "Plus, I thought I deserved some one-on-one time with my twin."

"They're going to kill you," I tell him seriously, despite the fact my lips are still twitching.

"They can try." He waggles his brows at me jokingly. "Greater men than them have tried and failed."

"True." I reach across to grab his hand, giving it a squeeze because I know the grain of truth that lives within his words.

He looks down at our entwined hands for a moment before lifting his head and looking back at me with a serious expression. "Do you want me to kill them?"

"Don't be so dramatic, Macallan."

"Fine then." He sighs. "Can I at least beat them up?"

I give his hand another squeeze and smirk. "Not yet."

"No fun, Els," he complains. "I knew you were spending too long in the south. Place'll suck the life right out of you."

"Shut it, you." I give him another roll of my eyes. "So did you finally decide on a room name?"

"Revel." He smiles at the reminder of our club opening this week.

We had decided to call the club Labyrinth in Greece and a labyrinth it would be, with twisting hallways leading inward to a central room that branched off into individual ones for each of us. Each of our rooms reflected our personalities and evoked a different experience for patrons to choose from. Stef had chosen the name Reminisce for his, I had dubbed mine Fractured, and Kai, of course, had gone with Forbidden. And now it appeared Mac had rounded us out with Revel. He had known his design immediately, but getting him to commit to a name had been a bitch. I had given up on it before I left for Landing Point.

"Appropriate." I laugh, turning as the sound of a car coming up the winding hillside road draws my attention and I see the guys' Uber pulling up behind us.

"I thought so," Mac agrees, eyes sparking with amusement before he reaches down and clicks the gate opener in the center console.

He slams the top of the console shut and drives through the gate as it opens, continuing up the short drive before pulling to a stop in front of the grand marble entry. I open the door and step out of the car at the same time Coop opens his behind me. Our eyes lock as we stand there for a second, allowing me to see all the dark conflict playing out behind his shuttered gaze. There's only so much you can hide from someone once you know them as intimately as we once knew each other and right now… he was toeing that line. I could see it plain as day, but I was at a loss as to what to do with it, because what he had done was unforgivable. That much I was sure of.

The sound of the front door opening draws my gaze and I see Kai step out, bronze paint-flecked and tattooed skin on full display as he jogs down the front porch in nothing more than a pair of loose sweatpants. His whiskey eyes eat me up from head to toe as he walks to me and wraps me up in a bear hug, swaying side to side and leaving me breathing in the smell of turpentine that's always clinging to him. He pulls back in the next instant, grinning down at me like a kid in a candy shop before biting his tongue and flashing me the metal piercing it.

An answering grin splits my face at the display and I reach up to ruffle his overgrown black locks affectionately. "You need a haircut, Kaison."

"Well now that you're here to hold my hand, I can go get one," he jokes, grinning even wider as he pulls me in and proceeds to squeeze the breath out of me.

I squirm in his arms and laughingly push back just as Stef's deep voice calls out to me from the entryway.

"Cara."

I turn at the familiar name, feeling my heart clench up at the sight of the small, secret smile on his classically handsome face. And dammit but even my eyes start to prick at the sight of him. His light-brown hair is stylishly pushed back with a few strands hanging loose around his forehead and he's sporting his trademark white button-down that's rolled up at the sleeves with fitted navy pants. Way too dressy a look for LA, which I've told him a million times despite the fact he always refuses to listen. I run forward and throw myself into his arms in the next instant, breathing in the earthy smell of the person who's always made sure I knew I was cared for above all others. Whether I liked it or not in the beginning.

He laughs in that deep baritone, wrapping his arms around me and bringing one hand to the back of my head before whispering. "You were missed more than you know."

I pull back and look into his near-black eyes, bringing my hands up to cup his face. "What the hell is this?" I laugh, feeling the scruff there.

He tips his head to the side once, giving me a slightly embarrassed look. "Macallan wasn't the only one who grew bored in your absence."

"I like it." I laugh again. "I bet the girls go even crazier now when you start speaking that Italian nonsense to them."

"Just a bit," he admits with a barely there smile before looking over my shoulder, expression going carefully blank. "I see you brought extra baggage," he surmises quietly.

I shake my head at him. "Careful now. You're starting to sound like Mac."

"Noted," he muses, narrowing his eyes at said baggage.

Turning with a sigh, I see that an epic showdown has indeed ensued between my two worlds of men. Coop and Jace stand with the luggage, Jace with a taunting grin that Mac's mirroring where he's perched against the back of his McLaren while Kai stands with crossed arms and Coop arches a brow back at him in challenge. Dear lord, I really should just hang a sign proclaiming it as the Wild West and be done with it.

"Do something," I mutter to Stef, lacking the energy to deal with this little display after days of pure hell followed by travel.

He looks down at me and an indulgent expression rolls across his face. "Only because I'm so happy you're home."

I give him a bratty smirk, nudging his shoulder with mine. "I'll take it."

"Mac, Kai," he calls, raising his voice with authority and drawing their reluctant gazes. "Let's go eat. We don't want to let the Indian food we got for Els from Cinnamon grow cold." He pauses for a beat. "We would never be so careless when it comes to her, would we?"

I see the fuck-off smile flash across Kai's face as he gives Coop one more look before turning to jog back up the front porch steps while Mac just laughs openly before doing the same. Kai stops to wrap his arms around me, lifting me into the air and making me squeal before he sets me down and walks inside with Mac. Jace grabs his bag and I take advantage of the opportunity to dart my eyes up to Stef, narrowing them on him in warning.

"Was that really necessary?" I scold.

"Absolutely," he answers, wrapping his arm around me before looking back out and I watch the dangerous look take over his face.

Turning my head, I see Coop staring right back at Stef, not backing down an inch as they size each other up silently. Jace comes up the front porch steps and gives me a mischievous grin as he threads a couple of our fingers together before letting them lightly trail apart on his way inside. Another long, tense moment passes before Stef eventually looks back down at me and squeezes my shoulders with another small smile.

"Don't take too long."

I give him a nod and he drops a kiss to the top of my head before turning to head inside. I wait until he disappears around the side of the front door before turning my head, looking back to Coop and seeing his narrowed eyes on the door Stef just disappeared into. The tension on his face is clear as his eyes sweep over the house before coming back to rest on me with a rare bit of unsureness peeking out from their depths.

And as much as what he did is unforgivable… a part of me can't just leave him out here in the cold either, not knowing the state he's in. I'm intimately familiar with it and it calls to me in some way. I can't help it.

I cock a brow at him. "Coming?"

His lips ghost up at my question and I see the flash of our shared memory play out on his face. He grabs both his bag and mine from the ground before walking up the marble steps of the house and coming to a stop beside me, night-forest eyes sparking with pleasure as they lock with mine.

"Always, Princess. Always."

Chapter Twelve

I shove another bite of naan and curry into my mouth from the seat on the back porch, flavors exploding across my tongue while I watch the guys move around inside the house through the windows. Stef is pouring the wine into a decanter, because his pretentious Italian ass refuses to drink it without letting it properly breathe while Mac is loading his plate up with *my* tikka masala of course. Kai had taken Coop and Jace upstairs to drop their bags off at Stef's direction. But when I see the three of them trail into the kitchen, one after the other, I shove another bite of naan into my mouth and chew it with possibly more force than necessary at the sight.

Kai immediately goes to grab a plate and begins to load it up with every dish in sight, food vacuum that he is. He's been that way since we were kids, ate everything in sight and somehow always managed to maintain more of that lanky punk rocker look. Jace scans the kitchen, pulling his bottom lip through his teeth before spying me through the back windows and flashing me a small grin. My lips twitch up in response and I watch him grab a plate, opening his mouth to speak as he does, charm probably in full force in an attempt to win over my family.

But Coop… Coop doesn't even look at the food before making a beeline straight for the back porch and causing any semblance of a smile to fall from my lips.

I look down at my plate and spear a piece of chicken with definitely more force than necessary this time, suddenly really regretting my choice to sit on one of the outdoor couches as I hear him open the back door. Should've foregone the view of inside and opted for a chair instead of my usual seat. I drag the chicken through the curry and rice before popping it into my mouth, looking up only when he comes to a stop at the couch. He doesn't even make eye contact with me, only looks at the spot to my right for not even two seconds before sitting down and making himself right at home. Not bothering to leave any space between our bodies and almost causing me to choke on the chicken I'm swallowing.

I shoot him an annoyed look and reach for my water on the glass table in front of us, using it as an excuse to resituate and put at least a little bit of space between our bodies. Trying my damndest to not focus on how the heat from his is practically radiating against mine. As I swallow down my water though, my eyes snag on the tattoo of our words on his arm and I set it back down with a sigh before leaning back into the couch to spear another bite. But the tension I can feel locking up his body next to mine grates at me as I chew, like an incessant thrum that's trying to work its way under my skin and cause me all kinds of anxiety. It leaves me so edgy after barely a minute that my stomach gives a twist and I can't take it anymore.

"Breathe, Cooper," I snap, tearing off a piece of naan and refusing to look at him. "And chill out before I make you smoke a blunt or something."

It's a beat before I hear him take a deep breath, his response coming with it. "I'll chill out when my cousin stops putting his hands on you."

I dip the naan into some curry, rolling my eyes. "Let it go."

"Let it go." He laughs low and humorlessly. "Let it go, she says."

"Yes, let it go," I repeat in a hard voice, finally looking at him and meeting his frustrated gaze before shoving my plate into his lap. "And for the love of god, fucking eat something and breathe."

He looks down at the plate and I see the flash of surprise on his face before his lips twitch. "Thank you."

"Whatever," I mutter, watching out of the corner of my eye as he takes a bite.

Feeding Satan now, El, really? Is it hot or cold? Care or don't care? Which is it because even I'm getting confused now.

Oh shut the fuck up, I order my inner voice, reaching over to snag the samosa off my plate because regardless of whether he's Satan or not, I'd never be that nice.

Coop swallows the food and leans back, spreading his arms wide and blatantly staring at me for a moment before he starts. "I was thinking."

"For once?" I quip, turning in time to see his lips twitch up again.

"Maybe when it comes to you." The dark in his eyes sparks with amusement and I look back down, flipping the samosa in my hands to give me something else to focus on. "Jace is definitely off base… I know that for a fact. But I can call Alec, have him look into the Morrisons at least. See if maybe he can find them."

My brows drop with displeasure at the mention of the fucker and I look back to Coop. "Wouldn't he get in trouble for that? They're not exactly high-level criminals or anything." Not that I particularly care when it comes to him.

"Trust me." His gaze rakes over my face before coming back to meet mine with a ghost of lips. "He owes me one."

The back door opens then, drawing both our gazes and I watch Mac's eyes move between us as he walks out, surprise flashing on his face when he spies my plate in Coop's lap. He shoots me a questioning look which I choose to ignore as he sits down in the chair to my left, instead darting my eyes away to watch Jace come out the door. Jace stops for a second at the sight of us, plate held aloft in the air as his eyes flick between us before he shakes his head with a small laugh and swaggers over to wedge himself in on my other side without any hesitation.

Leaving me sandwiched between my past and my present and having to remind *myself* to breathe now.

Kai ambles out then, shoving a whole samosa into his mouth and when his gaze lands on me, I see the way his whiskey eyes fill with laughter. He walks to the couch across from the one I'm on, setting his plate down on the glass table and chewing while his eyes flick between Jace and Coop before coming back to land on me.

"So." He swallows visibly before giving me a wide grin. "I put them in the first and third rooms on the left side of the second floor. I thought it was…" Chuckle, chuckle. "Appropriate."

I narrow my eyes on him dangerously. "Fucking hilarious, Kaison." Flipping him off, I take a bite of my samosa while Mac starts to laugh and I try to mumble. "Thanks."

"What's up with that?" Jace hedges, making me shove the rest of the samosa into my mouth to avoid having to explain and watching as Mac just narrows his eyes at him.

Uh-oh, apparently your charms need some work in the male department, Dawson.

"We all have rooms here, as I'm sure Els told you. Stef and Kai are down on the bottom floor, because apparently they have no appreciation for views," Mac explains after a moment, digging his Juul out from his pocket and nodding to me. "But our choices tend to mirror each other."

"You told me you were quitting!" I protest, words coming out garbled because of all the food I'm chewing.

"I am." He inhales the nicotine. "One day, when you quit too." I give him a confused look. I quit when we came back from Europe, like we had agreed to. There had even been a pact and all. "Everything," he tags on.

I roll my eyes in response and grab for my water to wash down the food as Kai picks up where Mac and I got distracted.

"As the twins were saying." He leans forward and begins to scoop up some food on his plate. "Mac has the second room on the right side of the second floor, which means…"

"El has the second room on the left side," Jace surmises quietly.

Coop's scoff of a laugh sounds, causing me to turn and look at him in surprise.

"Appropriate," he mutters with another dark laugh while spearing the last piece of chicken from the plate.

I shake my head with a sigh and look back to see Kai pulling the marble box on the table that we keep our paraphernalia in toward him. He opens the top and snags a lighter from inside before holding up a perfectly rolled baseball bat blunt out to me with a grin. Giving me the green as my welcome home present from him. My lips twitch up in answer and I reach out, grabbing the blunt and the lighter from him as Jace slides his plate onto the table in preparation for one of our favorite pastimes. Bringing the blunt to my lips, I flick the lighter, sparking up the end with a deep inhale to get it going.

I hold in the hit while passing the blunt to Jace, partly out of habit and also because I know without asking that Coop's ass is way too much of a control freak to get high despite my earlier threat. Jace takes the blunt from me and lifts it to his lips as Stef walks out, decanter in one hand and several wineglasses in the other. He walks around to place them on the glass table before grabbing one and pouring the wine into it. The deep red of what I'm guessing is my favorite cabernet fills the glass with a swirl and he cuts off the pour with a twist of his wrist before passing the glass to me.

"Caymus." He smiles.

Leaning forward, I grab the stem of the glass with a grateful grin. "I figured."

I take a sip of the wine and the warm, rich taste of cherries and licorice rolls over my palate, immediately making me sit back with a happy sigh as utter contentment washes over me for the first time in days. I hold the glass up to the light coming through the back windows, tilting it side to side and admiring the way the legs of the wine trail down the inside of the glass.

"Damn, Els." Mac laughs softly, drawing my gaze as he takes a hit of the blunt Jace must have passed him while I was in the midst of my wine obsession. His eyes roll over the two men caging me in before coming back to rest on me as he lets out the smoke with a shit-stirring grin. "That pussy really must be magical."

I feel Jace and Coop tense up on either side of me, still not used to Mac's and my borderline insulting dynamic of closeness.

"Having second thoughts?" I tease haughtily.

"Nah." He laughs again, shaking his head and passing the blunt to Kai. "It'd be like fucking myself. Too weird even for me."

"And here I thought you would be used to that."

Mac opens his mouth to no doubt instigate further when Stef slashes a hand through the air, cutting us off before we can really gather any steam with such an Italian move that I can't help but roll my eyes at it. "Enough, you two."

"Ah, come on, Stef. We were just playing." I take a sip of my wine before continuing. "Plus." I dip my head toward Jace. "This one has a pierced cock, so really, he's the most magical of us all."

You could hear a pin drop in the silence that follows my declaration as all eyes turn to Jace, and Coop's body winds impossibly tighter next to mine, pissed-off energy pouring out of him against my skin.

Really, El? Are we pushing or pushing away? And who, exactly, are we pushing? Because I'm pretty sure you don't even know what you're doing at this point.

I said shut the fuck up.

My brows drop down at the reality of my impulsive comment and I lean forward, snagging the blunt out of Kai's hand despite his sound of protest. I take a deep puff and pass it back to him before dropping back onto the couch and watching his eyes spark with interest on Jace.

"Seriously?" he hedges, flicking his tongue ring between his teeth.

Jace laughs lightly, dropping his hand to my knee and tapping a beat out against it thoughtlessly. Drawing my gaze to his face as he answers laughingly. "Seriously."

And despite his casual, laid-back posture, I can see a determined glint in his firework eyes that makes me think his hand placement is maybe not such a thoughtless gesture. Especially when Coop goes to put his now empty plate on the table and pauses midmove at the sight of it. I take a healthy gulp of my wine and grasp for anything to break up the tension now lacing the air because of my own stupidity in bringing his pierced cock up at all.

One of these days I *would* learn to keep my mouth shut and not give in to my impulsivity.

I would. Probably.

"So uh…" I start, still racking my brain and looking around aimlessly before my eyes land on the flash of white through Steff's hedge on the side of the house. "Yvie doesn't know I'm here yet."

Stef tips his head at me in question. "And why is that, *cara*?" He follows up the question with a sip of his wine.

"Because well…" I wave my hand to Jace and Coop on either side of me, giving him a come-on look. "I was hoping you could help me figure out how to explain this."

He narrows his eyes and flicks them between the two of them before shrugging. "Tell her the truth."

My mouth pops open for a second before I pull a disbelieving face. "The truth?" Surely I misheard.

"Why not?" He motions at Jace with his wineglass. "She knew you were bringing him." A dip of the wineglass toward Coop. "Just tell her his cousin tagged along."

"Right," I mutter.

"Keep it simple, *cara*."

"Simple," Coop scoffs darkly next to me.

Stef turns his eyes on him with an icy expression. “Would you prefer she tell her what really happened with you?” A tense beat passes between them and I see Coop clench his fists out of the corner of my eye before Stef looks back to me and continues. “Besides, Yvie will be at Nona’s gala the day after tomorrow and she’s expecting you back for that so it’s not like you can hide. Invite her for dinner tomorrow night and get it over with.”

“Sure. Okay.” I nod, trying to convince myself that this plan will go over as smoothly as Stef makes it sound.

“And then,” Mac chimes in merrily. “I have that epic party you requested planned for the next day.”

“Let me guess.” I smirk at the distraction. “There’ll be foam machines?”

“We aren’t in Vegas, Els,” he jokes. “It’s just a pool party. Intimate guest list of about a hundred, including Miss January through December.”

“Of course.” I laugh. “Whatever would I do without them?”

“Wallow for eternity,” he laments dramatically. “As would I.”

“So.” Kai leans forward and holds the blunt out to me, but I shake my head to pass, not looking to wind up on another bender after my adventures the day before. He passes it to Jace with a nod downward and lifts his brows in question. “How bad did that hurt?”

God, he was such a masochistic fuck sometimes.

I roll my eyes as Stef sighs wearily across from me at the question.

Jace takes a hit from the blunt. “Bad,” he breathes out with the smoke.

Kai grins, leaning back into the couch. “Interesting.”

"Crazy fucker," Mac mutters with a shake of his head, our eyes meeting and both of us grinning at the twin thought.

Jace looks between our two identical expressions before shaking his head with a laugh. "Okay, I get it now." He looks to me. "That is kind of creepy, Ellie."

Mac whips his head to Jace. "She lets you call her Ellie?"

Oh god, here we go.

Jace tilts his head toward him. "Define let."

"She kneed me in the balls when I kept trying to call her that in eighth grade."

"Well then I guess she lets me." Jace grins, dimples flashing and voice filled with satisfaction as he starts to trail his fingers up my leg.

My stomach gives a flip of anticipation that I definitely should not be feeling at this particular moment and I panic, popping up on my feet. "I think we need more wine." Grabbing for the decanter and quickly stepping over Coop's feet.

No need to pay attention to the fact that it's half-full, everyone.

Nothing to see here.

Avoiding eye contact with everyone, I walk to the back door and step inside before shutting it behind me with a sigh of relief. My eyes trail over Stef's familiar home as I walk through the living room and into the large, chef-style kitchen that his nona insisted on when moving here. The whole place is done in dark marbles with streaks of caramel running through them and creams accentuate everything in the home. From the walls to the leather furniture to the dark mahogany wood covering everything. Blatant wealth on full display that you could only get away with in LA and maybe a handful of other places.

I walk over to the wine chiller next to the oversized black-and-bronze fridge, opening it up and grabbing a bottle of Caymus. Turning around, I place it on the island and open the drawer to find the wine opener just as I hear the back door open. My head lifts and I see Coop closing the door behind himself softly, eyes already zeroed on me.

Of course, I sigh, looking back down and riffling through the drawer to avoid him for a minute more. I should've known he would chase when I fled. It was what he was good at, but the truth part, not so much. I come up empty in my search and close the cabinet before opening the next to see the wine opener lying right there on top. All the while hearing his footsteps draw closer and trying to distract myself with inane thoughts.

They must have switched the drawer we kept the wine opener in while I was away. It definitely used to be the other one.

Coop comes to a stop beside me, grabbing the wine bottle from the counter and plucking the opener from my hand. "It's nice," he muses, drawing my reluctant gaze as he begins to twist the metal into the cork. "Seeing your life here." His head dips toward the back porch, lips twitching. "I see what you meant. You and Mac are definitely… cut from the same cloth."

"It's always been that way." I give him a shrug as he pulls the cork from the bottle with a strong pull and dart my eyes away. Not wanting to feel the things I do when I look at him. That flare of attraction I'm trying with everything in me to snub the life out of. "We have… a lot in common, you could say."

"Hmm," he muses, smoothly stepping behind me and reaching around to pour the wine into the decanter. Putting his body bare millimeters away from mine and causing me to freeze completely, breath and all.

"What are you doing?" I manage to stutter out, looking into the decanter and forcing myself to take a shallow breath.

But the only thing that hits me is the smell of sandalwood and my favorite wine.

"Helping you," he answers quietly, pausing as he pours the last bit of wine and sets the bottle gently on the counter. Not moving for a beat before he whispers. "I miss you." I feel his head dip down next to mine and his upper body crowd closer as he braces his hands on either side of me, yet still, somehow, not quite touching. "God," he breathes heavily, the air fanning out against my ear and sending a few strands of hair tickling. "You have no idea how much I missed you."

My brows drop, face pinching up at the pain his words unearth and I reach out to grip the edge of the counter in front of me.

"Then why did you never call?" I whisper haltingly.

The question is ripped from me, ripped from some part of that broken girl who secretly, in some part of her most hidden inner heart, spent months wishing he would. Who wished for damn near a year.

He pauses. “That part of the story is… more complicated, Princess. It’s not my secret to tell.”

“Of course,” I scoff, gripping the counter tighter. “Because nothing is ever simple with you, right? What the fuck does that even mean?”

“Don’t you think I would tell you if I could?” he snaps, that demanding voice in full force. “Don’t you think I would give anything to be able to tell you? Is that not clear by now, Eleanor?” He closes that last barely nothing space between our bodies, letting me feel how taut his is against mine. “I’ve laid everything else at your feet… but this, it’s not my secret to tell.”

I remain silent in response, staring down into the wine and unable to properly sort through his cryptic words or my own feelings about them when he’s drowning me in his presence. Lighting my skin on fire with the heat and need I can feel leaking into my body from his.

“But I can tell you this,” he continues, dropping his voice low again. “I wasn’t lying when I said I chased you around the damn world this past year. Do you know the closest I got to actually catching you?” For a second, I think he’s waiting for a response until I feel him breathe me in, running his nose along the side of my hair down toward my neck. “You remember that little villa you stayed at in Seville? The one with the blue room?”

Shock fills me before I snap quietly. “How?”

I can still perfectly picture the blue room. The wrought iron double bed, the airy lace drapes, the tiny vase with white flowers on the bedside table.

He pauses for a beat, voice coming out rough when he speaks. “I got there the day after you left.”

His words hit my heart hard, chipping just a bit with the possibility of their almost and digging deep with the impossibility of what never was. I see his hand, the one with our words starting at the top of it, drop from the counter and when I feel his fingertips at the bottom of my tank top a second later, my whole body locks up. Tense and electrified all at once as he starts to lightly play with the edge of the fabric. Testing me, pushing me.

"It just about gutted me." He whispers the confession brokenly. "To know I had been so fucking close to actually being in your presence again." I feel his fingertips touch the skin at the top of my shorts with the lightest possible touch and my breath catches in response. "So I stayed in that room for the night." He drags his fingers back and forth along the curve of my hip, each pass a little harder than the last. "Just so I could be some kind of close to you for a night. To soak up something of your essence for a moment."

I see his other hand drop from the counter in the next breath. "Since you all had rented the whole villa, they hadn't cleaned it yet." He lifts his hand to my hair, brushing it gently away from my neck and tucking it behind my shoulder before dropping his mouth to my ear with an intimate whisper. "So it was a special kind of torture." His words have me held completely in a trance, waiting for the next bit of the story he's feeding me, anticipation ratcheting at the feel of him at my back again. "I could practically smell you on the pillow. That damn smell I can never figure out where it comes from… it's like…" A breath of his low, dark laugh flows over my skin. "I don't even know, something like the ecstasy of your cries when I'm inside you. Could practically hear your bratty taunts hanging in the air."

I feel his thumb run along that spot between my neck and shoulder that's gone without his worship for a year. And god help me, but my head dips to the side just the barest hint. "Could practically feel this spot under my lips."

A long moment passes as his fingers trail along my hip, his breath fanning across my ear and I feel him start to harden against me. "Do you know what else I did in that room that night, Eleanor?" He trails his lips down my neck so close that I can practically feel them and it causes the most delicious chills against my skin. "When I was lying in that bed, the closest to you I had been in months. Can you imagine it?" And between the wine and weed and his voice… that demanding voice that's pushing at me with every low and intimate note. I can. Staring down into the wine, I can picture it perfectly. "Can you fantasize it like I did about you when I took my cock in my hand?" My pussy gives a throb of need at the imagined picture and I'm wound so tight that when I feel his lips land on that damn spot in the next instant, I jolt in surprise, gasping as I raise my head.

And the first thing I see is Jace's narrowed eyes staring back at me.

It shatters the carefully crafted fantasy instantly.

I whip around, pushing at Coop's shoulders and looking up at him with furious accusation. "You did that on purpose."

He arches a brow at me, dark arrogance filling his night-forest eyes. "All's fair, right?" An insolent smirk rises to his lips. "Or does Jace get to play by a different set of rules?"

I heave a few breaths, face heating with embarrassment as I try desperately to get my body back in check. “I can’t do this.” I shake my head and take a few steps to the side, needing to escape. To run from the pressure I can feel bearing down on me from both of them. “Tell everyone I went to bed.”

“They’ll ask why.”

“I’m sure they all caught the show. But in case anyone missed it, you can just come up with a story.” I cock a brow in challenge. “You’re good at that, right?”

I watch frustration edge out any satisfaction in his eyes as he takes a step back toward me. “You can’t ignore this between us, Eleanor,” he argues, voice tight. “I know you feel it too. It’s not just going to go away.”

His words spark nothing but defiance, making me lift my chin. “Just watch me,” I toss out, turning away and walking from the kitchen. Picking up my pace as I make it to the foyer and begin to climb the grand, arching staircase that leads to the second floor.

And with every step upward, I try to convince myself that he’s wrong, that I really don’t feel anything for him at all.

Chapter Thirteen

Jace

One Year Ago

"So you really fell in love with this girl, huh?" I shake my head with a grin at the ridiculousness of my cousin's story. "Some random girl you met at a bar in Costa Rica."

Coop smiles just a bit from the hospital bed next to mine but I can see the happiness filling up his usually broody-ass eyes at the mere mention of her. "Yeah, I did."

"Man." I laugh and then suck in a breath as the incision in my stomach gives a sharp twinge in protest. Coop looks at me with concern and I grin, letting him know I'm okay, except for the little problem of every part of my body fucking *hurting*. "Fucking nuts. I can't believe she puts up with your sullen ass."

"Well." He lifts a brow at me. "I'm not so sullen where she's concerned."

I stop myself from laughing again by grabbing the empty Styrofoam cup from my bed tray and tossing it at him. "Don't make me laugh, asshole. I'm an invalid." I lift my brows at him in question. "So what's her name?"

He looks down at the Styrofoam cup now in his lap and he picks it up, clearing his throat as he answers. "Della."

"Damn." I sigh, trying to imagine the girl who finally brought my cousin to heel and somehow feeling like I'm coming up short. "That's a hot name. What's she look like? I need some visuals to go off while I'm in here, if you get what I mean."

"Shut the fuck up." Coop laughs, tossing the cup back at me before I see the pain come over his face, cutting him off.

"Nah." I grin. "I'm just kidding. Don't worry. Nurse Abby has become quite a fan since I regained consciousness."

"I noticed." Coop smirks, shaking his head.

Silence falls, and I pick up the cup, starting to tear it up as best I can with my one free hand just for something to do, going crazy with how confined I've been since the accident. Plus, it'll give me a reason to call the sexy nurse back in here to dote on me some more.

"Hey, Jace," Coop calls quietly.

I turn to him and see a more than usual serious expression on his face. "Yeah, man?"

"If anything ever happens to me—"

"Don't start." I shake my head, gut clenching at the thought. "Noth—"

"You can't let it be her," he orders, cutting me off in a hard voice. "If anything were to happen to me. If I ended up in a coma like you and someone had to pull the plug. You can't let it be her."

"Coop…" I drawl, feeling my heart fucking spasm at the mere thought of a world without him. Maybe getting a little dose of what I put him through.

"Promise me, Jace," he demands, eyes going a little crazy. "You don't know what she's been through already."

It takes me a minute to swallow down my protest but I finally sigh, knowing I owe him this a thousand times over. "Fine."

"Swear it."

"Fine!" I agree. "I fucking swear it, happy now?"

His eyes narrow on me for a second before he lets out a breath. "Thank you."

I look down, shaking my head and pulling more pieces of the cup apart. Trying to ease some of the tension pulling at me before speaking. "The same goes for you, Coop."

"What do you mean?"

"I don't ever want to live like that." I look back at him and see the way his forehead is all puckered up at my request.

Yeah, doesn't feel great, does it, cousin?

"I don't think I liked what was there, Coop. When I was out the past few days, I don't know… it just left me with this weird feeling. I don't want to be stuck there. You can't leave me to that."

A heavy moment passes between us as I stare into his eyes that are so similar to mine, just a few shades that separate our similarities. Eventually, he gives me the same nod of acceptance in return and I know I don't have to ask him to swear it. Coop was good by his word like that.

"So does this mean you're planning on marrying that girl?" I grin, trying to lighten the mood now. Being in the hospital was rough enough without all this talk of death.

He looks down with that bit of a smile. "Something like that."

"That tattoo for her?" I prod.

"Yeah."

"Man, you really have lost your fucking mind." I laugh, ribbing him, but really, I'm sort of wondering what that kind of love must feel like.

"Definitely." He laughs quietly and looks back at me with this forlorn kind of pain on his face. "I fucking miss her, man."

"Dude. You only have like two more days left in here." I snort. "I'm in here for at least another two weeks."

"You're right." He sighs. "I just… no, you're right."

"And didn't your creepy-ass coworker say that she said to tell you she'd be waiting in bed for you or something like that before he broke your phone?"

"Yeah." He smirks. "Something like that."

"Fucking idiot." I grab my phone off the hospital tray next to me for something to do now that the cup is an obliterated mess in my lap. "How the fuck do you drop a phone down the stairs in the span of like five minutes?"

Silence sounds from the bed next to mine, and I look to Coop, seeing how his eyes are narrowed on the hospital blanket covering him. Bastard was a needy pain in the ass now that he was in love.

I hold out my phone to him. "Want to use mine?"

Coop looks at me, eyes moving to my phone and sticking there for a moment before his brow puckers and he shakes his head. "No, that's okay." He looks back to me and his expression clears. "You're right. I'll be back in two days. It's fine."

"I see how it is." I lift my brows at him and pull my phone back. "You just don't want me to have her number."

"Fuck off, man." He laughs before that twinging flashes across his face again.

"Probably for the best." I grin widely, looking back down to my phone and unlocking it to pull up Hinge. "She'd probably talk to me once before falling madly in love and leaving your sullen ass."

I see him grab for the remote on his bed out of the corner of my eye and quickly hold up my arm, ducking to miss the thrown projectile while pain-racked laughter grips us both.

Chapter Fourteen

My eyes pop open the next morning to the sound of Mac's grunt in his sleep and the first thing I see is the way his face is screwed up as if he's in pain, blond hair sticking out every which way against the navy silk of his pillow. I reach up, placing my hand on his shoulder to shake him awake, used to the routine by this point in our lives. I was far from the only person in this house who suffered from bad dreams. His body gives one last jerk before his eyes fly open, darting around in panic at whatever horrible memory he was reliving before finding mine. He stares at me for a moment as his eyes clear before exhaling a deep breath and rolling over, flopping against his bed and lifting an arm to pull me against him. Seeking comfort just as I did last night when I chose to sleep in his room and not mine.

I feel his body slowly relax and ask the question that's always filled with uneasiness. "How is she?"

He shrugs under my cheek. "Okay as she can be, I guess."

"And Wells?"

"Good, actually. Enjoying being at college and out from under my father's thumb. He decided to stay there through the summer, shocking, right?" He laughs sarcastically.

"Hmm." I sigh. "Well, at least there's that."

A beat passes and I feel him tense up again. “He’s thinking about running for governor.”

“Wow.” I scoff, unable to fathom how the world still can’t see Mac’s dad for the evil that he really is.

“It would mean him being home year round instead of splitting time in DC.”

“There’s nothing you can do,” I interrupt quickly, tipping my head back to look at him. “You’ve tried to help her so many times, Mac. You can’t help someone who won’t accept it. This is not on you.” Repeating the words I’ve told him countless times despite the fact I know they do little to ease the weary pain in his eyes.

He stares at me for a moment, gaze unfocused and my mind dredges up all those bruises I helped him hide when we were young, knowing how much worse it would be if he said anything.

We had tried that once.

It had only led to broken bones that, though they may have healed, never quite mended properly.

“You’re right.” He finally nods, squeezing me with his arm. “So why the hell did I find you in my bed last night and not one of your boys? I was looking forward to making a big fuss about it this morning.”

“Because.” I give him a shrug and answer honestly. “I just needed my twin last night.” Needed the familiar comfort of family. “I just needed a minute to myself and fucking Kai made that impossible when he put them on either side of me.”

I could feel it as soon as I stepped into my room, that usually felt like a refuge. The way that pressure still lingered when I was lying in my bed. The tight anticipation running through me at the thought of when they came to bed and were both only feet away from me. The probability that one of them would knock on my door. I would have never slept. So I had fled, walking down the hall and closing myself in Mac's room before anyone else came up. Sleep had come easily then.

"You know they probably checked and know you weren't in your room last night." He chuckles. "They're going to be pissed."

"I don't care."

"Yes, you do," he counters. "You wouldn't have brought them here if you didn't care, Els."

"Whatever," I humph, looking down at the giant flat screen mounted in front of his bed to avoid his questioning eyes.

It's a moment before he speaks again, voice quietly curious. "Do you still love them? Even after what they did?"

"Jace." I narrow my eyes at the TV, trying to sort through the mess of feelings his question sparks. "Yes. Jace is…" Pausing, I tilt my gaze back to his as I try to explain. "He's all the bright impossibilities I had lost faith in come to life, Mac. He makes me a better person too. He hurt me and that—that shook me, because he was the last person I ever expected to." I look back at the TV with a sigh. "So yes, I still love him. He's impossible not to. It's what made me fall for him in the first place."

"That sounds… nice," he admits, reluctance clear in his voice. "And the other one?"

My lips twitch just the barest hint at his refusal to say Coop's name. "I don't know the first thing when it comes to Coop," I finally admit, sucking in a breath at the physical ache in my heart at the mere mention of him. Especially after last night. "Except that I think a part of me might always hate him a little for how he broke me. And I don't want to care about him. Me and him, it's just all kinds of wrong even without what he did to me."

"Yeah," he scoffs. "Hate to break it to you, but if there's one thing I've learned, it's that the heart is probably the most irrational part of our bodies. There's no reason involved there." He squeezes me again to soften the blow of his words. "You'd think such a vital organ would be smarter considering its necessity."

My brows drop at his words, at the horrible reality of them. "So what does that mean?"

I feel his chest move under my cheek with another shrug. "I guess we'll see."

We lie there for a while longer, both of us lost in our own struggles until I eventually feel his body go slack under mine. Soft snores pour from his mouth as he falls back into a hopefully peaceful and dreamless sleep. But my mind is running in circles after our conversation, making further sleep impossible. So I wait a few more minutes to make sure he's really out before sliding out from under his arm and off the bed, holding my breath as I tiptoe out of the room on the cold marble floor in an effort not to wake him. I open the door, stepping out quickly and looking down as I close it behind me. The soft snick sounds and I exhale a deep breath, shoulders dropping as I look up toward the other end of the hallway.

And there he is.

Dirty-blond hair hanging loose, shirtless perfection in a pair of joggers that are hanging just low enough to be considered indecent. That beautiful tattoo and lickable *V* cut on full display for the world to want or envy. Leaning against the door to my room as if he's just been casually waiting around for me to finally make my appearance for hours now. His playful eyes are narrowed on me with open curiosity and my lips twitch at the sight of him. It's an automatic reaction at this point that I probably couldn't stop if I tried and all he does is make me not want to. He tilts his head at me, flashing those dimples, and I cock a brow back before walking down the hallway to him. Unable to do anything but to give in to our playful game as he pulls me closer. His eyes run down the length of me, taking in my tank top and pajama shorts combo as I pass the massive media room filled with oversized couches that separate the two sides of the upstairs.

His firework eyes are swirling with questions when I come to a stop in front of him and he flicks them over my shoulder toward Mac's room. "Do I have another reason to be worried here, Blondie?"

"No." I laugh lightly, leaning against the door to my room before giving him a half shrug. "Just needed some space last night."

"Hmm," he drawls, looking down and reaching up to play with the ends of my hair where it's falling over my shoulder.

I see the hint of tightness pulling at his face and tilt my head at him in question. "Does it bother you?"

His lips pull up for a second before he tugs on my hair playfully. "A bit." He drops his hand from my hair, reaching down to grip my hip as he moves closer to me. "You're just lucky I have a big enough ego to deal with it."

But that admission has my brows dropping as guilt tugs at me. My carelessness hitting a bit too close to the currently raw nerve that is the reminder of my mother.

"I'm sorry," I start. "I wasn't really thinking… all of this is new and things last night got, uh—" I drop my eyes, unable to hold his gaze as the memory of last night in the kitchen flashes through my mind. "Intense and I just needed a minute."

He reaches up with his other hand to my chin, tipping my head back so that I'm forced to look him in the eye again. Seeing the way his brows are pulled down and his eyes crinkled at the corners with concern I probably don't deserve shining from their depths.

"I get it, Ellie." He tilts his head side to side. "I may not like it, but I get it." Giving my hip a squeeze, he nods to the door. "So you going to invite me in?"

His eyes spark with the question and I shake my head with a small grin. "I have to get ready to go see Yvie. Let her know about dinner tonight."

"Good." He runs his hand up my face, brushing my hair behind my ear. "Then you can get ready and we can talk."

"Just talk?" I pull a face, knowing his sneaky ways by this point and seriously doubting that I'm going to be able to get ready with him in there.

"Just talk, at least to start." He drops his lips to my ear, melodic voice filled with sensual promise when he speaks. "But I promise to reward you with wicked, wicked things if there's time."

My mouth pops open at his audacity and the next thing I know, he's snagging me around the waist while opening my door.

"Jace!" I laugh in surprise, feet hanging in the air as he holds me and walks into my room.

He carries me over to the bed and tosses me onto it before coming down on top of me, trapping me under his weight quickly and sliding his arms on either side of mine. His sea-spring scent washes over me as he scoots his arms in closer and nudges one of his legs between mine, leaving me feeling like a caterpillar in a cocoon. A very pretty, golden cocoon that's making all kinds of desire pool in me, but a cocoon nonetheless.

He looks around curiously, taking in the space with a frown as his eyes roam over all the shades of light purple that the room is decorated in, except for the ruffly white curtains and quilt we're lying on. "It's very… uh, delicate."

I roll my eyes at him with a soft laugh. "Nona did it for me before she passed. The decor wouldn't have been my first choice but I think she had always wanted a girly granddaughter and I wasn't about to upset her."

"That makes more sense." He grins down at me, eyes rolling over my face before coming back to meet mine, and I watch as his expression turns serious. Lips falling into a straight line and clueing me in on the fact that I'm going to hate what he's about to say before he even opens his mouth. "We need to talk about Coop."

I look up at the ceiling fan, focusing on its spinning as I fight the way my body is trying to tense up. "What about him?"

He's silent for so long in response that I'm forced to look back at him, and when I do, I see something that I've never seen shining out of his firework eyes before.

There's anger there, not blazing or furious, but the quiet kind that peeks out from the depths and is all the more serious for it. It makes my stomach flip in a way that has nothing to do with the desire that's now abandoning me, leaving nothing but a foreign unsureness in its wake.

"What?" I venture cautiously.

Jace didn't get angry, at least not at me.

His face tightens up with pain as he stares down at me for another moment, eyes flicking between mine as he sucks in a breath. "Why did you never tell me?"

Oh.

As I stare up into his eyes, it occurs to me for the first time that Jace Dawson has every reason to be as angry at me as I was at him when all of this came out. And that by the looks of things, he probably is, at least a little. I mean, technically, I was the adulterous, lying bitch in this situation with him. Even if Coop had built all the cards of this tower, I was still at fault here too. I had still kept the secret that caused it to fall and was probably just as much to blame, but Jace was just too empathetic to throw it in my face at first, like I did him.

My failure to recognize this, again, hits way too close to the raw nerve that is my mother and my brows pull down tight as I force myself to take a few deep breaths. Hating with every one of them that I'm not a better person like he is. That I didn't think through how much my omission might be hurting him through all this too.

That maybe I was a little more like Coop than I wanted to admit.

And Jace had waited, the stupid, self-sacrificing sun that I love so much had waited until he knew I was doing better to bring it up. Until I could weather the question.

It strips me bare and demands a naked kind of vulnerability that I rarely give in return, about why, exactly, I didn't just tell him. And I can give it to him, because staring up into his firework eyes now I know that even though he might've hurt me… he's still that safe haven that brought me back to life.

"Because," I whisper haltingly, forcing the words out. "I was embarrassed."

His brows pull down in confusion. "What?"

"I didn't know then what I do now." I bite down on my lip hard, trying to use the pain as a distraction as I wade through all the current and remembered feelings tearing at my heart. "I didn't know that he had left to save you, that it had all been… whatever it was from the beginning. I just knew—" My face scrunches up at the memories as I look away and Jace lifts his hand to my hair, beginning to run his fingers through it soothingly.

Cracking my heart open even more with that one move. "I just knew he had left me." I look back to him, seeing the start of understanding in his eyes. "That he had loved me, and left me, just like my parents. And in the months after… I think some part of me started to believe it was because he had realized my damage wasn't worth it. That I wasn't worth all the trouble or that… I don't know." I shrug as much as possible in my cocoon of him. "That he had gotten some sick satisfaction from playing me. That I was too much of an idiot to recognize either one that it had been. And it left this place in me." My words catch on a stuttering breath and I try to swallow down the tightness in my throat. "It left this place in me that *hurt*, Jace, hurt so fucking bad from the embarrassment of it all. That I was the one who had been left. Again. I blamed myself for not being smart enough to see what was happening with him one way or the other." A lone tear escapes my eyes and I blink rapidly against it, hating Coop so damn much in this moment for what he did to me. "And that maybe, just a little bit… I blamed myself for not being good enough to make him stay. That—" I inhale a quick breath and hurry the rest of the words out before I can't manage them at all. "That I wasn't worthy enough to make him stay. To deserve that happiness after all."

"Oh, Ellie." Jace reaches up to brush the tear from my cheek. "Pretty girl," he whispers tenderly. "As much as I might hate to admit it for the broody bastard's sake… I can tell you for a fact that it wasn't any of those things."

Giving him a small nod, I look up into his eyes that are heartbroken for me and answer him softly. "I know that now. But at the time… I didn't. So I did what I do best." I shrug helplessly in his arms. "I buried it and avoided."

"And now?"

My brows drop in confusion. "Now what?"

"You still care about him," he states bluntly, eyes searching mine. "So is that what you're doing now? The avoiding?"

I shake my head, inwardly cursing Cooper Monroe and his very public display last night for bringing all this on but Jace just continues over my silent protest.

"Ellie," he sighs, breath fanning out over my face in all its minty freshness. Apparently he had time to brush before waiting around for me this morning. "You would have never let him that close in the kitchen last night if there wasn't *something* still there."

I close my eyes, unable to look at him and face the confession that it takes me a minute to finally speak. "I hate it," I choke, the words feeling like nothing but betrayal. "I hate it and I'm sorry."

Such useless words, I'm sorry, as if they're magically supposed to close the wound. In reality, they fix nothing. In actuality, they're really only something to make the person saying them feel better more than anything else.

Jace gives my hair a light tug and I open my eyes again, seeing nothing but the thoughts flying behind his own in our close proximity.

"It's okay, Ellie."

"It's not," I argue. "I don't want—"

"That's not what I'm saying." He lifts his head, bracing his arm on the bed to lift up a bit. "It has nothing to do with what anyone wants. I'm saying it'd be impossible to go through what y'all have and feel nothing for him. It's not…" His brows pull down, lips twitching at the same time. "A rational thing to ask of yourself. There's too much history there." He reaches up, lightly running his fingers down along my hairline, eyes tracking the movement as he speaks. "And you never got closure before. Never got to really heal completely because of it. So I'd be an idiot if I asked you to feel nothing for him. It'd be an impossible request and one that I'd lose." Those firework eyes find mine, filling with playful determination as he grins. "And Blondie, I have no intention of losing here."

"Who said anything about winning and losing?" I scoff softly. "I'm not a prize, you know."

"Mmm," he drawls, dropping his face a breath away from mine. "Don't kid yourself, Ellie. There's a war happening here. Even if you haven't caught on to it yet, and don't think you're getting away with that." Those dimples flash. "Because I know you're way too smart for that shit."

I see the spark of need in his gaze as he slides his leg up higher between mine, causing me to open my legs wider for him until I feel him press his thigh against me.

"I don't want a war." My breath hitches as I speak, pussy tingling at the sudden pressure and reminding me of just how well Jace Dawson knows my body at this point.

"Few do." He drops his lips to mine with a slow, barely there kiss and it hits me that this is really our first intimate moment since everything came out. That this is the first time I've let him this close again. But if I'm being brutally honest with myself, I want to. I want nothing more than to forgive him because of all the impossibilities he became to me. To bask in his light again.

"But sometimes…" He pushes harder against me and I roll my hips, desire urging me to chase that pressure as he whispers against my lips. "They're unavoidable." I feel him start to harden against me as he dips his head, trailing his lips down my neck before dropping a kiss to the center of my chest. He reaches down to loop a hand behind one of my legs and hitches it over his hip, flicking his eyes up to mine with a small grin. "So I'm just making sure you're still with me."

I heave a couple breaths, ridiculously keyed up from his little seduction. The thin cotton of my panties already embarrassingly damp as I widen my legs, searching for some kind of more to feed the rapidly growing need he's sparking inside of me.

My lips twitch up in answer. "I'm with you, Dawson."

He braces a hand next to my head, bringing his head back up to look down at me as he reaches down and hitches my other leg over his hip.

Pressing himself into me and causing me to gasp as he lets me feel just how hard he is. "You sure about that, Ellie?"

And looking up at him, I see it then, the same look I saw in his eyes the night before that sent me running from the kitchen. That unsure possession darkening them to almost the same night-forest shade as Coop's. It makes me pause and force myself to take a few steadying breaths as I try to find the right words, because the truth is, I don't want any of Coop's and my bullshit to touch him. Even if I had dragged him into this and would burn for eternity for that.

I would be damned if I took him with me.

Reaching up with both hands, I tangle one into his hair and pull him closer while cupping his face with the other, running my thumb along the place I love to see those damn dimples flash. Knowing that this feeling of unsurety is probably something completely foreign to him.

"Tell me something," I quip, trying for haughty and just barely making it there. "What happens to the world without the sun?"

That brilliant smile flashes, hitting me hard as I feel his dimple under my thumb and his eyes flick between mine, lightening immediately at our familiar play. "It goes dark."

"Exactly." I nod, cocking a brow at him with a warning look. "So don't ever come at me with that bullshit again, Jace Dawson." Softening my voice, I pull him even closer until there's nothing but a breath left between us. "Coop or not. You became my fucking sun and my world would go dark without you." I press my lips to his with a soft kiss. "But don't you ever lie to me again. Capiche?"

I feel him grin into our kiss as he deepens it, tongue swirling all his lightness against mine before he answers. "Yes, empress."

A shocked laugh leaves me at the term that is most definitely his version of a snub on the one his cousin uses for me, only granting him further access, and he takes full advantage. Quickly taking the teasing kiss, desperate as he pushes against me. I roll my hips again in answer, pulling him impossibly closer as our breaths become a needy mix of giving and taking until I'm light-headed with the wave of desire pulling me under. He breaks the kiss in the next instant, eyes filled with those wicked things he promised as he reaches down to push my tank top up and starts to kiss his way down my stomach. I drop my hands from him to the ruffled quilt, grip tightening with each kiss and skin sparking under his lips.

Pausing when he makes it to the edge of my shorts, he flicks his eyes up to mine before darting his tongue out and dragging it across the sensitive skin above the waistband as a gasp escapes me at the move. He ends it with a playful tug of the waistband using nothing but his teeth that leaves me digging my heels into the bed at the demanding pulse of need my pussy gives at the sight. Keeping his eyes locked on mine, he lets go of the waistband and turns his head to the side, blowing a soft breath across the skin he just licked that has my hips lifting off the bed, desperately chasing more of what he has to offer.

Jace's eyes shine with pure mischief as he raises a hand, lightly trailing his fingers over my pussy and flashing his dimples at me. "Does my girl want to play?"

"I don't know," I gasp, unable to resist the urge to tease him a little. "I'm not sure you're that forgiven yet, Dawson."

"Why don't you give me a chance to apologize properly then?" He nudges my underwear to the side, sinking two fingers inside of me as his voice drops to a husky kind of melody. "And then maybe we can both find it in our hearts to forgive a little, yeah?"

"Fuck." I throw my head back at his words, feeling him pump his fingers inside of me and drag his teeth over my clit through the fabric of my shorts.

What were you saying about forgiveness, El?

He's forgiven. Totally forgiven.

"Is that a yes, Delacroix?" he teases with another pump. "Still waiting on my answer here."

"Yes," I gasp, looking back down to find his eyes waiting for mine. "Fucking yes."

"Yes to the apology?" He dips his head, dragging his teeth along the outside of my shorts again and killing me with how close he isn't. "Or a request for my cock inside you?"

"Jace!" I snap warningly, narrowing my eyes on him.

"Okay, okay." He laughs lightly, sliding his fingers from me as he rises up with a smug grin and fingers the edge of his joggers. Taunting me with the large bulge I can see through them. "No need to make a fuss, Ellie. Despite what they say, you *can* have it all."

"I'm going to—"

"Good morning, *cara*!"

"Fuck!" I shout in an outburst at the sound of Stef's voice and it's not one of embarrassment. Oh, no. It's an outburst of primal fucking frustration at this point.

I turn my head to the door to give Stefano Garda the most deadly look I probably have in the history of our friendship as Jace drops his body back over mine immediately. Although why, considering I'm pretty much completely clothed, I have no idea.

Stef comes to a slow halt, a small smile playing across his face as Jace's heavy breathing fills my ear.

"Oh." His eyes move between us with fake surprise. "Am I interrupting something?"

I was going to end him. Years of friendship and family be damned.

"Get out!" I screech, reaching up to grab a pillow and tossing it at him over Jace's shoulder with all the strength I can muster.

The pillow lands on the floor at his feet and he gives me a reproachful look. "Come now, *cara*. You should really put a sock on the door or something like Mac if you plan on entertaining." I reach up, grabbing for a second pillow in agitation at his words and he just chuckles before walking back out of the room while speaking. "I was just letting you know I talked to Yvie's assistant and the only free time she has today is in an hour. So you better get going if you hope to make it. I left Kai's keys on the counter for you."

The sound of the door shutting cuts off his chuckle and Jace lifts his head, looking down at me with both amusement and frustration in his gaze. Although what the hell he found particularly amusing about this situation was beyond me.

"Don't take this the wrong way, Blondie." He drops his lips to mine with a small grin. "But I kinda hate him."

I snort a laugh. "Trust me, Dawson, I'm right there with you too."

Unfortunately for both of us, I had a feeling this was just the start of their games.

Chapter Fifteen

I push against the door of Yvie's law office, using my shoulder to move the ridiculously heavy glass across the tile floor before sweeping my gaze over the space. The harsh white and metal interior hitting my eyes with its usual harshness despite the windows on every side that offer priceless views of the LA skyline. The place had always reminded me of some kind of weird heavenly waiting room. One part purgatory, two parts apple genius bar, mix well for the perfect upscale law office that constantly puts you on edge. My dislike of the place had only grown through the years of visits and probably had something to do with what had pushed me toward a more aesthetically pleasing career instead of one in corporate America.

Walking up to the front desk, my lips twitch at the sight of the young receptionist giving my cutoffs and Converse an open sneer of disdain, and I can't help but wonder how long she's been here. They never lasted long. Typically, the stress drove them to quit within a month but this one looked like she had a bit more steel to her, so I might wager two this time. I prop my arms up on the quartz top of the elevated desk, eyeing the way the bun on the back of her head is pulling the skin on her forehead tight and the all-black ensemble she's dressed in that's practically the company uniform around here.

“Hi.” I give her an overly bright smile, getting way too much satisfaction out of the way her eyes narrow on me. “Is Yvie in her office?”

Her lips purse briefly before she snips back. “Do you have an appointment?”

“Never do,” I shoot back quickly. “Can you just tell her—”

“Eleanor!”

I turn at the bright voice, lips stretching into a genuine grin at the sight of the Driscoll part of the Driscoll and Barnes Law Firm. “Larry.” I laugh, walking toward the elderly man who had always made sure to sneak me extra sweets at all of the forced family events Yvie had dragged me to growing up.

“What are you doing here?” He hugs me quickly before leaning back, holding my shoulders and looking me over with a surprised smile. “Yvie said you weren’t supposed to be back until tomorrow!”

“Decided to surprise her.” I give him a half shrug in answer, nodding toward the hallway on my left leading to the back. “She in her office?” I take a step in that direction, not waiting for an answer because I already know she is, thanks to fucking Stefano.

“Uh, Elean—” The sound of Larry’s voice stops me, and I look back to him, cocking my head in question but he just looks at me for a second before chuckling. “Never mind. Go on ahead.”

“Okay.” I drag out the word in confusion, waiting to see if he decides to add anything more before shaking my head at him and turning back to the hallway.

I shoot the receptionist's now scared shitless face a smug look and continue on my way, throwing in a little skip just to shock her a little. Walking down the long hallway, I peek into the glassed-in offices on either side of me, seeing all the busy worker bees. Some hunched over stacks of paperwork or yelling into phones pressed to their ears. And by the time I make it to Yvie's corner office at the end of the hall, I'm counting my lucky stars that my aunt understood the fact that my soul would die in this kind of place and went along with me majoring in photography.

The sight of the drawn shades on her office not allowing anyone to see through the glass has my brows pulling down in concern though. Yvie typically only did that when she got one of her migraines and was trying to dim the light. I'd have to be sure to tread carefully. She was always particularly straightforward with her nosiness when that happened.

Grabbing the metal handle of the door, I pull it open and call out quietly. "Yvie."

"Oh my god!" My gaze jerks to my aunt's at the sound of her squeal, quickly finding her where she's sitting on the edge of her desk with her silk blouse undone and pencil skirt pushed up.

With a man I most certainly do not know standing between her legs.

"Oh my god!" I echo her squeal, slapping a hand over my eyes. "Yvie!"

"Ellie!"

"Bollocks."

Bollocks?

"Huh?" I mumble, vaguely registering the man's British accent through the damaging visual I just witnessed. "What the fuck?"

"Language, Ellie!"

"Really?" I snort, keeping my hand firmly over my eyes until advised otherwise. "I guess it's true what they say, 'when the cat's away, the mice will play.'"

"Ellie," Yvie chides before I hear the ruffling of clothes that have me openly cringing. "You can open your eyes now."

"Are you sure?"

But it's not my aunt's very American voice that answers. "Very sure, pet."

Excuse me? Pet?

Uh, I repeat, what the fuck?

I squint through a few of my fingers to make sure all their clothes are in place before dropping my hand with a sigh of relief. Taking in my aunt's disheveled brunette pixie cut framing her heart-shaped face as she tugs on her white blouse and looks at me nervously with our shared gray eyes. I flick my eyes to the man at her side, taking in his boardroom good looks wrapped up in a navy-pin-striped suit and topped with salt-and-pepper hair. Acceptable, I suppose, but I narrow my eyes at him all the same. Letting him know that no one could ever be good enough for my aunt, in my opinion.

And who's stopping someone from getting theirs now, El?

Yeah, yeah.

I roll my eyes at the irony and look back to my aunt, giving her a weak smile. "Surprise."

A sudden laugh leaves her lips, leaving her with a wide smile on her face as she walks across the office. "Surprise, indeed! What are you doing here, kid?" She pulls me into a tight hug, laughing again. "Not that I'm complaining."

"Mhmm," I mutter sarcastically, giving the man over her shoulder another glare and leaning into the comfort of her Chanel-scented embrace. "Just decided to come home a day early is all."

"And where's that boyfriend I'm supposed to be meeting?"

"At Stef's," I answer as she leans back, looking at me with open curiosity.

"Well." She lets go of me and starts to fidget in a way that is very much *unlike* the aunt I grew up with as she shoots the strange man behind her a nervous look. "This was definitely not how I wanted you both to meet but since we're all here."

Mr. Bollocks walks forward at her prompt, hand held out with a winning smile that makes me automatically suspicious. "Simon Taylor."

I reluctantly return the gesture, shaking his hand. "Uh-huh."

His smile falters briefly at my answer as our hands drop away from each other before he tugs it back up and tries again. "And you must be the famous Ellie I've heard so much about."

Catching my aunt's nervous glance, I manage to twitch my lips into a forced grin for her sake. Inwardly admitting that recent events might have made me just a tad jaded when it comes to the realm of men. "The one and only."

Awkward silence falls between us then and I look down, scuffing the toe of my Converse on the sparkly white tile floor as my aunt clears her throat.

"I guess your aunt wasn't the only one in for a surprise today when you got here."

A surprised laugh bursts from my lips and I look up to meet Simon's amused brown eyes. "That would be correct."

Okay, maybe I'd give him a chance.

He looks at my aunt and I see a dopey expression come over her face as she smiles up at him that makes me feel like I'm in some kind of weird, alternate reality.

"Why don't I clear out? Give you two the chance to catch up?"

"Okay." My aunt nods, going up on the tip of her Manolo Blahniks to press a kiss to his lips that has me darting my eyes away. "I'll give you a call after, love."

Love? Love?! What the fuck had happened when I went away this summer?

Yvie had never dated when I was growing up, and if she had any, ahem, relationships, she sure as hell kept them discreet. Completely out of my sphere of knowledge. I mean, logically, I knew she probably had. She was attractive, in her late forties, and a fucking catch. So obviously she had to be getting her extracurriculars in somewhere. But this was just throwing me into the deep end with no preparation in the shallows.

And to think, she had tattled to Stef about Jace and me.

My eyes go wide with realization but I manage to nod a semi-friendly goodbye to Simon with the accent before whipping my gaze to Yvie as the door shuts behind him.

"Did Stef know?" I demand, narrowing my eyes at her.

She bites down on her bottom lip for a second in the exact same way I do when I'm trying to buy time and I already know the answer.

"You little shits!"

"Eleanor." She sighs wearily.

"No, no, no." I hold up a hand. "Why is it a public service announcement when I date someone but not you?"

Shaking her head at me with an exasperated look, she walks back toward her desk. "Maybe because of the age difference and fact that I'm your guardian." She shrugs, taking a seat in her oversized leather chair and pressing the button on her desk to raise the shades along the walls. "But that's just a guess."

"Not fair," I complain, walking over and taking a seat opposite her. Quickly turning to lean back against the arm of the chair and lift my legs to hang over the other side. "Secrets don't make friends, Yvie."

"It's been quiet since you went away to college." She looks down with a small shrug. "I met Simon when he moved here from London a few months ago and… it's been nice. Having someone around again."

Well, that shut me up.

The last thing I wanted was for Yvie to be lonely… so if Simon made her happy, then I would find it in me to deal. Or at least put aside my jadedness enough to make sure he wasn't a serial killer or something.

Her eyes run over me with an amused look. "You know, every time you come here I'm pretty sure Larry sequesters all of the interns just so that they don't get any crazy ideas about boycotting and going on spirit quests."

"That's what I'm aiming for." I shoot her a bratty look. "It'd be a personal achievement for me. Would probably add it to my résumé and everything."

A smile stretches across her face even as she shakes her head. "I've missed you, kid."

"Likewise." I smile softly.

Yvie leans back in her seat, face falling into a considering look. "So did you find what you were looking for there?"

I dart my eyes away at her question, looking to the wall as shame grips me fiercely. Hating the truths I'm about to have to tell her and how they might change the way she sees me. It's been the worry nagging at the back of my mind since I stepped foot on the plane. That Yvie might feel differently about me when she finds out the truth about my mother. About that night.

But as much as it might terrify me, she deserves to know.

She deserves to know the truth of what happened. And I won't keep that from her the way it was kept from me.

"Yeah," I whisper, face pinching up. "Yeah, I did."

“And?” she prompts, drawing my gaze back to her carefully blank expression.

“And he did it.” I suck in a deep breath and force the rest of the story through my lips before I can chicken out. “But she had an affair and I’m not sure he meant to.”

My aunt’s face goes slack, and she blinks at me slowly. “What do you mean, not sure he meant to?”

“The uh—” I clear my throat, trying to focus on the facts and not the conflict this story is stirring up inside of me on so many different fronts. Blocking out any thought of Coop from my mind momentarily. “The person she was having the affair with was there that night. It’s possible Cane was trying to shoot him or that the gun went off accidentally. I don’t really know. It’s a messed-up clusterfuck and I’m sorry—”

“Ellie,” my aunt cuts off my rant, immediately rising from her seat and walking over to kneel down in front of me. Her face pained and eyes full of concern as she slowly takes my hands in hers, giving them a squeeze. “Ellie.” She sighs my name again and looks down for a second before bringing her eyes back to mine with a small smile. “I’m going to be honest with you. The truth about what happened that night has never mattered to me like it came to matter to you.”

My brows shoot down at her words and she hurries to continue.

“Don’t get me wrong. I loved my brother and even with what you’ve just told me, I still loved your mother too. Nadia was a force of nature. Irresistible. So in a way, it makes sense.” She shrugs, looking to the ceiling.

"But what happened in that room that night was not how I chose to remember them. We never talked about it much and that's on me. I should've… I don't know. Talked about them more. I was just so at a loss about how to handle it all. But still, I should've explained that I let it go a long time ago. I chose to not let the horrible memory of that night hold sway over me because I had the best parts of them still with me." Squeezing my hands, she gives me another smile. "So the only thing I'm concerned with right now is how are you doing?"

I exhale a shaky breath and break her gaze, looking back to the wall as I ask the question my soul needs answered. Even if the prospect of that answer terrified me in equal measure all the same. "Do you think I'm like her?"

The idea had been leaching its poison inside of me for days now.

That I was somehow reliving Nadia's most horrible, selfish, tragic history.

A girl sitting on the beach, caught somewhere in the dusk and using the heavens as her plaything to alter the fates of two men.

"Yes," my aunt answers softly, shocking me into looking back at her. "Yes, Ellie, in a lot of ways, you are. Like I said, Nadia was irresistible. She could walk into a room and change the mood with just one look. She was daring and opinionated and beautiful." Her shoulders drop as if she's carrying the weight of the world on them, her words coming out more gentle when she continues. "But she also rarely cared about anyone else besides herself. At least until you came along."

"But I—"

"No, Ellie." She shakes her head adamantly. "You don't understand. Nadia would know she was upsetting someone by doing something wrong but she just simply didn't *care*. Not unless it directly impacted her in some way. I told Cane—" She cuts herself off, looking down for a moment before meeting my gaze again with a small smile. "You're not like that. You may be impulsive, yes." She laughs quietly. "God knows that after all these years. But if you upset me or the guys… it bothers you to hurt someone you love, Ellie. You feel things in a way Nadia, I don't know, at least never let on that she did. And I think that empathy comes from Cane even if it deserted him at the end. So like I said…" Her hands squeeze mine again. "I got to keep the best parts of both of them."

"Thank you," I choke out the words, wrapping my arms around her suddenly as a deep sense of relief fills me for the first time in days. "Thank you. You have no idea how much I needed to hear that." Even if part of me still doubted her words.

Yvie returns my hug quickly. "Now, are you okay besides that?"

"Yeah," I murmur. At least for the most part. Somewhat. "The thing about it is, finding out that he actually did it wasn't even the shocking part to me. That was always just my reality."

"I know." She nods against my shoulder. "Now when do I get to meet this Dawson boy you brought home?"

"Uh." I laugh. "How about dinner?"

"Dinner sounds perfect." She leans back with a smile. "Mine or Stef's?"

"Stef's," I answer quickly, forcing a smile. "Oh, and by the way, he brought his cousin, so why don't you bring Simon too?"

Stroke of genius right there, El.

The more people to distract her from my convoluted relationships, the better.

Chapter Sixteen

The heavy garment bags weighing down my arm drag along the ground as I push open the front door to Stef's despite my best attempt to keep them aloft. I had killed as much time as possible after leaving Yvie's office, not quite ready after my conversation with her to go back and face the two men at the center of my turmoil. So I had gone to Bergdorf's and picked up my gown for the gala tomorrow night that I had preordered before ever leaving for Landing Point this summer. And then I had figured Coop and Jace definitely hadn't thought to pack suits so I had used that as an excuse to stay longer, sorting through the options with a salesclerk until I had something I thought suited both of them.

After that, I grabbed a smoothie and moseyed on over to the shoe department. Trying on Ferragamos to Venetas and everything in between. But it was as I was staring at the most perfect pair of jeweled Christian Louboutins on my feet that I was left with no more excuses and had to face up to the fact that I was being a coward.

And my bill now reflected that.

Hiding out at Bergdorf's like some kind of girl who couldn't handle her own mess of shit and that just didn't sit right with me.

So I grabbed my purchases and headed out to face the arduous drive back to Stef's through the nightmare that is LA traffic. Giving myself a firm talk all along the way that I would no longer be a cowardly avoider when it came to either one of my relationships or nonrelationships. That I couldn't be, if I ever wanted to figure anything out when it came to both of them. I had to face them and brace my heart for whatever the outcome may be. For whatever pain came from the journey.

But I had *totally* gotten the shoes to soften the blow.

The sound of cheers fills the air as I close the front door and I whip my head around, trying to find the cause of the noise but the living room at the end of the hallway is cut off by a wall. Curious as to what in the hell has transpired in my absence, I take a few steps in that direction before coming to the entrance of the office at the base of the stairs and stopping short. The double doors are open, revealing the generous space inside that's decked out with a giant, ornately carved desk, sitting area around the fireplace, and built-in shelves along the back walls with a collection of trinkets on display.

But it's the sight of shirtless Cooper Monroe in black basketball shorts, staring intently at something on the wall in what we generally consider to be Stef's domain that startles me into popping off. "What are you doing?"

His surprised eyes find mine through the door, face screwing up for a second before he drops his head. "Uh." He flips his phone in his hand before looking back to me. "Talking to Alec." He nods toward the wall. "And then I got distracted."

After a moment's hesitation, I throw the garment bags over my shoulder and step into the room. Walking to stand beside him and seeing what caught his attention.

"Oh."

"Yeah." He lets out a humorless scoff. "It's terrible."

"Yeah," I agree, eyes scanning my least favorite of all Kai's paintings and understanding what he means.

It's not that the painting itself is terrible. It might even be one of Kai's best, which was what he had argued when I demanded he get rid of the thing. It's the depiction of me that's heartbreaking. A huge portrait of my face alone, entirely painted in blues and grays with overly large eyes bleeding tears. The lines of misery etched deep in my face with carving strokes in the paint.

I fucking hate the thing. Wanted to burn it as soon as Kai had dragged it proudly into the living room as if he was looking for accolades on his latest work.

"Kai did it when we got back from Europe," I explain softly. "He uh, he said it's what I looked like when they got to me after you…" I trail off, looking to Coop and finding his eyes already on me. "Although, why the hell he would want to commemorate that is beyond me. I told them to get rid of it before I left so Stef must've hidden it in here."

He nods, voice tight when he speaks. "I see." Clearing his throat, he gives the phone in his hand a shake and arches a brow at me in question. "Alec said to tell Helen hello?"

"Ha." I snort. "You can tell him I said to go fuck himself."

His lips ghost up with quiet laughter. "I'll be sure to do that."

But when his questioning eyes don't leave mine, I sigh, determined to live up to my pep talk in the car about facing things. "That's what he said to me that day in San Jose, when you went to talk to Tiff." A small laugh of irony escapes me. "He called me Helen of Troy and warned me to not mess around with you and leave destruction in my wake." I cock a brow at him. "Little did he know, huh? How right he'd be."

He blinks slowly in surprise before shaking his head. "You're not the one responsible for this destruction, Eleanor."

"Maybe," I give him, looking back to the painting I want nothing more than to rip from the wall. "But I'm still playing the part pretty damn accurately."

A moment passes before he speaks again, voice softly curious. "How are you doing? Really?"

I can feel his eyes on me still and after a second of consideration, I give him the only answer I can despite the ache in my heart making me not want to. "Feeling a little lost honestly." Damn, this being a better person shit was hard.

"Yeah." He sighs, looking back to the painting as I look at him. "Yeah, I get that."

I watch his brow tense as he stares at the painting, expression turning a little lost as the pain starts to pour off him and wind through that space between us to pull at me. Instinct makes me want to ease it in some way, but there's nothing I can do for him here. I can't magically forget everything he put me through and he can't go back in time and change the decisions he made.

We're both just left to muddle through the catastrophe until we figure out what's on the other side now.

I drop my gaze from his face, unable to keep staring at what I see there and my eyes snag on the new thin line of a scar spanning across one of his pecs. "What's that?" He looks at me in question and I nod to the scar, brows dropping down at the uncomfortable tug in my stomach it incites. "The scar."

"Oh." He looks down. "Got it during my failed search for you this past year."

"How?"

"A knife."

I suck in a breath, eyes widening and dropping to it again. "Oh."

"Don't worry." He shrugs, drawing my eyes back to his in time for me to see his lips ghost up. "It was… uh, comical in the end, more than anything else."

I scoff, shaking my head. "Never a simple answer with you."

His eyes lock with mine and I see the thoughts rattling around in their night-forest depths as he gives me a small nod. "I guess not."

"How did you end up with Bainbridge?" I cock my head at him, reluctantly curious. "Jace told me, I guess you know that already, but he told me what happened to you both with the Morrisons. How he ended up in the Navy. So how did you end up with Bainbridge?"

"That answer I can give you." His lips twitch as he dips his head toward my shoulder. "But not until you let me take those bags that you look like you're about to drop."

"You won't find any complaints from me there." I laugh, passing them over and shaking out my arm.

His brows drop down as he holds them up, giving me a clear view of the new, harsher cuts of his body. "What the hell is in these things?"

I watch him throw them over his shoulder and clear my throat, forcing my eyes back to his before he catches me. "Uh, clothes. For me and Jace and you for the gala tomorrow night."

"Right," he mutters. "What's that for again?"

"Stef's nona, she died of heart disease so he's a big sponsor of the LA Heart Ball every year. It's a big event here."

"Gotcha." He nods, finding my eyes again. "So Bainbridge, they actually recruited me out of the Navy. Pulled me in my last year for specialized missions with them and then I kept working for them when I got out."

Well, I guess he did tell a roundabout truth about that. "How did that happen?"

"Jace," he sighs, looking back at the painting as his jaw clenches. "He, uh, did his time in the Navy and got out. Went home to Landing Point. He might've not hated it but in the end it was still a sentence to him. But I… I excelled." Looking back at me for a second, he shrugs. "It was a good fit. I liked the work and even more than that I liked that it got me the hell out of Landing Point and away from everything that came with it. It was the first time in my life that I was able to leave it behind somewhat. I worked a mission with Bainbridge as I was going into my last year and that was that."

"You never missed it at all? Home?"

He looks back down at me, face screwing up as our eyes lock before he admits quietly. "I never had a home, Eleanor. Not really. Not until you."

We stare at each other in the silence that follows, as I remember the home our two broken souls once made. Our eyes leaking out all the unsaid words and hurt into the space between us until the air feels thick with it. So damn heavy I can hardly breathe it in. Am scared to, because in the muck of all those painful feelings is a thread that terrifies me. That I can feel pulling taut between us, softly lighting up that entity of us that had gone dark with life again.

It's that echo of love. Love lost and found in the most painful of ways.

Love that probably should have never been but might possibly still remain.

Trying to work its way up to mend the bridge broken by secrets and betrayals, regardless of the reminders screaming out from my logical brain.

And it makes me want to run far, far away.

I bite down on my lip to fight the urge and see Coop's gaze drop to it, night-forest eyes zeroing in on the act as he sucks in a harsh breath before they flow over my face. Locking with mine again, a shade darker than before.

Another round of cheers sound from outside the office at that moment and I break our gaze, freeing my lip with a slow exhale.

I clear my throat and muster up a smirk, looking back to him. "What the hell are they doing out there anyway?"

Those plush lips tighten for a second before he answers. "*Call of Duty*."

"What?" I cock a brow at him. "Are you not a fan?"

"I am. But Alec called and..." His lips twitch. "They kicked me off because I just kept beating them."

"Shocking," I quip, lips twitching in turn.

"Brat." A low laugh leaves him as he takes a step toward me, forcing me to tilt my head back to keep him in my sight. "You know, I think this is the longest we've gone without fighting since I got back."

"Yeah, well, let's keep that trend up through dinner with Yvie, shall we?"

His eyes narrow on me, face tensing as silence falls between us and I know out of everyone tonight, he's the wildcard. Jace will behave for my sake and because he'll want Yvie to like him. The guys will go along with it, either for my sake or in Mac's case because he thinks it's funny to see me squirm. But Coop, he won't like playing that he's just the random cousin tagalong one bit. It's not in his nature, especially when it comes to me.

"Yvie." I shake my head. "I just don't want to throw this on her tonight." Softening my voice, I give him a rare, pleading look. "Please, Coop. It's important to me."

"Answer one question for me." He moves in closer, our bodies almost touching as his eyes rake my face. "I know that I owe you this. Hell, this is the least that I owe you. But I think we both know that I'm a selfish bastard when it comes to you so answer one question for me and I'll play my part tonight."

I'm silent in response, hardly breathing. Not agreeing to anything until I hear what he wants of me.

He drops his face closer to mine, gaze intense and filled with shadows. "Whose bed did you sleep in last night?"

My lips part in surprise. "You came into my room."

"Whose bed, Princess?"

I narrow my eyes at him, indignant despite the fact that I suspected he might check when no one answered the door. And I don't want to answer him because of it. Every defiant cell in my body is pushing me to toss some bratty remark in his face and leave him wondering. But I need him to play along for this dinner to work, and if I don't give him what he wants… in our current state, he will out me to Yvie.

Push back at me for not giving in to him.

I take a few more angry breaths before finally managing to make myself snap out. "Mac's."

His eyes drill into mine for a moment as if checking the truth of my answer before he nods. "Good."

"Good?" I scoff.

"Yeah, good." He shrugs. "Your golden twin is the least of my concerns, even if he makes me want to deck him occasionally."

"So happy I could make you feel better," I throw back snarkily.

"You should be, because now I'll bite my tongue and play nice. But Eleanor." He smirks. "I'll only be a good boy for so long."

I cross my arms, staring up at him with silent warning and trying not to pay attention to what his words are doing to me somewhere underneath all my indignant anger.

He lifts the hangers he's holding over his shoulder just a bit. "I'll take these up for you. I have to get ready for dinner anyway." Moving to take a step around me, he pauses when his gaze lands on the painting again and I watch his body tense up. "I am sorry, Eleanor." He breathes, looking back at me regretfully. "I hope you know that."

I stare into his eyes and debate whether to give in to the spiteful side of me that wants to get him back just a little before the honesty I see in his gaze eventually pulls at me, winning out. "Yeah," I sigh. "I know."

He waits a beat and for a second I think he's going to say something more but then he just swallows, giving me a single nod before walking from the room. Leaving me staring at the haunting painting of the girl he broke as another round of cheers sounds from the other room and his sorry hangs in the air.

Like I said, such useless fucking words. They didn't change anything. Not really.

Chapter Seventeen

Coop

Present Day

I throw the garment bag on the bed and lie down, mind whirling over my conversation with Eleanor downstairs. Obsessing over her every little word, little move, replaying the whole thing on a loop in my head as I try to figure out what my next move should be. Some part of her still wants me. I can see it, even if she won't acknowledge it yet. And that's okay. She deserves a little time after everything I did. A little time to forgive me.

I can give her that. Have to give her that.

Just for a little bit longer, and then, then I'll push. Because she has to forgive me. There's no other option. There is no me without her, that much became abundantly clear to me over this last year.

Plus, I've always been good at playing her game. Our game.

The ebb and flow of us as natural a language to me as pen on paper. Even from that very first day. So I'll know. I'll know when she's ready to be pushed.

The only thing I have to worry about in the meantime is the demand that pounds through my veins to physically remove Jace's hands from her body every time I see him touch her. I love my cousin, but fuck, my gut twists every time I see them together. The feel of their relationship an easy, foreign thing to me that I'm still trying to wrap my head around. Eleanor has never made things easy for me.

So yeah, I just have to worry about keeping that little urge in check, because I seriously doubt she would appreciate the fallout like I would.

My phone buzzes in my hand and I flip it open, lifting it to see the message.

Alec: I made the call. Will let you know what I hear from my contact about the Morrisons.

My lips twitch at Eleanor's words for him as I type my reply, getting an immense satisfaction she definitely didn't know she was gifting me by passing them along.

Cooper: Good. I told the princess what you said and she told me to tell you to go fuck yourself.

His reply is quick, as if he was waiting to see if I had passed his message along yet.

Alec: CLEARLY, if you're any indication, my little sister doesn't know what's good for her. So I won't let that bother me too much.

I scoff at his response and close the phone, tossing it into the air with a flip before catching it. He might be right about that, but I didn't care.

She was mine regardless, the rest of the world be damned.

Bound

Chapter Eighteen

I push the mess of my black tulle evening gown to the side and slip on the jeweled Christian Louboutins I purchased yesterday. Totally checking out as I complete the task like I have been all day. Yvie knew something was up. I had seen it in the way her eyes had slid curiously between the three of us last night despite everyone's best attempt to play the happy family. She definitely wasn't buying the show but I was pretty sure she hadn't figured out what wasn't adding up yet either.

The only true moment of panic I'd had last night was when I had seen her eyes narrow on the tattoo winding up Coop's arm. The sight of that had me promptly choking on the sip of water I'd been taking at the time and proceeding to spend the next thirty minutes racking my brain, trying to remember if she had ever seen my half of the tattoo before I'd left for Landing Point.

The distraction of Simon would have proved invaluable, to say the least, but unfortunately for me he'd been busy at some work event.

I had turned the problem over in my head over and over today, through breakfast and then the whole process of getting ready.

It was going to hurt her. I knew that and fucking hated it. Hated that my inability to open up was going to make her feel like she was inadequate in some way as a parental figure. The problem though, is I don't know how long we are all going to be stuck here and all three of us fucking suck at faking it. As Yvie's suspicious gaze on me at the end of last night had made clear. And as I stare down at the twinkling jewels on my shoes, I'm once again faced with an unpleasant reality.

I'm going to have to come clean with her about some of it at least. Hopefully, before she figures it out herself.

Fuck, but being an avoider could bite me in the ass sometimes.

And you're just *now figuring that out, El? Seriously?*

Brows dropping in frustration, I stand from the backless settee in my bathroom with a sigh and push down the overflowing tulle of my skirt. Looking in the mirror and seeing how I stand out against the all-white bathroom with striking contrast. I rarely got this dressed up, but there were a few occasions where it was absolutely necessary and when it was… well, I was never one to disappoint.

My hair is pulled back at the base of my neck in a messy updo, braided into a fishtail along the crown of my head, with a few pieces hanging loose here and there. Artful in its effortlessness, that was anything but. The black tulle ball gown is fitted along the bodice and accented with strips of silk that mimic the lines of a corset before falling loose to the floor. The full skirt peppered with hidden jewels and cut higher in the front. Perfect for showing off my new shoes. My makeup is heavier than I typically ever wear, a dark smoky eye paired with a nude lip that's tinged gold. And to top it all off, a gold, luminescent powder is glowing along the lines of my face and body.

The look is ethereal and haunting, just like I had felt when I picked it out at the beginning of this summer. Like the ghost of a once vibrant girl. But it fits now in a different sort of way too, because now I'm the girl being pulled apart in that breaking moment between the night and the day. Living somewhere in the midst of dusk or dawn, which yet, I wasn't quite sure if I was being brutally honest with myself.

I sigh again while stepping forward, grabbing the golden powder the makeup artist had sent home with me and giving one last dusting along my skin. Knowing Stef is probably pacing the foyer downstairs because I'm making everyone run late and his fussy ass can't handle being two minutes behind schedule. But he won't say a word after the limo ride he endured two years ago where I proceeded to tell him, in great detail, what goes into being waxed and done up for events like this after he had voiced a complaint.

He had looked a little green after that description.

I hear the door to my room open right before Mac's voice singsongs. "Oh, Ellie."

My lips twitch and I shout. "Knee to the balls, Macallan!"

"Are you naked?"

"No."

"Thank god." He steps into the open doorway of the bathroom and whistles at the sight of me. "Fucking killer, Els."

"Thanks." I smile, giving him a twirl before coming to a stop and taking in the classic cut of his Armani tux. Similar to the one I had chosen for Jace, except for one tiny detail. "Were you sent to hurry me along?"

"Oh, yeah," he admits. "But don't tell Stef I told you that." Walking toward me, he holds out his arm. "Plus, the strays are circling the bottom of the stairs so I figured you might want an escort to avoid that particular decision."

I raise my hand to heart, batting my lashes up at him dramatically. "Why Macallan Astor, chivalry isn't dead after all."

"Shut up." He rolls his eyes. "Before I leave you here to face them without any backup."

"Okay, okay." I laugh softly, reaching up and winding my arm through his. "And this has nothing to do with wanting to piss your parents off with pictures of us together from tonight?" The Astors were, ahem, not my biggest fans you could say.

That typically happened though when you called someone's dad an evil under lord after one too many mimosas at the family charity event.

"Maybe a bit, Els." He chuckles as we walk from my room. "You know me, gotta stick it to the man where I can."

"Well." I toss him a conspiratorial grin. "You can always count me in for that."

We come to the top of the stairs then and my breath halts for a second as I see what he meant. Both Coop and Jace are waiting at the bottom of the stairs, poses mimicked as they lean up against the wall. Jace leaning casually against it with one shoulder in the dark burgundy and black silk Armani tux I picked for him, hair pulled back and looking like every sinful temptation LA has to offer. Coop stands with his arms crossed, back against the wall and wrapped in the heavier fabric of his black Ralph Lauren tux that I knew his presence could not only handle but accentuate with his dark arrogance.

And both of their eyes are on the top of the stairs, waiting to lock with mine instantly. My gaze darts between them and I breathe out a slow breath as Mac gives my arm a squeeze and I take that first step down the stairs. Stomach flipping and heart pounding as I feel the tension in the air skyrocket, both of their gazes running the length of me as they push away from the wall. Leaving me with the sense of being intimately caressed by their eyes, unwrapped a little bit more with each step that I take. Some sensual essence of me unwinding in answer to the call I not only see but feel there. Until it's as if I'm naked under their gaze by the time I make it to the bottom, utterly exposed and fucking electrified as hell by it. Head dizzy as my pulse races and wondering what the hell that says about me.

If it's wrong to feel so high off the carnal energy, so empowered by the desire offered up in their eyes so blatantly.

Another me would've said no, but that girl never faced the reality of today. Of having the deepest, most secret heart of the night and the blinding power of the sun under her sway. In the palm of her hand to snuff out or save.

The raw need lacing the silent air is so palpable that I have to clench my hands to keep them from shaking, fighting the urge to bite my lip as I meet both of their eyes. Empty of any quips to break the tension and at a total loss as to how to proceed from this point. Completely sucked in by the demand for more I see in both of their gazes.

Thankfully, Mac saves me the trouble of having to speak, breaking the moment as he cracks. "So I thought I'd save you both the trouble of having to find a quarter to flip and call dibs on El. At least until we get in there."

I see Coop's jaw clench, his eyes never leaving mine, the pure awe swirling in their night-forest depths staggering as he gives a single nod, his reluctance clear with the jerky move. Jace, surprisingly, is the one with his brows pulling down at the declaration though, firework eyes flicking between us for a moment as he pulls his bottom lip through his teeth. Making me jealous he can still get away with such a move without ruining any makeup.

I cock my head at him in question, silently asking if he's really that bothered by it and he finally just sighs. "Until we get there."

He gives me a small grin and my lips twitch up as I remember that first bonfire with him on the beach. How he surprised me then with his subtle possession and how he keeps surprising me in so many ways, even today.

"Great," Stef snaps and I turn my head to see both him and Kai by the door. A shit-eating grin splitting Kai's face while Stef looks so on edge that he might break apart at any moment. "Now that's settled, please, *cara*." He opens the door, revealing the limo waiting before bringing his hands together as if he's praying. "I beg of you. Fretta."

A burst of laughter leaves me at his plea to hurry and I let go of Mac's arm to walk to him, reaching up to run the lapel of his gray tux through my fingers. "Stefano." I drag his name out with a teasing look. "Looking very dapper." Turning back to look at the others, the energy of the night starts to hum through my veins, making me want to live a little dangerously. To push out the concerns weighing me down of late and just live for this moment. Plus, it wasn't like obsessing over it all was helping me figure out anything anyway. And when you were lost, you never found your way again by freezing.

That much I knew at least.

So I cock a brow, looking between Jace and Coop, reckless audacity in full force as I tip my chin up with a smirk. "Now who's ready to have some fun?"

Who are you kidding, El? You've always liked to live dangerously. Case in two points right there.

Yeah, I wasn't fooling anyone here.

Chapter Nineteen

There are still spots dancing across my vision from the never-ending flashes of cameras as I sip my second glass of champagne inside the Beverly Hills Hotel. The low lighting of the Crystal Ballroom casting everything in a romantic glow and the steady buzz of conversation in the air is only dulled by the classical orchestra playing onstage. I had lost track of the guys pretty quickly as we made the rounds, catching up with our acquaintances from LA's finest and dropping subtle reminders with the youngest of them that Labyrinth was opening this weekend. Doing my part to ensure its success as I casually introduced Coop and Jace to some of the people I knew and watched the curiosity spark in their gazes. They knew I wasn't one to be seen with any guy at an event outside of *my guys*, much less two.

So I'd happily sipped my champagne without giving any explanation, knowing that the buzz alone would drive them to our club this weekend just to scope out the situation some more.

Predictable, to say the least.

My lips twitch as I eye the two men in question at the bar, getting something stronger than champagne, and damn, but I have to admit it's a little bit understandable too. Hell, even I'm fucking mesmerized staring at the stunning duo. I see Stef walk up to the bar then, joining them just as the music cuts off and a voice calls the room's attention from the stage. Turning to give the voice my attention, I catch sight of Yvie through the crowd and give her a smile as the organizer of tonight's event starts the lengthy spiel of thanking everyone for being here. Saving the silent auction and donations bit for the end I'm sure.

I tip the last of my champagne back, bubbles fizzing in my mouth as a body comes up behind me and causes me to tense for a moment before the faint whiff of sea-spring hits me as his head dips down next to mine.

"You know, I think I might have undershot a bit with that doctor thing."

Holding the glass to my mouth, I laugh softly, turning my head to meet his amused gaze. "Just a bit." I tease.

"Hmm," he drawls, bringing his mouth to my ear. "What about a model? Think that would do?"

I pause for a beat, letting my eyes flow over his face before purposefully cringing. "Not sure they'd take you."

"Oh, Delacroix." He laughs lightly. "It's a good thing that I have other attributes then."

"And those would be?"

"Follow me and find out."

I pull back to look at him, wondering if he's just joking, but the serious look on his face along with the temptation filling his firework eyes clues me into the fact that while he's definitely up to no good, he's also one-hundred-percent serious.

"Come play with me, Ellie," he whispers, the blatant intimacy of his tone making my lips part. "Promise it'll be worth your while."

The obvious invitation has desire pooling low in me, but I can't help pushing just a little more. Testing him in some way after everything we've been through recently. "You sure your promises are good, Dawson?"

He lifts a hand, pushing a few strands of hair away from my neck before bringing his eyes back to mine. "Like I said, follow me and see."

I'm silent in response but he must see the answer I already know in my gaze because that brilliant smile flashes across his face as he winds a few fingers through the hand hanging by my side and tugs gently. Dipping my head, I try to hide the smile wanting to break free on my face from the excitement pumping through my veins and follow behind him as he smoothly navigates between the bodies of the crowd. Quietly leading us out of the ballroom without drawing too much attention our way.

By the time we make it to the hallway, my heart is just about to pound out of my chest and I can't help but ask when he swings a right down a hallway. "And where exactly are we headed?"

He looks back over his shoulder at me with a grin and winks. "Shock and awe, remember, Blondie?"

"Hmm," I drawl, not having to wait but three more steps before he comes to a stop and my brows shoot up at our destination. "The women's bathroom?"

"Have you seen the bathrooms here?" He pushes open the door just a hair and peeks in before opening it to reveal the empty space within. The rust-colored marble covering everything from the faucet space to a lower area with cream cushioned chairs and mirrors where women can reapply makeup. Hell, there's even a sitting area with a couple of couches so you don't have to stand while waiting. "They deserve some shock and awe credit all on their own." Tugging on my hand, he gently pushes me in ahead of him before bringing both his hands to my hips and dipping his mouth to my ear. "But I thought we might shock these walls a little and give them some secrets to awe over, yeah?"

And I know right then that I'm his, at least for these next moments, without any reservation. My ridiculously blinding, charming sun that lights up all the places in me that remained barren and cold for far too long.

He grips my hips tightly, walking us forward slowly and whispering huskily. "Do you have any idea how fucking stunning you look tonight?" Turning me toward the couches, he lets go of one of my hips and slowly trails his fingers up over the silk covering my skin. "Fuck if it wasn't for—" He cuts himself off and sucks in a breath. "Let's just say we barely made it out of the house."

I feel his lips press softly to the skin right below my ear and my breath catches, head dropping to grant him better access as goose bumps erupt.

"And I know I should be the better guy here, give you space to figure it out. Work your shit out with him."

We make it to one of the couches then and he turns me around, bringing us face to face and letting me see all the conflict playing out across his. The crinkle of pain at the corner of his eyes paired with the stark need lighting up their depths.

He reaches up, bringing his thumb to rest against my bottom lip and pulling down gently. “But I can’t.” My stomach flips at his words, breath starting up at a rapid pace as the need in my own body answers his. “Because everything in me is screaming that you’re mine.” Moving closer, he wraps an arm around my waist and pulls me against him. Leaving absolutely no space between our bodies. “That you’ve always been mine, just like I’ve always been yours.” He dips his head, bringing his lips a breath away from mine. “That you were my Ellie long before you were ever his anything.” My heart cracks open in my chest at his words and a beat passes where we simply breathe each other in before he drops a hand, tugging on a loose strand of my hair. “How’s that for shock and awe, huh, Delacroix?”

My answer is simple. I press my lips to his.

His response is quick, pulling me in impossibly closer and dropping his hand to grip my hip. Teasing my mouth open immediately and swirling his tongue against mine. I drop my empty champagne glass to the ground without a care. Hearing the glass clatter against the marble as my chest heaves and I reach up to wrap my arms around his neck, immediately tangling my hands in his hair. Needing more of him with every breath. A closeness that’s definitely not appropriate in our current setting but sure as fuck is happening anyway.

He turns us without breaking our kiss, sitting down on the couch and taking me with him as he does. I drop a hand from his hair to pull up the front of my gown, settling myself over him and immediately gasping into our kiss at the feel of how hard he is against my pussy. And he follows my gasp, deepening our kiss and lifting his hips to grind against me. Grabbing his shoulder, I roll my hips down onto his cock and dig my nails into the fine fabric of his suit to convey the urgency of how badly I need him inside of me.

And the little shit has the nerve to laugh lightly into our kiss.

I pull back and narrow my eyes at him, gulping down a breath to speak. "Dawson, I swear to god if you—"

"You'll what, Ellie?" He reaches under my dress in the next breath, quickly nudging my underwear to the side and plunging two fingers inside of me. "Ride my cock like the world is ending?" The playfulness in his voice is full force as he pumps his fingers, causing me to throw my head back with a cry. "That's kind of the point." I feel his lips run along the edge of my dress, trailing the swell of my breast and causing my pussy to clench around his fingers. "Just had to make sure you were ready."

He slides his other hand under my dress then, reaching for the top of my underwear and starting to pull them down my hips. I look back to him and see the way his gaze is lowered, face uncharacteristically intense as he helps rid me of them. The act a little awkward considering our position but that doesn't seem to matter to him. His eyes are all blinding need and wonder as he looks at the most intimate part of me and reaches down to unzip his pants. Quickly pulling his shirt up and pushing down his boxers to free that incredible pierced cock as my eyes lock onto how it's wet at the tip for me already. My own need reflected in physical form right back at me.

He pushes my dress up even more, gripping my hips tightly as I raise myself up in the next breath and reach down to grab his cock. Putting him right at my entrance and feeling that tease of metal as he raises his eyes to meet mine and I start to slowly lower myself down onto him. Our eyes locked as I slowly take him inside of my body while my breath hitches and pussy spasms. His cock twitches inside of me when I finally seat myself completely and I feel that piercing brush up against the deepest part of me.

"And here I thought you were the one supposed to be earning forgiveness?" I toss out, unable to help the tease with words that are more gasped than spoken.

"Don't let our position fool you, Blondie." His dimples flash with a wicked grin and he sits up, grabbing my calves. "Now wrap those pretty fuck-me heels around me and let me apologize properly."

I do as he asks and lift up slightly, feeling him move inside of me as I tangle my legs around him. Locking them behind his back as he reaches to grab my hips again, immediately jackhammering up into me and causing a cry to escape my lips. I reach up, tangling my fingers in his hair just as he does it again and I grind myself down onto him. Trying to take him impossibly deeper as my pussy tightens around him and he drops his head back against the couch with a groan. I rise up and nearly lift off him before rolling my hips back down as his fingers clench on my hips. Pulling on his head to get him to cooperate, I bring my lips down against his and kiss him with a fierceness he quickly answers.

And this time when we move, it's together.

Completely in sync as we both feed our need for each other. Parting and meeting with each breath as if maybe, we can outrace the euphoric feeling barreling down on us and somehow manage to live in it forever. It's frenzied, desperate in a way Jace and I have rarely been. As if we both know this moment is a stolen thing. A retreat into each other's bodies from the uncertainty that is our lives right now. A mending memory to hold on to among all the hurt-laced days of late. A coupling of light, desire and a need for the kind of reassurance you can only get from the most intimate form of meeting another's soul.

I know we're both close. Can feel it in the way his body is tensing up under mine and the way my skin feels too tight, as if every nerve in my body is exposed to his touch. In the way my pussy is starting to clamp down on him tighter with every stroke of his cock inside of me, each thrust making that piercing drag over just the right spot and hit deep with the most dizzying kind of pleasure.

And right before we reach that peak, he pulls back. "I love you, Eleanor Delacroix." His fucking soul in his eyes for me to claim. "Promise."

It's a melodic kind of swear, almost a song, and it makes me come apart immediately. Curling my body into his as I cry out and lock up, body unbearably tight before coming apart with the rarest kind of rapture. Every part of me totally pulled under the wave, catching that blissful high that comes from reaching such a desperate kind of peak. The orgasm as intense and frenzied as the climb had been, as if each of those exposed nerves fell apart only to be remade with pleasure that left me gasping for breath against his neck.

I feel him follow me then, a deep groan leaving his lips as his cock jerks inside of me, filling me up with his heat. And I manage to turn my head, lifting my lips to his ear as my legs tremble softly around him. “I love you too, Dawson.”

Because I can’t not give him the words. Can’t deny him the necessity some part of me knows he needs after everything he became to me. Incapable of not soaking up a bit of his brilliant light during my stolen moment in the sun with him.

Chapter Twenty

I flush the toilet after cleaning up from Jace's and my little bathroom tryst, trying to ignore the fact that he's out there guarding the door as I go about my business.

"You about finished, Delacroix?"

My lips twitch as I open the stall door. "That would be an affirmative, Dawson." I walk over to wash my hands at the sink, eyeing the couch we, ahem, borrowed as I do. "Just one little problem."

"What's that?"

"I don't know where my underwear went."

"Oh, you mean these underwear?"

I turn my head and see him dangling the delicate scrap of black silk in the air with one finger, a wicked grin stretched across his face where he leans against the door.

"Yes, asshole." I laugh, drying my hands and tossing the paper towels in the trash before crossing my arms. "Those underwear."

"Hmm," he drawls. "I could be persuaded to give them back." Taking a step away from the door, he holds them out to me. "For a price."

I narrow my eyes at him playfully. "Which is?"

Jace opens his mouth to respond right as the door opens behind him and my heart stops in my chest. Not beating for the span of a few seconds at the sight of Coop in the doorway before starting back up at a frantic rhythm. Each pulse as we lock eyes sounding in my ears with a deafening cadence.

He doesn't even look at Jace, doesn't move an inch as we stare at one another.

And I know, he knows. Knows what just happened here without being told. Can probably see it all over me. In the mess of my hair and the flush of my cheeks.

Jace turns his head slowly, hand dropping to his side as if he too knows who will be waiting for him and I see Coop's nostrils flare. Night-forest eyes still on mine as his jaw clenches and his brows drop harshly. A dark kind of pain I've never seen spiraling out from the depths of his gaze.

"Get the fuck out, Jace," he orders harshly.

Jace pauses at the order and a hostile tension fills the air instantly. "I think that's up to Ellie."

Coop snaps his gaze to Jace, letting me know that things are about to get really ugly in here unless I intervene.

"It's okay, Jace," I interrupt, giving him a small smile when he flicks his eyes to me. "Coop would never hurt me." I sigh, looking back to see Coop's eyes back on me again. Right where I need them to be at this moment. "I know that."

Coop's shoulders drop the barest inch even as he narrows his eyes on me. As if he's trying to figure out what game I'm playing here.

Uh, trying to keep you both in one piece, dummy.

Jace waits a beat before giving me a single nod and walking to the door, stopping as he comes to stand before his cousin. Coop breaks my gaze to look at him, eyes narrowing as he stares at him for a second before taking a step back to let him pass. But dammit all to hell, Jace seems to choose that particular moment to remember he's holding my panties and looks down, stilling for a second before flicking his eyes to me in question.

Coop scoffs viciously at Jace's hesitation, unable to see what he's holding at the angle they're standing and misinterpreting what the holdup is.

"Never forget, Jace." He takes a small step toward Jace. "She was mine first. And I've kept her safe in ways you can't even comprehend."

Jace turns his head to Coop, lifting his brows at the challenge. "Debatable," he muses, dipping his head side to side with a thoughtful expression. "But even if that were the case," he answers Coop's step with one of his own and I take a step toward both of them, heart racing at the impending explosion I can feel barreling down. "I love you like a brother, Coop. You know that. But you had your chance and you fucked it up." A sigh leaves him. "And as much as I know that must fucking hurt, and as grateful as I am to you for leaving her to save me. It is what it is." Jace fingers my panties at his side and I see Coop's gaze drop to them, his body going that scary kind of still. "So while she might've been yours once, just now." He laughs softly, the taunt in it clear. "Well, just now, she was most definitely mine." Turning his head, he flashes those fucking dimples at me as I stare at him with wide eyes. Equal parts awed and terrified by his audacity. "Don't worry, Ellie. I'll hold on to these and give them back to you later."

Coop's body moves faster than my brain can process and he pins Jace against the wall in the blink of an eye. His forearm slams down against Jace's chest while his other hand grabs the one holding my panties, ripping them from his grasp as the open door swings shut beside them.

"Cooper!" I shout, scrambling forward.

"And let *me* be very clear about something, little cousin." Coop laughs darkly, not giving an inch as I make it to them and grab for his arm. "The only reason you're still in one piece right now is because I love you like a brother too." He leans in, bringing his face an inch away from Jace's and my eyes dart between them. Seeing the way both their eyes are narrowed, chests heaving, edging that line of true violence as Coop continues on a deathly whisper, "And the only reason you're about to walk out of this room breathing is because of the love she has in her heart for you." Brows dropping at his own words, he shoves Jace against the wall before stepping back and shoving my panties in his pocket. "So I'll be holding on to these, because she most definitely is still fucking mine." His chest heaves with a few deep breaths before he jerks his head to the door. "Now get the fuck out of here before I forget all that you did for her when I couldn't."

Jace stands from the wall, fists clenching at his sides and I can see the anger in his eyes. The desire there to fight back against Coop's words. To challenge his claim.

"Jace," I snap, the adrenaline pumping through my veins making me unbearably edgy. His eyes flick to mine and I try to soften my voice. "Please." I cringe, knowing how hard my next word is going to hit him. Almost as bad as the sight of me was to Coop when he walked through that door. "Go."

His eyes crinkle up at the corners, flicking between me and Coop rapidly for a moment before coming back to rest on me with a frustrated look. He gives me a single nod before turning and ripping the door open, walking quickly from the room and taking half my heart with him. Leaving a guilt in its place that I hate.

But I also know I did the best thing for everyone here.

Nothing was about to come of that besides violence and Coop, well, he needed me more right this moment. Satan or not. The pain I'd seen in his eyes was real, deserved to be acknowledged and not just shoved to the side out of spite.

Dropping my hands from his arm with a sigh of my own, I look up and see how his body is still locked up. Brows dropped, forehead tensed, jaw clenched, and eyes on the spot Jace just vacated as if still fighting the urge to go after him. An expression of true pain if ever there was one. And it tugs hard on the half of my heart still left in my chest.

"Coop—" I start softly.

"Don't," he interrupts roughly, darting his eyes to mine. "If you're about to tell me to let it go right now, Eleanor. I can't hand—"

"I wasn't going to—"

The door to the bathroom opens again and a high society matron walks in, eyes just about bugging out of her head at the sight of us.

I scramble internally for a beat before forcing an awkward laugh. “You’re absolutely right, honey.” Grabbing Coop’s hand, I give it a hard tug toward the door while watching her mouth pop open. “This is definitely not our room.”

Dragging Coop from the room, I give her a wide smile as we pass by and try my damndest to look clueless before exhaling in relief as the door shuts behind us. I walk the length of the hallway before realizing I’m still holding on to his hand and quickly let go now that he seems to have been shocked back into motion. The surprise twinge of loss I get from doing so causing my brows to drop just a bit as we turn the corner and walk to the entrance of the ballroom silently, not speaking a word. The energy between us taut, pressing against me with tones of his natural demand.

I stop suddenly as we come to the door and turn to look at him, mouth opening with an attempt to speak but what words I’m not quite sure. His eyes are narrowed on me, hands shoved into the pockets of his pants and staring into his eyes, I know it’s not about want. It’s a *need.* A need to give him a truth to ease the pain I know he’s in. And I can feel those almost words sitting on my tongue as I choose to swallow them back down.

Because while I do care for him still. I’m not sorry for what I did either. And while I may not be able to tell him the first, I won’t lie to him about the latter.

So instead I give him a helpless shrug, latching on to the first thing that pops into my mind. "What did you mean?"

"What?"

"When you said you've kept me safe in ways he can't comprehend?"

His expression shutters and he gives me an echo of my shrug in return.

I can't help but cock my head at him, taking a deep breath before wondering out loud. "Do you think we'll always be like this? Half-truths and withheld words?"

His lips tighten for a beat before he sighs. "I don't know, Eleanor." He takes a slow step toward me. "I hope not." Dropping his head, he looks down to my side and winds his fingers through mine. "But I do know something."

"What?" I whisper, heart starting up at a rapid pace in my chest again.

Fuck, I was going to have a heart attack by the end of the night between the two of them.

I thought you wanted some fun, El? Bite off a bit too much to chew?

I'm about to chew you.

His eyes come back to mine. "Dance with me."

"Huh?"

That savage smirk flashes across his face as he turns and opens the door, not waiting for my answer before tugging me behind him as the sound of a contemporary pop rendition played in classical strings fills the air. Coop walks through the crowd and it parts for him automatically, as if people can feel the authority of his presence and respond to it instinctually. He quickly makes it to the center of the room where the ballroom is and my brain finally catches up to what's about to happen.

I plant my feet, bringing us both to a halt and whispering in alarm. "What are you doing?"

He turns back to me, stepping right up into my space and dropping his head down closer to mine. "Come on, Princess." His lips twitch up. "I know they had to teach you how to waltz at that ritzy private school you went to."

"That's-that's not the point," I stutter.

He reaches up with his free hand, bringing it to my waist and dropping his voice low. "And the only way I'm going to keep my hands off my cousin right now is by keeping them on you." He arches a brow at me. "Or would you like for Satan to make a scene?"

I suck in a breath and stare up at him, scared and excited by the prospect all at the same time. The truth is I fucking loved to dance. It's one of the few things that keeps me coming to these events, but usually, I have to force one of the guys out onto the floor with me much to their displeasure. Typically Stef because he always indulged me more than the others.

I see the dark flecks in his night-forest eyes spark with pleasure. "I'll take that as a yes."

Using his hold on me, he guides us those last few steps onto the dance floor and slides us in among the other dancers. Quickly picking up the steps of the waltz, timing them perfectly to the song and reminding me of just how gracefully that body can move regardless of its size. And shocking the hell out of me as he begins to expertly spin us around.

I look up and narrow my eyes at him suspiciously. "You can dance."

His lips twitch. "Most can."

"No." I roll my eyes. "You can *really* dance."

He looks down and stares at me, pausing for a beat before giving me a small nod. "It was necessary for my job occasionally."

"Hmm," I answer noncommittally, darting my eyes away.

Trying my damndest not to get too swept up by him in this moment and failing miserably.

"I think," he starts after a few more steps. "This might technically be our first dance."

I look back to him, shaking my head at his very incorrect words. "No, it's not."

A low laugh leaves him. "I'm not sure if barely having room to sway in a bar in San Jose counts as a proper first dance." His eyes drift to something over my shoulder. "What was that song again?"

"You know the song," I argue softly. "And it counts."

"Fine. It counts." His eyes come back to lock with mine as those ridiculously full lips twitch again. "No need to get worked up over it."

I roll my eyes again, fighting the answering twitch my lips are wanting to give.

Pulling me in just a bit tighter, his head drops down next to mine. "And of course I remember the song." My breath catches as his thumb lightly caresses my waist, trapping a little bit of his sandalwood scent in my lungs.

“I hear it in my sleep and replay that day in my mind every spare moment I can.”

He spins me suddenly then and I falter just the barest bit in a very uncharacteristic fashion before catching up. And as he brings me back into his embrace, closer than before, I can feel their eyes burning into me. All the boys in my life scattered throughout the room. Every person in my world has their curious gaze roving over us, watching our touches that are probably filled with intimate familiarity. I can sense with every step that we’re being dissected, but as I look up into Coop’s eyes, heart swelling and tightening all at once… I’m not sure I care.

I tighten my grip on his hand, swallowing hard against the tightness working its way up my throat. Floundering as my brain and my heart war over everything staring into his eyes is unearthing inside of me. One reminding me excruciatingly of what came with giving in to him before and the other wanting nothing more than to sink into the dream that being here with him is.

But fuck, either way, I can’t make myself look away. Am utterly unable to force myself to break the spell. Locked in this moment with him that’s nothing more than music and magic and breaths stuttering out in an echoing answer. Each of our steps perfectly in tune, the ghosts of us reminding me painfully of how perfectly we once fit.

His brow tightens, eyes filling with that lost reverence I’d forgotten what it was like to possess as he breathes. “Princess.”

I cock a brow and shoot back. "Coop?" Trying to keep it light despite the levity I know we both feel.

That rare, breathtaking smile flashes across his face. "There she is." He laughs, the sound low as he runs his thumb along the back of my hand. "You know, I realized something tonight when you were standing at the top of those stairs stealing the damn air from my lungs."

I duck my head in defense. "What's that?"

"I've been thoughtless."

"You don't say?" I scoff softly, looking back to him in time to see his eyes narrow just a bit.

"Brat." He flicks his fingers against my side in reprimand. "I meant all we've talked about for the most part is me, or them, but not about you like we should have been."

I give him a careless shrug and look away, in no hurry to go down that particular road.

"Forgive me for that. It was an unacceptable oversight on my part." He pulls me in dangerously close, until there's barely room for us to continue the complex steps of the dance. "And one I intend to rectify immediately." His words have nerves shooting straight to my shoulders, tensing me up because I know that he's about to push me just a bit. Know it with the same surety I have that the stars twinkle at night.

"So tell me something, Eleanor." His voice drops with intimate demand. "What do you miss?"

"Miss?" I question, brows dropping in confusion as I look at him.

"What do you miss?" he repeats, slowly trailing his hand over my waist to rest at the small of my back. "Does your skin miss my words?" One lone finger draws a very distinct *C* over the silk of my dress. "That cheekbone my caress?" He raises our intertwined hands to my face and runs his thumb over the curve with a featherlight touch making my breath still. I see the pained need in his eyes as he lingers there for a moment before letting our hands drift down to his favorite place on my neck. "Does that exquisite curve of your neck miss my mark?" Running his thumb slowly back and forth over the spot, he drops his lips a breath away from mine. "Do these lips miss mine?" he whispers roughly, eyes locked with mine with unwavering intensity. And as my lips part against my will, I have to admit to myself that in this moment, I'm completely enchanted by him. "Or the ones under your dress?"

I suck in a breath at the blatant innuendo, filling my lungs with air again as need shoots through me with a shocking intensity.

He breaks our gaze, dropping his lips to rest just over my ear. "Are you quivering inside like your hand is in mine right now?" I clench his hand at his words to stop the shaking I hadn't even noticed, skin tingling where his breath is fanning over it. "Are you dripping onto this ballroom floor for my cock?" He trails his fingers lower on my back, dangerously close to territory that would be considered blatantly inappropriate, before pausing to run them back and forth. "So tell me, Eleanor, what do you miss?" He turns his head the barest hint, pressing his lips to my skin as he speaks and causing my heart to falter in my chest. "Do you miss me? Us?"

I bite down on my lip hard to keep the words from breaking free, because I do. In this moment I fucking ache for him, want nothing more than to reclaim the magnificent entity of us that's lighting up in a way it hasn't in a year with the steps of a simple dance. An entity threatened by shadows with a love that made it shine all the more vividly to spite the darkness. I can feel it between us to a painful degree, trying desperately to find some purchase to bind us together again. And it makes every part of me want to give in. To let the ghost of us come back to life again.

But I just can't. I can't give him the words.

The harsh reality of me on a book-strewn floor won't allow me to become lost in the dream again.

And as I let go of my lip, breathing out with slow purpose, I realize that deep down… I kind of hate both of us for it. Him for tempting me to take a bite of the forbidden fruit that only brought destruction before and me for not being brave enough to take it. To trust again. For not being brave enough to step out of Eden and see if the knowledge of the shadows live up to what my memory tells me it does.

"It's okay," he breathes against my skin. "I'm in no rush." His fingers swirl at the edge of impropriety again before he curls his arm around me and trails them up to my ribs, slowing down our dance. "Eternity, remember?" I feel his thumb run back and forth along the edge of our tattoo there. "But Eleanor." His voice drops to a dark note threaded with warning. "Next time he touches you, puts his hands on you, his cock inside of you, make sure you remember how this feels too." He brings us to a halt, untwining our hands and I'm left standing in shock at his words as he trails his fingers up my arm. "How every part of you answers to me, wants me, needs me. Just as much as I need you." I feel his arms come around me as he dips me without warning and brings his face to rest right above mine, looking down at me with night-forest eyes blazing an inferno of feeling. "Be sure to think of me."

A small gasp escapes my lips and I reach up to grab his shoulders out of instinct, watching as his gaze rakes my face. Feeling what he wants through that damn pull between us that's fighting for life with every breath. And when he drops his lips closer to mine… I do nothing.

Nothing to stop it.

Nothing but selfishly want it in the most secret part of my heart I'll fight like hell against admitting to. At least to him.

So I do nothing.

Not moving, barely breathing as he lowers his lips to mine with the softest, barely there brush of skin. I do nothing but close my eyes and clench the fabric of his suit in my hands, heart about to pound right out of my fucking chest as I'm drenched in him. Wrapped in the heat of his body and filled with the spark between us that always drove us both mad.

A long moment passes before he lifts the barest hint, leaving hardly enough room to breathe between us as our eyes lock. Entrapping us in a universe of all the things we won't speak.

"What did you do?" I whisper, desperately trying to throw what just happened back on him. To ease the immense guilt I know I'm going to feel when I find my way back from this moment with him.

His lips ghost up at my attempt. "Nothing some part of you didn't want me to."

My brows drop at his words. "I have to go." To get some space from all of this before I do something even more monumentally reckless tonight and create an even bigger mess. I never knew such recklessness could be found in doing nothing before.

He stands us back up, quickly dropping his lips to my ear. "Let me know when you want those panties back, Princess."

I take a deep breath, stepping back as he arches a brow in question, checking on me and challenging me all at once before I flee. Because he knows me, knows that when that particular urge strikes, it's because what I'm feeling is enough to scare me.

So just to prove him wrong, I cock my own in turn, keeping my movements slow and steady as I turn and most definitely fucking flee. Just a bit more gracefully than usual. Making sure I'm past a few dancing couples and obscured from his line of sight before letting myself crumble a bit. Chest heaving a little more with each step I take and hands clenching by my sides at the reality of what just happened now that the spell is broken. Thighs a little wet and pussy throbbing with fresh need that twists me up just as much as it makes me want him. Head spinning like I'm still in his arms circling the ballroom, unable to stop and see straight.

I've barely made it to the edge of the ballroom floor when a hand darts out and I startle in surprise, eyes going a little crazy before landing on the owner of the gentle grip stopping me.

Stef's near-black eyes look down on me with concern. "That looked…" His face twists up in what I'm guessing is an attempt to say it delicately. "Intense." He holds up a full glass of champagne to me. "Figured you probably need this."

"Ha," I scoff, riding that edge. "Yeah, intense is one way of putting it." I grab the champagne from him with a shaky hand and throw it back, draining the glass in one go. "Thank you." A sigh leaves my lips as I look back to him and find he's already holding out his own glass to me.

His eyes dart to the dance floor as I take the glass and they narrow for a moment before coming back to rest on me. "What can I do, *cara*? I want to fix this for you."

"You can't," I answer dejectedly, feeling Coop's gaze on my back still. "I'm not sure anyone can."

"I could have them both killed." He gives me that small smile. "Problem solved."

A small laugh escapes me before my brows drop at the reality my brain is just now beginning to grasp.

He gives me a questioning look. "What is it?"

"I think…" I clear my throat, face screwing up at the sense of my heart being too full. As if it's one pump away from bursting in my chest. "I think the problem is…" I shake my head, unable to find the right words to explain.

All of it still too fresh and raw, an unprocessed but instinctual kind of knowing.

I heave a breath, taking a sip of my champagne and darting my eyes away, trying to sort through it all. But when my gaze catches Yvie's through the crowd, I immediately know I'm in deep shit by the knowing look in her eyes. She dips her head toward the dance floor with a care-to-explain look, lifting her brows at me.

Whoops.

Having fun yet, El?

I cringe, using Coop's lame explanation, "It's complicated," I say, exaggeratedly mouthing the words to her before mumbling under my breath to Steff, "Think you can manage to snag me a bottle?"

Chapter Twenty-One

Mac

One Year Ago

I can't take my eyes off her.

So fucking scared that the moment I do, she's going to disappear completely into this agony I can see swallowing her up. We had all been edgy waiting for her in Berlin, already situated in our hotel room and pacing the floors. Going crazy imagining what had happened to her in Costa Rica.

And when she had finally gotten here… fuck, I had never seen Els that way.

My twin that usually blazed so rebelliously, was empty, a shell of a person compared to the one I had grown up with. It had caused me rage so intense it felt like I had fucking snakes slithering through my veins, pumping me full of venom. Rage that I had only ever felt toward my father now directed at this fucker she had met over the summer. This guy that had tossed her aside as if she wasn't as fucking miraculous as me.

We were fucking thoroughbreds, Els and me. The cream of the crop. Anyone we picked should feel nothing but eternally thankful to catch our gaze. Even more so because we so rarely picked anyone at all. Our damage too deep for most of the world to see.

But worst of all, it put me right back in that scary pit of a place where I felt helpless. Unable to do anything to save the person I loved from the pain they were experiencing, just like I had my whole life. First, at five, when I realized why my mother always had bruises underneath her perfectly ironed cardigan. Then at eight, when those bruises started to appear on me. And finally, at seventeen, when I had put a gun to my father's head and told him I'd never set foot in his house again.

His only stipulation had been that I maintain public appearances with the family, as long as I did that, he'd allow me to keep my trust fund. So I'd countered by bringing Els to every damn one, upholding my end and flipping him the finger all at the same time. It wasn't that she didn't fit in, she did, it was the fact he knew she'd never be someone he could push around that grated at the senator so beautifully.

And now, to see her like this, my twin that had iced my bruises and covered for me more times than I could count…

I can barely stop myself from going and turning this earth over to track the piece of shit down. To let loose on him even a fraction of the rage pumping through my veins. The only thing keeping me in place is her, watching the steady rise and fall of her chest in her sleep. I had finally gotten her to stop crying an hour ago, tucking her into the bed in one of the hotel rooms and sitting my ass in the chair next to it to start my silent watch.

I could hear Stef and Kai in the other room, quietly arguing over what was best to do with her. We were out of our depth here. None of us had ever had our heart broken besides Kai, not that any of us had known what to make of that particular situation. And Kai had locked himself in his studio for almost a month after it all went down but refused to talk about it, so who the fuck knew really. But the fact that Els had been the first to really be broken like this… to say we weren't taking it well was putting it lightly.

Her phone starts to buzz on the nightstand and I immediately pick it up, not wanting it to wake her. When I see an unknown number lighting up the screen though, my heart picks up at a thundering pace. I squeeze the phone in my hand and stand, quickly making my way out of the room before closing the door behind me softly. Turning away from the door, I snap my fingers to get Stef and Kai's attention before pointing at the screen. Kai's eyes fill with worry immediately but Stef's just narrow at the phone for a second before he gives me a single nod. Probably in the same mind as me of wanting to dish out some pain.

I slide my finger across the phone to answer before biting out. "Who the fuck is this?"

A condescending laugh comes through the phone before a slightly accented male voice speaks. "Someone with a mutual interest in that girl you've been watching sleep."

My blood turns cold and I see Stef's eyes flare with shock before he spins around, going straight to the hotel window that faces the street and peeking out as if he'll be able to see whoever the fuck is on the phone.

"Now that's out of the way," the voice continues. "We need to have a little chat."

"Not until I know who the fuck I'm speaking to."

"That's been asked and answered."

I grit my teeth and look to Stef, trying to figure out what the fuck to do here. He gives me another silent nod and that coldly amused voice sounds through the phone again. "Great. The team's all on the same page."

Fucker was watching us still.

"Do you love her? Eleanor?" The question is quiet, his voice a hint softer than before.

"Of course." My face tightens up at the absurdity of what he's asking. "She's one of the few people that matter to me."

"Good." A deep breath comes through the phone. "And what would you do to keep her safe?"

"Anything." Is the instant response from my lips even as Stef slashes his hand through the air as if to stop me. It didn't matter though, if this guy had been and was still watching us, he already knew what my answer would be.

"Even better." He chuckles quietly. "Truth be told, I've had a hell of a couple weeks. Scrambling, running around, trying to negate people's mind-boggling decisions and cover their tracks. It's been exhausting, honestly." Another sigh comes through the phone. "So I figured it was time for someone else to pull some weight."

I pause for a beat, gut churning, before I ask. "What do you mean?"

"I'm going to text a link to her phone here in a minute. I'm assuming you know her passcode?"

"Yes, but—"

"You're going to click the link, it will start a download on her phone and that's all that's required of you." He pauses. "Nothing too difficult."

I laugh. I can't help it. "Dude. I don't know who you are but I'm not clicking any link—"

"Do you want her to die?"

My heart stops, completely halts in my chest before starting up again. Raging in my chest at the idea of a world without her.

"What the fuck are you talking about?" I growl, pulling the phone closer to my mouth.

"I'm telling you that in a couple days, Cooper is going to realize she's not still at his house in Costa Rica. And to be perfectly honest, I don't know what kind of fucked-up game he was playing." He snorts. "That's really the least of my concerns right now though. But when he realizes she's gone, I'm guessing he will come looking for her. He will call her and if that happens, if the wrong people find out about her… *she will die.*"

My eyes find Stef's and I can see the gut-wrenching terror there that has me in a choke hold too.

The phone buzzes in my hand and I look down, seeing a new message pop up on the screen from that same unknown number.

"Don't do it," Kai mutters, eyes squinted at the phone. "We don't know what the fuck that is, Mac."

"Don't worry," the cold voice muses. "It's nothing more than something to block all calls from unknown numbers. She won't even know it's there and you can take solace in the fact I won't even be able to call her either. You'll have to distract her, keep her moving, but as long as she doesn't pay too much attention to it… she'll never suspect something is wrong."

"Don't do it," Kai argues, stepping closer to me as I type in the passcode and open up her messages. "This is Els's *life*, Mac. She should be the one to make the choice."

"Yeah, well," I scoff. "If this call is anything to go by then maybe her life needs a little redirection so that she still has one."

"Exactly." The voice on the phone encourages. "It'll be our little secret."

I won't let her be like my mother. I won't stand by uselessly this time while some guy breaks her over and over again. And I sure as fuck am not going to let my twin die.

"Do it," Stef says softly.

I look up, meeting his resigned eyes for a second before turning my gaze to Kai.

"Two against one, man."

I look back down at the phone, bringing my finger down on the link without any hesitation or remorse.

The line goes dead instantly.

Bound

Chapter Twenty-Two

Somebody's watching me.

I know it with the first stirrings of consciousness. A deep kind of instinct born from the days when we lived in caves, constantly on alert to avoid becoming the prey instead of the hunter. I keep my eyes closed, trying to fight against the way my body is trying to tense.

Breathe in, breathe out. Slow and steady, El. What do you sense?

Jace or Coop?

But when faint tendrils of turpentine wind their way up through my nose, I know it's neither of the boys I spent the night tossing and turning over. As if I could feel them both pressing in on me from their rooms on either side.

Snapping my eyes open, I meet the whiskey-colored pair of my intruders and immediately suck in a breath to yell. "Kaison!"

"Els." He sighs.

"What the fuck are you doing?" I roll over, smacking his arm. "You almost gave me a heart attack!"

"Staging an intervention."

"An intervention?"

"It's needed." He sighs again worriedly and lifts the hand lying by his side, holding out a weed pen to me.

I roll my eyes at him. "Pretty sure that's the opposite of an intervention, Kai."

"Fine." He shrugs. "Call it a man-tervention then."

"A man-tervention?" I repeat dumbly. It was way too early for this shit and I was way too uncaffeinated. "What time is it even?" I squint my eyes at him.

"Ten. We let you sleep late." He holds the pen closer to me. "All of Mac's party people are going to be here in a couple hours for that epic party you demanded, and after last night I figured you might want something to take the edge off before then."

Understatement of the century. I had never endured a more awkward ride home in my life. There had only been stony silences, deadly looks, and the occasional grunt being traded between all *five* guys in the limo. Needless to say I hadn't stuck around to see what transpired when we got home, just left them downstairs when they all sat down silently to play *Call of Duty* and bid them a-fucking-dieu.

Letting them work out their issues virtually sounded pretty fantastic to me.

"Fine." I snag the pen from him and bring it to my mouth, quickly taking a hit. "Just make it quick."

"I think you should ditch Danny and Sandy and marry me." He throws out casually.

I blink rapidly, trying to process what he just said through the haze of leftover sleep. "Excuse me?"

"You know Danny and Sandy from *Grease*."

"I know that!" I smack his shoulder again. A bit more forcefully this time to make sure I'm not dreaming or some equally probable shit. "I meant the other part."

Because I could not be waking up to another marriage proposal.

"Oh, yeah." He grabs the pen from me and takes a hit, rolling over to look at the ceiling as he blows out smoke rings. As if what he just said is no big deal. "Well, I was thinking you ditch them, and we get married eventually." I stare at him stupidly as he takes another puff, followed by a few more rings. "I mean, I know we don't have the twin thing going on like you and Mac, and I know Stef and you have this weird connection thing going on too. But I figured we get along well enough, love each other and never fight." He shoots me a pleased grin as if he's discovered the magical recipe for all successful relationships. "Plus, we'd have fucking gorgeous kids if you ever wanted them but don't worry, we could keep that all artificial, so things didn't get weird."

I narrow my eyes on him, trying really hard to make sure I've got this right. "Artificial?"

"Yeah, like a doctor." He shrugs. "Come on, Els, keep up. But really, the main point is this way we could get rid of Danny and Sandy before they fuck up your life any more."

I stare at him for a few blinks before snagging the pen out of his hand and taking a huge hit. Looking up at the ceiling and thinking through how to make this abundantly clear to him while still saving his ego a bit, because he is Kai after all.

"Kaison." I exhale the smoke.

"Yeah, Els?"

"I'm going to be honest with you. I currently have a semi-estranged husband, a boyfriend who's my semi-estranged husband's cousin, and three big brothers in you guys. The last thing I need in my life right now is more testosterone." I look back at him. "So if things don't work out with either one of them, I'd be more likely to date your ex-girlfriend than you." Reaching over, I pat his shoulder consolingly as a look of utter horror comes over his face. "And I mean that in the nicest way possible."

He snags the pen from me in the next second, huffing a pout. "That's just mean, Els."

"But true, even considering how much I dislike her." I laugh.

"You just took something hot and made it… not. Fucking vicious."

I give his shoulder a push, laughing harder. "I seriously doubt that."

"It was a close call."

I hold out my hand, rolling over and taking one last hit when he passes it over. Just enough to take the edge off like he said but still keep my head.

His curious eyes find mine when I pass it back. "So what did Yvie say last night?"

"Uh." I laugh without humor. "Asked me if I was a polygamist now and if you all were planning on joining my harem too."

"So it went well?"

"About as well as it could." I sigh, giving him a small shrug. "I just kept telling her it's complicated and I was figuring it out. Then I reminded her that she had raised me to solve my own problems."

"I bet she loved that." He chuckles.

I turn my head to the side, giving him a small grin. "Let's just say it was a good thing there were people around."

Comfortable silence falls between us then and we both just lie there, enjoying the high within the twists and turns of our own minds. The truth was, when I'd been faced down with it, I couldn't tell her about Coop. About his dad's involvement in my parents' deaths. I'd looked into Yvie's face minutes after coming off the dance floor and I just… couldn't. But when my own thoughts turn a corner of the maze in my mind, they snag on the task I had tossed and turned over for most of the night, causing guilt to hit me hard.

Jace.

"I need to go talk to Sandy." I sigh.

"Yeah, he should be a little better by now."

I roll my head to look at Kai, narrowing my eyes at the shit-eating grin spreading over his face. "What do you mean 'better by now?'" I snap sharply.

"Well I had to distract them somehow so I could have this little man-tervention this morning."

I pause for a second before demanding. "What did you do?"

"Might've laced his morning coffee with some THC so he'd take a nap."

"You didn't."

"At least he's not locked outside like Danny," Kai grumbles. "Fucker's unnatural. There was no way to dose him."

"Kai!"

"Hey!" He holds up his arm to ward off the multiple smacks I'm attempting to give him. "Don't just blame me! Stef and Mac agreed it was worth a shot too."

"Fucking testosterone-addled brains," I huff, throwing back the covers and giving him a warning look. "No more drugging or locking outside my-my—"

"Harem?"

"Ugh!" I stand from the bed before turning and pointing my finger at him threateningly. "No more, Kaison! And you can pass that message along!" I stomp to the door and grab the handle before pausing to shoot a guilty look over my shoulder. "But maybe leave Danny outside for a few more minutes while I talk to Sandy."

Kai chuckles, taking another puff. "I got you, Els, I got you."

Taking a deep breath to fortify myself for the conversation that's coming, I open the door and try to get my slightly sluggish thoughts in order while walking the few steps to Jace's room. Pausing outside the door as I flounder in a sea of guilt for a moment. I knew he had to have seen Coop and me last night, it was why I had avoided his gaze the entire way home.

And I wouldn't blame him one bit if he was pissed.

Hell, part of me wanted him to be pissed. Wanted him to rage against me with all the mixed-up emotions I was currently dealing with myself. I deserved it. Any and all flack I was about to take over what was most definitely not my finest moment of going from one guy to the next.

That should be laid at my feet and no one else's. My fucking waltzing feet that had been a little too weak to stop it… and that I still wasn't sure could stand against either of their onslaughts.

Channeling your inner Nadia, El? Tut, tut. You might prove Yvie wrong yet.

My stomach gives a vicious twist at the thought, the comparison I can't quite seem to escape. It's more complicated than that, I reason, trying to push out the self-destruction slowly trying to work its poisonous tendrils into me. It wasn't like any of us intentionally set out to be in this mess. Well, besides Coop that is.

You sure about that? Take a second look and you might notice some striking similarities between the two.

Sometimes I really do wonder whose side you're on.

I hurriedly push open the door to stave off the self-hatred that's growing the longer I stand there, heart clenching up immediately at the familiar sight of Jace all sprawled out in bed. Closing the door softly behind me, I walk to the bed and pause to simply take him in. The way his lips are parted just a little bit like always, paired with the peaceful expression on his face. It looks like he literally collapsed onto the bed, fully clothed in his favorite joggers and threadbare white T-shirt. Looking as cute as he did when we woke up from that first nap together on his boat. I can't stop the lift of my lips at the sight, despite my disapproval of the reason for his little siesta.

And I'm undoubtedly a selfish fucking bitch because the next thing I do is climb onto the bed and curl my body around his. As helpless in my need for him as I was for Coop last night during our dance. I quickly tuck myself into him without giving him the chance to protest, laying my head on his chest and sliding a leg over him, trying to ignore the prick in my eyes as I do.

He doesn't deserve my fucking mess. He deserves someone better, undamaged and whole. Someone selfless like him. Someone who can offer him even a fraction of what he does by just simply lying here and letting me breathe him in.

He sighs under my chest. "Stop it."

"What?" I counter, looking up to see his eyes closed, the peaceful expression in place as if he's still asleep.

"I can hear you thinking." He brings a hand up, starting to trail his fingers up and down my spine and causing me to relax instantly. To let go of the tension I didn't even know I was projecting. "And I'm still too high for that. So get out of here with that shit, Delacroix."

His lips pull up just a bit with the order and my face scrunches up in turn. "Jace—"

"I told you there was a war happening." He opens those almond-shaped eyes just a sliver, meeting my gaze. "Ready to admit it yet?"

I drop my eyes from his and swallow. "Why don't you hate me?"

His soft, melodic laughter sounds under my head. "Ellie—"

"You should at least be a little pissed," I argue, tightening my grip on him despite the glaring contradiction to my words in the action.

"Oh, trust me. I am." He scoffs, reaching down with his free hand to grab me behind the knee, pulling my leg higher till it's wrapped around his hip. "But only because I didn't think of that dance move first."

"Jace." My voice cracks a little on his name and I feel him go still. "I need you to hate me here. At least a little. I deserve it."

"Ellie." His voice is all soft care and I feel him tug on my hair a second later. "I could never hate you."

I'm silent for a long moment before quietly giving voice to my biggest fear of what's happening here. Facing it with the person it concerns, the one I'm desperate to save from the fate I endured. "I don't want to hurt you." The confession is so quiet it's the kind a too-loud breath could erase.

"It's okay." He tugs on my hair again, trying to lighten the mood. "You've got to figure it out and there're not too many ways to do that."

"It's not okay!" I argue again, anger sparking as I look back to his half-open, amused gaze. "It's not okay or fair and I don't want to hurt—"

He holds a finger to my mouth in the next instant, lips pulling up just a bit. "Blondie, the only way you could ever really hurt me would be if I lost you."

"That's not going to happen." I shake my head, feeling his finger brush against my lips as I do.

Those dimples flash with a quick grin. “I know that.” He lifts his finger from my lips, brushing my hair behind my ear and lingering there to rub the strands back and forth in a gentle grip. “But do you know what would hurt me?”

It takes me a second to force the uneasy question out, voice quiet when I do. “What?”

“If you picked me and then woke up five years from now with doubts.” He flicks his eyes to the hand playing with my hair, running the strands through a few times before continuing. “That would kill me.” Clearing his throat, he looks back to me with a sad grin. “So yeah, you figuring it out might be a little uncomfortable, might make me feel possessive as hell. But I would rather that than have five years with you, only for you to realize you had made the wrong choice.”

“Jace.” I sigh.

“Don’t forget, Ellie,” he interrupts softly, brows pulling down just a bit. “I share the blame here too.”

I shake my head. “Not till the end.”

“That’s not entirely true.”

I’m silent in response, staring into his firework eyes as trepidation rises fast and quick due to all the secrets that have split my world recently.

I see the clear struggle playing out on his face as he pulls his bottom lip through his teeth before speaking huskily. “Coop was right, you know? When he asked if there was a moment when I saw that tattoo.” He sighs, dropping his hand from my hair and running it over his face before looking back to me. "There was." His eyes turn pained with the quiet confession. "There was a second where something about it just *tugged* at me… and the thought crossed my mind. But I pushed it to the side, told myself it was impossible, because all I wanted in that moment was you." He shakes his head and looks up to the ceiling with a humorless scoff. "And even when I knew for sure, I still didn't say anything. So this is on me too, Blondie."

I let him work through his own blame for a moment before reaching a hand up and tugging on his hair, echoing the way he always plays with me. When he takes a deep breath and looks down to me again, I give him a small grin. "None of us are perfect, Dawson." I push myself off the bed before planting my hands on either side of his shoulders and sliding up so that I'm holding my face right above his. "And if you can forgive me for my massive secret, I can damn well forgive you for your slightly smaller one."

His eyes search mine for a moment. "Aptly put, Delacroix." He grins, narrowing his eyes on me. "When did you become the zen master?"

"Trust me, I'm not." I sigh dramatically. "And you're handling that little dance scene like Yoda himself, so I'd say that title still goes to you."

He shrugs. "Well we stayed up till four in the morning silently beating the shit out of each other on *Call of Duty* so I think that helped some."

My brows drop at the picture, hating the rift I know I am between them right now.

"Stop beating yourself up, Ellie." He lifts his head, pressing a soft kiss to my lips. "It's not like we don't know what's going on here. This war is a consensual one."

"You're not making me feel better."

"I can think of something that would."

"Incorrigible." I roll my eyes.

"Mhmm," he drawls in agreement, eyes pure mischief as he lifts his lips to mine again.

And I can't help but whisper. "I don't deserve you." Because it's true.

"True." A soft laugh leaves his lips. "No one could hope to. Really, you should feel blessed that I picked you." He finishes with a wink, dropping his head back to the bed.

Rolling my eyes at him, I roll over and scoot to the edge of the bed before standing, sparing him a look over my shoulder as I walk toward the door. "Shake off the high and go get your bathing suit on, Dawson." I toss him a bratty smirk. "You're about to see how we royals like to party."

Chapter Twenty-Three

My bones are already rattling from the bass pumping from the speakers outside as I walk down the stairs inside Stef's house. The white cover-up I'd left completely open in the front trailing behind me, perfectly showing off my favorite bright-emerald Brazilian bikini I had chosen to rock today. I stared at it for about two seconds before grabbing it out of the drawer. The suit was one of my favorites and I sure as shit wasn't going to allow the fact that it might push Coop and Jace over that edge they were toeing dissuade me now. There was consideration, and then there was changing who you were for someone. And while I definitely would make every effort to not get into any sticky situations today… I made no apologies for who I was or what I wore. If they had a problem with it, well, they could politely go fuck themselves.

I looked hot as shit and that made me happy. And my happiness was damn well as important as theirs.

Peeking over the railing, I see that, thankfully, the festivities seemed to have been contained outside. At least for the cleanup crew's sake. Although the hooting and hollering drifting through the air to me as I walk to the kitchen makes it apparent that things are already in full force. A few people that are lingering inside with Kai cast curious eyes my way as I come into the kitchen and head straight for the island. Eyeing the assortment of fancy drinks and liquor bottles littering the large space along with a bowl of edibles, because why not, right? Grabbing a glass of champagne, I figure there's no harm in keeping it light since it was still around noon.

I bring the glass to my lips, still feeling their eyes on me in the silence that's filling the space at my arrival and know they're waiting for me to pander a bit like some random newb. I've been out of this scene for two summers in a row now, plus my year abroad, and there are probably going to be a hell of a lot of new faces. Too many people that don't recognize me or my place here. I tilt my head and run my gaze over them, cocking a brow like a queen holding court before letting my lips twitch just a bit. Dismissing them with a flick of my eyes, I walk right up to Kai and give him a passing peck on the cheek before walking through the rest of them without a word. Heading to the back door while fighting the grin trying to break free.

God, I lived for this shit in a way.

And I was going to have so much damn fun today reminding the top tier of LA just who Eleanor Delacroix was.

Why she was still spoken about like a myth in hushed tones during drunken two a.m. conversations.

The music hits me hard as I open the back door and my gaze immediately lands on Stef standing at the stone column that encloses the porch with the exception of the two stairways leading down on either side of us. His hands are braced on the top of the low wall and even standing in nothing but a pair of black swim trunks he looks every bit the picture of a king overlooking his domain. I take a sip of my champagne and walk up to stand beside him, eyes rolling over the debauchery below as I place my glass on the stone.

The massive pool that had taken practically a year to complete stretches out a level below, the water inside appearing to topple right over the edge and down into the California hills below. The only thing keeping swimmers from being able to hang their hands right into open air is the glass wall shooting up from the side that Stef had added when our parties became decidedly more lively with each year we aged. There are two shelves with loungers built into them on either side of the pool for sunbathing, with a massive, raised platform smack in the middle to match.

And every available surface is covered with people partying.

There are girls dancing on the shelves to the music pumping from the DJ, who I'm guessing is set up on the ground floor patio below us. There are people lining the edge of the pool, doing shots off each other's bodies with complete abandon. Guys with huge double-sided knockout jousts are on the center shelf, trying to topple each other off while Mac plays referee with a whistle in his mouth and a bottle of Dom in hand.

Give it a few hours and we would be putting the playboy mansion to shame.

I scoff a laugh at the sight. "Typical."

"You know Mac." Stef chuckles quietly next to me. "Rage all day. Plus, you did ask for it to be epic."

"True." I sip. "Have they been down yet?"

"The Dawson boy stumbled through here a while ago."

"And?"

"Said to tell you he was still too high for this shit and to let him sleep through it all."

I laugh softly, looking at Stef. "Where is he?"

He nods his head down to the shelf on the left and I follow his eyes to see Jace sprawled out in one of the loungers, hair pulled back and chin dipped to his chest with a baseball cap covering his face. Gorgeous cuts of his suntanned body on full display. I try to fight the goofy smile breaking free at the sight and fail miserably, looking back to Stef.

"I take it Kai passed along my warning?"

"He did." He nods.

"I mean it, Stefano."

"And I don't care, *cara*." He finally looks at me and I see the iciness in the back of his eyes. "They hurt you and can shoulder the burden of what that means to us until I've decided they've paid the price for their actions."

"Stef." I sigh, floundering as I try to figure out a way to make peace between them all when I don't even know how to do that myself with half of the equation.

"No, *cara*." He shakes his head with a sharp move before speaking quickly and quietly. "Ti voglio molto bene." *I love you deeply*. "But I won't budge on this. Especially considering they've both made their current intentions very clear."

I sigh again, knowing there's little hope when he really gets set on something. "No bodily injury." I wager.

That small secret smile flashes across his face for a split second before he hides it. "Fine, but self-defense is allowed."

I narrow my eyes on him suspiciously, not at all liking his easy agreement and the condition tagged onto it even less.

"Take the deal." He chuckles, waving a hand in the air as if to motion someone forward. "It's the best I'll offer." A girl in a string bikini walks forward then and sets a bottle down in front of him, along with two shot glasses, before going up on her toes to give him a quick peck on the cheek. And the indifferent bastard in front of me doesn't even break my gaze to give her the time of day through the whole thing, not even sparing her a glance when she walks away. Most of the time, Stef is so warm and caring with me that I forget how he could be with the rest of the world. Then there are moments like this when I remember how very intimidating and cold he can be. I remember where the origins of his formation occurred.

As if sensing the train of my thoughts, he gives me a wider smile than usual and slides the bottle in front of me. "I dug this out of the cellar to celebrate your homecoming. I know it's your favorite."

I look down to the bottle and immediately have to fight the smile trying to break free. It's an añejo. A very old and expensive añejo by the looks of it.

Damn, but the girl that finally broke through to that soft indulgent center one day… I almost envied her, or I would, if it wasn't for the fact she'll have to make it past me first.

He slides a shot glass in front of me. "Make peace with me, *cara,* and enjoy the day."

I look up and meet his questioning eyes, lips twitching. "Only because I love you too, Stef."

He looks into my eyes for a moment before giving me a pleased nod and grabbing the tequila to pour us both a shot. I quickly grab mine and sip, eager to try the añejo and it does not disappoint. The liquor rolls over my tongue, all earthy and rich, delighting me into giving a happy sigh as Stef cringes next to me.

"I don't know how you drink this shit."

"Probably the same way you drink scotch."

"True." He chuckles, forcing himself to take another sip before setting the glass down.

Taking another sip of the tequila, I try to muster up the courage to ask the question buzzing at the back of my mind. "And Coop?" I look back to the party, steadfastly ignoring Stef's gaze. "Has he come down?"

"That was the other reason for the tequila."

My brows drop, eyes shooting back to him quickly. "What do you mean?"

Stef's lips purse before he sighs and points to his right. I follow his finger to the edge of the pool where Coop stands shirtless in his gray swimsuit with Marcie fucking Gibbons of all people. The bitch who had outed what had happened to my parents to the whole school in seventh grade. Her head is cocked to the side flirtatiously and she's fucking *pawing* at his chest while

Coop just stands there, not participating by the bored look on his face but not backing away either.

Stef clears his throat. "Not to do him any favors, but I have a feeling Mac had a hand in this. As you know, she's never invited to our parties."

Oh, I'm sure. This has Macallan written all over it. I'm sure all he had to do was point her in his direction and give her a swat on the ass as she headed that way.

Motherfucker.

I throw back the shot in one go, trying to quell the sudden surge of possessiveness roaring through me. So much for taking it easy. Grabbing the bottle of tequila, I quickly fill the shot glass again and bring it to my lips. Taking a small sip and hating that I'm unable to keep from looking their way.

Coop's waiting for me this time.

Our eyes lock and he slowly arches a brow at me, holding my gaze for a long moment before looking back down to Marcie as if he's giving her his undivided attention.

Fucker was provoking me.

"What was that?" Stef asks curiously, drawing my gaze away from the scene currently causing my blood to boil.

"That." I take another sip of the shot and blow out a deep breath. "Was Coop pushing me, giving me a taste of my own medicine to try and force a reaction."

Stef pauses. "And is it working?"

I let my eyes drift back down in time to see Marcie take a step toward Coop, quickly wiping any sense of reason from me. "You know what?" I throw back the shot before carefully setting the now empty glass down on the stone. "I think it is."

The humor in Stef's eyes is clear when I meet them briefly before walking slowly past him. My pace measured and calm, completely at odds with the reckless anger riding me. I practically skip down the stairs, just like any other carefree girl coming down to party before swinging a right at the bottom. Coop's eyes rise to meet mine over Marcie's shoulder as I walk toward them and I see that arrogant smirk flash across his face before he ducks his head. And the thing is, right now, I don't even care that he won this round of our game. I just know this churning inside me demands to be poured into something. No matter whether it proves his point or not.

I don't pause or hesitate as I come up on them. Hell, I'd even call my turn toward Marcie as I come alongside them worthy of a ballerina. And then I lift a hand and shove her shoulder with all the mediocre strength packed into my five-eight frame, sending her toppling into the pool with a splash. I resist the urge to look at Coop when I hear that rare, open laughter pour from him next to me, along with the sounds of surprise from the people surrounding us. Somehow managing to just lift my brows and wait for the piranha to surface.

She comes up as a sputtering mess of sandy-blonde hair with mascara streaming down her face.

I look down and hold up a hand as if checking my nails, droning her name. "Marcie."

"You, you—"

"Me? Me?" I mock, looking back at her with a bored expression.

"You're not supposed to be here," she argues indignantly, treading water. "You've been gone for like ever."

I crouch down beside the pool, giving her a vicious smile. "That little rule I made about you not being allowed at our parties applies whether I'm in town or not." Standing, I wave a hand in the air carelessly. "You never know when I'll decide to pop back in." I turn away from both her and Coop without a second look, calling out over my shoulder loudly. "Now get the fuck out of here and don't make me repeat myself again."

I can feel Coop's eyes burning a hole in my back as I walk back to the stairs but seriously, fuck him. If he wants to play, we'll play. And to think I came down to this party with the best of intentions. I jog up the stairs, trying to keep the same relaxed air as I'd had during my descent and ignoring the bit of guilt settling in my stomach over my actions. The sight of Stef's smiling face greets me when I make it to the top, causing me to roll my eyes.

He holds out a full shot glass as I come up to him. "I think I'll tell Mac it was worth inviting her just for that moment alone."

"Oh, I'm sure he caught it." I snort. "And don't you dare encourage him."

The music cuts out the next second, drawing both of our gazes to the pool where the man in question stands on the center shelf alone now. A bullhorn in hand he pulled out of his ass from somewhere and a delighted expression on his face that should strike fear in the hearts of everyone here.

Oh no.

"Always the showman." Stef sighs wearily.

Mac lifts the bullhorn to his mouth. "Welcome!" He holds out his arm wide, turning from side to side to no doubt show off the flaming wings stretched across his back that dip down below his white swim trunks.

I seriously can't help but roll my eyes.

He brings the bullhorn back to his mouth and begins to walk slowly around the shelf. "Friends! Strangers!" His walk slows just a bit and I see him eye a redhead in the pool not too far away. "Soon-to-be friends." That sinful smile flashes as he lifts his head. "This is typically about the time we like to do away with the inflatables and move into straight, bare-knuckle knockouts. And we'll get there in a minute!" He pauses and drops the bullhorn for a moment, casting a purposefully pensive look across the pool before bringing it back to his mouth. "But today, today, I wanted to take a moment to reminisce with you all. Reminisce about how me and mine have risen to be fucking royalty in this town throughout the years. The kings and queen of the hills!" His eyes zero in on the left shelf and I look that way, seeing Kai sitting with not one but two girls on his lap and a grin spread across his face. "And then I wanted to take a moment to talk about all the forbidden things that we've done to get there because they have been… delicious." He laughs, dropping the bullhorn from his mouth and I can see the way he's sucking up all the crazed energy flying around before bringing it back to his lips and speaking quietly. “But why settle for being a mere royal when you could be a deity?” He shakes his head as if the idea alone is sickening. “And today we really have reason to revel, because with the opening of Labyrinth this week…” A beat of suspense fills the air before he roars into the mic. “We’ve become fucking gods this year!”

Laughter spills from my lips as the crowd grows wild, eating up the show he’s putting on. And right now, it’s impossible to not join in on his fun, because he’s right. This is the pinnacle of our debauchery. All those years of being heathens, the scandalous children of the hills, was finally being thrown into something productive.

I catch Stef’s eyes as he chuckles next to me and Mac starts to speak again. “But one more thing.” I look back and see his eyes are dead set on me, causing anticipation to fill me. “Most of you have heard of her, but there’s been a fracture among us these past couple summers. A goddess that was missing from our Olympus.” That troublemaker smile spreads, inviting me to join in on his fun. “So I thought Eleanor Delacroix might like to make an entrance for old times’ sake.”

I know what he means instantly. The years of epic parties paired with our shared recklessness leave no question as to what he’s suggesting. It’s actually incredibly sweet, in a Mac kind of way. Adrenaline and excitement flood my veins the next second and I don’t miss a beat.

I flash him a conspiratorial grin, throw back my shot, and dart inside as the first electric chords of “Jamie All Over” pound through the speakers below my feet.

Bound

Chapter Twenty-Four

It's always been Mac's and my favorite song for this particular stunt.

Stef and Kai had called us insane. Stef had even offered to pay me to stop doing it at one point. But alas, we had kept on throughout the years so much that they eventually grew bored and figured if we hadn't died by this point… it was probably okay.

I slide open the window in Mac's room that's closest to the deepest part of the pool and the dry air hits me instantly. Reaching up to brace my hands on the window ledge, I push up and stretch my leg out. Tentatively placing a toe on the tile roof and knowing it's going to burn like hell for a minute before my feet adjust to the heat. But the song is playing, each note filling me with further excitement and driving me forward. I clench my teeth with a firm reminder to not be a little bitch and step out onto the tile, carefully hopping from one foot to the other to help with the momentary temperature adjustment. My gaze finds Mac in the pool, openly laughing at me, and I lift my hand to promptly flip him off.

Lifting a hand toward me, he brings the bullhorn back to his mouth. "And there she is, ladies and gentlemen." He points to the deepest part of the pool. "Clear the landing space, assholes."

I immediately stop my hopping as every eye in the place turns to me, lifting my chin with just enough of a smirk to be seen from the level below. It's almost comical, the way their jaws drop in unison as they spot me. Even the guys littering the crowd look nervous at the sight of me on the roof.

And I do get it. I'd seen Mac up here before and it was a heart-stopping sight despite the fact that it was technically only a one level jump down. It was the gap between the roof and the patio that made it so questionable though. You had to really launch yourself to make it to the right part of the pool. But really, that's what made it so fun. Plus, with the angle and the way you could see over the edge of the pool to the sharp drop-off… fuck me but it felt like you were about to base jump straight off the California hills.

A pure, supercharged adrenaline high every time I did it.

"Eleanor!" a demanding voice shouts below me and my gaze immediately finds Coop, standing right in the path I'll have to jump over. "Don't you fucking dare!" he growls.

I lift my chin defiantly at him, shrugging my cover-up off my shoulders and holding it out between two fingers. Pausing for a beat, I let a fuck-off smirk fill my face before letting go of the cover-up and watching it float down to him on a gentle breeze.

You wanted to play, big boy. Let's play.

I watch the dark fury fill his face and don't even bother trying to deny that I love the edge it gives to the excitement vibrating through me.

Hands clenching at his sides, he opens his mouth to no doubt shout at me some more. "Elean—"

"Blondie!" Jace cuts him off and I look over to see him standing on the shelf now, head tilted up at me with a nervous expression on his face. "Come on, don't give the old man a heart attack!"

I shake my head and yell. "I'll be fine!"

That bullhorn sounds through the air again as the chorus plays. "What do you say, Els?" My eyes find Mac's goading ones. "For old times' sake?"

I answer with a reckless smile for about two seconds before taking the three lunges off the roof at a run and launching myself into the air. My stomach flips wildly as I practically fly and am filled with split-second thoughts. That instant wondering of whether I really did get the angle right or launch myself far enough that intensifies my adrenaline with a touch of fear right before I come down. Sucking in a breath as my feet hit the water just on the right side of deep enough and my heart pounds hard with a thrilling kind of relief.

I don't even bother surfacing for air or going back to the patio, just swimming forward under the water to the center shelf. Knowing Mac's going to be waiting for our moment of glory. I come up out of the water and grab his waiting hands without hesitation, letting him haul me up onto the shelf as the crowd hollers around us. A full-blown smile splits his face as he leans down and throws me over his shoulder, spinning in a circle and flashing my ass to the crowd as he screams into the bullhorn.

"Eleanor Delacroix has returned!"

The laughter is falling freely from my lips as he sets me back down and carelessly tosses the bullhorn into the pool before starting to scream more than sing the song in my face. I give in immediately, singing with him and starting to jump around together like we always have. Reveling in the moment with absolute abandon as water splashes around us. Hands in the air and completely on display as the goddess he claims me to be. I catch Jace's eyes over his shoulder and see the amused grin filling his face before he shakes his head at me with an exasperated look. But I just toss him a grin and turn in a circle, shaking my hips, catching sight of him collapsing back into the lounger and lifting his hat back over his face as I come back around.

Apparently, Dawson was still too high for my shit.

I can't help but giggle a bit over it as the song comes to an end.

Mac holds up a hand to me and motions taking a shot. "Shots?"

"Absolutely." I nod, giving him a smug look. "Stef broke out the good stuff for me."

He rolls his eyes. "Of course he did."

"Be right back." I laugh, turning and diving back into the water.

It takes me a minute to swim back across the length of the pool, considering I didn't fly through the air over part of it this time and I notice more than a few appreciative looks being thrown my way by the attendees. I steadfastly ignore them as I make my way back to the patio though, having no wish to deal with more jealous drama and, quite frankly, just no desire for them at all. When I make it to the edge of the pool, I grab it and push up, sliding my butt onto the grainy ground before standing. Bringing both my hands up, I start to squeeze the water from my hair right as a viselike grip closes around my elbow and gives a hard tug, almost causing me to stumble if it wasn't for that same hand holding me up.

I jerk my head around, locking eyes with Coop and my breath comes to a halt at the barely contained rage I see there. Those night-forest eyes drilling into me with nothing but shadows.

"What?" I snap.

You really never learn, do you, El?

He scoffs a humorless sound and jerks me a few steps toward the lower patio where the DJ is set up before I plant my feet.

"What are you doing?"

He whips around and looks down at me. "I let you have your moment, Princess," he grinds out, voice filled with the promise of retribution. "Now I get mine."

"Um, yeah, no thanks." I manage a weak laugh as nerves fill me.

His grip tightens to near bruising on my arm. "Either you come with me, Eleanor…" He drops his head down close to mine and continues in a low voice. "Or I will smack that pretty ass so hard out here in front of god and everybody that you won't be able to sit for a month."

My mouth pops open in shock and I stare at him for a second before muttering. "You wouldn't."

"Just try me." He smirks tauntingly. "Push me just a little bit harder right now, *please*, because half of me wants to do it just so they know who you belong to."

My eyes widen at his words, heart skipping a beat, and he takes full advantage of my momentary lapse. Dragging me past the DJ and through the glass back doors of the house. I can feel the tension vibrating through his body and into mine thanks to the tight grip he's maintaining as he continues right through the poolroom and into the hall before pausing to look both ways. He walks us a few more paces before opening a door at random and pulling me into the wine cellar. His hand lets go of my arm suddenly, sending me stumbling a few steps past him as he slams the door behind us.

Anger flares to life in me at his manhandling, strong enough to match his as I spin around. "What the hell is your problem, Coop?"

His hand is still braced on the door, head bowed and I watch his shoulders rise and fall with a few deep breaths before he speaks quietly. "My problem?" He turns slowly, eyes meeting mine before dropping to my toes and slowly working their way back up my body. "My problem, Eleanor, is you."

Our eyes lock and I can sense us teetering on the edge of a true fight right before I scoff. "Well that can be easily fixed." Throwing him right over that edge.

A beat passes before he starts to walk toward me so fast that I can't stop my gut reaction of backing up, stumbling back as his strides eat up the space between us until my back hits one of the floor-to-ceiling wine shelves and I'm forced to stop. His eyes pin me in place as he pushes into my space, both of our chests heaving and his sandalwood scent wrapping around me like some damn vine I can't escape.

"That wasn't reckless, Eleanor, that was stupid," he spits out, face dropping even closer to mine. "And you don't get to be stupid with your life like that."

Tense silence fills the air for a second before I shoot back. "Let's be honest here." I narrow my eyes on his. "You're not pissed I jumped from some roof into the pool. You're pissed because you have no control over me anymore." My lips twitch up into a smirk. "And as you saw, you fell in love with a princess without realizing I was a motherfucking deity. So it's not my fault you don't care for the reality."

"So fucking stupid." He laughs a low sound that's all kinds of rough. "Much as you might not like to face it, you're not invincible." Those night-forest eyes practically blaze with a universe of barely contained feelings. "All it would have taken was one slip of your foot, one misplaced step, a million little things that could've gone wrong and you would have been *gone*."

"Oh, like you were?" I toss out carelessly, immediately regretting taking it there as it settles like gasoline on my anger, feeding the flames. "Let me make something abundantly clear, Cooper. You gave up the right to have any say over how I live my life when you left me on that beach in Costa Rica."

His head pulls back just a bit, nostrils flaring and eyes raking my face before coming back to mine. "Liar."

"Excuse me?"

He narrows his eyes on me. "If you didn't want me to have any say, why not just ask for a divorce?"

I cock my head at him, copping an attitude to try and cover up how many holes his question punches into my own story. "There hasn't really been time for that."

"More lies." His lips twitch as he drops his head right back into my space. "If you didn't care, Eleanor. Why bring me here?"

The full weight of his demand pushes at me, the determined look in his eyes letting me know that he's not just going to walk away this time. And it has me swallowing to ease the sudden dryness of my throat.

"I don't know," I mutter distractedly, breaking his gaze to dart my eyes to the side and search for an escape.

"If you really hate me so much, why not leave me behind?"

"I don't know."

"If there's no hope, why put us all through this?"

"I don't know!"

"If I really am Satan, why do you still *care*?"

"I don't—"

"Yes you do," he cuts me off, reaching up and grabbing the wine shelf on either side of me and causing panic to grip me as he cages me in. "You still care." A beat passes and I'm left with nowhere to look but back at him, gaze going to that tense brow before dropping to lock with his eyes. "Even if I am unforgivable, you still love me."

His words crack something inside of me that I've been desperately trying to patch since his reappearance and I bite my lip, fighting the urge to gasp for breath. My chest so fucking heavy it feels like all the gravity in the room is pressing on it.

"You still love me," he repeats, eyes demanding the truth from mine and I shake my head, trying to block him out. "You still *love me*."

I can feel myself coming undone, toppling right over that edge I pushed him over myself.

"You still love—"

"Loving you broke me!"

"And what do you think losing you did to me?!"

Our shouts echo in the air, words overlapping until the painful truth and our angry breaths are all that fill my ears.

He lets go of the shelf next to my head with one hand and brings his fingers to his favorite place on my neck. "Maybe we're broken right now." His voice comes out dangerously soft as he trails his fingers up to rest on the frantically beating pulse of my neck, brows dropping while he stares at the life-giving spot for a moment. "But let *me* tell *you* something, Princess." His fingers wrap around my throat with a barely there caress, the touch so careful and light and all the more powerful for it. Making me excruciatingly aware of just how much bigger he is. How much strength he's holding in check under all that heated olive skin.

He brings his eyes back to mine as my stomach flips wildly and an exhilaration I hope he can't see starts to pound through my body with an aching acuity. "Maybe take into account the next time you decide to go putting your life at risk that if something ever happened to you… I'd follow you straight into whatever comes after." Those ridiculously full lips smirk humorlessly. "And yeah, I know what those words do to you." He drops his head so close to mine that there's a scant inch between us, leaving our eyes darting between each other's. "But if that's what it takes to get it through that thick fucking skull of yours that I'll always love you." His fingers tighten the barest hint. "So be it."

I suck in a breath, trying to stave off the dark desire in me that's answering his demand and emphasize every quiet word from my lips. "Back the fuck off."

He narrows his eyes on mine, searching for the thing I'm trying to hide as my betraying pulse feathers under his touch. "No."

"Back off," I snap, bringing an arm up and batting his hand from my neck.

His response is instant, immediately stepping into me and using the weight of his body to keep me trapped against the shelf. My heart thundering and breath catching at the shock of his bare skin against mine. He drops his eyes to my chest at the sound and I go perfectly still, trying to calm my heart and rapid breathing. But his eyes fill with satisfaction as he watches the rise and fall of my chest and I can see the victory swirling in their depths when he brings his gaze back to mine.

His lips ghost up. "You fucking want me."

"No, I don't," I scoff.

"I can see it all over you."

"I don't!"

"Your body's practically begging me." A disbelieving huff leaves him before his voice drops roughly, laced with the need I can feel pounding through me. "I bet all you can think about right now is how good it would feel to have my cock inside of you while I fuck this horrible feeling from us both."

"You're insane." I laugh in his face, the sound a little too forced for even me to believe and it drives me to bring my hands up. Pushing them against his chest and trying to wiggle a desperate escape as I continue in a vicious voice. "The last thing I want is you."

He reaches up and grabs my wrist, quickly pinning one of my hands to the shelf above my head and I gasp when I feel his other hand push into my bathing suit bottoms the next instant. His fingers slide through my drenched pussy without hesitation and spread my folds wide before he spears them roughly up into me. And my whole body goes taut, completely locking up as my pussy clenches violently around his fingers.

He drops his head down next to mine and a quiet, arrogant laugh fans against my ear. "You sure about that, Princess?" He pulls his fingers out, swirling his thumb around my clit before pumping two into me deeper than before. "Because from where I'm standing… you're," Pump. "Fucking." Pump. "Dripping." Pump. "For me."

He pulls back and arches a brow down at me, those night-forest eyes nothing but shadows and need. "Or would you like to keep playing this little game for a while?" A careless shrug rolls off his shoulders that I feel all the way to where his fingers are curling inside of me. "I'm good either way."

My eyes flow over his face as I lose all semblance of control, every fucking part of me zeroing in on the feel of his fingers inside of me. The aching throb happening there. The painful desire for more of him. He pushes down on my clit again, causing my body to give a soft tremble and when a quiet moan escapes me, we both know there's only one way we're finishing this fight.

His lips come crashing down onto mine the next instant and as my eyes close I can practically see our stars collide in brilliant ecstasy. Creating a black hole that sucks us both in, fighting its pull an impossibility I don't even attempt as I give in to the undeniable need inside of me.

Our kiss is a raw thing, a clashing of teeth and delving of tongues that can't quite get deep enough to satisfy but try to all the same. His grip loosens on my wrist and I drop my hand into his, our fingers winding together to grip tightly. He spreads his fingers wide in me and I gasp into our kiss as an answering groan of satisfaction leaves him and he brings his thumb to my clit again. I feel him circle the sensitive nub a few times before pinching it and causing my hips to jolt against him as he nips at my bottom lip.

He pulls his hand from my bathing suit the next instant and grabs the side, beginning to roughly push it down over my hip. And I yank my hand from his to help him forcefully push the clinging fabric from my skin. Needing more of him in this moment to a degree that's fucking excruciating. He leaves the task to me and immediately grabs the strings at the back of my top, tearing at them until my top drops to the ground at the same time as my bottoms fall from my hips. I move to kick them to the side and he leans back, eyes raking my naked body and stopping to linger on my intimate areas. My nipples pebble under his gaze and an arrogant smirk flares to life on his face as he brings his gaze back to mine. The smug satisfaction rolling off him so palpable that it makes me want to slap him.

So I do.

I bring my hand up and smack it carelessly across his face. Not with a punishing strength but just enough to check him a bit. To remind him that he's not playing with some meek body.

His head whips to the side and I watch the shock play over his face, cheek reddening a bit before he jerks his gaze back to mine. Our eyes locking as a dark heat flashes in his gaze and probably mine too right before he drops his head and we begin to devour each other again. Fighting for dominance as my hands go to the front of his bathing suit, jerking on the strings there frantically until I feel them loosen enough that I can push the fabric over his hips. I hear his suit fall to the floor as that magnificent cock springs out, hard as a rock against my stomach. Ripping my mouth from his, I drop my gaze to look at him and bring a hand up to wrap my fingers around him tightly.

That inferno of blood pulses under my fingers in response and I start to give him a stroke but he steps back. "Nuh-uh." His lips twitch. "There'll be time to play later." He reaches down, grabbing the backs of my knees and I don't hesitate to lock my arms around his neck as he lifts me. "But I've waited a year to be inside you and the only touch I want right now is that fucking paradise between your legs throttling me."

I wrap my legs around his hips and feel him nudge at my entrance with unerring accuracy, his forehead dropping against mine as he starts to sink into me without a second's hesitation. His eyes snap shut, air hissing out between his teeth that I suck in with the little gasps coming from my lips at the feel of him stretching me again. That glorious pain-edged pleasure that borders on release already and has me digging my nails into his shoulders as my pussy does exactly what he wants. Throttles him greedily as he pushes in and seats himself to the hilt, until I'm barely able to breathe with the feeling of being so full. No space inside of me left untouched by him.

His eyes pop open after a moment, locking on to mine as we both stay perfectly still. And I can feel the shift between us happen then. The precious agony of intimacy that comes with being one with him again pulling me apart piece by piece until I can't help but squeeze my eyes shut against it.

He moves a hand around to hold me up from behind and the next moment I feel his thumb bush against my cheek with gentle reverence. "Talk to me, Princess." He thrusts shallowly, causing my breath to catch. "Speak our language."

My face screws up, eyes squeezing impossibly tighter. "I fucking hate you," I choke out.

He grinds against my clit and answers with a soft whisper. "I fucking love you."

I dig my nails even harder into his skin, deep enough that I know it has to hurt. "You broke me."

His thumb brushes my cheek again. "And I will always hate myself for that."

I open my eyes and meet his pained ones. "You left me," I accuse quietly.

His fingers dig into my ass. "I found you."

"Too late."

Anything to keep him at bay.

I see the possession roar to life in his eyes, practically blacking them out as he drops his other hand to my ass, fingers digging into both cheeks as he pulls back and slams into me. His mouth comes down on mine, pulling at my bottom lip and dragging it through his teeth punishingly. Hard enough I know it's going to leave a bruising mark. And the next thrust is so powerful that it almost has my eyes rolling back in my head as a gasping cry rips from me. Sure that I've never been so intimately invaded before as he slides his cheek along mine and brings his lips to my ear.

"Fuck around with my cousin if you need to," he snaps, grinding against my clit. "To punish me. To make me pay." He pulls back before thrusting deep again. "I'll allow it because I know I deserve that agony." Those fingers dig into my ass just a touch harder. "So I'll take whatever punishment you give me. I'll pay the price for my mistake," he whispers roughly, dragging his nose along my cheek and reaching a hand up to grab my left one from his shoulder. "But you are mine, Eleanor *Monroe*." His eyes lock with mine, demanding my gaze as he pulls back and brings my hand up, sucking my ring finger into his mouth. He swirls his tongue around it, causing my pussy to convulse around him before he drags it through his teeth to release. "I made sure of it."

My eyes prick at his words and I look away, knowing that as much as a part of me might still hate him… the other part knows he's right too. That he still owns some part of my heart that I never got back from him. That I gave him when I finally fell that first time into the mud with him on that rain-soaked day.

He winds our fingers together, bringing them to my cheek and nudging my head back before dropping his forehead to mine as he picks up a slow pace inside of me. "Your every moan, cry, laugh, and scream." His lips drop to mine with a soft kiss. "Every inch of your skin and the air in your goddamn lungs belongs to me." I feel my throat start to tighten and try to swallow down everything his words are ripping up in me. "You want to know why?" Trying to will myself to break his gaze that's so full of love it's breaking. "Because there is no one, no world, no universe for me without you." His breath stutters out against my lips. "I am *lost* without you, Eleanor." The first tear falls onto my cheek and his thumb is already waiting there to brush it away. "You have me for eternity. Without you, there is no past, or present, or future. You alone are my captivating insanity. The only infinity for me." He chokes. "My whole fucking existence in one being."

The tears are falling freely onto my cheeks by the time he finishes. My heart blown wide open by his words, into so many pieces, littering the air he spoke them into. So I do the only thing I can. The thing we're good at. I wrap my arm more tightly around him, pulling him even closer, and roll my hips. Answering him in the way we speak best. A rough laugh leaves his lips before he drops them back to mine and kisses me demandingly, never letting up as he picks up the pace inside of me.

It's not punishing like before, but the possession riding him is clear in every thrust, along with my answering reprimand. Each of our moves toeing that line we love to push each other over. Every caress that's just a touch past gentle. That tug of my hair that's just hard enough to sting before his fingers massage. My bite of his shoulder that's sure to leave a mark for days before I kiss the spot softly. It is the embodiment of carnal reverence that's been laced with remembered pain. Pain that's still there, but that has lessened just a bit in this moment of broken need.

It's not long before I feel us both start to truly be pulled into each other's gravity. His skin turns burning against mine, those smooth thrusts losing their steady pace here and there. And every inch of the skin he's claiming becomes hypersensitized, aching and needy under his touch as my pussy convulses around him over and over again. As if my body is trying desperately to cling to him forever so that it never has to suffer his loss again. He finds his end before me, thrusting hard and deep before going still, cock jerking inside of me as I balance on that edge.

But Coop knows me better than most.

Knows what I'd never admit that I like.

So he drops his head to that curve between my neck and shoulder, sucking the skin deep and dragging it through his teeth.

Setting me off as my universe compacts, centering suddenly on the feel of him coming inside of me before shattering outward with ecstasy on a scream.

And on the end of that scream, I gasp, the confession rattling through me. “I miss you.” I give him my words for once, the ones he’s been seeking.

Chapter Twenty-Five

Coop

One Year Ago

My incision is aching like fucking hell by the time I make it back to our home in Cahuita. The doctors had warned me that it was too soon to travel when I checked out of the hospital early this morning, but I had told them to go to hell, much to Jace's amusement as he chortled through it all next to me. Screw them all though, I was getting back to my girl. Today. Right fucking now, before the anxiety of not being able to hear her voice ate me alive.

And then I was spending the next twenty-four hours with her naked body all pressed up against mine. Even if I couldn't do anything about it quite yet.

Fuck 'em though, I might still try.

She was the only painkiller I needed.

I push open the red door of our home with my backpack in my hand, calling out for her as I do. "Princess?"

But my foot never even lands, just pauses in the air midstep, because I know.

I know as soon as that door swings open that something is horribly wrong here. I know it before I even see my books strewn and torn across the floor. Before I step farther into the house and smell the tequila in the air. Before my heart is torn right from my fucking chest and left as nothing more than a shredded lump of muscle resting beside her ring sitting atop our words on our bed.

I know it instantly because there's nothing reaching for me. Pulling at me. No vibrant brush of her presence against my skin to soothe the calamity in my head.

She's not here.

She's gone.

I rush forward, ignoring the sharp slice of pain from my still-healing wound until I stand in the middle of our home. My eyes darting around from one disastrous scene to the next, fucking gasping for breath at the nightmare before me.

How?

I press my eyes closed, trying to shut out what I'm seeing as my body begins to shake. Wanting it all to be some drug-induced nightmare I might wake up from, still stuck in the hospital. Or better yet, wake up in her arms.

Fuck… God, I've never begged you for anything but I'll give you whatever you want to make this a nightmare. To bring her back to me. To let me see her just once more.

But when I open my eyes, the tragic heartbreak screaming at me from every corner of our home makes it clear that this agony is reality.

But how? How the fuck did this happen? She was supposed to be waiting for me.

Terror claws its way up my throat with the sudden realization that she had to have figured out what I've been hiding, followed quickly by dread at the suspicion that she'll never forgive me. Never forgive me for not telling her the truth about our parents.

No. That's not possible. I wouldn't let that be possible. She had to forgive me. I couldn't have lost the answer to all the never-ending questions in my head. I couldn't lose the one person whose soul fit with mine so perfectly. That spark that had brought color to my monotone world. That couldn't be our story. Not after everything that we had been through side by side, even if she hadn't realized it, didn't remember it all.

My thoughts are jumping around in my head like fucking Ping-Pong balls and all I know is that I have to talk to her. I have to explain, to make her understand.

Dropping my backpack, I jerk the zipper open frantically and dig inside to find the new burner phone I had purchased at the airport. My hand closes around it and I whip the phone open, close to breaking it with how tightly I'm grasping it as I punch her number in.

Bringing the phone to my ear, I listen for the ringing to start, but it never does.

Only a dull buzz comes through the other end.

My whole body locks up as I quickly end the call before calling her again. Trying to place where I've heard that noise before. It's not the normal sound you get when someone's out of service but I'm so fucking panicked I can't think straight. Horrified at the thought of one more night without her.

But the same sound comes through the phone a second time. And a third.

What the fuck? Did she change her number?

No. That makes no sense if she changed her number…

It hits me then. Where I've heard that noise before.

It's the sound some of the spyware programs make at Bainbridge when we're trying to intercept a call or redirect it.

I can feel each slow pump of my mutilated heart lying on the bed beside the destruction of the girl that I love more than anything as my chaotic thoughts start to find a focus.

He had broken my phone.

He had… he had never called Eleanor, and he had broken my phone.

That moment of doubt when I was lying in the hospital bed and Jace popped off with the comment of how he managed to do that comes roaring back into my mind.

There was no way. Alec could shoot the top off a fucking soda bottle from three-thousand yards away. He was one of the few people at Bainbridge who was quite possibly better than me. No way was he dropping a fucking phone and breaking it.

And somehow, he had gotten that fucking trojan horse of a program onto her phone.

She must've… she thought that I left her.

I stare at the books on the floor, slowly blinking with the horrifying realization for a moment before a page from *Wuthering Heights* catches my eye and a primal scream rips from my throat. I reach down, flipping the mattress and sending our words and her ring flying. Uncaring about the stitches I can feel stretching and tearing in my stomach. The pain they bring is nothing in comparison to the absolute agony I feel throughout every inch of my body. Agony that shreds more deeply with every breath I heave.

She thought that I left her. And that would break her in a way I knew nothing had before. Because above anyone else, I was supposed to keep her safe, cherished, protected. I had sworn it to her in the mud and rain and then again when she married me. When I had imagined a whole beautiful, never-ending infinity with her. Only her.

And I had failed her.

I drop to my knees as my scream tries to turn into a sob, clenching my teeth against it as tears fall onto my cheeks for the first time I can remember since I was a boy. Swallowing down the cry, I force myself to take deep breaths through my nose. Using the oxygen to push through the pain eating me alive and to *think*.

There was only one person who held the answers here.

And he better hope whatever answer he had for his actions was adequate.

Because if it wasn't, if he had taken her from me without a fucking vital reason… I'd end him. If he turned out to be a threat to her for some unknowable reason, I'd squeeze the oxygen from his lungs without an ounce of remorse. Just like I had fallen in love with her with only the barest hint of guilt where Jace was concerned. Even when I knew she was the childhood memory he still held close to his heart. The girl that had been planned for him in a way.

But it hadn't mattered, not like it should have.

Because with each teasing word that brought me back to life, each cock of her brow that made me play in a way I hadn't in years, each hard-fought confession that made her immeasurably more precious to me. I knew.

No one else had mattered when it came to this one girl.

Because she was mine, our souls one and the same. Hearts timed perfectly to an answering call. Two broken parts of one mesmerizing whole. And I didn't care if it was because of some darkness that had invaded us at the sound of two gunshots and one crash of metal on a thundering night. Whatever we had become since, whether by miracle or fate or tragedy, there was no one else for her or me. And even if we were doomed to tragedy, it was an end I'd happily meet.

If only so that my fate could be written in the stars with hers for eternity.

So Alec had better hope he had an explanation for me. Or else, pretty soon, his heart would, quite literally, be the one mangled at my feet.

Chapter Twenty-Six

Present Day

I ran.

And I'm not even a little ashamed to admit it.

I fucking fled like someone had lit a fire under my ass, completely ignoring Coop's attempts to draw me into a conversation about what had happened.

No way was that happening.

I had felt utterly turned inside out after the postorgasmic haze had lifted enough for me to really start processing what had happened between us in the cellar. Every word we had spoken ringing through my head as I stood with wide eyes, watching his mouth open but not really hearing him. And the feelings… I'd needed space to even begin to unravel the feelings. Not to mention my orgasm-induced confession of missing him.

So I had thrown my bathing suit back on, jerked my head like some guy and muttered a "catch you later" before fleeing like my life depended on it. Only stopping long enough to grab a weed pen from the bowl on the kitchen counter before retreating to my room and locking the door. I had even texted the guys and told them I started my period like a little bitch to avoid them coming to look for me. And did I regret it? Nope, not one bit.

One proud little bitch right here.

Hell, I had even ordered a dozen cupcakes at one point and snuck downstairs to get them before absconding back to my room and shutting out the world. Hiding from reality despite all of my prior pep talks because all it would have taken was one look at me to know what had happened between Coop and me. It was, quite literally, written all over my skin.

So I had eaten cupcakes all day and watched reruns of *Survivor*, a show that, for the most part, guaranteed no romance and enough mental stimulation to keep me distracted. Distracted from the fact that my pussy was still throbbing with need despite being sore. And when a quiet knock had sounded on my door, I had tensed, but whoever it had been only knocked that once before soundlessly walking away. So it was no surprise that I had spent all night tossing and turning, filled with conflicted guilt and trying desperately to not compare myself to my mother.

When morning came though, I knew I couldn't hide anymore. So I pulled my big girl panties on, or in actuality, took them off to shower. Pausing to look at my naked body in the mirror and take stock of the damage done yesterday, the bruised lip and mark on my neck as telling as I knew they would be. I had turned from the reminders before they got to me too much though and stepped into the spray, washing the lingering scent of Coop from my skin. The act helped to settle my inner conflict into more melancholy. After that, I pulled a brush through my hair and threw on an oversized vintage Beatles shirt to match my mood before finishing it off with my uniform cutoff shorts.

Left with nothing else to do, I steel myself with a deep breath and open the bedroom door. Firmly reminding myself that it's still early and after the rager yesterday, entirely possible no one else is up yet. The quietness of the house as I walk down the hall to the stairs reflects my assumption but when I spy the empty drinks on the staircase, I can't help but roll my eyes at the obvious signs that the party had made it inside at some point. When I hit the bottom of the stairs though, the smell of coffee has guilt flaring back to life, making me want to run back to my room before I force myself to push through it and keep walking.

I round the corner to enter the kitchen, expecting it but still coming to a halt as my gaze finds Jace. A coffee cup in his hand and fully dressed already, the same as me. Our eyes meet and he searches mine in the silence, as if trying to place what he sees there before his gaze dips to my lip and stills. And I don't move, don't make excuses for what obviously happened. Just take the full weight of his gaze as he puts two and two together about why, exactly, I disappeared yesterday.

His hair is pulled back, allowing me to see the tension filling his face along with the pain in his firework eyes as he forces them to move again. Slowly flowing down the length of me before coming back to rest on the mark at my neck. He flicks them away quickly, clearing his throat and looking down into his coffee cup for a moment before lifting them back to meet mine.

And this time I see only resignation in his gaze.

Because this is what he told me to do. Maybe not explicitly to go bang his cousin in the cellar… but to make sure. To be sure of whatever decision I make.

But right now, I think he might be hating himself for that as much as the guilty pit in my stomach is trying to swallow me.

A small grin pulls at his lips that's so forced there's not even a hint of those dimples I love so much. "Don't feel guilty." He finally speaks.

"That's impossible."

"Yeah." He sighs, looking to the ceiling for a moment as an ironic laugh pours from his lips.

My brows drop in confusion. "What could possibly be funny about this?"

"Nothing." Another short laugh leaves him as he brings his eyes back to me. "Just thinking this must be what it felt like for him when he found you at my boat that day. Gotta say, I'm surprised he only hit me once."

His words have my face pinching up as I fight the urge to just fucking leave and remove myself from this equation entirely, to not be the wedge between them anymore. But at the end of the day, my heart won't let me and even I'm not stupid enough to deny that.

"Want to get out of here today?"

His voice breaks through my thoughts and I meet his gaze again, seeing the same heaviness there that I'm feeling. "Yeah." I nod. "Yeah, Dawson, I do."

***

I take Stef's Pagani and drive us to the PCH, the winding coastline road a must-see for anyone visiting LA. And the sun-drenched day was perfect for it. Nothing but endless miles of the Pacific dotted with surfers on one side and mountains on the other. It was a very Jace scene. I knew that, it was why I had picked it. Just like I knew that putting the top down and letting the drive to nowhere unwind us both would probably do a hell of a lot more for us than talking. The speed of the car helping us to come to grips with the ground shifting beneath our feet.

Plus, he had already said it, it wasn't like any of us didn't know what was going on here.

And sometime during the drive, I'm forced to admit that he was right, there is a war happening here. Because while I may have confessed to missing Coop yesterday, that confession alone meant that somewhere inside a part of me, I still loved him too. But out here on the road, away from him and with Jace at my side, the idea didn't seem as terrifying as it did in his presence. As fucked up as that was to admit. I blow out the realization with a breath though, letting the wind carry it back to the house we left behind to be picked up and examined at another time.

We drive for damn near three hours down the coast before I finally force myself to turn around. Hating that I can't just keep chasing the sun in front of us forever with him. Our drive back is just as silent as the one out had been, but it's a blissful kind of silence. Not a hint of pressure or awkwardness between us, only mutual release of the worry plaguing us both at Coop's very visible presence in my life again.

A much-needed break from reality.

But when we make it back into the city, Jace stops me from searching for food by placing a hand on my arm and pointing to the right. "Turn here."

"Why?"

He rolls his eyes with a hint of dimples. "Just do it, Blondie."

"Fine," I grumble, making the turn and then the following three he directs me through while checking his phone despite the hunger gnawing at me.

We're on Santa Monica Boulevard ten minutes later when he points to pull alongside the curb in front of a pink stucco structure with a black awning proclaiming it as a tattoo studio. I cock a brow at him in question but he just shoots me a mischievous look in answer and I park the car, the sleek black convertible earning a few appreciative looks from bystanders. Cutting off the engine, I open my door and step out, looking the shop over and seeing the neon-pink signs in the window offering piercings too.

I shoot him a teasing grin as he gets out of the car. "You thinking about adding another piercing to the merchandise, Dawson?"

"No." He laughs as I walk over to where he stands on the sidewalk. "That is not an experience I'm looking to repeat." A small shrug leaves his shoulders and he reaches up, brushing some of my windblown hair behind my ear. "This detour's for you."

My brows shoot up in surprise. "I hope you're not expecting me to add a piercing to my merchandise."

"No." Another quiet laugh leaves him before his voice turns as soft as his eyes. "But I know you have me and Coop pulling at you right now.

Tearing you in two different directions." He grabs my left wrist with his other hand, running his thumb over the tattoo there. "And I know you have one for him and me, but I thought you might like something for just you too." Dipping his head a little closer to mine, he lets the hand in my hair fall to tug at the ends playfully. "A little bit of Ellie, to remind you that we can never take anything you aren't willing to give." Those dimples flash with a small grin. "That your heart can only be captured willingly and that you were a badass long before we ever came along."

My heart melts right there on the sidewalk. Fucking dissolves in my chest into nothing but a light, comforting goop that's filled with sunrises and songs and firework eyes. A beat passes before I throw my arms around him, locking them behind his neck and breathing in his sea-spring scent. Eyes pricking just a bit as I do, his presence and priceless gift allowing me to let the last of my stress out on a deep sigh.

Jace fucking Dawson. What am I going to do with you?

He wraps an arm around my middle and brings his other hand to the back of my hair. "So I take it you like the idea?"

"I love it." I nod into his shoulder. "And I love you."

The arm around my middle squeezes a bit tighter as he answers quietly. "Glad to hear it, Blondie."

I don't let go of him for a minute, worried that if I do, I might lose the lightness he's shining on my soul. But then I remember his words and that he's right. Before Coop and him, I might have been a little more closed off and reckless, but I liked that girl just as much as the versions of her I became with them. Maybe not the ghost who existed in between so much, but I still learned something from her. From the heartbreak. And that maybe, with each experience, each of them, the unearthing of my parents' secrets, I was evolving into a better version of myself.

A version that at its core would always be based on that reckless girl that had left LA to see the world through the simplicity of her lens.

But who had found a world filled with so many brilliant spectrums that it had forced her to see the picture for the intricacies she had originally refused to acknowledge.

Because nothing was ever simple, not even a picture, not when you really looked deep enough.

"Thank you." I sigh, loosening my hold on his neck and leaning back to look at him.

"Of course."

I see the thread of hesitation in his questioning eyes and my lips twitch as I bring them to his in answer.

Don't worry, Dawson. I'm still with you.

"Yeah, well." His lips pull up against mine. "Ready to go pick something out?"

"Hell yeah." I laugh.

He grabs my hand and walks backward with a grin, tugging me into the shop that's just as eclectic on the inside as it appeared on the outside. Everything about it exuding that West LA vibe, from the plants hanging from the ceiling to the neon lights and wood paneling mixed with slate-blue walls. The faux fur chair at the entrance and random assortment of artwork are just the icing on the cake. Along with the large sign proclaiming that beauty is pain, because you know, we are in LA after all. A young, dark-haired girl with multiple piercings in the back of the shop notices us first.

"What can I do for you today?" she calls, walking forward to greet us.

"A tattoo," I answer her while thinking that I'm definitely going to have to get her number for Kai. She was just his type.

"What are you thinking?" She raises her brows at me in question. "Want to look at a book or something?"

"No." I shake my head and see Jace turn his head toward me in surprise. "Have you ever heard of a firebird?" I ask her.

"You mean the car or a phoenix?"

"No." I shake my head again. "Similar to a phoenix but not the same. It's a bird with more of an internal golden glow than flame."

"Hmm." She brings a finger to her chin, face turning thoughtful. "Let me go do a quick search and then we can sit down and I can sketch a few options out for you. Sound good?"

"Sounds perfect." I smile as she turns away before turning to meet Jace's curious gaze.

He tilts his head at me with a bemused look. "A firebird?"

"Yeah, uh," I start, darting my eyes away with rare hesitance. "It's one of the few memories I have of my mother. She would tell me this story sometimes about a firebird who stole golden apples from a king." I meet his gaze again with a half shrug. "I don't know, I remember her saying something about the bird being as likely to bring blessing as doom. Kinda a catch twenty-two. They were hunted for their rarity but also feared for the trouble they brought. It was a Slavic myth from where she came from I think."

"And you want this catch twenty-two doom bird on your body… why?" he drags out with an increasingly concerned look.

"Because," I shoot back quickly. "She also told me they lit up everything around them with their glowing golden feathers and jewel eyes." His look of continued confusion has me fighting the trickle of embarrassment that comes with revealing this story. "I kind of liked the idea of the bird which was hunted being able to decide whether to bestow blessing or doom. It made the idea of being caught not so scary, I guess. As if the prey held more power than the hunter for once."

A look of understanding fills his face and he reaches up to loop a hand around my shoulders, pulling me in tight. "I got you, Blondie."

"Plus…" I wrap my arms around his middle and sigh. "I'm trying to take Yvie's and your advice."

"What's that?"

Head pressed against his chest, I stare at that neon sign proclaiming beauty over pain and it takes me a moment to answer him softly. "Choosing to remember the good and not let her ghost haunt me."

Chapter Twenty-Seven

Present Day

I laugh while pushing open the door to Stef's, looking back at Jace and holding out the take-out bag from Neptune's Net teasingly. "I told you nothing beats the tacos here."

"Yeah, yeah," he drawls. "No need to rub it in, Delacroix."

We had stopped off at the famous local restaurant to feed my hangry self after the tattoo session before heading to the beach. Spending the rest of the day lying around in the sun and lightheartedly playing in the way Jace and I always did. The afternoon a soothing balm that I think he in particular might have needed after the shock of seeing me this morning.

And when he had asked to pick up takeout from the same restaurant on the way home, I had laughed my ass off, knowing I had just created another little addiction for him to sit side by side with his closet *Bridgerton* fandom.

His phone starts to ring as we come up alongside the stairs and he stops, pulling it from his pocket. "Uh." His brows pull down as he stares at the screen. "I got to take this."

I cock my head at him in question. "Everything okay?"

"Yeah." He clears his throat before looking up with a grin. "Yeah, it's just Zane. I think he's been missing me."

I narrow my eyes at him, unsure what's not settling right about his words. But when he reaches up and gives my hair a tug, I can't help the twitch of my lips.

"I'm sure." I roll my eyes, going up on my toes to give him a quick kiss. "Alright, well, go tell your boyfriend you're still alive."

"Will do." He laughs, turning quickly and taking the stairs two at a time as he flips open the phone. "Hey, man."

I watch him until he gets to the top, and he turns, flashing me those dimples one more time before walking down the hall.

A minute more passes before I shake my head at my own paranoia. Fucking seeing monsters where there were none now. A snort leaves me and I continue to walk through the foyer, intending to drop the takeout in the kitchen before seeing what everyone was up to.

But when I make it to the entry of the living area, I stop in my tracks at the sight that greets me.

Oh dear god, no.

Yvie and Coop are perched on opposite ends of the couch from each other, eyes narrowed and tense silence filling the air. Yvie's lips are all pinched up in the way they typically only get when she loses a case at work and the small, insolent smirk Coop's giving her in return clues me in real fast that they've probably been sitting there for a while now.

"Uh." I step into the space and both their gazes snap to me in a way-too-close imitation of the exorcist for my liking. "Hello?"

Apparently, I really should have paid more attention to that constant buzzing from my phone.

"Ellie," Yvie answers shortly before turning her suspicious glare back on Coop.

His lips twitch up as he meets my aunt's gaze head-on while greeting me, voice all kinds of intimate. "Princess."

Fuck my life.

My feet are moving before my brain even catches up to the fact I probably need to do some massive damage control here. And that's saying something coming from me.

Yvie lifts a hand in the air, pointing her finger toward the foyer. "Anyone without the last name Delacroix, out!"

I see that savage smirk spread over Coop's face and am already sucking in a breath in preparation. "Actually—"

"Cooper!"

He turns his head slowly and I see the spark of amusement in his dark eyes dim some at the obvious panic I'm sure he can see on my face. "Fine. Whatever you want." A purposeful pause fills the air before he continues with a ghost of lips. "Princess."

I roll my eyes as he stands and starts to walk toward me, his gaze immediately going to the gauze taped to the space below my right ear now that I have his full attention.

His brows drop harshly, voice coming out all kinds of tense. "What happened?"

"Nothing." I shake my head as he comes to stand before me. "Just a tattoo."

Surprise flashes across his face before he looks down at the spot curiously. "Of what?"

"I'll tell you later." I give him an exasperated look and shove the take-out bag at his chest. "Here. We got extra for everyone."

He looks at the bag for a second before taking it and dropping his lips to my cheek. "Did you have a nice run today?"

The quiet taunt is spoken against my skin with a soft brush of lips and I freeze for a second before narrowing my eyes at him as he lifts his head. "I don't know what you're talking about."

"Of course you don't." His lips twitch one more time before he turns toward the back patio. "I'll take this outside. Your boys should be back in an hour or so, they went to check on final preparations for the club opening tomorrow."

"Right," I mutter, watching as he walks to the back door and feeling a little guilty for being MIA on those preparations but considering everything I had going on in my personal life at the moment. I'd say it was pretty understandable too.

Plus, Stef's need for absolute control rivaled that of even Coop's, so there really was no point in the rest of us being there anyway.

"Oh, Eleanor?" Yvie calls mockingly, snapping me out of it and making me realize I was still watching Coop as he unpacked the food on the patio table.

Turning my head to her, I can't help but cringe at the no-bullshit look I find there.

"Come take a seat, dear niece." She pats the couch next to her. "Tell me about this situation you've gotten yourself into and I don't mean the new tattoo you're sporting."

Fuck, but it still feels like being called into the principal's office. Even at twenty-three. I drag my feet walking over to her, trying to get my bearings about me before collapsing onto the couch.

"What situation would that be exactly?" I quip.

She gives me a silent look of warning and I sigh under the pressure of her gaze, my inner child crumbling just a bit. "What do you want to know?"

Her gaze drifts to the back porch for a moment before coming back to me. "Cousins, right?"

I dart my eyes down at her question, reaching for the rolled edge of leather sealing the couch cushion and running my fingers along it while answering vaguely. "Mhmm."

"That would make him Adam's son, correct?"

"Guess so."

"I remember Adam well."

I lift my head in surprise, brows dropping at the small smile on her face. "Really?"

"Oh, yes." She laughs. "He was quite the Casanova growing up."

My mouth drops in horror. "Please tell me you never—"

"No." She waves a hand with a laugh. "No. I was too determined to make it big back then to really pay attention to guys."

A huge breath of relief bursts from me. "Thank fucking god."

"But it did make me think." Her eyes narrow on me, and I can sense her sliding into full lawyer mode. "If I remember correctly, Adam died right around the same time as your parents."

I drop my eyes from hers again, not needing to give her the answer she's already figured out.

"Oh, Ellie." She sighs, reaching over for my hand that's still playing with the leather of the couch. "You have gotten yourself into a little bit of a mess, huh?"

"Just a bit." I scoff tightly before clearing my throat and telling her softly. "I'm sorry."

"Whatever for?"

"I don't know." My face screws up as I bring my eyes back to hers. "It's a kind of betrayal, isn't it? To fall for the son of the guy who my mom had an affair with?"

Her eyes pick mine apart for a moment in the oddly comforting way only she's ever been able to manage. "Listen to me." She squeezes my hand with a sad smile. "It never seemed much of a fair concept to me that the sins of the parents should be visited on their children, would you agree?"

A beat passes and I give her a hesitant nod before voicing the argument I'm still struggling with. "It still seems like a fucked-up thing though."

"The world is full of fucked-up things, Eleanor." She shrugs. "You know this more than most. But for something beautiful to come out of tragedy, well, that's something worthwhile in my opinion." An irritated look rolls over her face as her eyes drop to my bruised lip. "Even if the boy's arrogance irks me to no end."

A small laugh leaves me at her obvious annoyance with Coop.

I got it, I really did.

"I'm guessing there's more to this story though?"

Her question silences my laughter instantly. "Yeah." I admit. "Yeah, there is."

"Well I'm all ears."

But your ears won't be hearing the whole truth, Yvie.

I know that absolutely. If I tell her the whole truth about Coop… she would flip. And right now, I was still trying to figure out my own feelings about it all way too much to have anyone else's in the mix, there were too many others here already.

So instead I shrug and use Coop's lame words again. "It's complicated."

"Really?" I'm the one on the receiving end of her irritated look this time. "That again?"

"Listen," I sigh wearily, dropping my head back against the couch and rolling it to look at her. "I could tell you more of the story, Yvie. I could, but that would only lead to more questions and frustration on both our parts.

And I don't want that." I give her a helpless shrug. "Right now, I just need to know you're there if I need you. I can promise you that I'm working on figuring it out, but I want to be able to do that without any background noise. I hope you can understand that."

A frustrated expression fills her face. "You've got to give me something here, Ellie." She holds up her fingers, bringing them almost into a pinch. "Just a tiny smidgen to explain how this all came to be."

I roll my head back to look at the ceiling, knowing she's not going to let up until I give her something and consider what to share. "Coop and I," I start, having to swallow down some of the lingering hurt that's still right there alongside the memory before forcing the rest out. "Coop and I actually met last summer. In Costa Rica. So I actually fell for him before I met Jace."

I can feel her shock in the silence that follows before she quietly muses. "That's why you ran away to Europe. Whatever happened between you and him. I always wondered why you abandoned your whole plan."

"Yeah," I answer softly before blowing out a breath and turning my head back to force a twitch of my lips. "So there you go. A tidbit."

"You're right, that just made it worse."

"I did warn you."

I watch her face pinch up, lips pursing with the effort it's taking her to keep from asking any more questions and can't help but laugh quietly.

"I'll be okay, Yvie." I squeeze her hand, ignoring the tug of intuition that comes with my next word. "Promise."

A beat passes before she shakes her head. “You always were a difficult child.” A small smile pulls at her lips as she continues. “Never could do things the easy way. Never would listen to advice. Even when you learned to ride a bike, you wouldn’t accept my help.” A puff of laughter leaves her and a wide smile breaks across my face at the memory. “Fell so many times I was sure you were going to break a bone, but you did it. Finally rode that bike down the driveway, dripping blood all along the way.” Her brows drop as she stares at me worriedly. “Just always had to do it the hard way.”

“What can I say?” I tease, tossing her a bratty smirk. “I like to keep things interesting.”

We stare at each other for a long moment before she sighs in defeat and gives my hand one last squeeze. “Fine.” She lets go, holding up her hands. “But if you need me…”

“I know,” I tell her before continuing softly, wanting to give her something for what I won’t. “You know I wouldn’t have made it without you, right? You were as good a parent as I could have ever asked for, Yvie.”

A taken aback expression fills her face in the silence that follows before she clears her throat. “Don’t make me cry, Ellie.” She stands from the couch. “I have to go meet Simon for dinner and that just wouldn’t be a good look.”

“Oooh Simon,” I drag out dreamily.

“Eleanor,” she chides.

“No, no.” I laugh, standing up and wrapping my arms around her. “I’m happy for you, really.”

"Good." Her voice is filled with relief as she hugs me back. "And Ellie, if you take any one bit of advice in this life from me, let it be to listen to your heart. Whatever it's telling you."

"Noted." I step back, giving her a smile. "Now go have fun at dinner."

Problem is, Yvie, my heart doesn't know what it wants any more than my head does.

"Alright!" She turns, starting to walk toward the foyer and calling out over her shoulder. "Oh, and don't let any of the assholes push you around either."

"Never!" I smile, watching her go and waiting until I hear the front door close before turning to the back porch.

My eyes find Coop immediately, his back to me from where he sits on the couch, looking at the sun setting over the California hills. Uncharacteristically respectful in his attempt to give me privacy. And I can't help but sigh at the confusion that just looking at him sparks.

We're the definition of convoluted.

But do I still want him, us, as convoluted as we are?

That's what I don't know.

Because Jace and I, we're black and white, perfectly balanced, effortless in a way that soothes every part of me. But Coop and I are every painful shade of gray in between. The heart-stopping dream and the beautiful tragedy. I shake my arms out, trying to dislodge the direction of my thoughts while walking to the back door.

Coop's head turns to me as I open the door, our eyes locking as he arches a brow. "I take it she wasn't my biggest fan?"

"Well," I start sarcastically. "You do make it hard sometimes with the whole silent antagonization bit."

He scoots over on the couch as I walk up and pause, not quite sure what to do.

I'm not stupid enough to try and delude myself that what happened yesterday doesn't change things between us but I also don't want him to assume it means more than it did. I don't want to give him the impression that everything is okay between us when it still very much is not and might never be.

"Sit, Eleanor," he demands with a small smirk. "Promise not to bite unless you beg me to."

I roll my eyes, taking a seat but leaving some space between us to maintain my boundaries.

Clearly someone's in a good mood today despite my disappearance.

"So can I see it?" He nods his head toward my new tattoo.

"Oh." I reach up, touching the gauze below my ear. "Uh, yeah."

Gently fingering the tape keeping it in place, I slowly pull it off, revealing the small firebird below that's all sweeping wings and a tail depicted in vibrant shades of red and gold.

He dips his head closer to look, brows dropping. "A phoenix?"

"A firebird."

He leans back with a soft laugh. "Appropriate."

"You know the story?"

"I do." He nods. "They're still big on their superstitious myths in some parts of Eastern Europe."

"I forget sometimes." I tilt my head at him in consideration. "How well traveled you must be from your work."

His eyes drill into mine for a moment. "Almost as well traveled as you after last year I'd wager."

"Right." I clear my throat and break our gaze. Knowing I need to clear a few things up with him after yesterday so that he doesn't get confused when the dynamics here don't magically change. "I wanted to tell you that you were wrong yesterday."

"About what?"

"It's not... not what you're assuming." I take a deep breath, trying to find the right words to explain before looking back at him. "I'm not using him to make you pay, Coop." His face tenses and I have to fight the urge to just abandon this conversation for both our sakes. "I already told you how bad it was for me after we, uh, after you left. I really did lose myself there for a while. But Jace." I clear my throat again awkwardly. "He showed me how to let it all go, to find some measure of peace. He brought me back in a way that made me better than before."

He stares at me for a long moment, tense silence flowing between us before giving me a single nod. "And I've already said I know that he was there for you when I..." He pauses, skirting the truth he still won't give me. "When I couldn't be. And as much as it fucking kills me, I am grateful to him for that." A quiet, humorless sound leaves him, and he looks away, jaw clenching for a moment before his eyes find mine again. "But Princess, don't give him too much credit either. He may have shown you the way, but I know you, and you'd never let anyone change you unless you were already halfway there yourself." He reaches up, running his thumb lightly over my cheek and continuing in a low voice. "And Eleanor, as much as you may give me a fucking heart attack sometimes, there's not a damn thing about you I would change. The only thing you ever needed help with was believing in the good, so if he gave you that, I'll give him anything in return except for you."

My heart gives a hard tug, breaths turning shallow as I stare into his night-forest eyes that are darkening by the second before I force myself to pull back and look away. *Needing* him to understand what I'm saying here despite what his words are doing to me.

"I won't give him up, Coop," I whisper. "He means too much to me."

"As much as I once did?"

"In a different way," I admit, looking back and meeting his now-shuttered gaze. "I told you. You broke me, and he dragged me into the light again. I won't throw him into the darkness in return."

A long moment passes between us, our gazes darting over each other and trying to figure out where we go from here before he responds. "I get that, Princess. I do." His lips part and he pauses, as if choosing his words carefully before continuing. "I mean, he's more than my cousin, Eleanor, he's like a brother to me and despite all this… like I said, I would give him anything. Anything but you." He blows out a breath, shaking his head before continuing. "Consider this though, is it right to keep dragging him through this when we both know how it ends?"

My eyes widen, imploring him to understand. "That's what I'm telling you, Coop," I argue softly, trying to ease the blow I know is about to hit. "I don't know *how* this ends yet."

He says nothing in return, just stares into my eyes intently as his brows drop. But I see the true fear there, peeking out from his shuttered gaze despite how he's trying to hide it from me. And for the first time since he walked onto that boat, I think he might actually believe me.

I think he finally understands.

Chapter Twenty-Eight

Present Day

My knee won't stop bouncing during the limo ride to Labyrinth, like all the nervous energy coursing through me is focused on that one part of my body, completely acting with a mind of its own. It's irritating the shit out of me, knocking around the dangling silver sequins of my flapper-esque minidress and making this annoying jingling noise as I stare at it threateningly. But I can't seem to control it any more than I can ease the nerves riding me, the cause suspected but undetermined.

Might have something to do with Jace Dawson sitting in the spot he quickly snagged next to me while Cooper Monroe sits across from us, staring through narrowed eyes. As if he's trying to work out how anyone else besides him could have ever worked their way so deeply into my heart.

Shocking, I know.

I let my eyes roll over the white button-down he's wearing that's standing out beautifully against his olive-toned skin before swallowing and looking back down. Catching sight of Jace's black one out of the corner of my eye. Apparently, they'd had a lovers-of-El meeting earlier and decided to really fuck with my perception of our reality tonight.

"Fucking hell, Els," Mac groans, quickly reaching across the limo from where he sits next to Coop and gripping the top of my knee. "Stop." He keeps his hand on my knee for a second, giving me a questioning look before slowly removing it as if he's ready to jump back into action at the first bounce. "Everything is going to be fine, you saw the club this morning. It's epic, everything we dreamed it would be."

I swallow again, trying to force the nerves down before managing an unenthusiastic. "I know."

"Don't get too excited or anything." He rolls his eyes, causing Kai and Stef to chuckle where they sit on the seat to my left.

I roll my eyes at him in turn as Jace drops his lips close to my ear, whispering with that playful sensuality. "You owe me a dance tonight, Blondie."

Coop's gaze narrows even further, and I suck in a breath, stomach flipping right as the limo comes to a slow stop and Stef's deep voice announces with amusement. "We're here."

"Oh, thank god."

A soft, melodic laugh sounds next to me as I exhale a deep breath, fully ready to get out of this confined space.

Stef slides across the seat, grabbing the handle of the door and buttoning his suit as he opens it, letting in the sound of the crowd and never-ending nightlife that is West Hollywood. Kai shoots me a wide grin, flashing that tongue ring, completely dressed down in his usual punkish attire before getting out next. Mac lingers, of course, briefly sliding his gaze between my two, uh, men and me before shaking his head and crouching to climb out after them.

Men? Lovers? Boyfriend? Husband? Bel amis?

Gosh, this was fucking confusing.

When neither of them makes a move to exit the limo though, I realize they're having yet another stare-off while waiting for me to go first.

I shake my head, sliding down the seat and trying to keep my legs closed so that I don't pull a Lohan while stretching my shiny black platform heels out of the limo. Stef is there waiting for me, hand outstretched to help me stand, and I meet his near-black eyes with a small twitch of my lips that are painted a bright red to hide the bruise still there. Bright flashes from the photographers covering the club opening come in quick succession as soon as I place my hand in his, their frequency increasing as he pulls me from the limo, helping immensely in keeping the indecently short dress in its proper place. I blink rapidly, keeping my hand in Stef's and that barely there smile on my lips, tilting my chin up in both defiance and invitation at the cameras.

Playing my part perfectly, if I do say so myself.

After a few more moments, I turn my head to make sure Coop and Jace are out of the limo and behind me before letting go of Stef's hand. Leading us forward and down the sidewalk with a teasing grin thrown over my shoulder for the cameras. One last money shot for the social sites tomorrow, despite the anxiety still filling me at being thrown into the spotlight more spectacularly than ever before. The large industrial light-brown brick building of Labyrinth looms before me with its large windows flashing different colors from the lights inside the club. And some, well, some windows don't show any light at all. One person's nightmare was another's fantasy, or something like that was how the saying goes.

And if not, it should.

I tilt my head to the side, taking in the line of people stretched around the building that we're completely bypassing, not even breaking my stride as scary-ass-looking bouncers unhook the red rope and let us pass without question. One of them pulls open the heavy, double black doors and I walk into the entrance chamber of the club before coming to a stop. The door slowly shuts behind us as we all come to stand inside, completely cutting off the sound from outside as it seals silently. Dark light fills the all-black chamber that's shaped like a half circle with four doors painted different colors and a neon-white script sign above them that simply reads one word, *Choose*.

I had laughed my fucking ass off when I saw it this morning, so much so that tears had leaked from my eyes and even Stef had started to chuckle. The irony of the sign we had picked at the start of this summer was definitely not lost on me. Stef's gold door lies all the way to the left with Mac's red door beside it, Kai's black one is next, with my silver one rounding us out on the right.

Decisions, decisions, decisions.

Choose, choose, choose.

That was the root of my problem tonight, I knew it. The nerves that were itching under my skin like a creature that was gnawing. And it had only gotten worse now that everything was out in the open, so to speak, both men very much aware of where the other stood. All of us knowing a decision had to be made eventually. Maybe not today, maybe not tomorrow, but I could feel it bearing down on me all the same. For someone that had lived their whole life with minimum attachments, I really had stepped off the ledge this past year. Free-falling with the ground rushing up at me, destruction or salvation just one tug away.

Wars have been fought over pussy. I'd heard that somewhere.

Should've paid better attention, I guess.

You're more than pussy to them, El. Stop being dramatic.

Well, true, but still… valid.

"Come on, Els," Mac calls, walking forward and grabbing the large brass handle on his door with that troublemaker smile. "You saw yours earlier, but you haven't seen mine in all its grandeur yet. You can show the strays yours on the way out."

I fight against the grin wanting to answer his before tossing out haughtily. "Fine."

Walking up to him, I bop him on top of the head when I make it there. Knowing the show I'm about to see is sure to impress, but still, can't ever let his ego get too big. Not even on a night like this.

I put my back against the door, keeping it open as Mac goes in and cocking a brow at Jace and Coop. "Want to come see what Mac's definition of fun is?"

Stef and Kai just shake their heads, going to their respective doors while Coop's lips twitch. He walks forward first, coming close enough that our bodies brush against one another's and making mine tense until he passes.

Jace just lifts his brows, walking up while muttering. "This should be interesting."

"You have no idea." I laugh as he passes by, stepping in after him and letting the door shut behind me.

Every surface is covered in red. Red walls, red lights, red velvet floors. The only part of the long hallway stretching out in front of us with twists and turns that aren't red are the glass displays built into the walls. Similar to what you would see a mannequin inside of and spaced out every ten feet or so along the hall.

Except these most definitely do not have mannequins in them.

They have people, people in various states of dress and undress, in everything from regular party clothes to lingerie and costumes. People of every shape and size, male and female. Some inanely innocent, just sitting in a chair with their legs propped up reading a book, and others, well, others decidedly less so. A heady, bass-pumping beat plays in the air as we walk and I watch Coop and Jace take in the hedonistic display curiously, finding no judgment in either of their gazes.

Jace's too-perceptive eyes eventually slide to Mac as we round one of the turns at about the halfway point. "You like to watch," he guesses, tilting his head at him in question.

Mac just smiles. "I like a good many things, stray."

Coop's brows drop down as we come alongside a particularly interesting display with a couple inside, playing what I believe is a game of *Twister*. Involving Saran Wrap.

"They're like Barbie dolls in a box."

"Exactly!" Mac throws up his hands in victory. "Somebody gets it. Finally."

I roll my eyes, making sure they land on Coop on the way down. "Did you really have to encourage him?"

"Just making an observation, Princess." His lips ghost up, eyes locking with mine and darkening with desire instantly.

And I do understand it.

The environment of this whole club practically invites you to play out your most forbidden fantasies. We designed it that way.

Quickly breaking our gaze, I look forward and breathe out a sigh of relief at the sight of the door at the end of the hall. Needing a little space to get my bearings.

Mac jogs forward, holding open the door for us and I pause, letting Jace and Coop go first as we come alongside him. I look up into his sapphire eyes and give him what I know he needs. "You did good, Macallan." I grin, because he is my twin and my opinion matters most to him. "It's fucking killer."

"God." He shakes his head. "You're such a head trip sometimes. Always sour before sweet."

"You need it." I shrug.

"I'm not sure what I need."

"You'll know when you find her."

He looks like he swallowed a lemon at my words. "Don't put that shit on me. You're the only one of us who's probably going to procreate one day and even that came as a shock to me."

I throw back my head, laughing openly at the blatant refusal that he'll ever find love and causing his distasteful expression to deepen. "I'll remember that." I giggle.

"You do that."

I'm still laughing under my breath as I step onto the second-story landing that all of the doors lead to. The VIP section sits on either side of it, enclosed by wrought iron gates and looking down on the circular first-floor bar area below. There's a floor-to-ceiling bar in the center of the space, something from a bygone age that looks straight out of *The Great Gatsby* with its wraparound ladders and selection of liquors on display. The ceiling is a mosaic of fractured mirrors, reflecting the scene from the first floor in disorienting detail while the walls of the space are painted a deep burgundy and couches made of black leather litter the space. And directly in front of us is the main walkway that leads down onto the first floor for all the non-VIP visitors.

Our individual rooms are evenly spaced out around the circular space, the name of each written above it with the little taglines we came up with in smaller letters either below it, above it, or both. *Reminisce over days past*, for Stef; *Revel in the present*, for Mac; *step into the Forbidden future*, for

Kai; *and Fracture from the memories*, for me. All decided on after quite a few bottles of wine for our own reasons, besides Mac of course.

But what immediately draws my gaze are the acrobats hanging in the air around the bar, going up and down, doing tricks on their aerial silks as the audience looks on with awe. Because why not, right? If you're going to do something, do it right or not at all.

Even if that liability insurance was a bitch.

"Damn, Delacroix." Jace whistles in front of me, delight in his voice as he looks back at me with a grin. "You weren't lying about that bartender gig."

"Me?" I give him a grin and wink. "Never."

"Come on," Mac calls, drawing my gaze over the steady thump of the DJ setup to our right. "They're waiting." He nods to the left and my eyes find Stef and Kai, already sitting in our private VIP area for the night.

I follow behind Mac, dodging a few people stepping out from one of the doors and onto the landing before arriving at the VIP area, where he's holding the gate open for me. Stef gives me a nod from where he sits on the couch, standing as I enter and holding out a glass to me silently that I'm sure is already filled with añejo. I give him a smile of thanks as he passes the glass to me, the hard glint in his eyes clueing me into the fact that I'm not the only one on edge tonight. Although, his nerves probably have more to do with the club opening than any kind of romantic situation.

I take a sip of my tequila, watching as he nods to Mac and Kai, giving them the silent signal to stand before catching the DJ's eye. He makes a quick slashing motion across his throat and a few moments later the music in the club cuts off, plunging everyone into silence as a spotlight lands on our VIP section. Every eye in the place immediately turns to us and Stef wastes no time in stepping up to the railing, slowly bracing his hands wide on it as we gather around him.

One of the staff quickly walks over, passing him a mic, and he brings it to his lips. "Welcome." His deep voice booms through the club with the quiet word and I see the doors to our rooms open as people peek out to see what's going on. He turns his head, running his eyes over all the people below before continuing. "The idea for Labyrinth came to us this past year while we were traveling Europe. Particularly when we visited Rome and Greece." That secret smile briefly plays across his face. "Although *Moulin Rouge* might've played a part in its inception too, *non sei d'accordo?*" A few of the girls in the audience actually swoon a little at his casual Italian and I have to take a sip of my añejo to hide the roll of my eyes. "But the idea of bread and circuses, the lost appreciation of myths and legends, the seductive beauty of the forbidden oracle. The invitation to step into the labyrinth and slay the modern-day monster that is inhibition." He pauses, letting his gaze flow over the crowd again. "To indulge in the fantasy for a moment. That is Labyrinth… and I invite you to partake."

Dropping the mic, he nods to the DJ and the music starts back up instantly but at a slower, more hypnotic rhythm than before. I grab his arm as he turns, lifting my lips to his ear as he passes the mic off to a waitress. "This place is all you, Stef. It never would've happened if left up to Mac,

Kai, and me. So thank you." I lean back, giving him a teasing smile and reaching up to wiggle his tie, loosening it a bit. "Now try to enjoy it a bit tonight, yeah?"

He reaches up, cupping my cheek as his eyes turn soft, an indulgent smile pulling at his lips. "Of course, *cara*."

My smile grows wide at his words and I turn, seeing that Jace and Coop have settled themselves into opposite ends of the couch behind me. Pausing, I dart my eyes between them, meeting both of their expectant gazes before shaking my head with a laugh.

"Nope." I take a sip of my añejo before continuing to laugh quietly while walking to the leather chair beside the couch. "Not happening."

Kai wastes no time in settling himself between them while Mac and Stef take the couch across from me.

"Shots!" Kai shouts and brings his hand up before slapping their legs on the way down.

And it goes like that for a while, all of us taking shots and talking. Laughing over stories from Europe and enjoying the atmosphere of the club we created, the hard work put in, theirs slightly more than mine. But I brought the feminine touch because god knows none of them knew what a girl really needed in her restroom so they had lucked out. And eventually, between the alcohol and the familiarity of family, I feel the nerves that've been coursing through me start to fade. My shoulders drop and loosen as the tension eases under the steady pounding of the music.

Eventually Coop leans over from where he's sitting near me on the couch, sipping at the beer in his hand while eyeing me consideringly.

"What?" I prod, the tequila loosening my tongue and shortening my patience per usual.

He lowers the bottle from his mouth. "Do you enjoy it?"

"Enjoy what?"

"The mini-socialite thing?" He dips his beer toward the club. "You never talked about all this in Costa Rica. Just seemed happy to escape."

I pause, sipping at my añejo and considering his question while casting my gaze over the club. "All of this hadn't really come to life yet back then but a part of me does. I like the spotlight, the—"

"Attention," he guesses.

I meet his gaze and a beat passes before I reluctantly admit, "Yeah." My lips twitch. "Not a great quality. Trust me, I know."

"We're all vain in some way, Princess," he muses. "It's not a crime as long as you're aware of it and don't abuse it."

"I'm sure I have a time or two." My brows drop with the confession and I look down into my glass as I continue. "Really though, I like it because it reminds me that no matter how many times they whispered about me," I shrug, lifting my eyes back to his. "I don't know, it was stupid kid stuff that shouldn't matter really. But it reminds me that I rose above it all. Above them. Used it to rise higher than they could reach." The memory of Cahuita brings a small smile to my lips though, and I give him, "But I did enjoy the escape too."

His eyes soften on mine, those full lips opening and sucking in a breath to respond right before he stops and his eyes drop to the front pocket of his jeans. He blows out the breath he just inhaled, digging the phone out and his expression shutters at the sight of whoever's on the other end. And just like that, the air between us turns heavy, filled with so many unspoken words that he won't give me.

"It's fine," I snap, voice deadening at the reminder of everything still between us.

His eyes dart up to mine and I see his hand tighten on the phone. "Eleanor…" He drags out with regret.

"It's fine, Coop." I take another sip, trying to burn away the twinge in my heart and looking away toward the first floor below. "Go take your call. It's not like your shit is new."

He only pauses for a second longer before I hear him blow out a deep breath and watch out of the corner of my eye as he stands, working his way out of the VIP area. My heart gives another little twinge when he makes it out of sight, which only serves to piss me off more. Hating that I just gave him something, however small it may have been, and yet again, got nothing back in return. Nothing real at least. Nothing truthful and meaningful about the things he's still holding out on where we're concerned. I roll my shoulders with a deep breath, determined to not let him tense me back up again while staring blankly at all the happy clubgoers.

A few minutes pass before someone comes to stand in front of me and my eyes lift to see Jace's too-perceptive gaze looking down at me. Hair pulled back into a messy bun at the back of his head and looking a little more sinful than usual with the way he left a few more buttons than necessary undone at the top of his shirt.

"What do you say, Blondie?" He leans down, bracing his hands on the arms of my chair. "Wanna take me to your room?" His beautifully arched lips lift with a playful grin. "Show me your moves?"

My heart immediately lightens as I stare into his firework eyes and I throw back the last of my añejo before bringing my lips to his with a soft kiss. "Absolutely, Dawson."

He takes the empty glass from my hand, eyes never leaving mine as he passes it to Mac behind him and winds his fingers through mine. Tugging me up to stand and wrapping an arm around my waist as he brings his lips to my ear. "Let's go have some fucking fun, yeah?"

Chapter Twenty-Nine

Present Day

My hips sway to the sensual beat of the music pumping through my room at Labyrinth. Body covered in a light sheen of perspiration already and a wide smile on my face at the absolute perfection of it. The entire room, with the exception of the floor, is covered in a mosaic of reflective surfaces with columns sprouting out of the ground here and there that I had Kai design to look like modern art pieces. The effect is disorienting, but in a hypnotic kind of sense. Making it seem as if the crowd around you is both pressing in and not really there at all. As if there's no beginning or end to the room. Only an infinite space of music and dancing that you could get lost in, never able to find your way out again. Leaving the body pressed against yours the only reality for your senses to anchor themselves in.

And oh what a body it is.

All hard planes pressed against me, shining with the glorious temptation of the sun. I watch the refracted pieces of him behind me in the column of mirrors closest to us, his body moving with mine in that perfect synchronization we have together. Our hips swaying in an effortless translation of the beat with his hands on my hips. His eyes catch mine in the mirrors and I can't help but throw my head back with laughter at the wicked grin he flashes me. The brilliant energy of him thrumming against me in a far more intoxicating beat than anything the music or room could offer. I lean my head back against his chest and look up straight into his firework eyes, seeing how those dimples are still on full display.

He lets go of my hip, beginning to lightly trail his fingers over my stomach teasingly and I know he's hard already, can feel him pressing against my ass with need. But it's kind of unavoidable considering the way we're dancing and that we're two people who are very much aware of the desire we have for one another. When his fingers start a path downward though, my smile falters a bit. And when he drags them lightly over my pussy to the borderline scandalous edge of my dress, I reach out to grip his arm but not to stop him. His dimples fade, expression still playful but more heavy with desire as he traces his fingers back and forth high on my thigh. The teasing touches causing desire to pool low in me until my pussy is practically throbbing with it. My lips part as I stare into his eyes and those dimples make an appearance again as his eyes dip to the sight.

"Jace." I try to scold, although it ends up coming out a bit too breathy to be taken seriously.

"Yes, Ellie?" He blinks innocently.

Such a little shit. Always playing with me.

I narrow my eyes in warning. "Don't play unless you plan on doing something about it, Dawson."

"Oh, Delacroix." He dips his head closer to mine and blatantly slides his hand under my dress, running his fingers over the edge of my underwear. "I very much plan on doing something about it." I feel two of his fingers push my underwear aside and quickly find my clit, causing my pace to falter as he circles it while speaking. "This whole place is a fantasy. Y'all definitely did it right." His fingers dip down, plunging inside of me and stroking against that glorious spot. Not a care in the world that we're in the middle of the dance floor and starting up a far more carnal kind as my hips grind back against him. "But Ellie." He dips his head, pressing his lips to mine with a teasing upside-down kiss before lifting to speak in an intimate voice. "You're the only fantasy I want tonight. Just you, with me, all night. That's the only fantasy I need." I feel his fingers leave me and my mouth opens in protest, thoroughly fucking confused as to why he just denied me the very public orgasm we were working toward until I see him lift them to his lips. And my mouth stays open as I watch him suck the fingers that were just inside me into his mouth as if they're his favorite lollipop.

His eyes are practically glowing with mischief in the dark club as he pulls his fingers from his lips, immediately dropping them to mine and sweeping his tongue in. My eyes close as he feeds me the taste of myself, almost causing me to combust right on the spot from how fucking hot it all is.

He pulls back just a bit, speaking against my lips. "So what do you say? Want to get out of here and go indulge in each other, huh?"

I only pause the briefest second, the first thought in my mind for Coop and the second filled with the reminder that he's given me nothing while demanding everything.

"I thought you'd never ask." My lips twitch against his. "And I just happen to know the back way out of here."

***

We crash through the front door of Stef's, stumbling and laughing into our kiss as I clumsily try to unbutton his shirt while he kicks the door shut behind us.

"I think we scared that Uber driver for life."

"Nah." I get a button undone, somehow managing to not trip over my own feet. "Just gave him some spank bank material for later."

He reaches down, hooking his hands behind my legs and I quickly catch on, jumping as he lifts me before walking to the stairs. "Trust me, Blondie. You in that dress is material enough."

"Jace Dawson," I tease playfully, pressing my lips to his and successfully undoing a few more of the buttons on his shirt as he walks us up the stairs. "You are a charmer."

I feel his lips pull up to grin against mine. "Just one of my endless attributes."

I laugh into our kiss again, abandoning his shirt to bring my hands up and cup his face as he walks us down the hall. Passing my room without pause and taking me straight to his. He opens the door with one hand and walks us in before letting go of my legs to grasp my waist, slowly allowing my body to slide down his. I look up at him when my feet hit the floor, feeling the electric charge in the air between us as he brings his hand up to gently brush my hair behind my ear. Letting my eyes run over his face as I take a moment to appreciate the beauty of him. It still knocks me on my ass sometimes. In moments like this when it catches me by surprise, as if I'm seeing him in that bar for the first time all over again. Those arching cheekbones, defined lips and playful almond-shaped eyes all shining with blinding sensuality that somehow manages to warm the soul.

"Go get on the bed, Ellie."

I cock my head at him. "And if I don't?"

His eyes narrow at me just a hint in our play. "Then you won't get to see all the wicked things I have in store."

I sigh dramatically, tilting my head up toward the ceiling as if to ponder the decision before answering indifferently. "I suppose."

"Oh you suppose?"

"That's what I said, right?"

A grin flashes across his face about a second before he reaches down, gripping the bottom of my dress and pulling it up suddenly. Leaving me laughing as it tangles in my arms before he lifts it over my head and tosses it to the side. The sound of sequins hitting the ground fills the air as his eyes land on my almost naked body and turn heated as they run over the matching red lace bra and panties I'm wearing underneath.

"Oh, yeah." He swallows visibly. "Go get on the bed, Delacroix."

I give him an inviting grin and reach out to grab his hand before slowly walking backward to the bed. Already knowing the layout of the standard beige guest room and not needing to look to see where I'm going. His eyes stay on me as we walk, running over my body again and again as if he can't drink in the sight of me enough. And the feeling is mutual, because when the back of my knees hit the bed, I sit and let go of his hand so I can undo the last couple buttons of his shirt.

The shirt finally opens up completely and I jerk my head up at him. "Your turn."

"Of course, empress." He grins, shaking the shirt off his shoulders and causing me to suck in a breath as my eyes immediately go to that *V* cut, dipping down teasingly below his pants.

Unable to resist the temptation, I lean forward and dart my tongue out, running it over one of the deep lines with slow appreciation and causing him to groan. His hand immediately goes to my hair and I give the other side the same treatment before leaning back with a smirk to blow lightly against the wet skin.

How do you like those tables turning, Dawson?

"Fuck."

The groaned word escapes him as I bring my hands to the button of his pants, wiggling it free before pulling the zipper down and pushing them over his hips along with his underwear. His pierced cock springs free and I waste no time, immediately taking him in my mouth as he groans again. Swirling my tongue around the head and playing with the metal there.

Flicking it in the way I know pushes him right to the edge before sinking down, taking him as far back as I can until he hits the back of my throat and makes me have to swallow to keep from choking. I rise back up to flick at the tip again and his hand tightens in my hair, tugging me back gently.

I let him slip from between my lips and lift my eyes up to his. “What?”

“As much as I’m enjoying this.” He unwinds his fingers from my hair, reaching down to run his thumb over my bottom lip and spread the wetness there as his gaze follows the motion with a regretful look. “I have big plans for tonight.”

I cock a brow at him. “Which are?”

A mischievous look fills his gaze as it comes back to mine. “Lie down.”

“Someone’s feeling bossy tonight.”

He rolls his eyes, giving my shoulder a light push. “Lie down, Blondie.”

I do as he asks, scooting back on the bed before lying back and propping myself up on my elbows. Genuinely curious as to where he’s going to take this, what corner our play is about to turn and whether I’m going to like the street we land on.

He steps out of his pants quickly before reaching up to grab the top of my underwear. “How many times have you ever O’d in a row?”

Oh dear lord. I think I’m going to like this street very much.

Maybe buy a house. Put a pool in. Could even learn to cook if it means I get to live here.

“Uh.” My stomach flips, pussy tingling with desire as he slowly slides my underwear down my legs and I stutter. “T-two? Three?”

He gives a casual nod, lifting my underwear to dangle them on one finger. "Thought so." His brows lift as he tosses them behind his shoulder carelessly. "Let's see if we can top that, yeah?"

I'm the one cursing this time as he grabs my heels, pushing them up and spreading me wide on the bed before trailing his fingers up my legs.

"You know," he muses, kneeling on the bed when his fingers reach the top of my legs. "People really are like instruments." I suck in a breath as his fingers begin to lightly run over the lips of my pussy. "You have to take the time to learn them, which movements strike just the right chords." He dips his fingers inside of me and I clench the sheets in answer as my pussy does the same. Body tight with anticipation and unbelievably turned on by this little lesson he's giving me. "How to play those notes together to actually make music instead of just random noise." Bracing his hand on my leg, he dips his head down to give my clit a quick lick before flashing me a grin. "Which type of music that particular instrument favors."

"Right," I gasp, damn well ready to agree to anything he would ask of me right now.

He hooks those fingers inside of me, running them back and forth over that perfect spot while moving the hand on my leg up to my pussy. Spreading me before him as he dips his mouth to my clit again and begins to run his tongue over it mercilessly. My hips buck immediately at the brazen contact, head falling back to hit the bed, but he only uses the bucking to his advantage. Pushing his mouth harder against me, relentless in his pursuit of the orgasm that's barreling down on me. He starts to circle the sensitive nub a couple times before making a pass over it, pushing down hard as he does and it only takes a few more passes to set me off like a rocket.

I scream his name as I come, thrashing underneath his mouth but he doesn't let up, just continues to flick that tongue over my clit. Pumping his fingers deeper inside of me as he does and pressing down harder with his mouth. Leaving my body shaking as I gasp for breath, still under the throes of one orgasm while quickly locking up with the next. He brings his fingers right to the edge of my opening, almost pulling them out before adding a third to the mix and thrusting them back inside of me. Picking up the pace of everything and making me abandon all pretense as I let go of the sheets to grip at his head. Desperate for anything he's willing to give me.

And when he starts to hum against my clit I barely have time to process what's happening as a second orgasm rips through me viciously, more powerfully than the first. Making my entire body go tight right before my pussy gushes against his mouth and a scream rips from my lips. My vision spots and I'm panting by the time it ends, focused only on the feeling of Jace still licking at me. Gentle now though, as if he's seeing me through and making sure the crash on the other side isn't too hard.

He stops after a moment, giving my pussy a soft kiss. "Not a piano or violin."

It takes me a few breaths to process what he said, coming up empty. "What?" I manage to gasp, rolling my head to the side to look down at him.

He flicks those firework eyes up to mine and I find them full of delight. "You."

"What?"

I'm definitely losing brain cells here, but I'll happily show them the door if it means I get more of this.

"You." He lifts up to place another kiss just above my slit and this time I'm coherent enough to feel how wet his mouth is from me. "Eleanor Delacroix." Kissing his way up over my stomach, he continues. "Are not a piano or violin. Too delicate an instrument for you although your beauty rivals them." He makes it to my bra and quickly finds the front clasp, flicking it open and letting my breasts fall out as he dips his mouth. Pulling my nipple into his mouth and rolling his tongue over it, making me wiggle with fresh need even though my body is already on the edge of being spent. He lets my breast pop free of his mouth and brings his hands up, placing them on either side of my head. Finally looking down at me with a soft look.

It's one I know well. It's the one that made me fall for him in the first place. All care and mischievous play that I just couldn't resist. It's the look that brought me back to life and it has me reaching up to wrap my arms around his neck as my heart grows in my chest.

"Not a guitar either." He dips his lips to mine, pulling at them teasingly while lowering his hips. Pressing them against mine for a moment before I feel him nudge against my entrance. "Too simple. Straightforward in a way I don't think you've ever been." I feel him push into me an inch, lingering there for a moment and letting the anticipation ratchet up to the point that

I'm just about to pop off with a bratty comment right before he thrusts into me. Sliding home without hesitation or issue because I'm beyond wet for him.

"Jace!" I shout his name, feeling that piercing nudging inside of me as he rolls his hips.

My legs come up, hitching over his hips as I roll up to meet him, pushing him deeper as he speaks again. "Maybe drums." His voice comes out sharper than before, as if he's having to hold himself in check and he leans back to look down at me thoughtfully. "Deceptively straightforward when they're really anything but." He brings a hand up, pushing my hair back and winding his fingers through it. "A little in your face, setting the tempo for the whole damn band. And man, when that solo hits," His eyes roll over my face with a mesmerized look before coming back to meet mine. "Nothing's more spectacular."

He pulls back before thrusting into me with a slow kind of torture and dipping his lips to mine again. "Yeah, you're a drum girl. One of a kind. The kind of instrument you can work at forever and still not manage to master."

His words have my heart hurting with a pain I just want more of and when he starts to move inside of me, I grip at his shoulders to pull him as close as I can. Quickly finding that even with him inside of me, our bodies as close as you can ever get to another human being, it's still not enough. I move my heels up, digging them into his ass and he thrusts as deep as he can before going still. Keeping himself there as he slides a hand between us to my clit and begins to circle it with his fingers. My back bows immediately, chest pressing against his as soft cries begin to pour from my mouth, the hypersensitized nub hardly able to handle his attentions. And it's not long before I feel my pussy begin to lock down around his cock with more force than before as if it's greedy at finally having something there.

He starts to move right when the third orgasm hits, prolonging the pleasure until it borders on almost too intense. Almost more than I can take. Leaving me biting my lip to keep the word stop from escaping before he finally lets up on my clit and begins to thrust inside of me in earnest. Not even giving me a chance to catch my breath before he starts to roll his hips, dragging that piercing over my inner walls that are still clinging to him with aftershocks and sending little twinges of pleasure through me that have open-mouthed cries leaving my lips.

He dips his mouth to my neck, trailing a path of kisses to my ear before whispering. "What do you think, pretty girl?" I feel him bite down on the lobe, gently pulling it through his teeth. "You got one more in you for me?" He lifts up, meeting my eyes and flashing those dimples before bringing his lips to mine. "Promise I'll make it worth your while."

I give him a nod, beyond coherent speech at this point and he flashes those dimples at me once more before rising. Sliding his hands down to my hips and grasping them gently as he quickly flips me over, completely in control of my loose body. He lifts my hips, putting us at just the right angle as he runs a hand over my ass and starts to thrust slowly inside of me again.

I feel his fingers press into my ass cheek, pulling it to the side and causing my body to tighten up with hesitation before he speaks.

"See, now I'm torn, Blondie." His voice comes out in a husky kind of melody and I can hear that thread of possession in it. "Because I want to blow your mind a little." He presses a finger against the tight entrance of my ass, making me gasp. "But I also want to come inside of you more than my next breath. Leave a little bit of myself inside there." His proclamation is followed up by a powerful thrust that has a soft cry leaving my lips as I roll my head back to look at him, sheets moving underneath my cheek. I find his eyes on my ass, flicking a few times between where he's entering me and higher up on the place he wants to for a moment before coming up to meet mine.

A slow grin spreads on his face. "But why not both, right?"

"Uh—" My unintelligible start of a question is cut off at the sight of his mouth moving, cheeks sucking in a bit as his eyes drop back to my ass right before he lets a small stream of spit out to land against the tight entrance of it with unerring accuracy.

I narrow my eyes on him. "You've done this before."

He flicks those playful eyes up to mine with a shrug. "A time or two." I watch as he brings two fingers up to spread the lube of his spit around, the tattoo on his arm a swirling murk of ink in the low lighting of the room. "But all for your gain in the end." He starts to press those fingers inside of me and I suck in a breath at the foreign feeling. "That's it, Ellie." He thrusts shallowly into my pussy while sinking those fingers in a bit more. "Just relax and let us have both."

I do as he asks, forcing my body to go loose again and not letting it tense up as he fills both of my entrances up. Thrusting shallowly still as he works his fingers in enough to start the same motion up with them. Most definitely blowing my mind with the way I can feel him pressing them against his cock inside of me. He gives me a minute to adjust before picking up the pace and my whole body starts to shake uncontrollably in response. Cries pouring from my mouth as I watch what he's doing to me and feel him hitting me with that piercing with every hard thrust. And I'm so on edge from the previous orgasms, toeing that pleasure-filled line of being too sore yet still slick, that I know it's going to be quick.

But when he lets go of my hip to loop his arm around and slide his hand down to my clit again, I manage to gasp. "I can't."

His eyes search mine for a second. "Don't quit on me now, Delacroix." He flashes his dimples and circles the bundle once, making my whole body jerk back onto his fingers and cock. "You with me?"

I pause for only a second before giving him a nod. "Yeah." He circles my clit again, leaving me practically screaming as my hips buck again. "I'm with you!"

"Good girl."

He lets loose on me then, thrusting and circling, hitting every single sensitive spot on my body in quick succession and it's only seconds before I break apart more completely than I think I ever have. Screaming my throat raw and locking down around him with every muscle as wave after wave of the orgasm drowns me in euphoria. I feel him follow me then, continuing to thrust as he fills me up just like he wanted to and I manage to somehow keep my body aloft until he's finished.

I collapse onto the bed, barely even noticing his fingers slip from my ass until he laughs lightly and presses a soft kiss to my shoulder. "Be right back, pretty girl."

"Hmm," I mumble drowsily, mind and body totally spent.

I hear the water from the sink run for a minute before it shuts off and the bed dips beside me as he slides in. He reaches for me, gathering me up in his arms and pressing my back to his chest before sliding a leg between mine. And I'm almost asleep when he speaks again, completely swept up in the boneless bliss of my body and his sea-spring scent.

"The thing is…" His voice comes out hesitant as he brings a hand up to play with the ends of my hair. "Coop may be your stars and I may be your sun, but Ellie, you're our goddamn sky." His chest heaves against my back with a sigh. "I'm not sure what place we have, how either of us is supposed to exist without you."

I'm silent for a long time, heart clenching up painfully in my chest before I bring a hand up and grasp his arm around my stomach, squeezing it as I answer. "You won't."

But for the second time since I met him, I'm not sure whether I'm speaking a truth or telling a lie because the reality I'm coming to terms with is that I'm not sure I can bear to lose either of them. Even Coop, with all his withheld words he might only ever write on my skin. It'd be like losing half of my heart and I just can't wrap my head around how it's supposed to keep beating after a loss like that.

How I'm supposed to survive something like that again.

Chapter Thirty

Jace

Present Day

I wait until I'm sure Ellie's asleep before slipping from the bed, thirsty as hell after blowing her mind in the most satisfying way. My inner caveman fucking basking in the fact that I now had achieved what no man before me had. But I knew my girl. And she was *my girl*, even if she was Coop's a little too. Just for right now though, or at least that's what I kept telling myself. I pull my bottom lip through my teeth at the unpleasant jealousy spreading through me at the thought and quietly pull the door to my room closed. Not wanting to wake her and make her face who I know got back about an hour ago when we were still in the thick of it.

But he needed a reminder that this game wasn't his to win after all those fucking marks he left on her the other day. So yeah, I had left the door open a crack so that he could hear just how much she was mine now too. Even knowing what a blow it would be to him and hating myself a little bit for it. I still did it. Knew he would follow us home from the club after it was clear we had left and knew he wouldn't intervene after he figured out what was going on. It wasn't Coop's style, he was more of a bide his time and strategically strike back kind of guy. At least most of the time. And he wouldn't have been able to handle seeing her with me, hearing it was enough.

But I wouldn't let Ellie take the fallout for this.

This part of the war was between him and me.

I make my way down the stairs, wondering where he's posted up, but I don't have to wait long. The sight of him sitting in a chair pulled up to the island with a glass of what I'm guessing is whiskey in hand is the first thing I see when I enter the kitchen. It appears my little show did the job, Coop rarely drank liquor.

He doesn't even lift his head as I walk into the kitchen, just brings the glass up and takes a sip before asking casually. "Is my wife satisfied, or does she need me to make a visit?"

A laugh leaves me as the guilty pit in my stomach grows, but I push through it, grabbing a glass from the cabinet and filling it up. Waiting to respond as I walk to the other side of the island from him and take a sip to ease some of the tightness in my chest that happens every time I'm reminded that she fucking *married* him. He looks up and I see the fury lingering there in the back of his eyes as I lift my brows at him in question. "Couldn't you tell by the sound of her screams?"

His eyes narrow on me and my body goes tense at the violence filling the air between us. "How was it?" A smirk fills his face. "Fucking her while seeing my marks all over her skin?"

Fucking excruciating. Not that I'd ever tell her that. Probably as excruciating as it had been for him to hear what she sounds like when I'm inside of her. But instead I just shrug, maintaining just as casual a front as he is and both of us knowing how phony it is.

"Marks fade." I let a small grin rise to my lips, mimicking his. "But what I just did to her"—I lift my glass into the air as if in cheers—"that's bound to stick around for a long while."

I see the blow hit him. The pain fills his face before he wipes it clean, hiding behind the mask he never used with me before her, and I'm reminded for a second of how much I really do love my cousin. How much some part of me does hate what this is doing to us.

I brace my hands on the counter, looking down to blow out a deep breath before asking the question I haven't had the balls to until now. "Why did you do it, man?" I lift my head, wanting to see his face when he answers. "No bullshit."

He knows what I'm asking. It's the only thing I never asked when everything came out that day. I'm not sure I was ready then but now that I'm faced with just how much this is going to destroy either him or me in the end… I have to know now.

I see his jaw clench before he takes another sip of the whiskey, looking down into the glass when he's done. "Because she was the one thing I couldn't let go of. Even after all those years."

"Then what happened?" I press, anger growing at his response. How fucked he made all of us. "Why did it take you a year to catch up with her? Why—"

"I can't tell you, Jace," he cuts me off, looking back up with resolve in his eyes that just pisses me off more.

"Why?"

"I can't." He shakes his head. "I swore."

I look down, taking a few breaths and knowing that he won't give me anything here. Because if there's one thing about my cousin that I know, that I used to idolize about him, it's that he never breaks his word. And right now there's nothing I hate more about him.

"You never talked about her," I finally say after a minute.

"And you never looked for her." I look up and see the questioning look in his eyes. "Never reached out even though you had more reason to from day one than I ever did." He pauses as if waiting to see if I'll answer before prompting. "Why?"

I give him a shrug, uncomfortable for some reason at the question, as if he's implying I did this instead of him. "I guess I figured whatever had happened to her, she was probably better off without reminders of where it had begun."

He stares at me for so long in response that I'm about to just walk away when he nods, as if finally understanding something. "That's the difference between us, you know." He clears his throat and looks down into his glass again, swirling the liquid inside in the similar way we always have.

I hesitate for a second, not sure I really want to know at the end of the day before making myself ask. "What?"

He looks up, a rare show of pain in his eyes for me to see as he gives me a humorless smirk. "You were always selfless enough to leave her be and I was always too selfish to let her go."

My heart grows heavy at his words, because even if I'm mad as fucking hell at him right now. Willing to fight him over this girl who's both of our worlds. At the end of the day, he's still my big cousin. The one who I could always count on and I don't think anything will ever change that. Not even seeing the worst in him. It makes the words that have been circling around in my head for days tumble out in quick succession. "Do you ever think we're just living on repeat? Like the people we're here with today, we've been through a thousand lives with? Always finding each other and losing each other only to meet again? Like some horrible joke of fate. Just throwing us together over and over again to see if we ever change the story it's laid out for us?"

His brows shoot down, eyes moving over my face. "That's a little broody for you, Jace." He takes a large sip of the whiskey, cringing before continuing. "Leave that shit to me. I'm better suited for it." A heavy breath leaves him as he looks back down into his drink and I can see how tightly he grips the glass even from where I'm standing. "Go back to bed, cousin. If memory serves me right, her nightmares start soon on the nights they hit and she should have someone there."

I'm the one swallowing this time, trying to keep the guilty pit in my stomach from coming up as I give him a nod and silently walk from the kitchen.

But all that pit does is just roll and turn with every step.

Chapter Thirty-One

Present Day

I slipped out of bed after pressing a lingering kiss to Jace's lips this morning, a goofy smile on my face as I looked at his sleeping face despite the little bit of tension I saw there. Although really it was afternoon, considering how late everyone had slept in after last night. But regardless, I had hopped in the bath to let myself have a good soak after last night's extracurriculars and pulled up Uber Eats on my phone. Quickly ordering a good spread before washing up and throwing on an oversized concert tee with a pair of pajama shorts.

When the notification came through that the food had been dropped off, I quickly darted downstairs. Practically skipping down the steps from being so hyped up on postorgasmic bliss. I had gathered up the bags of food and walked them toward the kitchen with that goofy smile still plastered across my face before being met with a sight that quickly wiped it away.

Cooper Monroe sleeping on the couch and a glass lying on the floor beside him as if it had slipped from his hand.

That had pretty much been the end of my bliss.

He had barely looked at me when I had woken him up, making my heart fill with hurt and guilt. Then when he had come down later to join everyone for breakfast, that was really late lunch… well, let's just say there had been nothing but dangerous energy pouring off his skin. Everyone could feel it and was shooting both him and me questioning looks, but all I could do was shrug. I had my suspicions but wasn't quite sure how to approach it either. I mean, it wasn't like I had done it in public right in front of him. It had been in the privacy of a room and it wasn't like he wouldn't have suspected this would happen.

I had *told* him. I wasn't giving Jace up.

To cut right to the core of it though, it was all just a mess.

It was now two hours later, quickly approaching evening as we all sat in the living room making awkward small talk and trying to decide what to do for the rest of the day. Toeing around the eggshells littering the ground as they slowly deduced the reason Coop was so pissed and that it had everything to do with Jace and I disappearing the night before. Everyone besides Mac, that is.

He throws a tennis ball up into the air in front of where I sit on the couch, lying on the ground and tossing out ideas. "Strip club?"

"Nope," Stef and I reply at the same time and I give him a grin where he sits on the couch next to Jace and me.

"Racing?" That ball flies into the air again. "Stef never lets the Pagani loose, it's one of the most depressing realities of my life."

Stef chuckles before stating simply. "No."

"Hmm." He throws the ball into the air before catching it and turning his head with a look that spells trouble. "Want to go play kamikaze from the roof, Els?"

"Uh—" I've barely opened my mouth to respond when Coop cuts me off.

"If you ever try to get her to do something like that again," he snaps roughly, immediately drawing my gaze to where he sits in the chair diagonal from me. "I will show you the definition of bare-knuckle knockout, pretty boy." That savage smirk spreads. "Twin or not."

The ball Mac's been throwing stills, finally silent as I feel the air turn thick. Coop not knowing what those words will do to Mac, and Mac not knowing just how far my reckless act pushed Coop that day.

Kai clears his throat from the chair on my other side and I dart my eyes to him, seeing that he can feel what's brewing too by the nervous look on his face. "So," he starts. "What were you saying about a strip—"

"Um, sorry." Mac laughs mockingly, dipping his head to stare back at Coop. "Pretty sure Els is fully capable of making her own decisions."

"She is." Coop nods. "And if she suddenly wants to go jump from the roof, fuck, it'd kill me, but I've come to terms with the fact I can't always stand in her way. Just wait underneath to catch her if need be." He leans forward with narrowed eyes, bracing his arms on his knees. "But don't push your fucking death wish on her."

"Coop—" I start as Stef interjects.

"Settle down, everybody." My eyes go to him and I see him trying to catch Mac's gaze, attempting to rein him in. But when I look at Mac, he's completely ignoring us, rising up to sit as his face grows thunderous.

"Pretty sure we're not the dangerous thing to her here." He pauses. "That'd be you, right? The one who broke her heart to begin with."

I watch him slowly stand, stomach clenching up with nerves as I echo him and take a step forward. Praying I'm not going to have to intercede but knowing that wish is most likely about to go unanswered.

He smiles down at Coop tauntingly. "Yeah, you didn't have to deal with that fallout though, did you? That was everyone else."

"Mac!"

Coop shoots up, taking a step forward. "Careful, twin." His voice comes out dangerously low despite the twitch of his lips and I know right then that both of them are spoiling for this fight. "You wouldn't want her to find out I'm not the only one keeping secrets here." He arches a taunting brow as mine shoot down. "Would you?"

I see Mac pause, mouth opening but not speaking as his eyes widen before quickly shooting to mine.

My heart starts to race in my chest. "What is he talking about?"

"Enough, Monroe," Stef orders shortly, standing from the couch but making no move forward. "You've made your point."

Coop just laughs viciously though, eyes going dark in a way that lets me know just how far gone he is. How much pissed-off energy is really bottled up inside of him at the moment. And he's not one to ever take orders, except maybe from me.

"Really, Stefano?" He turns to Stef, voice dripping sarcasm and narrows his eyes. "Garda was it? Such a common Italian last name."

"Coop!" I shout. *Not your secret to tell.* Although how the hell he knows that particular one is beyond me.

Mac shoots forward at his accusation quicker than I can react to and gets right up in Coop's face as he smiles humorlessly. "Don't put this on them." I hear Kai mutter a quiet "Fuck" while Coop just narrows his eyes impossibly more, shoulders tensing as Mac finishes, almost proudly. "It. Was. Me."

And in the time it takes me to suck in a breath, knowing whatever this is has reached its boiling point, Cooper Monroe pulls his arm back and brings his fist crashing down on Macallan Astor's face.

Mac falls to the floor and I start to dart forward but an arm wraps around me from behind, pulling me back against a body that smells like sea and spring while Mac just laughs.

Planting his hand on the ground, he turns back to Coop with blood trickling from his mouth. "What? That's all you got? Do I need to repeat myself?" he mocks. "It was me!"

Mac's shout is cut off by Coop's quick kick to his gut and I watch him fall back to the floor before planting his hands again, turning his head back to meet Coop's furious face.

I start to fight Jace but he quickly drops his mouth to my ear, whispering with rushed intensity. “No, Blondie. I love you, but they need this.” He squeezes me more tightly, not giving an inch despite the fact I’m still trying to break free. “*Look* at them, Ellie. I don’t know what’s going on here but even your boys aren’t interfering.”

Coop’s fist comes down on Mac’s face again and the only response he gives is to laugh, as if welcoming the pain that’s being doled out to him as my heart twists painfully in my chest. And I know at that moment that I’m missing something big here. Some part of the story that everyone in this room probably knows besides Jace and me.

But I’m too frantic at the sight of two of the people I love tearing into each other in front of me for logic to matter right now. One physically and the other in some verbal way I can’t grasp. And when Coop brings his fist down on Mac’s face twice more in quick succession, sending blood spraying across the floor, I don’t give a damn about Jace’s reasoning.

I go crazy, thrashing in his arms. “Let me go, Jace!”

“No,” he answers regretfully, bringing his other arm up to help keep me contained.

Coop leans back, shaking out his arms as if to walk away but Mac pushes off the floor once again. Spitting some more blood out as he comes up on his knees and manages to smile through his already forming bruises. “It was me.” He coughs, mumbling the rest. “Think about what that year cost you.”

This time when Coop hits him, it’s as if all the pain he endured at my loss is thrown into it, and I hear something crack. My stomach twists right along with my heart this time at the noise and when he pulls back his fist again, I scream with every bit of fear inside of me. "Cooper!" That powerful arm stills midair, a second passing where I hold my breath before his eyes dart to me, raking over my face as I let the air out with his name. "Coop."

His eyes lock with mine and a long, tense moment passes before his arm falls from the air and his chest collapses on a deep exhale.

He gives Mac one last look before starting to walk slowly toward me, and I feel Jace's arm drop from my middle as he comes to stand before us. Looking down at me with night-forest eyes that are fucking broken as he raises a hand to brush away tears that I didn't even realize were on my cheeks and his brows drop.

"I did call you, Eleanor." His voice comes out rough with feeling. "And after I made sure you were safe, I would've kept calling you. I would've called you a thousand times until you had no other choice but to answer. I would've called you and chased you from one end of this earth to the other if it meant I got to see you just one more time." He chokes on the end of his words, dropping his hand from my face before jerking his head to where Mac is lying on the ground behind him. "You can ask him why they never came through."

My eyes flick to Mac, seeing the fear in his eyes as he pushes up off the floor and in the time it takes for me to look back to Coop, he's already walking away.

"Coop!" Jace calls.

And I want to call for him too, but I'm too scared of this secret, locked up with shock. But when I hear the front door slam, echoes of terror fill me, all laced with the loss of him a year ago, and my chest starts to heave with panicked breaths.

My eyes go to Mac. "What did you do?"

"Els." He rolls over, sitting on the ground and looking up at me with a lost expression.

"What did you do?!" I scream, feeling the ripple of surprise roll through the room at my hysteria.

"*Cara*," Stef starts carefully, moving closer from where he stands beside me.

I whip my head to him, tear-filled eyes blazing. "No." I shake my head. "Fuck no! Someone better come clean right now."

Stef's gaze moves to Mac and Kai before coming back to me with a solemn nod. "When you got to Berlin," he starts slowly. "We got a call. The person on the other end said you were in danger and that the only way to keep you safe was to make sure Cooper couldn't find you." A pause fills the air as his expression turns horribly apologetic. "So we did what the man asked, we made a choice and downloaded something onto your phone to keep him from being able to reach you."

My brows drop in confusion, because this… I could have never imagined this. Not from them. "Excuse me?"

"Not them." Mac coughs on the floor and I turn my head in time to see him spit more blood before looking back up to me with those scared, little boy eyes. "Me. Don't blame them."

"We took a v—" Stef starts but Mac just cuts him off, shaking his head.

"It was me, Els," he says. "I'm the one who pressed the button. Downloaded the program. No one else."

"And who the fuck was on the other end of the phone?!" I shout, trying to push through the panic filling me long enough to figure out why this ludicrous idea that caused me so much further pain would have ever seemed like a rational plan to them.

Mac hesitates for a second and Stef answers quietly for him. "We're not sure."

"Oh, brilliant. Trust the stranger on the phone," I scoff acidly. "Fucking idiots!" I march over to where Mac sits on the floor, dropping down to squat in front of him and letting him see every bit of violence in my eyes that matches what he just endured at Coop's hands.

He opens up his mouth and I hold up a hand. "Do not speak to me right now, Macallan. You won't like what I have to say, and we'll both regret it if you do." I blow out a stuttering breath, feeling my eyes prick as I stare into the ones that had always had my back before this. "I love you and I will forgive you eventually because you are my family. But be happy he got to you first for this." I smile sadly, mustering up a bravado to edge it a bit because he deserves to be a little afraid of me right now. "Because what I would have done to you for it would've made his punishment look like child's play." Cocking a brow, I stand and keep from running from the room long enough to finish mockingly. "And you should know that well, *twin*."

I turn without looking at another person, completely ignoring them and walking as quickly as I can out of the living room. My mind a mess as reality shifts beneath my feet again, leaving me with the sense that the earth is spinning too fast for me to ever have a hope of catching up. All I know is that right now… I need Coop. I need him to explain why he didn't throw those fuckers under the bus to begin with. It sure as hell would've helped his case.

And the only reason I can think of as I walk through the foyer is that he didn't want to do that to me. That he wanted to save me the pain of that betrayal on top of everything else. But then he was pushed just a bit too far and the whole mess had been confessed through violence, the truth sprayed across the floor in blood just like that of my parents.

I suck in a breath that holds his name, heart pounding in my chest as I throw open the front door… and find nothing but empty air. My eyes dart around the driveway, panic skyrocketing and when they land on the open gate, I can't help the quiet cry that escapes my lips at the sight. The terror in my veins turning visceral as two words repeat in my head on an endless loop again.

He's gone.

Chapter Thirty-Two

Coop

One Year Ago

It had taken me two days to track Alec down, one to make it back to the states and another to discreetly check in with a few people at Bainbridge to make sure he wasn't out on a job. I already knew where he based himself in New York whenever he had some downtime. It was the only apartment he kept, to my knowledge, which meant he knew that I would be coming. Or at least suspected it and was prepared for the possibility. That in itself already put me at a slight disadvantage. But the added fact that my body was wrecked from surgery and the lack of sleep I'd had since finding her gone two days ago put me firmly in the spot of the underdog.

At another time, it would have made me pause and take stock. Maybe put off confronting him for a couple weeks and take the time to plan a strategy. If this had been about anyone else, I would have been able to think clearly. But he had taken her from me. Deceived me for some unknown reason. Driven us apart. And that left my usually clear vision clouded with rage while the demand to make him pay pounded through the shredded muscle in my chest that was empty without her.

So I had staked out his apartment from the building across the street and as soon as I had seen him leave, I had made my move. Pulling a ball cap onto my head and jogging across the street. Keeping my head turned away from the concierge and cameras at the ritzy building he lived in on the Upper East Side as I ducked into the elevator. I had walked right past his door, knowing there was no way I would be able to get inside his apartment without setting off some sort of alarm he had in place. The only thing that allowed me to calm the jittery feeling in my limbs as I stepped around the corner of the hall to settle in and wait was the reminder that this would bring me that much closer to her again.

An hour had passed since. A few people had passed by during that time and I had given them a fake smile, holding my phone to my ear as if I was simply lost and trying to find my way. A painful thump in my heart happening each time at the accuracy of the analogy.

I drop the phone from my ear along with the act when a sound catches my attention though. Or more so the lack of sound. The silent steps that barely brush against the carpeted floor around the corner. Each step a touch too carefully placed and telling me that my target was finally here. I wait until I hear him pull his keys from his pocket to make my move, stepping around the corner with my head down silently.

Barely making it another step before his body barrels into mine, slamming me against the wall as he smirks down at me. “Cooper.”

I grunt, ignoring the pull on several of the stitches I hadn't managed to tear yet as I shove him. "What the fuck did you do, Alec?" I growl as he jumps back a couple steps on the toes of his feet, light as a fucking bird and obviously full of energy.

"Really, Coop?" He narrows his eyes on me, smile turning vicious as we begin to circle one another. "I think the better question, brother, is what did you do?"

"What are you talking about?" I push down the guilt his question churns up and keep my body tense, prepared for attack, my eyes trying to take in every move he makes all at once. "You're the one who lied to me."

"Ah." He nods mockingly, coming to a stop a split second before I do. "But you deceived her first, didn't you?"

He knows. I narrow my eyes at him in turn, staying silent as I take in his face and see that somehow, for some reason, he figured out the secret I was keeping from her.

But why the fuck does it matter to him?

Regardless, I was done with this. I knew him and he would continue on with this cat-and-mouse game for another hour if it was up to him. It was part of what made him so good at his work with Bainbridge, but today, it was going to end right here.

I look down as if his question has taken the fight out of me and let my hands drop at the same time, putting them a purposeful inch away from my back pockets. That much closer to where the switchblade I'm carrying is concealed. I typically favored a gun, but they are harder to conceal and ever since Eleanor… they just didn't carry the same.

"The truth is, Alec," I start slowly, lifting my head back to meet his eyes. Keeping his gaze on mine as I let my hand drift that much closer to my back pocket. "The truth is…"

I grab the switchblade, flicking it open the next second and lunging forward to slam my forearm against his chest, intending to bring the knife to his throat. But his eyes go wide and he manages to dodge the move, the blade nicking a thin line across his cheek as he ducks under my too-slow limbs and comes up behind me. I spin around, immediately feeling the cold pain of the knife I know he always carries on him slice across one side of my chest. It makes me falter briefly, the added pain to my already wrecked body and that's the only opening he needs. He pushes me against the wall, holding his own knife to my throat and landing a fist on my barely healed incision.

It knocks the air out of me, my stomach rebelling from the pain and bile trying to work its way up my throat as he stares at me. "You're smarter than this, Cooper," he muses, eyes looking over my face. "You had to have known you were in no shape to face me today." I gasp for air, trying to keep my throat from pressing on the blade there as he continues. "So why? What the fuck were you doing with that girl on the beach?"

It takes me a few more breaths before I manage a solid. "Fuck you."

"Wrong answer." He laughs icily. "I would have been happy to leave you alone now that I made sure she's out of your reach, but now that you're here, why don't we air the dirty laundry?"

He nods toward his apartment then and I know I have no option but to comply for now. Until I can manage to work myself into a better position to strike at him again. Plus, if I can manage to get some answers out of him in the meantime, all the more convenient. I turn toward his apartment and he keeps the knife pressed to my throat, moving to my back as I walk forward with spiders crawling up my spine. His keys are already in the lock of the door and I reach out to turn them, knowing the drill here. It was one we had forced others through before a time or two. I push open his door and an alarm immediately starts to beep on the wall next to it, drawing my attention as he speaks.

"Seven-two-six-two-zero," he starts, and I reach out, typing the numbers as he recites them. "Two-two." The alarm beeps as if disarmed and he continues in an amused voice. "Now press the button to arm it and type in one-zero-one-four-two-zero-two-two." The alarm gives a slightly different beep this time, actually disarming as Alec pushes me forward into his sterile, white apartment.

I knew it.

There were probably traps upon traps in this place. The biggest difference between Alec and I being that he was slightly more prone to paranoia than I was. When we make it to his white leather couch, he lifts the knife from my neck before pushing me toward it and I turn in time to see him grabbing a gun from the bookshelf behind him that's mostly empty.

He motions with the gun to the couch. "Sit down, Cooper. You look like you're about to collapse."

I hesitate, eyeing the gun at his side before replying. "I'd rather stand."

"That's nice." He takes a step toward me. "Now sit the fuck down and tell me about what a bad boy you've been."

I narrow my eyes on him, feeling my forehead go tense as I slowly take a seat. "Why the fuck do you care? About Eleanor?"

"You first."

We stare at each other in a silent standoff for a minute before I sigh. "I don't know what you want me to tell you."

"Tell me why you were shacked up on the beach with the daughter of the woman who your dad had an affair with." He pauses, waiting for my response but I hold my lips closed, making him scoff before he continues. "It wasn't that hard to figure out once I started to look into her. Both of you were born in Landing Point, both with parents that died on the same night. Add the murder-suicide bit into the mix, along with the fact that your dad's car crashed on the main road that led out toward their home and the writing is on the wall with that one."

"And again," I retort, pissed off that he's been digging into our business. "What the fuck business is this of yours?"

"There's no way you'd go off with some girl without knowing her full name," he muses, eyeing me hard. "It took me a minute to put that part together. The fact that you had to have known who she was already. Which made you the one with questionable intentions. So what was it?" I tense up as he grips the gun at his side a little tighter. "All a play to make her pay for how her mother wrecked your life? Were you just going to have fun fucking her over? Or was it more twisted than that? Did you want to feel the closest thing you could to what made your father abandon his family?"

"No!" I shout, stomach churning again at his words. My chest heaving as I try to control my rage. "No." Resting my elbows on my knees, I drop my head into my hands with actual exhaustion this time and confess roughly. "I fell in love with her. I knew who she was when I met her. It wasn't… I just wanted to meet her, but then, fuck, it was already too late. I fell in love with her and couldn't let her go."

He's silent for a long moment before sighing. "Damn, Cooper. And that's what I was hoping it wasn't."

"Why?" I snap my head up, meeting his brown eyes. "What are you? Her keeper?"

"No," he answers quietly, face going tight. "But you have no idea what you were about to drag her into."

"Then tell me!" I shout again, so fucking done with his vague answers.

"Did you ever wonder," he starts tightly. "About who Nadia Delacroix was before she came to Landing Point?"

"No." I shake my head quickly. "I never really thought of her as anything beyond the person who'd played a role in my dad dying before Eleanor."

"Understandable." He nods. "Let me enlighten you. Before she moved to New York and later became the Nadia Delacroix that moved to Landing Point, her name was Nadia Petras." A sigh leaves him as he leans up against the bookshelf, gun at his side dropping just a bit. Probably because he knows I'm too curious to interrupt at this point and make a play. "She was born an orphan in Czechia and after she aged out, she began to work at one of the higher-end bars in town, trying to save enough money to make it to America. Everything I've learned indicates that she was a smart individual if not a little cutthroat and one day she caught the eye of one of the wealthy men who came into the bar." He pauses purposefully. "Nicolai Novikov."

"Fuck." I exhale in shock, because I know Nicolai Novikov. He's the director of operations at Bainbridge, the person my boss reports to. And if the rumors I've heard are true…

"Now you're beginning to understand." Alec smirks humorlessly before continuing. "She became his lover and for a time was content with the role I believe. But Novikov's lovers had a habit of disappearing after either he tired of them or they learned too much about his dealings. And I think Nadia felt her time ticking down." He eyes me consideringly before asking. "What do you know of Novikov's dealings before he came to Bainbridge?"

"What everyone hears," I answer sharply. "That he was head of one of the major crime syndicates in Eastern Europe before he got busted and became a pawn for the US. After a time, he managed to convince the people at Bainbridge that he would be more useful using his connections for their profit. He rose quickly through their ranks after that with his newfound freedom."

"Correct." He nods. "And who do you think turned over the information the US needed to capture him in return for a new name and citizenship in their country?"

"No way." I shake my head with a quiet scoff. "You're telling me…"

"That Nadia Petras was responsible for the downfall of Nicolai Novikov?" He tilts his head at me. "She always was always resourceful, it seems."

I pause, processing everything he's just told me before asking. "I still don't understand why that would make you—"

"Come on, Cooper," he scoffs as if in disgust. "You know what men like Novikov believe. No debt goes unpaid. It doesn't matter if the parent's already dead, the child will pay. Nadia's crime against him was a blood debt. He would extinguish her line if he ever found her. If he ever found out about Eleanor. Reformed director at Bainbridge or not, he'd just use their resources to do it now." He exhales a deep breath. "I think that's in part why she married Cane Delacroix. So she could hide out even farther in the middle of nowhere Alabama." His hand tightens on the gun again and he uses it to motion at me. "And you were about to undo all her work. You don't start turning down jobs at Bainbridge without them at least looking into the reason. Especially not if you're one of their top agents. As soon as her information and picture circulated across his desk, he would have known. She looks just like her."

I nod, finally understanding. "Then he's dead."

Alec stares at me with a shocked look before starting to laugh. "You really have lost your mind."

"You just told me that if he ever finds out about her, he'll kill her." I shrug. "So it's simple, really. He won't be breathing by the end of the week."

"It's not simple, Cooper."

"You're right." I narrow my eyes on him. "Because I still don't understand what you're doing here, going around playing her knight in shining armor when that should be me."

He stares at me for a moment, eyes rolling over my face in consideration before speaking in a hard voice. "You have to swear to never tell her any of this."

"Why?"

"Doesn't matter." He shakes his head. "My reasons are my own, but if you want my help to ensure her safety and I promise you will need it, you have to swear."

"Fine, I swear," I agree, part of me unsure if it's a promise I'll be able to keep and dirtying up my soul a little bit more for her anyway. But really, at this point, I didn't care if the whole thing was stained black as long as I could keep her safe and have her in my arms again one day.

Alec narrows his eyes on me suspiciously, something about it pulling at my gut and reminding me of when I woke up in the hospital before he sighs. "Nadia." His head drops for a second before looking back at me. "Was pregnant with Novikov's child when she made the deal to get out of the country. She went into labor shortly before the deal was done and left the child at an orphanage in Slovakia on her way to America."

I put two and two together immediately, my eyes going to his platinum hair the same shade as hers. Such a rare color to have naturally. Almost white in its coloring with streaks of light woven through it. The color Nadia had too.

"You're her brother."

"Half," he retorts quickly with an uncomfortable look. "And it's not like I grew up with her. Novikov finally found me in college and told me the story then recruited me to Bainbridge." Looking down, he shakes his head. "I think part of the reason he didn't do away with me for the crime of being Nadia's child is because he thought I could be useful to him. But I only put it together about Eleanor because she spouted off about us looking alike when I met her that day and I thought there was no fucking way but her words kept nagging at me."

"Alec," I start slowly, trying to work out how to approach this with him. "You kept her safe."

He shrugs. "I didn't think it was fair that she pay for whatever fucked-up games you were playing."

"I wasn't playing any games," I shoot back in frustration. "I love her."

"Didn't know that then and there wasn't time to ask you." He pauses. "And it doesn't matter, Coop. You can't ever leave Bainbridge without them keeping an eye on you. You can't stay without them keeping an eye on you either. It's a miracle they didn't find out about her already and I had to wipe all the evidence so that they can't now." Another careless shrug leaves his shoulders. "You can't be with her without him finding out."

"Which is why I'm going to kill him," I state again. "Problem solved."

Alec's eyes narrow on me dangerously. "That's my father."

"And you already chose her over your loyalty to him once," I argue. "Do it again."

"I don't even know her." He exhales a humorless laugh. "And I didn't much like her the one time I did meet her."

My lips twitch. "Pretty sure that feeling was mutual."

"Exactly." He nods. "So let her go and leave my father be."

"Can't do that." I shake my head. "Trust me, that ship sailed pretty much the second I laid eyes on her."

"Cooper—"

"Do you like him?" I interrupt. "Your father?"

Alec pauses. "It's not a matter of like or dislike."

I nod because I get that, I really do, but the bastard has to die. No way was I going to allow some threat to her to walk freely, regardless of whether she was with me or not.

"I'm going to be straight with you." I lean back on the couch to give off the appearance that I'm relaxing when really I'm doing anything but. "Your father's a dead man walking and if you'd like to stand in my way and join him, be my guest. But I won't allow a threat to her to keep breathing as long as I'm alive." I shrug. "So you have a choice. Either your father or her."

He narrows his eyes on me and clenches the gun in his hand. "And why the fuck would I choose her over him?"

You already did, man.

"Because she's your little sister," I tell him simply. "And I have one of those, so I know that big brothers always protect their little sisters. Regardless of whether they like them or not."

His eyes drill into me for a beat before he snaps defiantly. "Fuck you." Reminding me so much of her in that moment that it makes the shredded muscle in my chest clench up in pain. But a minute later, he places the gun on the bookshelf behind him and says weakly. "I can't be the one to do it, Coop."

I nod in understanding. "That's fine. I'll take the shot."

"You're a shit shot," he scoffs. "It will take planning. You don't just take out the director of operations at Bainbridge without causing waves. If we do this… it will need to be planned perfectly."

"And then…" I stand, walking toward him with a smirk and feeling blood drip down my chest. "You're going to help me find what you took from me."

Chapter Thirty-Three

Present Day

I've been sitting on the marble steps outside the front door for at least a couple hours now. And I know it's been that long by the way the sun has made its way across the sky, sending the hills into the shadowy light of early dusk. Even an amateur like me can guess that. Not moving an inch even though my ass shot past numb to downright painful a good while ago. Arms wrapped around my legs and trying to hold it together as I watch the day fade with an internal excruciation that far surpasses any physical discomfort. My eyes are burning from the way they're peeled on the open gate, holding my breath as I wait for him.

Heart cracking just a bit more with every minute that passes without him reappearing.

It's terrible. A brutal reminder of everything from last summer that leaves me feeling horribly weak from how much I need him to walk through that gate again. Need him to not be gone so damn much that it makes me hate him just a little bit for existing in the first place and myself for ever letting him push into my heart again. It's a suffocating kind of fear. The kind that leaves you completely frozen and hiding under the covers while you wish the monster in the closet away.

I bite my lip at the realization that I really might have just a touch of PTSD from last summer. Going to have to make an appointment with myself to deal with that later.

But for now… for now, I'll sit here and hope the monster is really just a coat made greater by the shadows of fear. Hope that he's about to walk back through that gate any second now.

Jace had come out at some point, wordlessly leaving a bottle of water beside me, but besides that one interruption, everyone had left me alone to my silent vigil. They knew better. Knew I had meant what I said to Macallan and that nothing but ugliness would erupt from me if they dared to speak one word before I was ready.

The thirst finally breaks me when I swallow, dryness in my throat grating like sandpaper and my eyes move to the water bottle on the step next to me. I briefly consider taking a sip before discarding the idea. Fuck that, I'll hydrate again when he's back. There's something about fasting answering prayers, right?

And when you pass out from dehydration, El? How are you going to keep up this idiotic protest then? Also not sure God answers prayers if you're wishing for Satan.

Fuck you too.

I scowl at the water bottle as if it's been sent to test me and look back to the gate in time to see Coop round the corner, head bowed and hands holding either end of the shirt that's wrapped around his neck. Chest heaving from exertion as sweat drips from his body. I shoot to my feet, the rush of blood back through my legs causing them to go crazy with pins and needles as his head lifts.

Our eyes lock and his brow drops in confusion as he comes closer. "Eleanor?" I can hear the question in my name as his gaze runs the length of me. His face going tense as he comes to stand on the step below mine and looks up at me. And I can see the exhaustion in his face, in the bags under his eyes as we eye each other again. "What is it?"

I open and close my mouth a few times, swallowing down some more of the sandpaper in my throat before managing. "You left." My voice cracks at the end and his eyes go wide, raking my face and filling with concern.

"I'm sorry." He clears his throat, an echo of my pain flashing on his face. "I wasn't thinking. I just needed to get out of there and run off some of the…" His jaw clenches and he shakes his head, blowing out a breath. "I wasn't thinking. I'm sorry." He raises a hand, running a thumb along my cheek. "It would take an act of God to get me out of your life again. Even if you never forgive me. I'll still haunt you for eternity."

My face pinches up, brows dropping because I'm not sure what to do with his words. What to do with the harsh clarity that came with the terror that filled me when I thought he was gone again. And despite that, honestly not sure what it's going to take for me to finally forgive him completely besides the one truth he won't give me.

But I do know one thing.

I throw my arms around him in the next breath, wrapping them tight around his neck and feeling his body go still against mine as I tell him softly. “Don’t do that again.”

It takes him a minute to get over the shock before he slowly wraps his arms around my waist, pulling me in tight and up into the air as he answers quietly. “Okay.”

And for once, it’s that simple with us.

He holds me as he walks up the couple of steps, squeezing me even tighter as he whispers. “I’m right here, Princess. Not going anywhere.”

I nod against his shoulder, finally feeling some of my anxiety fade as my body relaxes against his and he lowers me back to the ground again.

My eyes meet his as I lean back, seeing the happiness within their shadowed depths. “I do need to go shower though.”

“Oh.”

His lips twitch. “There’s that eloquence again.”

I roll my eyes and reach out to grab his hand before turning to open the front door, dragging him behind me because the truth is I’m not sure I *can* let him out of my sight right now.

At least not for a little bit.

The panic lingering at the edges of my heart is still too real.

So I pull him behind me up the stairs, both of us silent as we make our way to my room. I let go of his hand long enough to grab the handle of the door and push it open, standing back to let him walk in and narrowing my eyes at the amused look he gives me. As if he knows that I need to be in control right now but is allowing it because it suits his needs just perfectly this time too.

I watch his curious gaze roll over the room as I close the door before walking forward and snagging his hand again to lead him to the bathroom. Not up for another commentary on its girliness at the moment. I flip the light switch just inside the bathroom, flooding the space with bright light before bringing us to the middle of the space and coming to a stop.

Pulling up the hand I'm holding, I look down and inspect his bruised knuckles peppered with a few shallow cuts. "Not too bad." I run a thumb over his knuckles, brows dropping at the scars that are already there. "Shower first, then we can clean them up." I dart my eyes up to his and pause at the look I find there. "What?"

"Nothing." He shakes his head, winding our fingers together. "Just." His ridiculously full lips tighten for a second. "You know, there's this moment every morning before I open my eyes. Before I even realize what I'm breathing really. That I still think I'm on that beach with you and I'm just so… fucking content." A sad smile ghosts across his face. "And then I open my eyes and it hits me all over again. Every morning. Like I'm living in some kind of never-ending purgatory of your loss."

My lips part as I stare into his eyes, unable to speak because I know what he means. Exactly what he means. It was the reality I endured for a year too.

The agony of that loss endlessly repeating until the sun drove out his shadows.

I clear my throat, breaking our gaze and walking to the shower to flip it on before coming back to stand in front of him. Reaching up, I grab his shirt where it's hanging across his shoulder and toss it on the ground.

"Why didn't you tell me, Coop?" I ask, staring at that new scar on his chest and trying to sort through the mess in my head. "What they had done?"

"Because." He shrugs. "It did you no good and just would've led to more questions I can't answer."

I cross my arms, bringing my eyes up to his. "Because it's not your secret to tell?"

He nods, gaze filling with wariness as if he knows I've just about reached my end with this bullshit.

"But it has to do with me? Right?" I cock a brow. "That's the only thing that makes sense which means I have a right to know."

"Yes," he answers reluctantly, an uncomfortable expression playing across his face. "But I swore, Eleanor. I swore that I'd keep my mouth shut. It was the only way I could make sure you stayed safe."

I can't help but snap in frustration. "Safe from what?"

"It doesn't matter." He brings his hands to the bottom of my oversized shirt, quickly pulling it over my head. "Not anymore. I took care of it."

My brows shoot down at his choice of words. "It or them, Coop?"

He pauses, staring into my eyes for a long moment before giving me, "Him."

A breath whooshes out of me at his confession, conflict of a whole new kind filling me as I try to come to terms with what he just admitted to. What he did to keep me safe from some kind of apparent threat. It turns my stomach, the idea that there was someone out there so bad that they needed to be dealt with that way as I continued on with my life obliviously. Completely unaware that someone wanted to do me harm. Because I know Coop well enough to know if there was any other option, he probably would have taken it. So it had to be bad, really bad, for him to deem that necessary to keep me safe.

Who the hell would have that much reason to hurt me besides the Morrisons?

You can be a bit of a bitch sometimes, El.

Well, yeah, but hardly enough of one to provoke violence. At least I hoped not.

And it pisses me the fuck off that he won't explain more to me than what he already has.

Narrowing my eyes at him, I reach out and grab the top of his basketball shorts. "You know." I shove them over his hips before grabbing his left arm and digging my nails into the tattoo there. "You swore a vow to me too."

"I know." He nods.

"Doesn't that mean more?"

"It means I'll protect you at all costs." He reaches forward, sliding his fingers underneath the top of my pajama shorts and underwear to rest against my skin. "Even if that cost is me pissing you off a bit."

I snort. "A bit?"

"Fine." He steps into me with a smirk. "A lot."

My face scrunches up as I look up at him, heart battling it out in my chest because as much as I want him, I need answers too. "I'm so confused." I finally admit, letting my hand drop from his arm.

"I know." He sighs, looking down and running his fingers along the waistband of my panties before pushing them down over my hips. Dropping to his knees as he does to help me step out of them before his eyes roll up my naked body, taking their time to come meet mine. "Only girl to ever bring me to my knees right here."

My lips twitch and I can't resist the urge to reach a hand out, running it through the new feeling of his buzzed, dark-chocolate hair.

His hands go to the back of my bra and he raises his head, bringing his lips to the tattoo under my left breast.

He runs his lips over it slowly, reverently, making my breath catch. "I still mean them, you know." I feel his lips move against my skin, air fanning out as my bra falls to the floor. "Every damn word."

"I know." He repeats the move and my breath catches again, head falling back as I manage to finish. "I know, Coop. The problem is whether that outweighs all the truths you withheld in the first place and won't give me now."

His hands wrap around my waist and I look back down to see him gazing at me intently. "Then what will it take, Eleanor?" He stands, pushing his boxer briefs down over his hips and freeing that magnificent cock that's already hard for me. "For you to stop punishing me."

"I told you, Jace isn't—"

"I'm not talking about Jace," he cuts me off, shaking his head and using his hold on my waist to walk me backward toward the shower. "Leave Jace out of this. I'm talking about you and me."

I hear the spray of the shower behind me and turn, buying myself some time to gather my thoughts as I open the door. Trying to separate out Coop and me from what I have with Jace while stepping underneath the spray with him right on my heels.

And when I turn back to him, I see the droplets of water I can feel on my own skin sliding down his, clinging to his dark lashes and dropping from his strong jaw to run down his olive skin. I shrug helplessly and give him the only honest answer I can. "Whenever this pain finally goes away."

"It might never, you know. Not completely." His voice is hesitant, scared even as his eyes rake my face. "It might be something that takes us a lifetime to work through, to not panic when the other leaves the room."

"Then whenever you give me an explanation worthy of forgiveness."

The truth.

His eyes narrow on me in understanding. "Okay, Princess." He cocks his head at me, bringing his hands to my waist again and backing me up against the shower wall. "Does it still bother you though? The rest? About them."

"Not as much as it did," I admit, biting my lip for a second before continuing. "It bothers me that you lied but I'm trying to let go of what they did." I pause, brows dropping down with my next confession. "I think if I don't, it'll taint everything good in my life. Eat me alive. So I'm trying to not let it determine how I live." My lips twitch at the memory of the words

I once told him in Cahuita. "We're more than the sum of their mistakes, right?"

His own lips twitch in turn as he drops his forehead to mine, our eyes locking. "Good." He nips at my bottom lip in that rare show of playfulness. "And I'll think on the rest."

I can't help but quip. "For once?"

The darkness in his eyes sparks with amusement as he pinches my waist. "Brat."

"Ass."

His hands slide up my waist, palming his next retort. "Breasts." He rolls my nipples between his fingers and I gasp as he drops to his knees again with an arrogant smirk. "I do some of my best thinking with the taste of you on my tongue." His hands drop from my breasts and he grabs one of my legs, throwing it over his shoulder. "So excuse me for a *bit*, Princess. I've missed having your pussy coming in my mouth for a fucking year."

He brings his mouth down on me then and my leg locks around his shoulders as a soft moan leaves my lips. I bring my hands to his head, missing the short length there that I used to grip as I dig my fingers into his scalp and he sucks my whole damn pussy into his mouth before lightly raking his teeth over it. Setting my nerves alight with the rush of blood to the area before he licks me from entrance to clit. Lazily circling the sensitive nub a few times before dropping back down to spear his tongue inside of me.

He brings his hands around to my ass, gripping both cheeks as he presses me harder against his mouth, going deeper with his tongue and licking at me like what he said is true. That he really can't get enough of my taste on his tongue. The whole thing is so erotic that it has my breaths coming in little gasps in no time. My pussy trying to clamp down around his tongue and my lone leg shaking so bad that it's barely able to hold me up. But he quickly remedies that, wedging his shoulders forcefully between my thighs and spreading me wider for his mouth as he nudges my other leg over his shoulder too. Completely holding me up as he licks inside of me one more time before bringing his mouth up to my clit and nibbling at it.

A gasped scream falls from my lips at the move, head falling back hard against the tile wall of the shower and a sound of satisfaction rumbles out of him against my sensitive flesh right before he pulls back.

"My name, Princess."

"What?" I gasp.

He runs his teeth lightly over my clit. "Scream my name."

"O-okay."

"Yours."

"Huh?" I lift my head, looking back down into his eyes as he presses a kiss to my thigh and my brain cells finally manage to fire enough that I understand what the stark possession I see there is demanding of me. "Oh."

His lips twitch against my skin. "Always with the eloquence."

I keep my eyes on him this time as he presses his tongue down on my clit. That night-forest gaze demanding mine as he increases the pressure, rolling it under his tongue before lightly running his teeth over it and causing my pussy to jerk into his mouth in response. Inner walls spasming as his fingers dig into my ass and he smirks against my intimate flesh before doing it again. Another cry falls from my lips but I keep my eyes on him as he drops to my entrance, thrusting his tongue in there and ramping up the pace as my whole body starts to tighten. My legs lock around his shoulders as he quickly moves back to my clit again, sucking it into his mouth as he presses down on it with his tongue all at the same time. Setting me off suddenly with an orgasm that shocks me with its intensity and rips his name from my lips.

"Coop!"

He drops his tongue back to my entrance, pushing through the resistance to taste my orgasm just like he wanted to. Lazily licking at me until my body goes slack and he turns his head, pressing another soft kiss to my inner thigh before narrowing his eyes on mine.

"That wasn't the name I wanted."

I scoff breathlessly. "I was a little distracted."

"Hmm." He trails his lips up my leg to my pussy again, making me tense up with anticipation before he moves back from between my thighs and drops his hands from my ass to scoop me up. One hand going underneath my legs and the other behind my back. Using his elbow, he shuts the shower off before pushing open the door and walking us to my bed. Uncaring of the fact that we're soaked as he lays me down and comes down over me, arching a brow. "You know what they say. If at first you don't succeed, try, try again."

I can't help the soft laugh that escapes me right before his lips twitch and he brings them down on mine with harsh demand. Kissing me like I'm the universe he's always claiming I am to him and after everything that came out today, I'm actually starting to believe him again. Believe in us again in a way I haven't let myself before now. And I kiss him back with that new hope, scared as I still am of the unknown truths he harbors. Opening my legs and letting him move between them as I push through the fear and feed that little seed that wants him to prove everything he's claiming to be true.

He breaks our kiss, dropping his forehead to mine and pausing for a beat before he slides into me with one hard thrust. Making me gasp at the sudden intrusion, our eyes never leaving each other's as that pull I'm finally starting to admit is our souls touches and tangles, settling together again with a blissful sigh. Easing the pain of all those mornings filled with loss as we come together again. He runs his hands up my body to thread our fingers together, stretching my arms above my head with a pained expression.

"You are love to me, Eleanor." He drops his lips to mine. "This." Another brush of lips. "Right here." He lifts his head, thrusting shallowly. "Is home to me."

"I know that, Cooper Monroe." I lift my lips to brush against his again as I unstick the words from my throat and force the terrifying truth out on a hushed breath. "And yes, I still love you too."

Some part of me mends with the admission. I can feel it there, deep within my heart in the corner of darkness that even Jace never managed to reach. Stitching back together and healing with a terrifying warmth.

He pulls back, eyes drilling into mine for a moment before that rare, breathtaking smile transforms his face and he drops his lips back to mine, starting to move inside of me. Picking up that lazy, intimate pace that we made love with so many times on the beach last year before we knew what it was like to lose each other. An unhurried dance of stars defying gravity, shining despite the shadows of reason we exist in.

I roll my hips underneath him, meeting him at every thrust despite the part of me that wishes this moment would never end. That we really could be immortalized in the heavens just like this. So that I wouldn't have to worry about the truths and lies, the staying or leaving. Just simply existing forever with him like this. And I know he feels it too when he lifts his head to stare into my eyes. Can see that he wishes it was all just as simple as this moment of us too.

My breath starts to come in little gasps and he tightens his grip on my hands, dropping his lips to trail down my breast before sucking my nipple into his mouth. He pulls on it deeply, causing a moan to escape me that turns into a gasp when he lets go with a rake of teeth. I know I'm close and can feel him right there with me as he grows even more inside of me, stretching and hitting me so deep I'm left with that delirious kind of pleasure-filled pain.

And when I start to lock down around him so hard it makes me think my body is trying to secretly trap every precious thing about this moment somewhere inside of me, he brings his lips to my ear right before the scream leaves my lips. "*Your* name, Eleanor."

His demanding voice rings through my head as I shatter underneath him, screaming the name I've never had anyone call me besides him. "Monroe!"

He slams into me harder than before, somehow managing to go even deeper before his whole body goes taut and he pours himself into me as a gutted kind of sound leaves his lips. A few minutes pass, as if we're both reluctant to end the moment before he presses a soft kiss to the curve of my neck and lifts his head to run his nose along mine. "There she is."

I stare into his eyes, seeing the light shining out from their depths, the love that's the only thing that makes them go a shade lighter and squeeze his hands in mine. "You're still not forgiven, but…" I lift my lips to his with my question. "Stay? Write some words on my skin?"

"Always, Princess. Always."

Chapter Thirty-Four

Present Day

I wake up early the next morning. Way earlier than normal for me because Coop and I had fallen asleep wrapped around each other early last night. He hadn't even tried for round two, just wrapped the inferno of his body around mine and wrote endless nonsense on my skin until sleep had eventually claimed me.

And I hadn't even tried to fight the snuggling.

I roll over in his arms and look up to see that, for once, he's wearing a mostly peaceful expression on his sleeping face. Only the faintest hint of tension on his brow. As if he can finally rest now that he's with me again. My eyes flow down his body, noting with a small smile that he's put back on a little of the weight he'd lost and I can't resist the urge to press a soft kiss to his chest. Breathing in his sandalwood scent and feeling my heart clench at the love I feel there.

All equal parts need and fear with him.

My bladder gives a twinge of protest and I grimace, realizing what woke me to begin with and sighing against his skin. I press another kiss there before wiggling out of his arms, trying to be quiet as I scoot off the bed and walk to the bathroom. Not wanting to disturb what I know is probably the deepest sleep he's gotten in a year.

And it's not until I'm in the middle of relieving myself, sitting on the porcelain throne, that my brows drop with the realization of how royally fucked I am.

Because I can't imagine losing either of them.

Like truly can't in a way that's different now than before that blood splattered across the floor yesterday. Than before I screamed the last name I've refused to use since Costa Rica and admitted that I still loved him.

My brows are still pulled down tight with the tension his face is finally missing when I make my way out of the bathroom, pausing to stare at him asleep in bed for a minute before going in search of coffee for us. I open the door and blow out a breath while closing it behind me, rolling my shoulders as I make my way down the hall to ease the tension there. My eyes narrow as I come to the top of the stairs though, and see that some of the lights in the house are already on, meaning one of the fuckers is already up.

Unless it's Jace, of course.

He was the only one excluded from my wrath. Although I had a guilt-laced suspicion that he would be giving me a little space this morning.

I dart my eyes around while walking down the stairs and through the foyer but it's not until I walk into the living room that I see the culprit through the windows overlooking the patio. Stef's light-brown hair peeks out from above the couch as if he's slouched there. But what brings me to a screeching halt is the sight of him raising a blunt through the air and bringing it to what has to be his lips.

Stef never smokes.

He's the responsible one. Not reckless or trying to smother demons like Mac and I. And definitely not a free spirit like Kai.

Which leaves me in a bit of a quandary.

I stand there for a minute more, staring at him in indecision before muttering a curse and walking to the back door. He doesn't get to go off the deep end right now. I'm the only one who gets to be righteously angry or lose my shit in this situation.

I throw open the back door in irritation, not even bothering to close it behind me before marching out to stare down at him. "What the fuck are you doing?"

He looks up at me, raising the poorly rolled blunt into the air. "Smoking, *cara*."

I watch him bring it to his lips, my face falling into a scowl as he inhales. "You don't smoke."

"Not true." He coughs, blowing out the smoke. "There's one exception."

"Yes, it is," I argue. "I've known you for long enough to know you don't smoke, Stef. Is this about what happened yesterday?"

"In part." He nods down to the couch. "Sit."

I hesitate, not quite sure if I'm ready to have it out with him yet but his near-black eyes come up to meet mine and I see the flash of pain there.

"Please, *cara*. Sit." He motions with the blunt and a stray bit of ash falls to the ground. "I need to tell you something that might help you… understand why I agreed with what Macallan did."

It takes me by surprise, the pain I see in his eyes, because Stef has always been the rock within the storm of us all. Steady and comforting in his consistency. And that, coupled with the curiosity filling me over what has him smoking and what he could possibly have to tell me after all these years, has me hesitantly taking a seat.

He passes the blunt to me, and I bring it to my lips because what the hell, if Stef, of all people, is doing it… I might as well join in.

"I never told you this," he starts, looking out to the pool as I inhale. "But I had a sister once."

I choke on the smoke, lungs burning as I cough it up and turn my wide eyes on him in complete shock. "Wh-what?"

He plucks the blunt from my fingers, bringing it to his mouth and continuing as if I'm not convulsing on the couch next to him. "Five minutes older than me." He blows the smoke out. "And when I met you, you reminded me so much of her." I watch that small smile pull at his face. "All attitude and defiance. It shocked me a little at first. But after I got past that, I knew that somehow, she had sent you to me. She had sent me a sister to replace the one I had lost." He takes another hit of the blunt as my eyes fill with tears. "Always looking out for me, my big sister."

A beat passes before I swallow and manage to ask quietly. "What happened to her?"

"You know the truth about my father."

He turns his head to me, and I jerk a nod, trying to hold it together because as much as this may be about me… it's not. Not really.

"When people eventually found out about my sister and me, the bastard children of the head of Sicily with the Hollywood starlet." He looks back out to the pool with a shake of his head. "It was only a matter of time before someone tried to make a play. Especially since my father insisted on keeping us in Italy even though we weren't afforded the same level of protection as his legitimate children." He passes the blunt back to me and I don't hesitate to take a deep hit, knowing I'm going to need it by the end of this story. "Shortly before I moved here, my sister and I were grabbed on our way home from school. The man that my father had assigned to watch over us was shot in the process." I take another hit before passing the blunt back to him and he nods his thanks. "Some enemies of my father's who thought they could get him to cede territory or cut a deal by holding us captive. But they didn't know my father, not as well as they thought at least." He pauses for a second, eyes narrowing at the memories. "Because if they did, they would have known that he would never allow himself to be seen as weak. And as much as he may have loved us, he couldn't compromise anything for his illegitimate blood without being seen as just that." He blows out an unsteady breath. "They made him pay for that. Tortured her for days and sent him videos of it. Me screaming in the background, trying to get to her before her body eventually gave out and they dragged her from the room even as I begged them to let me say goodbye." Bringing the blunt to his mouth, he sucks in harshly and rushes the rest out. "My father's men found me that night but they never found her body."

"Stef," I whisper, the anguish in my heart for him clear in my voice as I raise a hand to his arm.

"I'm telling you this, *cara*." He looks at me and I see the tears in my own eyes reflected in his. "Because you have to understand the terror I felt when we got that call in Berlin. The fear I know Macallan felt too and even Kai to some degree though he voted no." He brings a hand up, cupping my face. "I couldn't lose another sister. So you don't have to forgive me yet. I know what we did cost you and him. But I need you to understand why I didn't stop Mac."

I nod in his hand, choking out. "I understand."

"Good." He gives me a sad smile before dropping his hand and bringing the blunt to his lips again.

I suck in a deep breath, realization dawning about the rumors that always circulated about his mother and why she was hospitalized overseas. "That's why your mother…" I trail off. Stef had always just said she'd had a breakdown of some kind.

"The Hollywood starlet who fell." He blows out the smoke. "She never recovered. Nona moved here with me after my father was forced to face the fact that we weren't safe there."

I scoot over, leaning my head on his shoulder and offering what little comfort I can in the face of loss I can't even begin to comprehend. "Why did you never tell me?"

"Because you had enough demons to fight on your own. You and Mac both did."

My brows drop at his words but I'm silent in response, so many pieces of his personality falling into place in my head under this new light.

Several minutes pass before he finally speaks again. "So what are you going to do?"

"About what?"

"What do you think? Those boys sleeping in my beds upstairs."

I can't help but choke a laugh at his insulted tone before admitting, "I have no idea."

He pauses for a beat. "Why not keep them both?"

"It's not in their nature." My face scrunches up at the idea. "They're both too possessive. Both want all of me just to themself."

"Let me tell you a little secret, *cara*." He chuckles deeply and I tilt my head up to look at him, meeting his amused eyes. "A woman holds more power than anything else in existence. You can make savages of us, cause us to go to war, and at the same time, are what makes us *more* than mere savages. You hold the keys to the creation of life. You are our greatest weakness because the truth is no one holds more power over our hearts." His smile dims. "It's why we fight it so hard. Those of us who have known true loss."

"So." He passes the blunt to me, and I take a much-needed hit at his words. "If you demand it of them, if you tell them that's the only way they can have you… they'll give in, because you hold their hearts. Even a blind man could see that."

My brows drop as I dart my eyes away, taking my time to blow out the smoke before looking back at him. "And do you really think that's fair to either of them when it's not what they want?"

"Only you can decide that, *cara*."

"I think I'd spend the rest of my life hating myself," I confess quietly. "Constantly comparing myself to my mother when I'm trying to let go of that."

"It's different," he counters softly. "You know that."

"I do." I nod. "But that damage… it just hits too close to home, Stef. I think I'd always feel like I do now, like I'm betraying one or the other and I'd never be able to stop worrying that I was giving them less than the life they both really wanted."

"So you choose."

"I choose."

"But, who?"

"Your guess is as good as mine." I give him a sad smile. "One I can't bear to lose again and the other I can't imagine losing for a first time."

"You'll know," he tells me, voice filled with all the confidence my heart lacks. "When that moment comes, you'll know. It'll be like a gut check, I guess. Just like Mac and I had in that hotel room. We knew that we would gladly suffer your anger forever as long as you were here to be angry at us. So you'll know, when the time comes, you'll know which pain you can take and which half of your heart you can't bear to lose. We all do." He pauses, eyes taking on a worried look. "But be sure, *cara*. Don't mistake the moment because whatever you choose… you'll be bound by your decision. Even the little ones. We all are. Even if it's as simple as asking your sister to take a different way home from school."

Anxiety presses in on my chest at his words, stomach twisting acutely at the prospect and some of it must show on my face because he nods down to the blunt with a small smile. "And in the meantime, it's the anniversary of Camilla's death and I think she would approve of her little brother getting stoned out of his mind with the sister she sent him."

And how can I not give him that after what he just told me?

So I push off my worries, avoiding them for now and smiling as I bring the blunt to my lips. "For Camilla."

Chapter Thirty-Five

Present Day

By the time Coop comes out an hour later, Stef and I have made our way through another blunt, this one more expertly rolled by yours truly and are pretty much collapsed against each other. Completely successful in our mission to forget about all the worries that sobriety brings. And extremely obvious about our state of mind when we both jump as he seems to materialize in front of us out of thin air.

I meet his narrowed eyes with a wide smile, taking in his shirtless body and giggling. “Hi.”

His eyes flare just a bit with surprise before moving to Stef. “You two are fucking blazed, aren’t you?”

“Aye, aye, captain!” I giggle again, brows dropping in confusion at my choice of words.

His eyes come back to me, lips twitching up before he stops them just short of a smile. “You do realize it’s eight in the morning, Princess?”

Stef salutes him next to me. “Keen observation, Captain Monroe.”

Apparently the pirate talk was catching.

Coop shakes his head, taking a seat on the couch next to me as Stef continues thoughtfully. "Actually, if you're waiting to take your shot at me. I'm asking you to do it now when I'll feel it less and not care enough to strike back."

Coop pauses to lift me into his lap, wrapping his arms around me and making me sigh happily in the inferno of his body before he answers in a careful voice. "I've heard the rumors of what happened to the Corleonesi head of Sicily's bastard children before he hid the son away. I know what today is for you. So you get a free pass."

I watch the pain come over Stef's face in a way he'd never allow if it wasn't for the weed before he clears his throat. "You are well informed, Monroe."

"I have a friend with ties to similar circles."

"Scary friend."

"We're all monsters to someone."

I lean back, looking up at Coop with a dopey smile and forcing my brain to pay attention to what they're talking about. "For someone."

This time he can't stop the twitch from turning into a smile as he looks down at me. "You are stoned."

"Mhmm." I lift a hand, bopping him on the nose with my finger. "What woke you up? I was trying to let you sleep."

He shrugs. "You left the bed."

My heart fills at the memory of his words and I wrap my hand around the back of his head, pulling it down to brush my lips against his. "I'm right here."

"I know."

Stef makes a puking noise next to us and I laugh as Coop lifts his head, narrowing his eyes on him.

"Alright, kids." He stands, lifting me in his arms as he does and kicking Stef's leg lightly. "Time for a field trip."

"Oh!" I shout. "I love field trips. Where are we going?"

"Don't make me," Stef groans. "My entire school career was spent keeping her and Macallan from getting expelled on field trips."

"Don't worry." Coop laughs in a low voice. "I'll keep her from getting expelled this time." He kicks his leg again. "Come on, we're going to stoner's paradise."

***

It turned out that stoner's paradise was really Dylan's Candy Bar, but sometime around when we passed over the threshold, I started calling it heaven on earth.

At least for me it was.

"I want the giant lollipop."

"The colors, *cara*. There's too many of them."

"I'll give you a giant lollipop, Princess."

I narrow my eyes, shooting what I'm hoping is a truly terrifying look at both of them. "You." I bring a hand up and poke Stef. "Enjoy the wonder that is heaven while you're still stoned. The colors are your friends. And you," I turn my eyes to Coop and whisper. "Keep your voice down. Satan isn't allowed here."

He throws his head back with a laugh and reaches up, snagging the lollipop off the top of the carousel for me. "It's the size of your head."

I snatch it from his hand. "And I'll enjoy every lick."

"Now you're just teasing me."

"Possibly." I unwrap the lollipop, scowling at the dirty look the clerk is throwing me before purposely giving it a dramatic lick. The clerk's face turns scandalized and I toss Coop a bratty smirk, quite pleased with myself.

"Fuck," he groans. "Stef, you okay here for a bit?"

"Oh, shut up." I roll my eyes at him before grabbing Stef's arm and dragging him over to the jelly bean dispensers. "Alright." I grab a bag from where it's hanging off the wall. "These disgusting little things are your favorite, right?" Shoving the bag into his hand, I push him toward the bins. "Go crazy, Stefano."

His head turns back and forth a few times while I lick my lollipop, quite content, before he looks back at me with a lost look. "But how am I supposed to choose, *cara*?"

"I don't know. You just do." I step up beside him with a shrug as his chuckle hits my ears. "Wait a second, are you fucking with me?"

He looks down at me with an indulgent expression as Coop laughs quietly behind us. "Only a little."

"Bastard."

"Okay, but really." He looks back to the bins. "I understand your dilemma now. Because there's root beer, but then there's apple, and then there's—"

"Oh my god," I groan. "Stop bitching. You can, quite literally, have them all in this case, Stef."

"I can't fit every flavor in one bag."

I roll my eyes. "Then get two!"

"Oh." He pauses. "You're right."

"Duh." Fucking newbs.

He reaches up to pull the lever on the dispenser and I shake my head, turning around to look up at Coop. "And what does Satan want?" I cock a brow and take a step toward him. "Red Hots? Dark chocolate?"

He shakes his head with a laugh before dropping a kiss to my lips. "Just you." The dark in his eyes sparks. "And maybe some dulce de leche, I am partial to it."

I cock my head and give him a winning look. "You know the Kardashians actually don't live too far from here."

He pulls back, raising a hand and running a thumb over my cheek with all kinds of tenderness before smirking. "Not a chance, Princess."

"Ahh—"

His phone starts to ring at that moment and my mouth snaps shut midcomplaint, eyes narrowing at the offending device in his pocket as my happy mood plummets.

"Eleanor…" he begins.

"It's fine," I snap in irritation, going to turn around but he grabs my arm, stopping me and keeping his eyes on mine as he digs the phone from his pocket.

He doesn't even look down at the phone before flipping it open and bringing it to his ear. "Yeah?" I can't hear the voice on the other end but his brows drop down after a minute and he nods. "Good. That was fast." Another moment passes before his lips twitch. "Yeah, I'm with her. Looking at her right now, actually." Whatever the person on the phone is saying has him exhaling a breath in irritation. "I don't care. Your countdown has started." A tense beat passes before he finishes. "I'm not losing her over your bullshit. Man up." He lifts the phone from his ear, closing it without waiting for whoever it was to respond and shoving it back into his pocket.

"That was Alec." He steps closer to me, wrapping his arms around my waist.

My stoned brain struggles to catch up. "So wait," I scowl. "Whatever this big secret is has something to do with the fucker?"

"Yeah." He nods. "And we'll get to that soon, because I just put him on notice. But right now…" His brows drop with a sigh that has me tensing up. "He found the Morrisons. Authorities arrested them about an hour ago."

My mouth pops open. "Oh."

"Yeah."

And looking up into his eyes, I know I should be happy that the threat has been neutralized. We both should be, but we're not, because that means this little escape from reality just came to an end.

It means everyone can go home and get on with their lives.

It means that the choice I've been putting off just came crashing down on me because it's not like I can hang around Landing Point forever, stringing them both along.

I clear my throat. "Let me be the one to tell Jace."

"Tell him what?"

"That you and he can go home." I shrug.

His eyes narrow on me. "And you?"

"I'll—" A sigh leaves me, and I try to start again. "I'll come back with you both and then…" But I trail off, darting my eyes away from his and unable to even finish my sentence because the truth is I have no idea.

He tightens his arms around me, pulling me into the warmth of his body. "It'll be okay."

"Will it though?"

Because if, in that moment, it's not him, we'll just be suffering that terrible loss of each other all over again. And this time, the cut would be final with answers, whereas before it was only filled with questions.

***

My high has almost completely deserted me as we trail back into Stef's, giant lollipop hanging loosely at my side and face permanently pinched up at the cold dose of reality that's just been poured on me. The only one of us slightly oblivious still is Stef, munching away on his bags of jelly beans as Coop shoots increasingly concerned looks my way. I hear the sound of everyone in the kitchen as we make our way through the foyer and force my feet to head in that direction, trying to brace myself for what I'm about to face on multiple fronts. And even though I've seen Mac bruised before, when I step into the kitchen and his head lifts, it still brings me to a halt. Fuck, I had seen it happen but didn't expect him to look quite so wrecked. His left eye and bottom lip split open and swollen to twice their size, cheek bruised black.

I didn't even want to see his ribs.

I look away quickly despite the uncomfortable tug my heart gives in response to his lost little boy eyes though. Not ready to forgive him. My eyes find Jace next where he stands against the counter by the stove, his too perceptive gaze flicking between Coop and I as if trying to judge whether the playing field has changed. His eyes finally still, meeting mine and I open my mouth to tell him the news when Kai interrupts.

"You went to Dylan's?!" he shouts, darting forward from where he stands at the island with Mac and snagging one of the jelly bean bags out of Stef's hands. "Fuckers. Should've woken me up."

I break Jace's gaze, looking at him with a small smile. "Next time, we will. This was an emergency run."

"For what?"

I nod my head to Stef, pulling a purposeful face and he gives me a confused look before turning to investigate.

His face goes slack as he stares into Stef's glassy eyes. "Dude."

Stef pauses with a jelly bean halfway to his mouth. "What?"

"Are you stoned?" Kai continues to search his face when Stef remains silent and then asks hesitantly. "What's the date today?"

"Wait a second," I interrupt, drawing his gaze back to me. "You know?"

He answers me with a solemn nod. "Who do you think usually smokes with him?"

"Know what?"

I turn my gaze on Mac at his interruption and give him a warning look as Coop walks up to the island across from him, taking his attention away from me. His eyes roll over Mac's face and he arches an insolent brow. "You really should learn how to dodge a punch."

"I know how to dodge a punch, stray. Trust me." Mac laughs roughly before sliding his eyes to me. "I just wanted that pain."

My heart gives another tug at his words but I keep my face blank, not giving him an inch because, as sorry as he may be, it still doesn't change the year in between.

"Care to try again?"

Mac's eyes spark at the invitation and the smile he gives Coop as he looks back to him is all trouble. "Absolutely."

Not really *sure that's a good idea, guys.* "Uh—"

"It's fine, *cara*," Stef interrupts me. "We'll go downstairs and use the gym." He holds up his bag of jelly beans while walking from the room. "And I can snack while playing referee."

They all start to trail after him, except for Jace and Coop says quietly as he passes by me. "You can pass along the news."

Silence falls as they head downstairs and after a minute, I'm left with nowhere to look but at Jace.

His eyes are already on me, expectantly waiting and pinched up at the corners as if preparing for the worst. "What news?" he asks tightly.

"The uh…" I start lamely before clearing my throat. "The Morrisons were arrested a few hours ago."

It takes a beat longer than it should for him to nod and say in a voice that sounds anything but. "That's good."

Good to know we were all on the same uncomfortable page about this little reprieve from reality coming to an end? Sure.

His eyes search my face for a minute before he sucks in a breath to ask the question I can see in the back of his worried firework eyes. "Am I about to lose you, Blondie?"

I shake my head automatically and open my mouth to respond but he steps away from the counter, interrupting me. "Don't tell me what you think I want to hear, Ellie. Tell me the truth. That's the only way we all come out of this not absolutely hating each other."

And staring into his eyes at that moment, I want nothing more than for the ground to swallow me up, because I had promised him like he had promised me once, but when it came down to it… I might end up breaking my word the same as him, turning myself into a liar too. Because he was my rising sun who had made me believe, but the horrible truth was that I might like to shine in the darkness a little too much to turn away. But I wouldn't lie and hide it like both of them had out of fear of losing me. I would confess the truth and fall at the altar of his mercy while I tried to figure out which loss my heart could bear. Hoping that he really was that much better than me.

That he understood that all of us, even him, were imperfect in the singular human condition that was love. Blindly stumbling around with our hearts outstretched, hoping that they didn't get too damaged along the way. Yet knowing that it was inevitable if you wanted to have a hope of winning the game.

I had learned that much at least.

So I swallow down the tightness in my throat, blink against the pricking in my eyes and choke out the admission I hate. "I don't know."

He looks up at the ceiling and reaches up to run a hand over the back of his head before breathing out. "Thank you." His eyes come back to mine. "Thank you for being honest at least."

"I'm not saying—"

"I know." He walks the rest of the way to me, quickly wrapping his arms around me and pressing a kiss to the top of my head. "I get that you haven't decided anything. But the fact you're still being honest with me means that we're still standing on solid ground at least. It means I still have a foot in the game so thank you."

I wrap my arms around him, pressing my cheek into his chest. "I'm sorry." Fucking useless words. "I just," I start, throat tightening up with tears that I refuse to shed. "I don't know how to lose either of you now."

He runs his fingers up and down my spine for a minute before answering softly. “You have to. Even if we were the kind of guys that were cool with that, there’s just…”

“Too much there.”

“Yeah.” He sighs wearily. “Never did like history. It was a bitch of a subject for me.”

I scoff a tight laugh into his chest. “Especially mine.”

“Not all of it.” He presses another kiss to the top of my head. “Just one part that probably should have never been.”

“Him.”

“Him,” he agrees quietly.

My brows drop as I think over his words though, because he’s right, Coop never should have inserted himself into my life the way he did. But he’s also wrong, because if it hadn’t been for what happened in Costa Rica, I might have never gone back to Landing Point and found him. And I can’t help but wonder who really started the first ripple in the pond that is us and whether it all stretches back so much farther than we can see. If it really started with a million little choices that had already set our course before any of us ever came to be. Something outside of our reach.

Chapter Thirty-Six

Coop

Nine Months Ago

It had taken three months.

Three excruciating months of not looking for her. Three months of not acting like anything was out of the ordinary at Bainbridge. Three months of planning with Alec to set up what was about to take place tonight. The end to the threat against my world.

"Wind?" I ask him, looking through the scope of my sniper rifle and scanning the three black SUVs we're looking down on.

"Ten KMs from the east," he answers in a tight, quiet voice.

And I know what piece of his soul this is costing him, but in the months of planning, he had never faltered once. Not as we laid trails of fake threats to some of Novikov's old enemies. Not as I faked a rapidly weakening body ever since the liver transplant to segue into my resignation after this, although the fact that I could barely eat without her helped that show quite a bit. Hell, the bastard had even bought a next-to-nothing house in a blip of a town in Colorado to use as a new safe house after this instead of his usual residence in New York.

He loved her. Even if he might not like her much. She was his little sister, and he wasn't going to let anything happen to her, even if he was the one who had taken her from me. Him and those fucking boys that she had called family helping him along the way. What they had done was going to make it that much harder to find her when this was over. I didn't even really have a starting point besides Berlin, and we couldn't use Bainbridge resources where she was concerned without drawing too much attention. Even after this, there might be someone from Novikov's old circle that connected the dots.

"Time?"

"Ten eighteen. Meeting should be ending any second now."

I take a deep breath, keeping my limbs loose as I hear the traffic of Istanbul far below where we're perched on top of a building near where Novikov is meeting a contact tonight. We had snuck into the country using one of Alec's contacts and would be sneaking right back out of here shortly.

As soon as I stopped a man from breathing.

I knew it should bother me more. I had only ever killed one person before. But I had trouble feeling guilty about anything that was done to keep those I loved safe.

"There he is," Alec alerts me. "Coming up on the last SUV."

I swing the rifle in that direction, looking through the scope and quickly finding my target in the shadowy light between buildings. A tall, middle-aged man with salt-and-pepper hair wrapped in an elegant suit, he disappears behind the steam from a manhole for a second before appearing again and I don't hesitate. Just exhale a breath that holds her name as I pull on the trigger, seeing his head explode and his body falling almost instantly.

Now I could find her.

It's the only thought in my head as I lift up from the rifle.

The only thing that matters to me.

I look to Alec beside me to check on him and find him looking a little sick. "You okay, man?"

He nods quickly before bringing his empty eyes to mine. "Just remember your promise. You fucking owe it to me after what we just did, Cooper."

"I will," I tell him softly. "But Alec, if it ever becomes a choice between telling her your truth or losing her. I'll choose her every time."

He pauses, expression turning shocked before he grinds out angrily. "You lied."

"I would do anything it took to keep her safe. I'm pretty sure I've already damned my soul where she's concerned." I scoff a laugh. "But I will keep my promise to you unless it comes to a point that I have no other option. I do owe you that much."

Even though I suspected it would reach that point.

Eleanor would never let it go without a full explanation, it wasn't in her nature and I didn't blame her.

"Fucker." He scoffs as I begin to pack up the rifle with precise moves. "If it ever comes to that… just let me be the one to tell her."

I look up at him with a nod. “That I can do. But first you have to help me find her.”

And I had to figure out some way to tell her my own truth and make her forgive me.

Chapter Thirty-Seven

Present Day

I'm tossing the last pair of shorts into my carry-on bag when a soft knock sounds on the doorframe and I lift my gaze to see Mac standing there. Face sporting one more bruise than it was yesterday and his upset eyes on where my bag sits on the bed. He brings his eyes back to mine and I give him an icy look, cocking a brow and waiting him out until he fidgets under my gaze.

"So I guess I'm going to miss out on this trip too, huh?"

I narrow my eyes at his lame joke before biting out, "What do you want, Macallan?"

"Uh." He looks around nervously, taking a hesitant step into my room. "I just didn't want you to leave without getting to say goodbye."

I look down at my suitcase and pull the zipper closed harshly. "I'm not going to be gone long."

"How long do you think?"

"I don't know!" I snap, jerking my head back toward him. "However long it takes me to figure my shit out. A week? Two? How long is a decision that's probably going to determine the rest of my life supposed to take?"

"Yeah." He pauses for another second before walking the rest of the way to my bed and collapsing on it, looking up at me with a pained expression. "Can I do anything to help?"

I stare into his eyes for a beat before grabbing the handle of my bag and dropping it to the floor. "No," I answer quietly. "You've already done enough."

"Els..."

"What?"

I bring my eyes back to him in time to see him cringe at my tone before he continues. "I fucked up." Looking down, he pauses and threads his fingers together. "I thought I was keeping you safe at first but then, fuck, it was probably only a month later that I knew." His head lifts, uncomfortable eyes coming back to me as I cross my arms. "I knew I had fucked up because you were still a mess over him and I knew how bad it was but there was nothing I could do."

I shake my head with a scoff of disbelief. "You could have told me."

"And what?" he counters. "Sent you to your supposed death? Fuck that. All I could do at that point was just try to see you through it."

I scowl down at him. "So you're not sorry?"

"I'm sorry..." He starts slowly. "I'm sorry for what it cost you and I'm sorry that I didn't, didn't," he stutters before throwing up his hands in frustration. "I don't know! I'm sorry that I played a part in hurting you and that I didn't take a minute to think it through but all I wanted was to protect you."

I stare down at him for a minute silently, at the discomfort on his face that's so uncharacteristic. Remembering all the times he had agonized over not being able to protect his mother and the years between us before deciding to throw him a bone.

"That…" I pause and his eyes lift to mine. "Is probably the shittiest apology I've ever heard."

A smile breaks free on his face before he tries to contain it, probably worried if he shows too much happiness I'll renege my olive branch. "Yeah, well, we've never been great at words, right?"

"True." I nod. "You're going to need to work on that if you ever want to land a decent girl."

"Told you, Els." He laughs. "Not on my agenda."

I snort. "Wasn't really on mine either but look at my luck, I got two."

"True," he echoes me with a smile, eyes dipping to my bag again. "So when do you leave?"

"In a couple hours," I answer softly, sitting on the bed beside him as my stomach flips with nerves at the reality. "Already told Yvie bye and everything."

"What'd she have to say?" he asks curiously.

My lips twitch. "To try and not disappear for another year, whatever the fallout may be."

"Yeah, don't do that," he agrees quickly, face falling into serious lines. "So this is it, huh?"

"Guess so." I look down, toeing the edge of my bag before looking back at him. "But don't get all dramatic on me, Macallan. It's only for a week or two."

"Better be," he humphs. "Hey Els?"

"Yeah?"

"I'll fucking miss you."

And I can't help but smile, bumping my shoulder against his even though I'm still mad as hell at him. "I'll miss you too, twin."

***

The flight back to Landing Point was opposite in every way as the one to LA had been. It was quiet, subdued, and if anyone did speak, it was with more politeness than any of us had probably ever used with each other. To put it simply, it was unbearably tense, but it wasn't the aggressive tension that we had practically been bathing in since this little war began. This tension was just… empty. As if all of us knew the minute that plane touched down, everything would change. It was the dread in the air that kept us locked in our worlds, barely able to look at each other because of the fear of what we might find there.

And when the plane lands with a skip, Jace Dawson opens his mouth and shocks me with just how much things really have changed.

"So Blondie," he starts hesitantly, dimples barely there on his face. "Coop and I talked, and we figured it'd be best to have Tiff pick us up. Give you some space to think for a few days, yeah?"

I dart my eyes to Coop but he's looking away, body tense as if he most definitely did not agree with this little plan but was going along with it for some unknowable reason anyway.

"Right," I agree weakly, looking back at Jace and somehow managing to lift my lips a bit. "Probably easiest that way."

At least that way, we would avoid the awkward car ride in Franny back to Landing Point.

"Good."

"Good."

I cringe. I can't help it. Everything was just so unnatural. And I knew it was my doing because I wouldn't choose. But I also didn't know how they expected me to. Even this horrible awkwardness was better than what would come after with one of them, or more accurately, what *wouldn't* come after.

So yeah, I was being a coward even though it settled like lead in my gut. Desperately trying to hold on even though it just made me feel like both of them were slipping through my fingers all the more quickly.

When the door to the plane opens, I stand and grab my bag with an audible sigh, forcing my feet to move despite the sense of being weary to my bones. Jace and Coop stand too, their heavy eyes on me as I walk past them before they grab their own bags and trail behind. The rural Alabama evening sky greets me as I come to the door of the plane, a stark contrast to the bustling city we just left that has me hesitating for a split second before taking that first step down the stairs. Knowing as soon as my feet hit the tarmac that the next time I left this state, it would be with one less person in tow. Forever.

I almost start fucking crying right then and there.

It's horrible and I just can't. I can't even picture it.

Keeping my eyes firmly aimed straight ahead to avoid theirs, I can't help my quick pace as I walk toward the parking lot. Trying repeatedly to swallow down the cry I can tell is trying to work its way up my throat. Now unsure of whether I want to demand they both come with me just to keep them in my sights or if I want to break apart privately. And ultimately, I'm left in this horrible gray area of indecision, the same as I was in with both of them. It's starting to fuck with every aspect of my life, our lives, and if I don't do something soon, we'll all hit our breaking points.

I know that.

My eyes go to Jace's jeep as soon as we enter the parking lot, sitting harmlessly beside Franny and making me want to throw a Molotov cocktail in it. To burn this whole place down and force us all back onto the plane. Away from this choice.

Jace's driver's side door opens quickly as we walk up to the cars and Tiff steps out, the dramatic pout on her face clear for all the world to see.

"I'm not talking to any of you," she declares, throwing the door shut and contradicting her words the next second. "All of you left me here and went to LA!"

"Tiff," Coop starts tiredly, taking a step toward her.

"Nope." She plants her hands on her hips. "Not today, big brother. You all went off to gallivant around the big city without even asking if I wanted to tag along!"

Jace sighs. "Tiff, it was more complicated than that—"

"Not today for you either, cousin." She scowls at him. "In fact, why don't you take my shift at the bar tonight so El and I can have a girls' night to catch up?" Wasting no time, she tosses the keys at him, shocking the hell out of me with her attitude. "And Coop, Mom is back home so…" She trails off awkwardly.

He nods. "I'll stay with Tommy. Thanks for the heads-up."

"Come on, El." She jerks her head up at me as if that's that before walking to the passenger side of my car and jolting me into following after her.

I unzip the side pocket of my bag on the way to the driver's side door, grabbing my keys and unlocking Franny before looking back over my shoulder one last time to see Jace and Coop both looking at me with pain laid bare on their faces. My heart gives a vicious twist at the sight, quickly making me look away and swallow convulsively as I open my door. Hurriedly hopping in the car and throwing my bag in the back seat before noticing the anxious looks Tiff is darting over her shoulder.

"Holy shit," she starts with awe in her voice. "I can't believe that actually worked. I was so nervous that they were going to be like, 'Oh no way, Tiff. Go to the bar and work.' But it actually worked." Sucking in a deep breath, her wide eyes turn to me. "I was channeling my inner you. How did I do?"

The mess in my head slows me down, and it takes me a second to give her a small smile. "You did great, Tiff."

"I know, right?!" she agrees excitedly, bouncing in her seat as I force myself to start the car. "I really did need a girls' night though. Jared has been hinting around about wanting to get married but I just think we're way too young for that still. I mean, small-town kids or not, shouldn't we want, I don't know, more before we settle down?" A sigh leaves her as I begin to navigate the road leading away from the tarmac, not allowing myself to look back in my rearview mirror no matter how bad I want to. "I guess I probably wouldn't have even realized I might want more if it wasn't for you. You kind of widened my worldview, made me wonder about what's out there. Even if *Jared* doesn't see it that way."

"Right," I mutter distractedly, pulling up to the stop sign leading out onto the main road and coming to a halt as she makes an impatient noise next to me.

"So!" she exclaims. "What do you think? About the marriage thing?"

Turning to look at her expectant face, I snort a laugh, incapable of keeping this particular secret any longer. "I think I married your brother a year ago in Costa Rica and fell in love with your cousin this summer, so I'm probably not the best person to ask for advice when it comes to the prospect of marriage."

Her eyes turn the size of saucers, mouth dropping open as she stares at me, shocked speechless for once before pulling herself together and answering quietly. "Holy shit, and I thought I needed a girls' night."

Chapter Thirty-Eight

Present Day

Coop and Jace had stayed true to their word. Leaving Tiff and me to our girls' night, even if it was a slightly depressing one. It had been filled with what explanations I could give her while still leaving everything about our parents out of it. Much to her confusion and frustration. And I understood that, I did, but that part of the story was still up to Coop to tell her. Arguably, I hadn't been the best company outside of convincing her that marriage was definitely not something to embark upon unless she was absolutely sure. That advice I figured was pretty sound regardless of my current circumstances.

I had woken up this morning slightly hungover and knew a store run was going to be necessary after opening my fridge to find all the food inside had gone bad. So I had thrown myself together and darted out the door, pushed by the hunger in my stomach. Stopping only long enough to throw Doreen a wide smile and a wave when her horrified face had turned toward me from where she stood on her front porch. But the second I had stepped foot into the store my heart had clenched up in my chest with memories of playful firework eyes and bartered coffee.

It had taken everything in me to make it through there without breaking down, constantly looking over my shoulder, thinking I had heard his melodic voice calling Blondie through the air. And each time I looked only to not find him there, the part of my heart he lived in broke a little more in my chest. Crumbling with each aisle I turned down at the memories of the first time he had sneaked past my wall a little without me realizing it. The first time he had convinced me to come play with him at a bonfire on the beach.

It was excruciating. As brutal a realization of what life without him would be like as the reminder of Coop disappearing from Stef's the other day had been.

By the time I'm driving home with god only knows what groceries I had managed to snag from the store in the midst of my breakdown, 'cause I sure as shit couldn't tell you, I'm missing him so bad my body aches. And when I see his jeep parked in the parking lot he always uses off the beach, I pull in without hesitation. Quickly parking next to him in one of the spots that looks out to the water. I unbuckle my seat belt frantically and reach out to open up the door of my car when it hits me who's out there with him, making me pause. Hand falling from the handle of the door at a sight that I sure as hell didn't expect to see.

Because Coop is out there with him. And they look happy. No tension to be found in their bodies as they sit loosely on their surfboards, waiting to catch a wave. I can see them talking from my vantage point, even laughing once or twice as the minutes tick by.

One dark and one light with me as the breaking point in between.

It makes me sick, the realization, physically ill as my stomach turns, and I see what this is in a way I haven't before now. Not until the truth is right before my eyes, leaving me unable to look away as I'm struck by the image of what they probably were before me. A happy family, allies even. What I suspect they'll never have a chance of being again after me. After I choose and wreck that bond between them completely.

Stef said a woman is the most powerful being in existence, but the truth is that power can be a terrible thing. The power to give life and end dreams. Like Atlas holding up the heavens to keep them from crushing the world. But even Atlas couldn't have hoped to be able to hold two universes in his hands. It was an impossible feat that would have crushed everything underneath.

So instead of getting out of my car and going to one or the other, I put it in reverse and quietly pull away. Leaving them to their moment of stolen peace without me. To one of the last untainted memories they'll probably ever have without the painful reminder of my choice in between. And by the time I get the groceries unloaded back at Gram's, I'm so fucking drained that I collapse in the bed without even bothering to eat. Quickly falling into a dreamless sleep.

***

When I wake up, it's to find a body wrapped around mine, long hair tickling my neck and a sea-spring scent in the air that's a little saltier than usual. As if he came here right after the beach and slid into bed with me without even showering. His fingers trail up and down my spine, letting me know he didn't join in on naptime even if he is breaking his own rule about giving me space.

I reach out without hesitation, looping my arm around his where it rests against my waist and pulling it more tightly. Holding on to him with everything I have and not saying a word. Unwilling to speak on the off chance that this is a dream because if it is, then the last thing I want to do is wake up. He brings his leg up a little higher between mine with a sigh, but besides that, he doesn't make a move to speak either. Content to live in the dream with me, hearts beating in painful sync and avoiding reality.

Because no matter who I choose here, we all lose someone in the end. Husband, lover, cousin, friend. None of us would ever be the same again.

It seems like we lie there forever but when he clears his throat to speak, I realize it's not enough, it will never be enough. I could live forever and still not have enough time to make this decision.

"Caught you at the beach today," he says quietly, breath fanning out against my hair.

I suck in a deep breath before letting out an empty. "Yeah."

"Why didn't you come say hi?"

I give a small shrug in his arms. "Didn't want to disturb you both."

"You're never a disturbance, Blondie." He laughs softly. "Sorry I picked your lock."

"It's okay." I squeeze his arm impossibly closer around me. "You can pick my lock any time, Dawson." My throat tries to tighten up at the thought, but I fight it, managing to force out a quiet. "I love you."

He pauses, body going a little tense before it relaxes against mine again. "I love you too, Ellie."

A minute passes before I can't help but wonder aloud. "Do you think you and he will ever recover from this? That things will ever be the same between you again?" Because I'm unable to get that image of them this morning out of my head.

And his reply takes just as long as it took for me to ask the question. "I don't know," he admits in a tight voice.

"Do you think it would be better if I left?" I roll over in his arm, face drawn with the question. "That you and he would be okay if I took myself out of the equation?"

Maybe I could bear it if I knew they would be okay. That they would have each other again and moments in the waves like today.

He looks down at me, eyes brimming with concern and reaches up to brush my hair behind my ear while answering. "No, Blondie. I think that would just make it worse. We would spend forever blaming each other for you leaving."

"Oh." I nod, burying my face in his chest before whispering. "I could refuse to choose."

Maybe I could. Maybe they could. Maybe there was something to grasp for to avoid this pain.

"You could," he agrees, fingers moving to my spine again as he adds. "But you won't."

"Why not?"

"Because you, Eleanor Delacroix, are not a coward." He punctuates the end with a playful tug to my hair before starting those soothing trails again.

My brows pull down at his words and I admit. "I feel like one right now a little bit."

"Maybe." He sighs. "But you won't be in the end once you're ready to face whatever your heart is telling you. It's not in your nature."

It takes me a few swallows while looking up into his firework eyes to get out. "Yeah."

"Plus." His dimples flash with a small grin. "You kinda suck at hiding your feelings, so we'll probably know the second you do."

"True." I laugh softly in surprise but when his face falls into serious lines, it quickly wipes the smile from my face. "What?"

He shrugs. "Just thinking how happy we could be. How easy this is, just you and me in bed talking. Even the hard stuff is easy with you. Fun even. I think that's how it's meant to be. Life is already hard enough, the person you're with should…" He shakes his head as if to order his thoughts. "Should ease the hard hits, not make them. Should make your days brighter."

It takes me a second to give him. "You're right." Fully understanding the hidden message in what he's saying. Clever boy.

"Just saying." He shrugs again. "How happy we'd be." His lips pull up just a bit. "Plus, multiple orgasms have been proven to make you live longer."

I shake my head, unable to fight the answering twitch of my lips. "Incorrigible."

"Promise me something though?"

"Of course." I scowl despite my response though, not liking the direction this is headed one bit. "What?"

"Promise me," he starts slowly. "That no matter what happens, you'll be happy."

I shake my head. "Jace—"

"Promise me, Ellie," he insists, a rare show of force in his voice. "Promise me that you'll keep chasing that sun no matter who it's with in the end."

"That's bullshit," I argue. "I'll promise when you do the same."

"Ellie—"

"No, no, no," I scoff angrily. "A promise for a promise, Dawson."

His brows pull down, the frustration clear in his eyes as they search mine for a minute before he swears roughly. "Fine, Delacroix. If that's what it takes, I promise."

And it hits me so hard that I exhale a sudden breath, because I hadn't expected him to actually say it for some reason. Twisting my heart up and making my voice catch as I give him my vow in return. "Promise."

We stare at each other unwaveringly then, as if we're holding our breath and waiting to see if the ground has shifted underneath the bed we're lying on for a good while before I see his expression relax.

And all I know right then is that I can't bear for him to leave. "Want to stay? Binge a little *Bridgerton* with me today and live in the happy?"

He pauses, eyes turning mischievous before he dips his lips to mine with a teasing kiss and replies in a voice that says volumes about just how much he sucks at faking it too. "Coop would kill me if he knew."

"So that's a yes?"

"Fuck yeah."

Chapter Thirty-Nine

Present Day

Jace had slid from my bed this morning as the sun came up with a soft kiss pressed to the top of my head, leaving before we had the chance to break his rule about giving me space for one more day. And my heart had hurt from it even as sleep still pulled at me. Wanting more happy days with him watching *Bridgerton* while he somehow managed to make something edible out of the disastrous assortment of items I had gotten from the store. My dreams becoming filled with an imagined life of sunrises, firework eyes, and all that we could be after he left. Seeing it all perfectly.

How our kids would have his playful eyes and my bratty smirk. How he would age into one of those old men who told stories that grew more exaggerated with each retelling. How light I would become throughout my life with him until, by the end, it would be as if I floated up to the heavens as nothing more than a wisp of a soul. How he would be there to ease every blow, make me laugh with every hurt, and convince me to play even on my worst days. How happy he would make me. How he was probably the one I was supposed to have ended up with from the beginning.

I see it all in my dreams, just as I once saw what Coop and I would be.

Leaving me with two vividly imagined futures that collide as a loud knock sounds on the front door, startling me awake.

It takes me a few minutes to blink away the images of both futures from my eyes and drag myself from the bed, trying to somehow figure out which I was willing to let go. The dull ache in my chest a constant I was beginning to accept as the inevitable reality that was my future. At least for a while. But as I push off the bed and stand, I'm also reminded of when I first came to Landing Point. And that no matter how broken we ever are, and even if I have to tear my heart in two, it always heals regardless of the scars that may remain. That while it might not be the smartest organ, as Mac would say, it's certainly the most durable to endure what comes with the loss of reason and embracement of feeling.

I shuffle to the door on tired feet, flipping the lock Jace had picked close and opening it to once again find an empty porch waiting to greet me. My brows drop in confusion and a trickle of fear shoots through me at the memory of the last time I opened my door to find no one there. It sends my eyes immediately darting down to where the front porch mat used to be before we threw it away and what I find there has me freezing up in shock. Totally taken aback but for a whole different reason.

It's a simple brown leather-bound journal that I would recognize anywhere. The strings holding it closed almost frayed completely, one tug away from breaking with yellowish paper peeking out from the edge. I had stared at it in one place or another in Cahuita for a whole summer, only ever getting little snippets out of it but never the whole thing.

I blink hard a few times to make sure I'm not still dreaming before slowly reaching down to pick it up with gentle hands, worried that if I handle it too roughly, it'll just dissolve into nothing and I'll never get to know the secrets it keeps. Holding the journal to my chest, I pull the door shut as my pulse picks up a rapid pace at the prospect of what I'm about to read. Fully awake now and in no need of caffeine as I walk quickly back to Gram's room. I slide onto the bed and lay the journal down in front of me, staring at it for a few minutes as my face pinches up. Intuition whispering a knowing up my spine about how fundamentally whatever is inside will change things.

Not just shifting the ground beneath my feet but cracking it completely.

I suck in a deep breath and reach out, lightly pulling on the strings holding it closed until they fall apart and slowly exhaling as I flip it open, trying to brace myself for whatever hit I'm about to take. For better or worse, just like him and me. My eyes land on a sheet of paper tucked into the journal on top of the first page and flow over the scrawling script there, stomach flipping at the familiar sight.

Hey Princess,

I know I'm supposed to be giving you space to think. Figured I'd go along with Jace's bullshit plan because, like I told you, I do love him. But as the past has shown us, I've never been great at space when it comes to you. So I figured this might help fill in some of the blanks while I wait for Alec to fill in the rest. He's dragging his feet like the fucker you call him but should be back in a couple days.

I never told you this, but I didn't start journaling until after I found your mom's as a teenager. Figured after reading hers, though, that it was as good a place to spill my secrets as any. This is my journal from our time in Cahuita. It starts shortly before we met and I hope it helps explain what I didn't at the time. What I wished I had every day after I lost you. Tommy's address is at the bottom if you want to talk after.

Always,

Coop

I pull the note from the journal with a shaky hand, eyes quickly moving to the page behind it and devouring his words there. Flipping through those first pages, I find them filled with random observations and bleak words. Yet still littered with a bit of beautiful poetry here and there. It doesn't take me long to get to where I came into the picture though. That part is obvious, taking up a whole page with two simple words.

She's here.

My heart skips in my chest at the relic of when we really started for him and I stare at it for a moment before hesitantly leafing to the next page to find his internal deliberation there.

Do? Don't?

I wonder if she remembers that night like I do.

I doubt that she does. She probably wouldn't want to speak to me if she did.

Maybe that's her secret. That she doesn't remember.

Or is it something more? Something I could learn?

Maybe I could just watch her and see if there's something I'm missing that she figured out.

I shouldn't do it.

It's a mess of thoughts on paper. One that obviously didn't end with the way that last words suggested he knew it should have. My eyes move to the next page, frantically reading and finding that it picks up after our night on the beach together. The self-hatred quickly gives way to obvious thoughts of infatuation that flow into poetry.

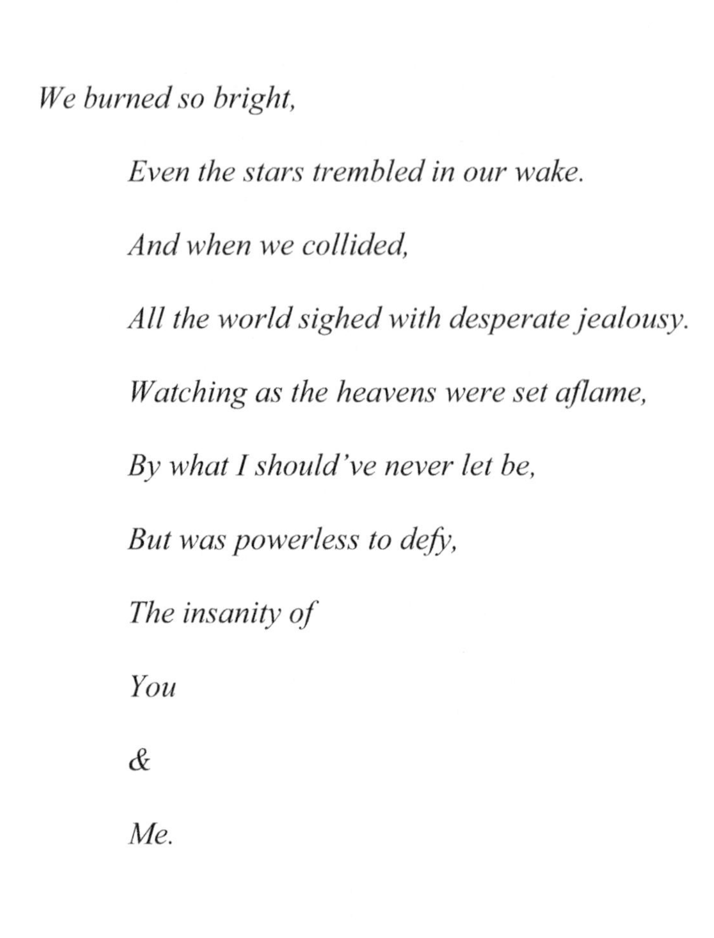

Bound

We burned so bright,

Even the stars trembled in our wake.

And when we collided,

All the world sighed with desperate jealousy.

Watching as the heavens were set aflame,

By what I should've never let be,

But was powerless to defy,

The insanity of

You

&

Me.

And a bit below that is the same words he gave me that very first day he came back into my life again with a shattering pain.

I think she might be a little broken like me. And I just can't let that be.

Can't let her be.

A stuttering breath leaves me at the written confession and I turn another few pages, finding that he did, in fact, look for me before randomly seeing me on his way to grab some food. I read about how he didn't really know what the hell he was doing when he invited me to Cahuita, except that he just simply wanted me. And the rest of it could be damned. The next poem comes after we had been in Cahuita for a short time, the best I can tell, and has my lips twitching with every line I read.

She's a tequila kind of girl.

Hair of light lifting in the sun-drenched air.

Baked in the sun till her skin doesn't care.

Smirking lips that draw me in with every quip.

Jaw so stubborn it won't give an inch, inviting every dare.

A world of secrets sparking in her gray eyes.

As she flips off the universe with no apologies to give.

It doesn't take me long after that to get to the day of our ice-cube breakdown. That first time he truly broke down my wall and I *did* give an inch which he turned into a thousand miles. I can tell how pissed he really was by the deep grooves in the paper where he was writing about what happened. But then, at the bottom of the page jotted down in light strokes that he must have written while I was asleep with a couple words scratched out in between.

They say

> *~~want needs~~*
>
> *like attracts like*
>
> *so…*
>
> *What does that say*
>
> *about*
>
> *you and I?*

I can tell it really starts to hit him after that, how deep he's in with me and how screwed he is by his lies. How already in love he is. It's plain as day in his writing, the love and the fear right there side by side. Pushing him to the inevitable end he had set up for us, the fear driving him to try and keep the love in any way he could.

Free-flowing ink is the truth that I speak while the lies puddle at my feet.

But the missing bits of paper and absent pages I notice among it all quickly have a few silent tears falling onto my cheeks as I remember each of the poems he had given me in return for the little pieces of my heart. And each new one I never saw pulls a fraction more of it his way.

I find my peace pressed up against you in sleep.

Would lie there for an eternity,

If it wasn't so tempting to wake you,

And see that smile that's just for me.

You can find the stories in her eyes that her heart can't bear to speak.

Push, pull, push some more just to see who falls first.

Endless versions of "Let's play a game" on the beach.

Forever cherishing each second of what I hope is always.

Pages and pages of poems about me, about us, saying more than any spoken words ever could. And when I come to the page with our poem on it, the breath whooshes out of me at the sight of the words permanently written on my body and I run my fingers over them. Tracing the lines that he had spoken to me the day after we fell in the rain with words of love ringing out through the air. I trace those lines and work up the courage to turn the page, knowing what comes next in our story. Honestly unsure of what I'll find, what I want to find. But I swallow down the fear and flip the page, expecting it to be a mess again but finding writing so neat it's perfect in its scrawling few lines.

What I would give to soak up this infinity of you, what I did to keep you.

How sorry I am that there was never an option, after that first night,

For a me without you.

And I realize then, staring at words that he probably thought would only ever be his, just how much what he always said is true. That I am the only eternity for him and his captivating insanity. That quite possibly, there is no him without me. Not really. Nothing but a phantom world left for him without a spark to light the way. I start to flip through pages after that quickly, eyes running over the words with increasing speed as I read about all of our happy days that followed.

But then it just stops. From one page to the next, there's nothing. My brows drop in confusion and I pick the journal up, fanning out the last quarter of empty pages before coming to the last one. And on the last page in ink that looks a bit fresher than what I've read through so far are a few simple words that break my heart in two.

There was nothing to write after you,

You took the words with you.

I clutch the journal to my chest as a sob escapes me, eyes screwing shut against the knowledge that's fracturing me. Because Jace is right, I would be so incredibly happy with him, and truth be told, I might even be happier with him. And if Coop had never come back, if he had never inserted himself into my life to begin with, things might've been different. I could have had that perfect life with Jace, basking in the day without ever knowing what I do at this moment. But Coop did step in, altering what might've been and then he came back and changed everything. For all of us.

So I know it then, in an instant, clutching simple words on paper to my chest that scream how I'm his world. It's my gut check.

Heads or tails, yes or no, stay or go, light or dark, day or night, dawn or dusk.

It's the break in the heart that speaks the truth to the soul. The one that told me which side it refused to be parted with again, even if I might always be a little pissed at him for being separated in the first place. That while Jace might always be the rising sun that I chased, it'd be from my place in the star-filled sky that, in so many ways, I'd been born into. Because I had chosen Coop before I ever needed the light of day.

And the horrible truth is that I think one of them needs me more than the other too.

The realization has me trying to stifle my sobs as I grab the letter Coop had left in the front of the journal and scoot off the bed, still clutching the journal to my chest. Snagging my keys from the nightstand using my pinkie finger of the hand holding his letter because I can't seem to make myself let go of any of his words at the moment. I don't even bother putting shoes on, just walk straight out the front door in my baggy shirt and pajama shorts with tears still streaming down my cheeks. It takes some awkward finagling, but I manage to hop into Franny before forcing myself to pull the journal away from my chest. Laying it gently in my lap and still open to that last page before I look at the letter he had written me.

I find the address at the bottom and quickly plug it into my car's GPS, seeing that it's taking me to the only apartment complex in all of Landing Point. My body is tight with nerves as I lay the letter on the open journal and pull out of the driveway. Swinging a left at the end of the street and quickly ending up on the main road that runs alongside the beach. I'm so fucking anxious with the need to get to him that the only thing keeping my free knee from bouncing is the desire to not disturb the journal in my lap.

The ten minutes it takes me to get there is excruciating, each stoplight in between seeming to last for an hour a piece. But the tears are still wet on my cheeks when I pull into the parking lot of the beachside apartments and waste no time in driving straight up to them. My eyes darting from one apartment door to the next as I drive down their length in a desperate search for apartment 5B. I find it when I'm three-quarters of the way down the complex and slam down on the brakes, bringing Franny to a jerking halt before throwing her into park. Closing the journal in my lap, I pull it back to my chest before cutting the engine and opening my door. Only stopping long enough to nudge it closed with my hip before taking off for the apartment door. I use my free hand to knock on it twice, reminding myself that there's no need to be quite so frantic. Not now that I know. Not now that we're finally going to be okay.

It doesn't take long for the door to open, revealing Tommy's smiling face. "Uh…" His smile falters at the sight of me and he calls back over his shoulder. "Hey, Coop?" He pauses for a second before some noises of movement sound in the apartment and he scoots by me. "I'll give y'all some space."

I nod a couple times, somehow managing to mutter. "Thanks."

He leaves the door open behind him, and it only takes a few more seconds before Coop steps into the doorway. Face turning all kinds of tense as he takes in the sight of me before his eyes lock with mine. I see his ridiculously full lips tighten up and know he's fighting the urge to say something. To push at me and see where I'm at after reading his most private thoughts. But he doesn't speak though, just stands there staring at me with desperate night-forest eyes as if he knows I'm working up to something big.

And I am.

"You had me," I choke out finally as a few fresh tears fall onto my cheeks. "That very first night you wrote your words on my skin." I see his chest expand with a deep breath as I take a step closer to him, looking up to keep our eyes locked and softening my voice. "When you became nothing but a lost dream that saved me from a nightmare as a kid. You had me the very first time you used an ice cube to break into my heart. You had me the second we fell in the rain that day and then again when I told you the name you already knew." My brows drop, face drawing tight as I continue. "And it doesn't matter if it should've never been because some things shine all the brighter in the dark to spite the reason trying to extinguish them. You had me and have me." I see his face screw up, his own eyes filling with tears as I fight to get the rest out. "You have me with dulce de leche on rainy days in Cahuita and sunny days in candy stores in LA. You have me with kids that are without a doubt going to be a head trip and dogs you're probably going to bitch about. You have thousands of days with me. Days where we won't keep any more secrets and the last one left between us, we'll face side by side." I cock a brow at him in question and he swallows visibly before giving me a quick nod. "Good."

"Eleanor," he begins, voice rough with feeling, but I shake my head, cutting him off because I need to get the rest out.

"You've had me, Cooper Monroe," I tell him softly, pressing the journal to his chest and closing that last step of space between us. "Since that very first night. Since before I even knew it. And I'll be your words for eternity."

He doesn't even grab for the journal, just wraps his arms around me and it stays that way, pressed between our hearts as he drops his lips to mine on a sigh.

Chapter Forty

Present Day

I run my fingers back and forth over the tattoo of our words on Coop's arm, head pressed against his chest and the steady thump of his heart under my ear. Lying on Tommy's couch in a tangle of limbs as we had been for the past hour since losing ourselves in each other's bodies, once again a magnificent entity of us with nothing but love in between. Tommy had been kind enough to leave us be. And even though my heart breaks a little more in my chest with each pump of his that I hear, I'm at peace, because I know this is where I'm supposed to be.

I know it with the certainty that everyone told me I would. Even Jace.

My brows drop at the ache in my heart, feeling it fracture a little more and I mutter quietly while staring at the front door. "I need to go talk to Jace."

His hand stills where it's writing words on my back and he clears his throat. "Yeah."

"Don't be upset," I murmur. "I told you, I'm yours."

"It's not that, Princess," he answers in a tight voice and I tilt my head back, looking up into his eyes. "It's that I know what he's about to feel and I hate it for him."

My throat tightens up and I look back down, nodding against his chest as he raises his hand to the back of my head. Pressing me closer to him and wrapping his other arm around me, holding me tight as I whisper haltingly. "You know he'll always have a place in my heart, right? That part of me will always care about him because of what he gave me."

Because it's true. And I won't accept anything but stark honesty between us from this day forward. No matter how painful that truth is.

"I know." He sighs. "It's my price."

"Don't say that," I snap.

"It's okay," he soothes in a low voice. "It's a price I'll gladly pay if it means I get to wake up with you in my arms every day. He can have his piece of your heart as long as I get your eternity."

"You do," I answer quietly, pressing a quick kiss to his chest and breathing in his sandalwood scent to hide the tears growing in my eyes. "But I should go."

I feel his body tense up under my lips. "Now?"

"Yeah." I look back up with a blink, resting my chin on his chest. "I don't want to keep him in this horrible gray place now that I know, Coop. He deserves better than that. I owe him more than that."

His brows drop down harshly and I can see how much he doesn't want me to leave in his eyes before he nods. "Okay. If you have to."

"I won't be gone long." I press another kiss to his chest before planting my hands on his shoulders and rising up to straddle him. "Maybe a couple hours? I'm not sure."

He raises a hand to my cheek and brushes his thumb over it, eyes tracking the movement before meeting mine. "I love you, Eleanor Monroe. I think I've loved you for forever actually."

My lips twitch up as I stare into his night-forest eyes that are as unclouded by shadows as I've ever seen them, only leaf-covered branches hiding bits of a night sky. "I love you too, Cooper Monroe." I drop my lips to his. "For always, right?"

"Always."

***

I pull into the marina parking lot with dread in my stomach. The part of my heart that belongs to Coop is tucked away for now and the part filled with Jace beats with a staggering pain. Each thump causing it to crumble and reform with my newfound realization into something that could weather what was about to come. Hoping with everything in me that his own would be able to do the same. That he really would keep his promise to always chase the sun, not for me, but for himself. To find his happy without me.

Parking in my usual spot, I stare down the dock for a long time, knowing that this might be the last time I ever walk down it. That fracture in my heart widening as the seconds tick by, and I fight the tears in my eyes. Knowing that I'm putting off the inevitable but unable to make myself move and take that final step that will end my days of firework eyes filled with melodies.

I'm left frozen in a trance as every memory he inhabits pulls me under, from that first flash of dimples to every sunrise in between that ends with all the songs he sang for me.

A flash of movement out of the corner of my eye finally breaks my trance and I jerk my head toward it, catching sight of something that flashes a coppery red in the setting sun before disappearing behind a nearby car. Shaking my head to clear the lingering memories, I feel the streams of a few tears that have fallen onto my cheeks without me realizing it and reach up to brush them away hurriedly. I blow out a deep breath and push open the door, not allowing myself to be a coward any longer, just like he knew I wouldn't. But the truth is it's not for me. It's for him, for both of them.

It's because what I discovered can make you as brave as broken.

The love I found with both of them.

I walk down the dock clad in my Converse that I had stopped long enough at Gram's to grab and shove my hands into the hoodie I'd thrown on too. Clutching my phone in my front pocket as I force each step forward into this new reality that's about to be my existence. And I see him before he catches sight of me. His perfect shirtless body standing on the *Miss Fortune*, hunched over with his arms resting on the railing and hair pulled back. Looking out over the water at the sun that's just beginning to set. It makes me halt, struck by how perfect he is in this moment that I'm about to bring crashing down around him. It makes me hate myself for every promise I'm about to break and how I'm about to taint his light-filled soul with new shadows.

It fucking shreds me.

And it almost makes me take back every word I just said to Coop. The part of my heart Jace lives in going frantic in its pace as if it knows it's about to become a past thing. Remembered, cherished, but no longer nurtured to grow.

It almost does, but not completely.

His head turns to me at that moment, dimples flashing at the sight of me for a second before his eyes start to move over my face. The grin falls from his lips slowly as his expression fills with realization and even with distance between us, I can see those firework eyes dim just a bit. I force my feet to move, pushing myself toward his pain and walking the last ten steps to where he stands. His eyes stay on me the whole time, but when I come to stand before him, he looks down with a blown-out breath.

"Jace—" I start to rasp, but he shakes his head.

"Don't say it." He blows out another deep breath, lifting his head and bringing his gaze back to mine. "Don't say it, Delacroix."

I have to swallow down the lump in my throat at the sound of his melodic voice before trying again. "Jace—"

"Please, Ellie." His voice comes out pleading, eyes crinkling up at the corners in pain. "Please. Just don't say it. I can't—" He cuts himself off, sucking in a breath this time and I drop my eyes to the dock under my feet. Trying to focus on the grain of the wood as I blink rapidly to rid my eyes of tears, letting them fall into the air so that he can't see. "Fuck!"

His shout has me quickly lifting my gazc back to him, seeing the way he's standing now with his hands grasping the back of his head. "Fuck," he breathes again, eyes searching mine as if trying to find any hint of doubt there as he pulls his bottom lip through his teeth. "I didn't think it would actually be him."

"Jace." My voice cracks on his name, and I bite down on my bottom lip as hard as I can. Almost drawing blood but welcoming the pain because I know it's probably only a fraction of what he's feeling. Because while I may be leaving half of my heart in the past, he's losing the whole damn thing. "Part of me wishes it wasn't." I finally admit a stuttering breath. "And you were right. We would have been so fucking happy. I know that, so please don't think this has anything to do with you lacking something."

His brows dip down in confusion, hands reaching down to grip the railing tightly. "Then why?"

"Because," I start slowly, looking down to try and order my thoughts, my face pinching up as I bring my eyes back to him. "Because I think he would always be the ghost between us. And maybe it would've been different if I didn't know what I do now, but…" I shrug helplessly, unable to blink away the couple tears that escape. "But now I think he would haunt us both forever honestly. That it would actually tear us apart because I would never be able to escape it, because—"

"Because you gave him parts of you that, for better or worse, you never got back," he finishes for me, expression turning tortured as he recites those words I told him the very first time we chased the sun.

I hold his gaze for another second before dropping my eyes to the dock with a quietly rasped. "Yeah."

He pauses, voice coming out empty when he speaks again. "It was always supposed to be us though. You know that?"

"I do." I nod, looking back at him with a mournful lift of my lips. "But I've never been great at following the rules, have I?"

His lips pull up in a reluctant answer to mine, even as his eyes bleed pain all over me. "No, you're definitely not great at that." He clears his throat, looking down. "It's part of the reason why we both love you so fucking much. You defy every reasonable thing and make the world fall at your feet." Looking back at me, he shakes his head with a humorless laugh. "Which actually means it makes sense that you wouldn't pick me."

I shake my head, hating how I can feel us changing already. "Jace—"

"No, Ellie," he cuts me off, chest heaving with a heavy breath. "I'm actually not sure if it's okay."

His words have me pausing, lips parting in quiet shock because he's never said anything to me like that before. I suck in a shallow breath, trying to figure out what to say, when I feel my phone start to buzz in the front pocket of my hoodie. My brows drop down in annoyance at the interruption and I want to ignore it, but a vicious tug in my gut has me pulling it out.

As soon as I see Coop's name on the screen, I know something is terribly wrong. I know it because he would never interrupt this if it was anything else.

The memory of him putting his number into the phone with an amused smirk before I walked out of the apartment flashes through my mind as I quickly slide my finger across the screen and bring it to my ear.

And I know I'm right as soon as I hear his voice quietly say my name through the phone. "Eleanor."

"What?" I demand. "What is it?"

He pauses for a beat. "I had to say goodbye this time."

Absolute terror grips my heart, strangling the words in my throat before I manage to snap. "What the fuck are you talking about?"

"I fucked up," he scoffs darkly. "I fucked up the one thing I needed to do right to keep you safe and I don't even know how. He should be dead."

"Coop. Tell me what you're talking about."

"I don't have time to explain it all," he replies in a low voice. "They're already here for me. I probably only have a couple more minutes before they, they…" I hear him exhale a breath. "Listen to me, okay?"

I can't help the panicked sound that escapes, so fucking scared by the resignation I hear in his voice before I force out, "Okay."

"You need to go to Alec's," he orders. "Don't stop, don't talk to anyone. Grab as much cash as you can from the nearest ATM and drive straight there. He should be back in a day."

My mind spins at his words and I question dumbly. "What?"

"Alec's, Princess," he repeats. "Address is 205 East Silver Street, Marble, Colorado. No one knows about it besides him and me. Now repeat it back to me."

"Coop," I call out for him through the phone weakly, heart spasming with the realization that I refuse to acknowledge.

"Repeat it, Eleanor."

Jace jumps down onto the dock, looking down at me with worry filling his face as I quickly rush out. "205 East Silver Street. Now tell me what the fuck is going on."

"There's no time," he tells me with rare hesitation. "You'll have to face this secret without me after all."

"Don't you say that," I gasp, choking. "Don't even think it. I can't—" My voice cracks and I gasp another breath. "I can't live without you again."

He pauses for so long that I start to hyperventilate, wondering if the line went dead before his voice comes through it roughly. "You'll have to face it without me but not alone. Take Jace with you. He'll help keep you safe until Alec figures this out."

"No." I shake my head adamantly with the refusal. "No, *I chose you!*"

"Princess." He speaks his name for me in a reverent voice, and I know it's because I am the most precious thing in the world to him. I know it in my soul so much more deeply than I ever did before. "You have to let me go. I won't be breathing by the end of the day, and you have to keep doing it for me."

"No!" I scream, falling to my knees.

"Go, Eleanor," he orders me again, voice breaking on my name. "Go to Alec. He'll tell you everything."

"No, no, no," I sob in frantic breaths as Jace drops to his knees next to me. "I won't do it. I can't—"

"I have to go. They're coming," he interrupts tensely, pausing for only a second before continuing softly. "Just know… know that I really will love you for eternity."

I gasp. "Coop—"

"Always."

The line goes dead, and I scream in agony, pulling the phone from my face to stare at the now blank screen, mind still refusing to accept what his words told me.

"Ellie," Jace calls in an anxious voice next to me, raising a hand to my back. "Ellie. What's going on?"

I turn to him, unable to speak as I stare at him through blurry eyes. Not willing to say the words until I see the reality before me. And maybe not even then, still.

"Tell me what he said."

I open my mouth, not to repeat what Coop said, but only to demand that he help me to get to him. "He—"

A sudden boom silences my voice, turning the world to fire in the next instant as a flame-filled wall of force explodes from the boat, throwing me backward into the watery embrace of the sea. And as the water closes over me, I realize I made a wrong choice, no matter how much it may have been made out of empathy.

I made a wrong choice. I'm in the wrong place.

A scream of defiance fills me even as my mind blacks out, salt water burning down my throat right before the darkness takes me. Bound by the choices I've made.

Chapter Forty-One

Jace

Somewhere In Between

Everything was so clear here.

In this place between worlds with timeless gods singing their stories in my ears.

I saw it all. All the lives we'd lived together. Each iteration of our story.

I saw all the countless times they'd thrown us together. I saw how they watched, waiting in rapt attention to see if he or she ever finally accepted the fate they'd defied that first time. How they waited to see if this time would finally be the one where they turned away from the impossibility.

But each time, no matter what roles they cast us all in; no matter whether it was enemies, lovers, friends, or family. No matter whether we were kings, warriors, princes, or peasants. No matter whether it took place on the shores of Greece, the banks of the Nile, or in a land of legend in Britain. No matter whether she was a princess, a queen, or even part deity. If they saw each other in the hall of a house that had long turned to dust or across a round table that had split. No matter the distance between them or how impossible it seemed.

His soul always found hers. Every time, in every life.

As if there was something there that even the gods couldn't see.

And every time, she chose him, dooming us all to death or misery.

No matter how much she loved me.

A millennia of their defiance of fate that left the gods wondering.

What had gone wrong when they had created these two souls? What unknowable part of the universes in which they played kept pulling them back together so desperately? Was there something greater than even them orchestrating things?

I see it all here with excruciating clarity. The only thing that was beyond my sight was how it would end this time. How the tragedy demanded by the gods for their defiance of fate would land its final blow in this version of the story.

The punishment for the choice her heart made endlessly.

Follow R. Phillips!

For the latest updates on future books.

@rphillipswrites

www.rphillipswrites.com

Facebook

Rachael's Tangled Readers

Instagram

TikTok

Goodreads

Amazon

A Very Unedited Letter of Acknowledgment

Okay, okay, I know… AGAIN with the cliffhanger?! But don't hate me! Lol. This is the last cliffhanger you'll have to live through with this trilogy and that right there is kind of crazy to me.

Bound was such a different experience for me than Entangled in pretty much every way. Writing El, Coop and Jace in the same timeline while making sure that each relationship still unfolded within its own unique story was such a balancing act. And I can only hope that I did it justice, because their story deserves that. It deserves all the epicness that I can give it and I'm honestly probably going to tear up writing every chapter of book three. I can't believe it's about to come to an end.

Bound touches on some topics that are fascinating to me. Have you ever met a person and felt like you've known them forever? Are we all just living on repeat? Are our lives destined or are we capable of defying the threads woven for us? The idea that our fates and decisions are all interconnected, layers upon layers, is something that has always interested me and I look forward to exploring all of these questions more in the final book of the trilogy.

But enough about all my philosophical musings.

Let me start off by saying… WOW! THANK YOU to all of the readers who took a chance on Entangled. I wasn't quite sure what to expect when I published it, but to hear how much you all loved it really was such a blessing to me. Never quit reading, never quit messaging me, y'all are everything.

Ellie, I'll say it again, you're a rockstar. And I promise to try and keep my towards, toward and my anyways, anyway in the next one and I'll try to catch on to the rest eventually lol. But seriously, once again, you've made this book a million times better and that means everything to me.

Clarissa, I know I probably drive you crazy with my whiplash cover design requests lol. But seriously, you make magic in bringing my visions to life and I cannot thank you enough for that.

To my mini. You've been such a trooper through mommy getting this book thing up and running and I love you more than anything lovey. I know in my soul you're going to grow up to move mountains one day.

To my mama. Where do I even start? I'm sure you never thought your daughter would grow up to write romance novels but the fact you love, support, and cheer me on means everything to me. You forged the steel in my spine so that I can stand proudly today.

To my sestra, Morgan. Have I driven you crazy yet? You might be regretting that day you decided to be my best friend by the end of book three lol. But seriously, can't ever thank you enough for dealing with my crazy and you do get to know how all the stories end so it's kind of an equal trade.

To my sister. I can't believe you read it! And I am so freaking proud of you for dipping your toe into the romance pool even if you skip the spicy scenes.

To my family. Thank you all for your support! Even if it comes with a healthy dose of teasing. Y'all are the best.

To Camille. You once told me to be shameless when promoting my art and I'm not sure Entangled ever would have gotten out there without those words playing in my head on repeat.

To my *INCREDIBLE* ARC team. Y'all showed up for me in such a big way and I am forever grateful to all of you. From bookstagram to TikTok to book clubs. Y'all know who you are and I could honestly go on for paragraphs thanking you. Just know that every review, post, and video genuinely means the world to me. Y'all are worth more than gold, each and every one of you.

Can't wait to chat with y'all after the final book!

XO,
R. Phillips

About the Author

R. Phillips is a contemporary and new adult romance author who loves to write stories full of angst, plot twists and a generous sprinkling of salacious scenes. She is a native Texan, reader first, and frequently imagines her book scenes to songs. Rachael is a lover of coffee, tex-mex, and is probably too particular when it comes to her choice in red wine. She credits any success to the long line of strong women she comes from who gave her a steely spine, taught her to know her mind, and to always rise.